the wedding
of the year

Jill Mansell

the wedding of the year

REVIEW

First published in 2024 by
HEADLINE REVIEW
An imprint of HEADLINE PUBLISHING GROUP

1

Cataloguing in Publication Data is available from the British Library

ISBN 978 1 4722 8793 9 (Hardback)
ISBN 978 1 4722 8797 7 (Trade Paperback)

Typeset in Bembo Std by Palimpsest Book Production Limited, Falkirk, Stirlingshire

Printed and bound in Great Britain by Clays Ltd, Elcograf S.p.A.

HEADLINE PUBLISHING GROUP
An Hachette UK Company
Carmelite House
50 Victoria Embankment
London EC4Y 0DZ

www.headline.co.uk
www.hachette.co.uk

2023 was the year I became both a happy mother-in-law and a besotted granny, so who else could I possibly dedicate this book to, other than Lydia, Arthur and my completely gorgeous grand-baby, Jessica Abigail? I love you all so much!

Chapter 1

Oh my God, it was him. *It was actually him.*

One minute Lottie was seated at the end of a pew halfway down the church, idly admiring the way bright sunlight streamed through the technicoloured stained-glass windows and breathing in the mingled scents of warm stone, old bibles and beeswax polish. The next moment she heard a laugh that caused all the tiny hairs on her arms to leap to attention.

It couldn't be, surely not. It just wasn't possible. But at the same time she knew who that laugh belonged to. All these years later, she'd still recognise it anywhere.

Straightening up, stretching her neck like a meerkat, she scanned the rows of pews on the other side of the church, tilting this way and that to see past the sea of decorative hats until she caught a glimpse of the back of his head. Again, instant recognition.

Max Farrell. How bizarre. The last time she'd seen him, they'd both been living in Oxford . . . until *the thing* had happened and his father had whisked him away to Ireland. And now here they were, thirteen years on, both attending a wedding over two hundred miles from Oxford.

Whoa, though, it definitely felt weird to be seeing him again.

'Who are you looking at?' Next to her, Hannah had noticed. 'Seen someone you like the look of?'

'Someone I haven't seen for years.' Lottie couldn't tear her eyes away. Max was chatting to a couple of the ushers, whom he clearly knew. 'Where did Cameron go to uni, any idea?'

'Um . . . hang on, I think he mentioned it once. Was it somewhere up in Scotland? The place where Prince William met Kate?'

'St Andrews.' Lottie nodded; that made sense. She'd heard on the grapevine that this was where Max had taken his degree. Cameron, about to marry Freya, had evidently invited several of his old university friends along to the wedding. And Max, it appeared, had been one of them.

She couldn't see that much of him from this angle – there was an elaborate arrangement of pink and cream roses and stargazer lilies in the way – but he was still Max, dark-haired and tanned, with that wide grin and those high cheek-bones . . . well, of course they were still high, he could hardly have had them lowered. And he was wearing a navy suit over a white shirt, but that was as much as she could tell from here.

Though as soon as the service was over, she'd be able to make herself known . . .

'Which one is it? The bald one?' Hannah gave her a nudge. 'Or that one in the purple tie?'

'He's to the left of them.'

'Ooh, I say, *nice*. Is he an ex? Always fun, bumping into an old boyfriend at a wedding, especially when he's that fit.' Indicating Lottie's scarlet silk dress, she went on cheerfully, 'And good that you're looking pretty hot yourself.'

This was true. In Lottie's experience, bumping into exes generally only happened when you were wearing a baggy old T-shirt with ice cream dripped down the front, or when you really should have washed your hair and shaved your legs but hadn't had time. Except . . . 'He isn't an ex. We just knew each other at school.'

Which was true, but also not completely true. There'd been a whole world of possibilities on the brink of becoming something more . . . until *the thing* had caused life as they'd both known it to change out of all recognition.

But she wasn't about to launch into that whole tumultuous story now.

'All the better. Maybe it's time to see what you've been missing out on. I tell you what, if I was single, I'd give him a go. He's *gorgeous*.'

'Ahem,' said Jerry. 'I'm sitting right next to you, in case you'd forgotten.'

'As if I could, my angel.' Hannah gave her fiancé's hand a reassuring squeeze, then leaned back to the left and stage-whispered to Lottie, 'I'm just saying, your one over there looks as if he'd really know how to kiss.'

'I'm still here,' Jerry reminded her good-naturedly.

'You should go over,' Hannah urged. 'Say hello!'

Lottie shifted her position on the wooden pew worn smooth with age and checked her watch. It was five to three and the wedding was due to start any minute now. Plus, she didn't want to do it with this much of an audience; she wouldn't put it past Max to pretend not to recognise her. 'It's OK, I'll wait until we're out of here.'

'Your eyes are all sparkly.' Hannah was annoyingly perceptive. 'OK, so maybe he's not an ex, but you aren't telling me

3

everything.' She raised her eyebrows at Lottie. 'I reckon there was something going on between you two. When did you first meet him?'

'When did you get so nosy?' said Jerry, on her other side.

'I was born nosy. Come on,' Hannah urged. 'Out with it.'

'Fine.' Lottie shrugged; it wasn't easy to appear calm when your insides were jittering. 'When we first met, I was six years old.'

'Oh, that's so *sweet*.'

'It might sound sweet. Trust me, it wasn't.'

Her memories of that first meeting had never faded; rather, the occasion had crystallised in her mind and she could remember every detail as clearly as if it had happened yesterday. She'd been a couple of weeks away from her seventh birthday, and Max was more confident than he had any right to be, seeing as it was his first day at Ashley Road Primary School and she'd been there for, like, *ages*.

Miss Philpott had seated him next to Lottie and told her to look after him, show him around and answer any questions he might have, which had made her feel special and important. Except the first thing he'd said to her when Miss Philpott had left them to it was, 'My friend used to have a pet mouse called Lottie. You look a bit like a mouse.' And he'd actually pulled a mousy kind of face that had taken her aback then filled her with outrage, causing her to retort, 'Well, my friend had a pig called Max and he was ugly like you.'

Whereupon he'd given her a pitying look and replied, 'But that's not true, is it? You just made it up.'

And as it had started, so it had continued from that day forward. Max had delighted in teasing and tormenting her at every opportunity, and she'd retaliated because . . . well, because

4

how could she not? That was just the way it worked. When Max had dipped the ends of her plaits in PVA glue, she'd bided her time then got her own back by tipping glitter into the hood of his green anorak. Whenever she found insects inside her school bag, she didn't have to wonder who was to blame. Similarly, when they went on a school trip to the Cotswold Water Park, Max knew at once who'd thrown his socks into the lake.

As the years went by, at least she'd had plenty of opportunities to up her repartee game after the shame of that very first and most feeble of retorts. Like flicking through the pages of a magazine, she was able to conjure up so many memories: in school, out of school, endlessly teasing each other and somehow never falling out over the pranks and the jibes. They might never have regarded each other as friends, but spending time together had always been good fun and entertaining in a love-to-hate-you kind of way.

Until the thing had happened to change everything.

'Look at you, you're miles away.' Hannah wasn't giving up. 'Seeing him again has really got to you. What aren't you telling me? OK, maybe nothing happened when you were that young, but how about later?'

What was Hannah, some kind of witch? Lottie exhaled; this was why she was glad to have had some warning before coming face to face with Max again, so she could give herself a good talking-to and have time to act all cool, calm and—

'Here we go.' Hannah raised an index finger as they heard the sound of the wedding car pulling up outside the church. 'Bang on time. You'll have to tell me later.'

But the next moment, just as the vicar signalled to the organist and everyone readied themselves for the imminent arrival of

5

the bride, they heard a voice outside shout, 'No, don't stop, don't get out of the car! Sorry, but could you drive off and go round again? We just need five minutes. Then you can come back and get married, I promise.'

Chapter 2

Seventeen minutes earlier

What Ruby Vale had been really looking forward to upon arriving home from a busy three-day work trip to London was a cool shower followed by a couple of hours out in the garden, relaxing on a sunlounger with a glass of wine and a great book.

What she was getting instead was horrible news piled on top of more horrible news, topped with the most horrible news of all.

She thought she might be in a state of shock, but when you found yourself on the receiving end of this amount of information in under two minutes, it was hard to tell for sure.

'Oh God, don't faint. Sit down. Here, chair.' Iris guided her into one before her legs could give way. 'Men, what are they? Total bastards, the lot of them. I mean, *I* already knew that, I've always known it, but I honestly thought yours'd be different. I couldn't believe it when I saw them. And if I'd had the vacuum cleaner going, we'd have been none the wiser. But I was still unwinding the lead all ready to plug it in when I heard him coming into the house. And I was about to call out to let him know I was here, but that was when I heard laughing and realised he had someone else with him.' She pulled an *eurgh* face. 'By then it was too late; they were all over each other. I could hear them coming up the stairs and there was no way I could say anything. They thought they were on their own. So I stayed where I was in the spare bedroom and they went into . . . well, yours.'

Ruby closed her eyes; she felt sick.

'They didn't take long. But it was pretty noisy.' Another grimace. 'And you definitely need to get that headboard fixed. Anyway, I waited until they'd finished and gone back downstairs, and they were still laughing and . . . you know, saying the kind of stuff you wouldn't want to hear. Then they left, and that's when I went to the window and saw who it was. My God, I nearly passed out with the shock. So I videoed them.' She held up her phone, like an actress brandishing a BAFTA. 'I thought I'd better film it; you never know when it might come in handy. This way they can't accuse me of making it up.'

She had a point. Iris, who cleaned for them twice a week, was feisty and opinionated, with some dodgy ex-boyfriends and impressively spidery false lashes. Her tops were low-cut, her shorts were high-cut and she had *LOOK UP* tattooed just above her chest. She was also a lovely person, and highly moral, but Ruby knew that some people who only knew her by sight were unaware of this and might judge her accordingly.

'Get this down you.' She thrust a tumbler of brandy into Ruby's trembling hand. 'OK, do you wish I'd kept my mouth shut?'

'No.' Ruby shook her head. 'No!'

'Good. I'd have felt bad if you'd said yes. I told you because I like you a lot more than I like him. Want to watch the video?'

8

'No, thanks.' Except she knew she had to; it needed to be done. Taking a hefty glug of brandy, she braced herself and said, 'OK.'

With Iris's warm hand resting supportively on her shoulder, she watched as her husband and the woman emerged from the front door together following their not-so-secret-any-more tryst. It had happened yesterday, while she'd been up in London. And there was no mistaking the body language between them as they made their way back to Peter's blue Volvo; her arm was around his waist and his hand was on her bottom as they leaned together, exchanging words Ruby couldn't hear but could probably guess at.

It was the identity of the woman she couldn't get over, not to mention the fact that Peter evidently preferred her and wanted to sleep with her rather than his own wife.

As if reading her thoughts, Iris blurted out, 'I mean, what man in his right mind would choose her over you? You're gorgeous!'

Exactly. Ruby nodded, the unfairness of it all rising like bile in her throat.

'She's older than you! And look at her *clothes.*'

Ruby looked. She'd always tried to wear nice things and make the best of herself, but maybe that wasn't what counted. The woman in the video was wearing a plain grey cardigan over a cream blouse, and a below-the-knee brown skirt with beige loafers. Maybe that was the kind of outfit her husband preferred.

'And to think she had the nerve to look down her nose at me,' Iris went on with a hint of relish. 'The times she called me into her office and tried to make me feel like a useless mother. Fucking liberty! You know what you've got to do, don't you?'

Ruby watched the last few seconds of the video, featuring

9

Peter and the other woman now wrapped around each other, kissing like besotted teenagers. Finally, reluctantly, they pulled apart, then climbed into the car and drove off.

She twisted round to Iris. 'Can you send me a copy of this?'

It only took a moment. 'Done.'

The initial spark of shock and disbelief was being fanned into flames now, rapidly turning into a bonfire of outrage. Ruby said, 'Go on then, tell me. What are you thinking I should do?'

Iris had had twenty-four hours to get her head around this. She checked the time on her phone. 'Well, at three thirty she's going to be standing up on stage opening the May Fair.' She gave Ruby a look of challenge. 'If it was me, I'd head down there and give her a piece of my mind.'

Ruby took a deep breath. An eye for an eye, a tooth for a tooth. *Retaliation.* Could she do it? Up until today, she hadn't been the kind of person who would confront another woman. But out of the blue, all this had happened, and it was as if Peter had suddenly become a whole different person.

In which case, why couldn't she become one too?

Adrenalin was rushing through her with nowhere to go. She'd been away for three days and her mind had gone blank. 'Where is he, do you know?'

'Up at the church,' said Iris. 'Along with everyone else.'

Of course. The wedding. Due to start just a few minutes from now.

'And straight after that,' she added, 'he's leaving for Liverpool.'

'He's what? Going *where*?' Peter hadn't said anything about Liverpool to Ruby.

'He mentioned it when I was last here, just after you left on Wednesday. Said it was some kind of retreat.'

Oh right, the alleged silent retreat; she'd forgotten about that.

'More like some kind of big *lie*.' There really was way too much adrenalin in her body and there was absolutely no way this could wait until he came back from Liverpool. Her mind made up, Ruby jumped to her feet. 'Right, they're not getting away with this.' There might not be an actual plan in her head, but she couldn't just sit here. Something had to happen, or she'd physically combust. And most brides were late turning up for their weddings, weren't they? It was a tradition Peter always found annoying, but if it gave her time to confront him . . . well, why not make the most of it?

'Good on you, girl. Whoa, hang on, wait for me.' Iris, her tone gleeful, raced out of the kitchen after her. 'I'm coming too!'

St Mary's Church, many centuries old and with a slightly crooked spire, was only a couple of hundred yards away. The sun was still beating down and Ruby's spine was damp, her dry-clean-only dress sticking to her in the heat. As they hurried up the driveway, she saw the wedding car had just beaten them to it and was turning in a slow circle. Damn, there was no way they could interrupt the wedding ceremony once it had started, which meant she had to get in there before the bride.

'Hey, over here.' Iris waved, then stuck her thumb and index finger in her mouth and executed an ear-splitting whistle to attract the chauffeur's attention.

When he looked around and lowered the window on the driver's side, Ruby took a panicky gulp of air and called out, 'No, don't stop, don't get out of the car! Sorry, but could you drive off and go round again? We just need five minutes. Then you can come back and get married, I promise.'

Freya Nicholson, the bride sitting in the back of the limo alongside her mother, Tess, looked surprised but not unduly

11

alarmed. Leaning forward and giving Ruby a little wave, she said, 'Are they not ready for us yet? OK, that's fine, see you in five. You look lovely, by the way. Fab dress!'

It *was* a fab dress, glazed white cotton splashed with big pink roses. Ruby's mouth might be dry and her brain in a spin, but she still knew how to respond to a compliment. Showing off the hip area in case Freya hadn't spotted the best part of all, she called back, 'Thanks. And it's got pockets!'

'Come on.' Iris gave her a push in the direction of the propped-open church doors. 'This is your moment. *Let's go.*'

'What's going on?' As heads swivelled to the back of the church to see who was sending the bride away, Hannah said excitedly, 'Oh wow, what if it's someone turning up to stop the wedding? Like in *The Vicar of Dibley*? I've always wanted to see that happen in real life!'

'I can't see it being that.' Lottie shook her head, because it just wasn't possible. 'This is Cameron and Freya we're talking about.'

'Maybe Cameron's already married. Or he's a murderer . . . or a fugitive from justice . . .'

The next moment there came a clatter of high heels on flagstones and a swirl of pink-on-white flew in through the door. Lottie and Hannah exchanged a look of disappointment, because it wasn't someone exciting after all, only the vicar's wife, Ruby Vale.

'Let me guess,' Lottie murmured. 'Either the Wi-Fi's stopped working at home or she's found a giant spider in the bath.' Because Ruby didn't mean to be overly dramatic, but sometimes she just couldn't help herself. She was one of those arty types. Married to the Reverend Peter Vale for many years despite not being a great churchgoer herself, she was well liked by everyone in Lanrock and, as the glamorous writer and artist behind a hugely popular series of children's books, counted as one of the town's minor celebrities.

'I need to speak to you,' she blurted out, pointing at her husband. 'In private.'

Peter Vale was standing beside the lectern, checking the order of service. He glanced up. 'I'm quite busy at the moment. The ceremony's about to start.'

'Peter. Just a few words, in the vestry. *Please.*'

'Darling, it's hardly a convenient time. Why don't you come back after we've finished?' With the faintest trace of irritation, he made a discreet get-out-of-here gesture with the hand holding the order of service, shooing her away as if she were an annoying wasp.

Lottie watched, intrigued by the exchange. Ruby was taking deep breaths now, her eyes like saucers and a sheen of perspiration visible on her slender neck.

'Later, darling.' Peter pressed the point home with exaggerated patience.

Out of the shadows stepped Iris Norton, known to most of the residents of Lanrock for her brash personality, excellent cleaning skills and outspoken remarks. Less traditionally dressed for a wedding than Ruby, in a fluorescent green crop top and frayed denim shorts, she was also less at a loss for words.

'Fine.' She addressed the Reverend from the lower end of the nave. 'We'll go. Your wife just wanted to let you know that she knows. But that's OK, we'll leave you to it, we have places to visit, people to see. One person in particular . . .'

'I'm sorry, I'm afraid I have no idea what you're talking about.' Peter shook his head, apparently mystified.

'No worries then, we'll be off. Don't want to miss our opportunity, do we?' Iris tapped her wristwatch in a playful way. 'Our big moment, if you know what I mean.'

Recovering herself, Ruby chipped in, 'I'm looking forward to telling everyone what's been going on. Can't wait!'

Peter's face turned the colour of fog. The entire congregation, having swivelled round in their seats, now turned back to view his reaction.

'Look, I don't know what you may have heard, but this is r-ridiculous.' He stumbled over the word and hastened down the nave towards them. 'I have a wedding to perform—'

'Your wife wasn't the one who heard it,' Iris said brightly. 'I did. And I recorded it all too.'

Everyone in the church was by this time agog. Next to Lottie, Hannah murmured, 'Oh my God, this is amazing. Are they saying what I think they're saying?'

'Mind you,' Iris continued, magicking her phone out of her bra, 'I wouldn't have guessed she'd be your type. Just goes to show, eh?'

'OK, that's enough,' hissed Peter through gritted teeth. '*Out.*'

'That's where we're going,' said Ruby. 'Heading over to see her now. I wonder what everyone's going to think when they hear what I have to tell them?'

He turned paler still. 'You can't do that. No, you *mustn't.*'

'Or, looking at it another way,' Ruby retorted, 'maybe you shouldn't have done what you did.'

The order of service crumpled in his tightening grip. 'It's not true, though.'

Iris mimicked his panicky tone. 'But it is, though. You know it and we know it.' She rested a hand on Ruby's arm. 'Come on, let's go. Feeling a bit better now?'

Ruby turned to look at her. 'Do you know what? I am. In fact, I'm actually starting to enjoy myself.'

'Wait!' howled Peter as they turned to leave. 'You can't do this.'

'No?' said Ruby. 'Watch me.'

'You're amazing. I knew you would be.' Applauding, Iris followed her out through the arched doorway.

Inside the church, everyone held their breath. A small child said, 'Mummy, I need a wee.' From one of the pews on the other side of the aisle, Lottie heard the familiar laughter of her childhood nemesis and felt her heart do a somersault.

After several seconds of being frozen to the spot, the Reverend Peter Vale suddenly said in a croaky voice quite unlike his own, 'I'm so sorry, I'll be back as soon as I can.'

And hitching up his black cassock, he legged it out of the church.

Chapter 3

Gasps of surprise, shock and poorly concealed delight rippled around the ancient church. Lottie saw Cameron Bancroft, on his feet at the front, absorbing this unforeseen hitch to his wedding but taking it in his stride.

'This is wild,' said the best man, next to him. 'What do we do now?'

Cameron was a doctor; he wasn't the panicking kind. With a shrug, he addressed the congregation in his customary good-natured, capable way. 'Not a lot we can do, is there? No worries. Apologies for the delay, folks. I guess we just have to wait until he comes back.'

'Shame we can't follow them,' Hannah whispered in Lottie's ear. 'I'm bursting to find out who the Rev's been shagging.'

The small child who'd complained minutes earlier announced in a high-pitched voice, 'Now I need a wee *and* a poo.'

While over on the other side of the church, where the ushers were clustered together, Lottie heard Max Farrell announce, 'And I could definitely do with a drink.'

★   ★   ★

From this position, high on the hill, you could see the sea glittering in the sunlight, as dazzling blue as the sky. And on this perfect late-spring day, the first Saturday in May, the streets of Lanrock were busy with holidaymakers.

But it was still pretty easy, amongst all the visitors in their multicoloured shorts, T-shirts and dresses, to pick out a vicar in a billowing white surplice over a black cassock hurtling down the road like a panicking penguin.

'There he is.' Ruby pointed him out. Having earlier vaulted a stone wall to take the shortcut and beat them into town, he was now pausing in a shop doorway to make a phone call. 'Trying to warn her, I expect.'

But as they carried on down the hill, they saw him give up without getting through and put his phone away, while visibly panting and catching his breath.

Moments later, he looked up and spotted them, and Ruby saw a mixture of emotions cross his features. She sensed his fear and felt a surge of power.

'I'm sorry, I'm sorry for everything,' he blurted out when they reached him, 'but you can't go and confront her. It'd destroy her career . . . both our careers . . .'

She nodded in agreement. 'I imagine it would.'

He moved into a side alley so they wouldn't be overheard. 'Don't do it. *Please* don't do it.'

'The thing is,' said Iris, 'I think you're mistaking us for two people who give a toss.'

He stared at her in dismay before turning his attention back to Ruby. 'You want me to beg? Fine, I'm begging you. Punish me all you like, but don't punish Margaret.'

It was almost three thirty; they were minutes away now from Margaret Crane stepping onto the stage, welcoming adults and children alike to the school's annual May Fair. Ruby marvelled at the fact that in under an hour, her entire world had imploded. There were beads of sweat running down her husband's neck and darkening patches spreading across the material of his black cassock.

'How long has it been going on?' she asked. If he said that yesterday was the first time, if it had been a moment of madness, a meaningless one-off, could she forgive him?

Peter's Adam's apple bobbed frantically above his clerical collar. 'Eight months.'

What?

'Fuck.' Iris shook her head, almost in admiration. She clearly hadn't thought he had it in him.

Fuck indeed. Ruby looked into the eyes of the man she'd been married to for the last decade. 'Do you love her?'

Out on the pavement, several yards away, a gull swooped down and made off with an ice cream cone, having knocked it out of a small child's hand. The child let out a high-pitched shriek and the next moment a second gull landed on the pavement to grab a broken-off scrap of cone, causing the boy's screams to double in volume and fury.

That was life for you. Full of unexpected incidents and nasty surprises.

'Yes.' Peter nodded. 'Yes, I do. Sorry.'

Ruby felt as if she were having an out-of-body experience, rising up and watching the three of them from above. She said, 'You need to get back. Everyone's waiting for you at the church.'

He stared at her in disbelief. 'I'm not leaving you down here. I don't know what you're going to do.'

'It's Freya and Cameron's wedding. You have to marry them. It's kind of your job.'

'But I don't trust you. I need to warn Margaret. I can't get

18

through to her . . .' He took out his phone once more and jabbed at the call button to try again.

Ruby watched his hands shake, saw a muscle jumping in his jaw and felt the waves of panic radiating from him. He was her husband, had been her husband for the last ten years, but it was like looking at a stranger, at someone with Peter's face and somebody else's brain. Well, if nothing else, it explained why his libido had packed up and left all those months ago. So much for having felt sympathy for him, thinking it had been stress-induced impotence.

'Why isn't she answering her *phone?*' Turning on his heel, still stabbing at the keys, he bolted back down the alley.

'Looks like we're off again.' Iris followed him. 'Are we having a race, seeing who can get to her first?' she called. 'Because I'm telling you now, I'm pretty speedy. Wouldn't bet on you to win.'

He broke into a sprint, reaching the main road ahead of them. Turning sharp right, he collided with a tourist wearing a Manchester United shirt and ricocheted off his extensive stomach. The phone flew out of his hand, clattered onto the pavement and bounced into the road.

'What the . . .?' snarled the tourist as Peter let out a yelp of desperation and dived to retrieve it.

'Nooooo!' cried Ruby as a car, unable to stop in time, slammed on its brakes and sent Peter somersaulting down the road.

Oh God, don't let him be dead. That would be too much instant karma.

Everyone in the vicinity stopped and turned, traffic and pedestrians alike. Pushing through the crowd rapidly gathering around him, Ruby shouted, 'It's my husband . . .'

There was blood trickling from a nasty-looking graze on his forehead. He gave a groan of pain, half opened his eyes, and murmured something unintelligible.

'I'll call an ambulance,' said Iris.

Ruby knelt in the dusty road. 'You're going to be OK. Stay where you are, don't move. What are you trying to say?' She wasn't a complete monster.

'Ph-phone,' he mumbled. 'Where is it? I need to call Margaret.'

'The car ran over your phone. It's smashed to pieces,' said Ruby. *Like my heart.*

'Where's Iris? Don't let her go to the school, *please.*'

And to think she'd actually been feeling sorry for him. 'Where does it hurt?'

'Everywhere. Shoulder. Ribs. Head. Left knee.' Shifting slightly, he winced and added, 'Pelvis.'

'Oh dear. Looks like it's going to be a while before you have sex again.'

He closed his eyes. 'No need to be sarcastic.'

'I'm not. I'm just glad it's not going to be with me.'

The ambulance arrived fifteen minutes later, having edged its way through the traffic, and the paramedics swiftly examined Peter before strapping him to a stretcher and lifting him into the back of the vehicle.

'Are you coming with us?' Having established that Ruby was his wife, the older paramedic gestured for her to hop up into the ambulance.

'No, thanks.' Ruby shook her head. 'I think it's time he learned to manage on his own.'

Everyone had stayed in the church at first, like small children waiting for their form teacher to come back and resume control of the situation. But as the minutes continued to tick by, still with no sign of the vicar returning, it wasn't long before the guests started leaving their pews and wandering outside to greet Freya and her mum, now waiting in their limo at the top of the drive once more, and discuss what on earth could be going on. The situation between the Reverend Peter Vale and his wife was obviously riveting, but that aside, when was he going to come back and perform the wedding ceremony?

Surely he'd be here soon?

Then again, surely he shouldn't have run off in the first place in such a panic. It was hardly professional.

Outside in the sunshine, Lottie lurked between a couple of well-tended graves and surreptitiously checked her face in the make-up mirror she happened – for once – to have in her bag. It was ridiculous, but a million butterflies were now taking flight in her stomach. Max was still in the church with the ushers and the groom. She patted her face with a clean tissue, applied a fresh coat of lipstick and squirted perfume from a tiny free sample vial onto her neck and wrists.

So this was how it felt to be the odd one out. Currently, everyone else here was agog at the revelation that the Rev had been having an affair and his wife had just publicly confronted him about it. Lottie glanced back at the entrance to the church; of course she was agog too, but right now the prospect of seeing Max again was having a more immediate effect on her.

And – her breath caught in her throat – here he came, emerging along with his friends, laughing at some joke or other and looking ridiculously handsome in his dark suit. He'd always been tall for his age, lithe and athletic. In the intervening years he hadn't gone to seed. Even the way he walked put other men to shame.

The next moment, he turned away from his friends and took in the scene, his gaze making a slow, steady sweep that included the bride's limo, the assorted guests avidly chattering away in groups, and the manicured churchyard beyond. Finally his eyes reached hers and Lottie held her breath, but there was no reaction, and now he was watching the other guests once more. Oh God, he had no idea who she was, he actually *didn't* recognise her. How *humiliating* . . .

Then his head swivelled back and his attention zeroed in on her once more, as realisation belatedly dawned. A brief head-shake was followed by an index finger being pointed at her while a slow smile lit up his face, and Lottie experienced a rush of relief. One of the ushers was speaking to him, but Max placed an apologetic hand on the man's arm and excused himself, leaving the group and making his way over to her with that loose-hipped, easy stride she remembered so well.

'My God. Of all the churchyards in all the towns in all the world,' he drawled, 'she had to walk into this one. How about that? Lottie Palmer. And looking fantastic, too . . . apart from that bit of something in your hair. Is it bird poo?'

Chapter 4

Lottie's hand was already halfway to her head before she realised he'd got her. Hastily pulling it back down, she said, 'Well done.'

Max was evidently delighted by his success. 'Just like old times. One up to me.'

'It's been a while. I'm out of practice.'

'I'll let you off, just this once. This is amazing,' he marvelled. 'I can't believe you're here. How *are* you?'

'Great. And you?'

'Also great. You must be a friend of the bride.'

'I know both of them. I live here in Lanrock. How about you?'

'London.'

'Let me guess, you and your friends were at uni with Cameron?' She indicated the group of ushers fifteen metres away.

'That's right, we were.'

'He's never mentioned you.'

'Never mentioned you either.'

Lottie couldn't help herself. 'So how come the rest of them are ushers and you aren't?'

'Ah, well. Cameron didn't trust me to behave myself.' His eyes danced.

'No change there, then.' Back in the day, pretty much all the girls had found Max irresistible, and he'd wasted no time making the most of this situation.

'Actually, I was asked to be an usher. But I was booked to be in New Zealand so I had to tell Cameron I wouldn't be available.' His mouth twitched. 'He was devastated, of course.'

'Goes without saying.'

'But I was able to finish up over there earlier than expected and brought my flight home forward so I could make it after all. And here I am.' He spread his hands. 'Still jet-lagged, but glad to be here. Even more glad,' he added, 'now that I've seen you.'

There was so much unsaid, and so many questions to ask. Lottie discreetly checked out his left hand. 'Are you here on your own?'

'Is that code for am I single? Pretty much. Well, more or less. No wife, no live-in girlfriend, if that's what you're longing to know.'

How had they fallen so effortlessly back into their old teasing ways? 'At least you know it means I haven't been secretly stalking you on social media.' She had been trying to, of course, on and off over the years. She just hadn't been able to find him.

'I'm not on social media.' He flashed a grin. 'But I expect you've already discovered that for yourself.'

'I wonder why you keep a low profile? Maybe it's easier, with all your countless live-out girlfriends. Less likely to get caught out.'

'Exactly, got it in one. How about you?' He glanced pointedly at her own left hand. 'Not been snapped up yet?' He looked over at the assorted wedding guests, milling around in the sunshine. 'Is there an angry boyfriend watching us right now, silently seething and wondering who his girlfriend's talking to? Oh Lord, is *that* him, the one over there?'

This time Lottie managed not to look. She waited until he knew she'd won this point, then followed the direction of his nod. 'The guy in the flat cap and wellington boots? That's Stan, one of the gravediggers. Apparently forty years ago he was quite a catch. And no, I'm very happy to be single right now. Concentrating on work instead.' She hesitated, then took a breath and said, 'How about your family? Are they . . . still around?'

There it was, she'd broached the subject. Well, it had to be done. Max's gaze met hers and time stopped for a couple of seconds before he nodded briefly and said, 'Still alive, thanks.'

'And . . .?'

'Still together.' Another pause. 'Yours?'

'Same.' She exhaled; so few words, with so much unspoken significance behind them. But even as she wondered whether to carry on, she became aware of heads swivelling in unison and conversation dying around them as the other guests turned to see who was coming up the drive.

There was no sign of Ruby Vale this time. Iris was making her way towards them on her own.

Maybe another bringer of news might have taken the groom or the bride-to-be to one side, but discretion had never been Iris Norton's strong point. Reaching the assembled group, she simply shrugged and said, 'Well, he's still alive, but he got hit by a car and carted off in an ambulance, and I can't see him being up for vicar duties any time soon. So if anyone's done one of those mad online courses that means you're allowed to perform

25

weddings, stick your hand in the air. Because now's your time to shine.'

'I can't believe this is happening.' Tess Nicholson, her pink lipstick having almost entirely vanished as a result of her increasing stress, clutched her daughter's hand. 'And to you, of all people. Oh sweetheart, you don't deserve this.'

'I don't know what else we can do.' Cameron was staring at his phone as if it might miraculously come up with an answer. 'I've phoned everyone I can think of, but no joy. It's not like *Les Misérables* on the London stage; there aren't any understudies ready to step in at a moment's notice.'

The photographer, in his ill-fitting suit, said apologetically, 'Look, I'm not being funny, but you booked me for four hours and Saturdays are my busy time. If you don't need me after all, I'm still going to need paying.'

Freya Nicholson turned to her husband-to-almost-be, who apparently might not be able to become her husband after all. She knew him well enough to know he was concealing the extent of his dismay, because Cameron was a planner, who liked everything to run smoothly, and this clearly wasn't on the cards today. Plus, he wasn't remotely mean where money was concerned, but neither did he enjoy seeing it go to waste. Weddings were expensive and they'd been saving hard for this day for the last eighteen months.

Freya made up her mind and waved her bouquet of pink roses and blue forget-me-nots in the air to attract everyone's attention. Once the chatter had stopped, she announced, 'Right, none of this can be helped, and we're all here, so we're going to have a great day regardless. The hotel isn't expecting us for another forty minutes, so could we all head back into the church and get some photos taken? And if anyone wants to stand up at the front and say nice things about us, that'd be brilliant. Then we'll make our way to the reception just like any normal married couple. How does that sound?'

Everyone cheered, because it sounded like an excellent plan, and once the organist had played her and her mum up the aisle, Freya turned to face Cameron and took his hands in hers.

'Cameron, I couldn't ask for a more wonderful husband than you. Thank you for everything you've done to make our lives so much better.' She smiled across at her mother as she said it, and Tess smiled back. 'I'm the luckiest girl in the world, marrying the nicest man in the world. And this is a day I'll never forget.'

'It's a day none of us will ever forget,' said Cameron with feeling. 'And I'm the lucky one. I've loved you since the day we first met, and that's never going to change.' He hesitated. 'I've got the ring here, obviously, but . . .'

Freya hastily shook her head. 'No, don't let's do it now. We'll wait until the proper wedding.' She glanced at the photographer, who was busy snapping away in the aisle.

'I can't wait to marry you,' Cameron went on. 'Whenever that might be. In the meantime, let's have an amazing day.'

The best man called out, 'You may now kiss your fiancée,' and everyone laughed. Freya leaned forward and so did Cameron, until their lips met. He was so lovely, he really was. And now everyone in the church was cheering and applauding while the organist, getting into the spirit of the occasion, broke into a jauntier-than-usual version of Mendelssohn's wedding march. Then the congregation spilled out of the church so they could be there when Freya and Cameron emerged together, and dozens more photos were snapped as handfuls of multicoloured confetti were flung into the air like a million escaped butterflies.

'You look bloody gorgeous.' Rushing up to them, Iris gave Freya a hug. 'And that was the best church service I've ever been to. Look, I know I wasn't on the guest list, but can I come along to the reception?'

'Of course you can.' Freya returned the hug.

'Sorry about messing up your wedding. I suppose it's my fault really.'

'From what I've heard, it sounds like it was the vicar's fault. Poor Ruby, is she all right?' For a split second, Freya wondered if Ruby could be persuaded to join them too. Well, probably not. She whispered, 'Who's he been having an affair with?'

Iris wavered, then pulled a face. 'Ruby asked me not to tell anyone until she's got her head around it.'

'OK.' Freya nodded; it was probably a sensible decision, for today at least. And they'd find out soon enough.

'Anyway, sorry again.' Iris was now vigorously brushing bits of confetti out of her fabulous cleavage. 'If it wasn't for me, you'd be properly married by now. I do feel bad about that.'

'Hey, don't worry. It's fine.' Freya sent up a prayer of thanks that nobody could read her mind right now. Whatever would they think if they knew that her uppermost emotion was relief? She gave Iris a magnanimous smile. 'Come on, let's head on down to the hotel. I think we could all do with a drink.'

Chapter 5

The plan, Ruby belatedly remembered, had been for her husband, the oh-so-saintly Reverend, to head off on his silent retreat as soon as the wedding was done and dusted. Since there was no sign of either his suitcase or the car keys here in the vicarage, she located the spare set of keys in the kitchen drawer and went outside to the car.

The suitcase was in the boot, and a cursory examination of its contents told her all she needed to know. God, how many more clues had she missed? It was almost embarrassing to think she'd had no idea about any of it. Had other people been aware for ages while she'd wandered around entirely oblivious? Had half the population of Lanrock been laughing and gossiping about it behind her back?

Although Iris was generally regarded as having her finger on the pulse when it came to local gossip, and she'd only discovered the subterfuge yesterday, so maybe not.

Ruby paced around the creaky old house until an hour had passed, then phoned the hospital to see what they had to say about Peter's condition. Much as she wanted to ask, 'Is he dead or alive? That's all I need to know,' she adopted her vicar's-wife voice – the one she hated and seldom used – to make the enquiry.

Once she'd been assured he wasn't dead, she headed upstairs and took an extra-long shower, enjoying the fact that, had he been here, Peter would have been fretting about the amount of electricity she was wasting.

Next, having dried herself and brushed her wet hair, she left the steamed-up bathroom awash with crumpled damp towels, happy in the knowledge that this would annoy him even more.

It was a shame, really, that he wasn't here to see it.

She blasted her long hair with the hairdryer, changed into faded jeans and a blue and white striped Breton top, then slipped her feet into orange espadrilles. Perfume, why not? And make-up, the full works.

Once she was done, she stood back from the mirror in the bedroom and gave a nod of satisfaction. She didn't look like a vicar's wife, which was good, because from this day forward she no longer was a vicar's wife. It was annoying that Peter was the one who'd get to stay in this house, seeing as it came with the job, but she'd never particularly liked it anyway.

Thank goodness she could afford to rent somewhere. At least money wasn't an issue; she knew how lucky she was in that respect.

Although it still stung a bit when she reached the school gates twenty minutes later and was obliged to hand over two pounds in order to get into the fete. *Two pounds?* Talk about daylight robbery. But she had to pay if she wanted to confront the other woman in her husband's life, and now that she'd been assured Peter's condition wasn't life-threatening, she was going to go ahead and do it. They both deserved that much, surely.

'The entrance fee gets you a free string of raffle tickets,' the annoyingly cheerful woman on gate duty explained. 'First prize is a meal for two at McCarthy's, isn't that fantastic?' She checked her watch. 'Ooh, and you're just in time for the dancing display, don't want to miss that!'

Ruby took the raffle tickets and imagined the woman's face if she replied, 'I'd rather pull all my teeth out with pliers than have to watch a dancing display.' But she smiled instead and passed through the gate, entering the playground adorned with bunting and crowded with enthusiastic fete-goers, assorted stalls and dozens of small children hurtling around in a state of overexcitement.

And there in the centre of the playground, surrounded by hyped-up tiny dancers in matching sparkly outfits, was the head of Lanrock Infants School, Margaret Crane, who was addressing the proud parents and grandparents gathering around.

'Now we have a real treat for you all,' she announced. 'Our wonderful dance troupe is going to perform . . . for you. Is everyone ready to be dazzled? Right, music, please!'

The moment of hesitation had occurred as she'd spotted Ruby in the crowd. Ruby perversely found herself enjoying the sense of one-upmanship. It was better this way, without Iris here at her side to goad her on. It felt good being in this position of power, aware of how alarming her presence must be for the woman who'd been having an affair with her husband.

The music began to play and the tiny dancers launched into their performance. Margaret Crane must know something significant had happened. Ruby was neither a parent nor a doting grandparent; what other reason could there be for her unexpected appearance here at the fete?

Was the head of the school inwardly quaking, maybe even feeling sick with concern? Oh, Ruby hoped so.

31

When the dance display was finally over – the children had been cute but clumsy – and the patchy applause had died down, Mrs Crane took to the microphone once more. 'Children, that was absolutely *wonderful*. Well done! Now, the next activity will be the bell-ringing demonstration at four thirty. And I promise none of you will want to miss that!'

Ruby definitely wanted to miss it. As the head teacher attempted to slip away in the direction of the school, she caught her up. 'Mrs Crane, I wonder if we could have a word? Maybe privately.' The original plan had been to let the whole school know what had been going on, but that had been before the accident; she wasn't completely heartless.

Although when the other woman hesitated, Ruby continued with a bland smile, 'Or we can do it out here, if you'd prefer that. Up to you.'

A fine film of perspiration was visible on Margaret Crane's thin upper lip. 'Can it wait until the fete is over?'

'Sorry, no. I'm afraid it can't.'

Her husband's mistress showed her into the office and closed the door firmly behind her.

'I hope he was worth it,' Ruby said pleasantly.

'Sorry, I don't know what you mean.' Margaret Crane sat behind her desk and steepled her fingertips. She'd evidently decided to brazen it out and deny everything.

'Oh, I think you do. Does sleeping with my husband ring a bell? Does *your* husband know?'

'Mrs Vale, I don't know what you may have heard, but I can assure you I have *never*—'

'That's not true, though, is it?' Ruby interrupted her with a raised index finger for added emphasis. 'The thing is, I have proof. On video. Which rather leaves you without a leg to stand on.' As she saw the colour flood into Margaret Crane's face, it crossed her mind to make a joke about the woman not doing much standing, but no, she wouldn't go there.

'Anyway, I just came to let you know that you won't be heading off with my husband this afternoon after all. The *silent retreat*' – she put the words inside air quotes – 'has had to be cancelled, due to an unfortunate incident.'

'What kind of incident?' From the look of veiled horror on Mrs Crane's face, she could have been wondering if Ruby had left Peter lying in a pool of blood on the vicarage's kitchen floor.

'Don't worry, I haven't murdered him. He was hit by a car on Beach Street and sustained a few injuries. Broken clavicle, smashed ankle, cracked pelvis . . . He's about to go into theatre to be patched up, but he'll definitely live. Oh, and I found these in his suitcase, but they're not my size, so I think they were meant for you.' Pulling a face, Ruby took the purple satin and lace camisole and matching knickers out of her bag and dropped them onto the desk.

Margaret Crane flinched and took an unsteady breath. 'Look, I'm sorry.'

'Don't be. I'm pretty sure I'm better off without him. OK, I'll head off now. Good luck with everything,' said Ruby. 'Especially that nasty underwear. It doesn't look comfortable at all.'

The trouble with being the wife of the local vicar was that a lot of people knew you. It meant always having to be aware that you might be being watched. Leaving the fete – thankfully before the bell-ringing got under way – Ruby made her way down to East Beach and surveyed the mix of holidaymakers.

Too many locals. Within the space of three minutes she'd been greeted by five people who knew her, the last of whom had heard all about the Reverend Peter's accident and was about to grill her for details. Word would spread and soon everyone would know. Plus, as well as asking endless questions, they'd start to wonder why she wasn't at the hospital, holding her beloved husband's hand.

Beloved, ha.

No, she didn't want to be in the vicinity of people who knew her. Nor could she bear to go back and sit in the house that would no longer be her home.

Leaving the beach, she made her way to the tiny taxi rank at the bottom of Long Street. She had her own car, but right now she didn't trust herself to drive. There were no taxis parked up, but one from a company she didn't recognise was just unloading a family of five.

She approached the driver. 'Are you free?'

'Sorry, love. Just finishing up now. Heading home.'

'Where's home?'

'St Ives.'

St Ives was good. It was also fifty miles away, on the north coast of Cornwall, and full of people she didn't know, which basically made it perfect. 'You know what? St Ives would do me just fine.'

Chapter 6

'I love this! Who'd have thought it?' Freya, pink-cheeked and tipsy after more champagne than she was used to, marvelled at what she was hearing. 'I mean, I remember you telling me ages ago about your Max, and I knew one of Cameron's friends from uni was called Max, but it never occurred to me that they could be the same person.'

'*Your* Max?' Laughing at Lottie, Max turned back to Freya. 'I didn't know I belonged to her. So now I'm intrigued. What's she been telling you about me?'

Lottie said, 'Just how unbelievably annoying you were at school.'

'But you were friends, right? You didn't *hate* each other.' Freya's eyes were sparkling as she gazed up at Max, visibly impressed. 'You're really good-looking, aren't you? Cameron didn't tell me you were this handsome.'

'I think my not-quite-wife is getting carried away.' Cameron slid his arm around her waist. 'Next thing we know, she might be asking you to marry her instead of me.'

'I just think you could have mentioned it, that's all. Mum?

Mum,' Freya called out as Tess Nicholson threaded her way between the tables. 'You won't believe this, Max and Lottie knew each other years ago! They were at school together! And doesn't he have lovely eyes?'

When the photographer had finished taking a series of informal, unposed photos of them, Max drew Lottie over to an empty sofa out on the hotel's terrace.

'Come on, we still have some catching-up to do. I want to hear all about you.'

Lottie was hyper-aware of his arm stretched out across the back of the sofa, the tips of his fingers millimetres from her bare shoulder.

'I work hard. I run my dad's property rental business, Lanrock Holiday Homes, and I love my job. And I love living here in Lanrock.' She shrugged, maybe a fraction higher than she would normally, and felt her shoulder tingle as it made contact with his fingers. 'I'm happy. My life is great.'

'That's good to hear.'

'And you?'

'Me?' Max's mouth twitched. 'You know me. Always happy.'

'Still snowboarding?'

'Only when there's snow.'

'What else do you do?'

He shrugged too. 'As little as possible, currently.'

'That's sad,' said Lottie. 'You always wanted to work in TV. Sports presenting, wasn't it?'

'That was the dream back then. Well, either that or score the winning goal for England in the World Cup.'

'So what did you end up going into?'

'IT. I'm a games designer.'

'Oh God, are you a giant nerd?'

'Maybe. But it means I can work from home, travel whenever I want to, and make people happy.'

'I don't play internet games.'

'Not even word games?'

'Oh well, that's different. I like Wordle. And Scrabble.'

He regarded her with amusement. 'Me too. Letterdox?'

'I *love* Letterdox.'

'One of mine.'

'One of your favourites?'

'Definitely.' He grinned. 'Especially since I sold it to the *New York Times* last year.'

Belatedly Lottie cottoned on. Letterdox had been created by him. Of course it had. Some people flailed and struggled through life, while others like Max simply floated through, with no pitfalls or obstacles occurring to hold them back. The sun would shine every day, opportunities would continue to fall into his lap, and other people did whatever was necessary to smooth his way to success. It was as if he was living a charmed life, mesmerising all who happened to cross his path.

'You always were so easy to read,' he said.

'You don't know what I'm thinking.'

'Of course I do. You looked at my watch, my shoes, my suit. You're bursting to know how much the *New York Times* paid me and you don't think I deserve it, because it's not as if inventing games is a proper job. And you're probably right.' He shrugged. 'What you don't know is how many weeks and months I put into coming up with Letterdox. Not to mention the years of work that went into learning how to create games in the first place. But you're still thinking everything comes too easily for me.'

Fine. He knew how to read her mind. Lottie nodded in agreement. 'Yep.'

'You're also secretly impressed and wondering how much my watch cost.'

'You're such a show-off.'

'I bought it for twenty euros last year in a flea market in Paris.' Max showed her the watch and she saw that it wasn't designer after all. Entertained, he said, 'Oh dear, are you disappointed now? I mean, I like watches, they're handy to have on the end of your arm. I just don't see the point in spending thousands of pounds in order to be able to tell the time.'

Lottie couldn't resist reminding him. 'When you were fifteen, you spent all your birthday money on a fake Rolex. You were *so* proud of it.'

'Of course I was.' He laughed. 'I was fifteen. I thought learning to do a ten-second wheelie on my pushbike was the pinnacle of achievement.'

'You were also proud of being able to burp the alphabet at the same time as juggling oranges.'

'Damn right. You have no idea how many hours of practice it took to perfect that skill.'

'You wanted to audition for *Britain's Got Talent* with it.'

'And I might have won. I could've been the Susan Boyle of burping-while-juggling. Sadly, it's too late now. We'll never know. Life could have been so different.'

'Of all the conversations I thought I might be having today,' said Lottie, 'I have to tell you, this wasn't one of them.'

A waitress circulating with a tray of drinks approached them. Max passed Lottie a fresh glass of Prosecco, then sat back and stretched his legs out in front of him. Long legs, casually crossed at the ankle, just the way she remembered them.

He cast a sidelong glance in her direction. 'Believe it or not, I've matured since then.'

'We only have your word for this.'

He touched the rim of his glass against hers. 'Oh Lottie, it's so good to see you again.'

'I bet you say that to all the girls.'

'It doesn't work if their name isn't Lottie.' He laughed when she rolled her eyes. 'OK, maybe it's been known to happen. But this time I really mean it. Tell me more about you. I want to hear everything.'

'Like what?'

'All the important stuff, like is Rihanna's "Umbrella" still your favourite song of all time? Can you still fit seven Jaffa Cakes into your mouth in one go? And do you still cry like a baby whenever someone wins a medal at the Olympics?'

Trust him to remember the silliest details about her teenage years. Lottie took a sip of her drink and wondered if he remembered the night they'd kissed, *that* night, the one before the day everything had changed and her world – both their worlds – had come crashing in.

Was he able to recall every spine-tingling detail about those kisses, how they had felt, the things they'd said to each other, the sensation that something tilting on the edge of momentous was happening to them, now that the pretence and the joking had at long last been stripped away?

Because if she lived to be a hundred, she knew she would never be able to forget that night. Each microscopic detail had imprinted itself indelibly on her brain.

As for the next two days . . . well, no one who'd been there could ever forget *that*.

But now wasn't the time. She quelled the memories and shook her head. 'No song will ever beat "Umbrella".'

'. . . ella, ella.' Max tapped his fingers on the back of the sofa

39

and eyed her playfully. 'Maybe I should see if the DJ has it in his playlist.'

Iris appeared in front of them, looking distracted and with her phone pressed to her ear.

'Everything OK?' said Lottie.

'Hope so. I've been over to the vicarage to check on Ruby, but she's not there. And her phone's switched off. I just want to know she's all right.'

'Poor Ruby.' Feeling guilty, Lottie put down her drink. 'Look at us, having fun and celebrating a wedding that didn't happen, while she's just found out her husband's been cheating on her. God knows what she's going through.'

'I know, and I thought I was doing the right thing telling her . . . Oh *hi*, thank goodness, I was worried sick about you! Your car's still there but you aren't at the house. Are you OK?' Iris listened, then patted her chest and nodded at Lottie and Max.

She was smiling, reassuring them. Lottie heaved a sigh of relief that Ruby was all right. Thank goodness for that.

Through the window of the beachfront café in St Ives, Ruby was watching the surfers riding on the waves rolling in from the Atlantic. The moment she'd switched her phone back on, it had begun to ring. Touched by Iris's concern, she said, 'I'm fine, I promise. No need to worry about me.'

'I can't help it. I feel responsible. Where are you?'

'Not in Lanrock. And I'm not going to do anything stupid. I just wanted to get away for a while, think things through.'

'Are you going to forgive him?' Iris sounded shocked. 'Take him back?'

Ruby already knew the answer. 'No. And no. That would definitely be stupid.'

'Well, hooray for that. He doesn't deserve you anyway.'

Drily, she said, 'I know.'

'Good girl. You're way better than he is.'

'Funnily enough, I think so too.'

'Want me to call the hospital, see how he is?'

'No need, I already checked. He's not in any danger, just a bit knocked about.' Ruby paused, watching as one of the surfers tumbled off his board in spectacular fashion. 'I went to see her too. Think I put the fear of God into her. It felt great.' It *had* felt great.

'You did? Told her in front of everyone? Whoa, good for you!'

'Not in front of everyone. I was discreet, in the end. Not that she deserves it, but there you go. I'm just too nice.'

'You are. We all think so. Don't we?'

'Who are you talking to?' said Ruby, because Iris was evidently speaking to someone else.

'Lottie Palmer, and some handsome chap. I've kind of crashed the non-wedding reception. Come and join us!'

'It's OK, I'm better here. Right now it's easier to be where people don't know me.' She was touched by the offer. 'But thanks for calling, and I promise I'm fine.'

'Oh, bless you.' Iris's voice softened. 'Look, if you ever need company, or anything at all, give me a shout. And I'm not just saying that. I mean it. You're a lovely woman and you haven't done anything to deserve this. That husband of yours is a prize dick. *Sorry.*'

'Why are you sorry?'

'I just said dick.'

Ruby had guessed that was why. Vicars' wives were widely regarded as too delicate to hear such words. She said, 'Don't apologise. He's definitely a dick.'

Which at least made Iris laugh. 'You go, girl.'

'Hey, I've already gone.' Ruby laughed too, but as soon as the call had ended, a great wave of sadness washed over her. It was the sympathy that did it. As soon as word got out, everyone would be feeling sorry for her, and the thought of it made her feel so . . . so . . . Oh God, please no, not now . . .

But some emotions simply refused to be squashed into submission, and here came the tears she'd been so determined not to shed. Sitting at the corner table in the café, relieved that she had her back to the rest of the room, she felt herself seized by a whole-body shudder as her throat closed up and the grief arrived, charging in like the cavalry. But it was OK, she could handle this, so long as she managed to do it quietly. If she stayed silent and just let the tears fall, no one would see and no one would know.

It might even have worked, if only her mascara hadn't begun to run and mingle with the tears and the suncream she'd sprayed over her face earlier, so the combination was now seeping into her eyes and making them sting. Reaching for her oversized bag and hauling it up onto the table in front of her, she rummaged until she located a travel pack of tissues, then groped blindly for the opening on the packet as the stinging intensified. The back of her hand hit her coffee cup, sending the contents sloshing across the table. At her wits' end, she made a despairing honking sound like a warthog in labour and squeezed her eyes shut in a desperate attempt to quell the burning pain, while lukewarm coffee dripped onto her feet. Ow, ow, ow and *ugh* . . .

Chapter 7

'It's OK, here you go.' A dry handkerchief was thrust into Ruby's free hand, a wodge of paper napkins appeared on the table and the pack of tissues was whisked from her grasp, deftly opened and returned. 'The handkerchief's clean, I promise. Let me just sort out this table. Oh dear,' said her rescuer as he caught a glimpse of her face, 'you might want to sort yourself out too. Go on, the bathroom's over there, through that blue door.'

He hadn't been kidding. The mix of mascara, sun protection and salty tears had left muddy tracks down her cheeks all the way to her chin. Ruby washed her face with liquid hand soap and dried it on a rough paper towel. Honestly, what a state. Although, on the upside, the panic of spilling coffee everywhere had brought the tears to a screeching halt.

And she hadn't brought any make-up with her, so that was that for now.

By the time she returned, the man had finished cleaning the table and her phone was sitting on a side plate.

'It didn't get wet,' he said, 'and I've ordered you another cappuccino.'

'Thank you. That's very kind.' The splatters of coffee had been mopped from the floor and the chair had been moved so she was no longer facing the wall. Her rescuer pulled it out and Ruby hesitated, then sat down and said apologetically, 'I'm afraid your handkerchief's wrecked.'

'I'm sure I'll survive without it.' The replacement drink arrived and he told the waitress to add it to his bill.

'You don't have to do that,' said Ruby. 'I can pay for it.'

'Hey, let me do something nice.' He sat back down at his own table with a laptop open in front of him. 'And forgive me, but I couldn't help overhearing some of your call. Sounds as if you aren't having the best day.'

He appeared to be around forty, quite nice-looking in an understated way. Light brown hair was swept back from a tanned face. He had a strong Roman nose, small pouches beneath kind grey eyes, and a jaw that was dotted with golden stubble. He was wearing a pale blue linen shirt, crumpled cream chinos and well-worn deck shoes.

Ruby nodded. 'You could say that.' She had a brief flashback to the video Iris had recorded on her phone. 'Isn't it weird how one minute life's just trundling along, then the next minute it's all been . . . I don't know, swept away. Like a tsunami.'

'And you find yourself spun round, suddenly facing a whole new world.' He nodded and added a spoonful of sugar to his coffee. 'Tell me about it.'

'Er . . .' Did she want to?

'God, sorry.' He sat back suddenly. 'I wasn't telling you to tell me about it! I meant that I've been there . . . everything changing, just like that.' Vigorously he shook his head. 'You don't have to tell me anything. I promise I wasn't being nosy.'

'Well, that's a relief.' Ruby glanced out of the window at the expanse of golden sand and the turquoise sea glittering in the sunlight. After a moment, she went on, 'Although the trouble is, now I'm the nosy one wanting to hear about your disaster.'

'And are you secretly hoping it'll be worse than yours?' He was smiling now. He had the type of face that people would describe as kind. Then again, so did Peter; it was pretty much a prerequisite when you were a vicar.

She nodded. 'It might help.'

'Would you like to hear the story?'

'Only if you really don't mind telling me. And if you're not busy.' She indicated the open laptop, on which he'd been doing something presumably business-related involving spread-sheets.

He closed the lid. 'You'd be doing me a favour. Any excuse to stop working. I'm Richard, by the way.'

She hesitated, then said, 'Ruby.'

'Well, it's nice to meet you. I'm just sorry it's under less than ideal circumstances. OK, here we go. My ex-wife has just asked me to be a sperm donor so she can have a baby with her new partner.'

Ruby blinked. 'Wow.'

'Indeed.' He pulled a face.

'So her new partner is infertile? Had a vasectomy?'

'Neither of those. Her new partner's a she, not a he.'

'Oh . . .'

'Yep.' He nodded slowly. 'One of those left-field reasons. Mel and I got married fifteen years ago and I thought we were great together. We moved to Henley-on-Thames and had two daughters, Sasha and Flo, and life really couldn't have

45

been better. Then three years ago, she told me she'd met someone else and fallen in love properly for the first time.' Drily he added, 'Which was obviously wonderful to hear. And weirdly, I guessed who it was right away. Over the previous months we'd got friendly with a couple called Dara and Graham who lived nearby, and I'd started to wonder if there could be something going on between Mel and Graham, because she always seemed to light up around him. Except then the truth came out and I discovered he wasn't the one who'd been causing her to light up.'

'It must have been awful,' Ruby said with feeling.

'It wasn't great, I can tell you. Much less comedy value in real life than when it happened to Ross in *Friends*.'

'And was it out of the blue for her? Like, a surprise? Or had she always known?'

He shrugged. 'Some inklings as a teenager, apparently. But when we met, she dismissed them. And she loved being a wife and mother. It wasn't until she met Dara that all the old feelings came rushing back, a hundred times more powerful than before. And she knew they had to be together.'

'I'm so sorry.'

'It wasn't anyone's fault. None of it was done deliberately. It meant I couldn't be angry, which wasn't easy, because I felt pretty bloody angry.' A faint smile. 'And it wasn't as if there was anything I could do to win her back. Plus, the kids were having to deal with the divorce, which neither of us had ever wanted them to go through, so we had to make it an amicable split for their sakes.'

'Are they OK now?'

'Better than we dared to expect. They're great girls and they've coped brilliantly. They split their time between Mel

46

and Dara's place and mine. They get on well with Dara. As far as my wife and her new wife are concerned, everything's perfect.' Richard paused to take a swallow of coffee and gaze through the window at a small boy who was having a tantrum in the street, throwing himself to the ground and yelling his head off. 'I know how *that* feels. Anyway, so here we are, three years on, a very modern co-parenting family, and everyone congratulates us on doing it so well. But last week Mel and Dara came to see me. They want to have a child together and have decided it'd be nicer if the baby was a full sibling to the girls. So apparently it makes sense for me to be the sperm donor. Which means I'd be the biological father. But I wouldn't be the baby's *real* father, because I wouldn't have any kind of say in its upbringing. It would be Mel and Dara's child.' He shrugged and watched as the tantrumming toddler was scooped up and hauled off by his parents. 'And they can't understand why I'm not happy with this apparently fantastic plan.'

'Well, if it helps at all,' said Ruby, 'you're making me feel so much better about my own mess.'

His gesture was magnanimous. 'There you go, then. Mission accomplished.' Another brief smile. 'Every cloud.'

'Would it be your ex-wife carrying the baby?'

'Yep. Via turkey baster, obviously.'

'How about Dara giving birth instead? Couldn't they ask her husband to do the honours?'

'Graham? They mentioned it to him in case I refused. He told them to take a hike. In so many words.'

'Awful for both of you. How's he coped with the break-up?'

'Put it this way, if you ever happen to bump into Graham, don't look him in the eye. Because if you do, he'll try to seduce you. He's spent the last couple of years sleeping his

47

way through the female population of Henley. I think he's desperate to prove to the world it wasn't his fault his wife left him for another woman.'

The trouble with being endlessly nosy was wanting to ask the kind of questions that were likely to make people look at you askance, if not back away in alarm. Ruby metaphorically sat on her hands and concentrated on not letting the next question blurt out of her mouth.

Watching her, Richard said genially, 'You're too polite to ask, but I know you're longing to know.'

'It's none of my business.'

'Hey, that was what helped Graham get over it. In my case, I just went in the opposite direction.'

'So the women of Henley were safe from you?'

He nodded. 'Oh yes. Completely.'

'You haven't met anyone else?'

'No one. Haven't wanted to. I have two girls to bring up; they're my priority right now.'

'And are they here in St Ives with you?'

'No, they've had school this week. I rented a cottage down here for a few days, fancied a change of scenery while I worked on a job. The joys of not being tied to an office. Heading home tomorrow, though.'

She barely knew him, but a bizarre thud of disappointment landed in the pit of Ruby's stomach. He felt like a friend, and heading home tomorrow wasn't what she'd wanted to hear. Finishing her coffee, she said, 'It really does make me feel better. You look at other people and they always seem to have their lives sorted. It's good to know they can be going through as much of a crappy time as you are.'

'Happy to help.' He laughed, glancing out of the window

48

as a tussle of gulls swooped down to demolish a dropped bag of chips, then indicated her empty cup. 'Can I get you another?'

Their conversation wasn't over; she hadn't even told him yet about her own problems. But nor did she want another coffee. Outside, the sun was bouncing off the sea; it was such a glorious afternoon, it seemed a waste to be sitting inside. On the other hand, he was meant to be here to work.

Noting the hesitation, he said, 'No worries if you want to leave.'

'Honestly, it's not that. It's just such a lovely day.' *Well, weatherwise, at least.*

'We could go for a walk? Again, just an idea. Feel free to say no.'

'I'd love to go for a walk,' said Ruby, relieved. 'But you don't want to have to cart your laptop around.'

'My cottage is five minutes from here. I'll drop it off. And please don't worry that I was supposed to be working. I'm now officially taking the rest of the day off.' Hastily he added, 'Don't panic, I don't mean you're stuck with me. The moment you've had enough, all you need to do is say goodbye. I'll take the hint, I promise.'

He paid the bill and they left the café. A few minutes later, they came to the world's tiniest cottage, on Carncrows Street, and she waited outside while he dropped off his laptop. Then they made their way back down to Quay Street and headed for the harbour.

'My turn now,' said Ruby fifteen minutes later, when they reached the golden expanse of Porthminster Beach. Having taken off her espadrilles, she curled her toes in the warm, dry sand and bent to pick up a piece of soft-focus azure sea glass.

'Only if you want to.'

She checked her watch. 'Three and a half hours ago I thought I was married to a man who was good, honest and completely trustworthy. I'd have bet a crazy amount of money on it. Then I found out he's been having an affair. For *months*. With someone he's apparently in love with.'

'Right.' Walking companionably alongside her, Richard nodded. 'Wow. I mean, I can say I'm sorry, but that doesn't actually help. And it only happened this afternoon. No wonder you're still blindsided.'

Kicking up sand, Ruby looked down at her feet, the toenails painted fluorescent pink. She wondered if Margaret Crane wore nail polish on her toes, or would she regard such decoration as frivolous? Maybe Peter secretly disapproved too; this was another possibility. She already knew he found ultra-long, highly decorated gel nails ridiculous. Then again, he'd bought that lurid purple satin lingerie for Margaret to wear during their sexy weekend away . . .

Now the sand was a blur and she pulled a tissue from her bag to wipe her eyes. 'Sorry. I promised myself I wouldn't do this again. I'm not normally the crying type.'

'I'd call this extenuating circumstances. If you want to howl,' said Richard, 'go ahead and howl away. You won't scare me.'

'Thanks.'

'Does he know you're here?'

She shook her head. 'No.'

'And where is he now?'

'In hospital.'

He looked momentarily startled. 'Did you . . . do something to him?'

'Kind of.'

'I think you need to tell me.'

'He thought I was going to publicly expose his . . . lady friend. In a panic, he dropped his phone in the road and dived after it, then got hit by a car. So technically I wasn't to blame,' Ruby explained. 'But it wouldn't have happened if I hadn't been there at the time, putting the fear of God into him.'

'Also wouldn't have happened if he hadn't been having an affair,' Richard observed. '*Were* you going to expose the mistress?'

Ruby shook her head. 'I honestly don't think I could have done that, at least not after he'd been carted off to hospital. I'm sure word will get out anyway. They'll both be at risk of losing their jobs.' Would that happen? She'd have to google it.

'Is he badly injured?'

She sidestepped a mound of dry seaweed. 'A few broken bones. He won't be getting up to much for a while.'

'And what *are* their jobs?'

He seemed so nice, so caring and concerned. But he was also a stranger. She said, 'You might be a journalist.'

'Very wise.' He gave a nod of approval. With a brief smile, he said, 'I'm not. But I could be.'

'One thing I will say.' A light sea breeze swept her hair across her face and she pushed it out of the way. 'Back when we got married, everyone told me he was the lucky one. And they were right. I was the better half.'

'I believe you.'

'If you'd asked anyone which of us was the more likely to go off with someone else, they'd have said me.'

'And were they right? Have you ever had a fling since you've been married?'

'No!' Ruby spread her hands in despair, because she hadn't.

'That's what's so annoying! He was lucky to have me, and now *this* happens.' The unfairness of it rose inside her chest like a cobra preparing to strike. 'And I know this makes me sound like a horrible person, but you should see this woman. She wears frumpy clothes *and* she's older than me . . . I've never been so humiliated in my life.'

Chapter 8

The sun had slowly sunk into the silver-blue sea, lights were starting to snap on across the town and the tide was now well and truly in, wavelets slapping against the harbour walls and gently knocking the hulls of the painted wooden boats against each other as they bobbed in the water.

The pretty waitress shared the last of the bottle of Sancerre between their glasses and said, 'There you go! Just the bill now, is it? Are you sure, or can I tempt you to another drink?'

Ruby hesitated, pleasantly relaxed after the excellent wine and food they'd already put away. One bottle between the two of them hadn't been enough. But another might be too much. They had spent hours together, talking non-stop and enjoying each other's company. If she was going home, now was probably the time to be calling a taxi.

If she was going home.

The candlelight here in the restaurant was golden and glowy. It had been a hell of a day, and now it was night. *Time to leave, Cinderella.* She reached under the table for her bag and said, 'Dinner's been fantastic. We'll have the bill, please.' And when the waitress had left them, she looked at Richard. 'I'm paying. You've done quite enough looking after me for one day.'

'It's been a great day. Not for you, obviously.' He tipped his glass against hers. 'But I've loved getting to know you.'

Her skin began to tingle. 'You'll have to show me where the taxi rank is.'

'I shall.' He lowered his voice. 'No need to go back if you don't want to. You're more than welcome to stay.'

Stop tingling, skin.

'Thank you. But I don't think I should.' He still had no idea what her husband did for a living. All he knew was that she deserved better than the hand she'd been dealt.

Outside, they made their way to the spot where a couple of taxis were waiting.

'You're amazing.' Richard enveloped her in a hug. 'Never forget that. And he's an idiot.'

'I know. We both deserve better.' Ruby stepped back. 'Thanks for today. And good luck with your wife too.'

'Ex-wife,' Richard reminded her, and on impulse she reached up to kiss him on the cheek. Quite close to the corner of his mouth, but not actually *on* it. She heard his intake of breath, then he murmured, 'OK, now you really should leave.'

She climbed into the first taxi and waved goodbye. Richard waved back, then turned away and headed in the direction of his tiny cottage.

The driver navigated the cab through the narrow winding streets, until they'd left St Ives behind them and were wending their way south, back to Lanrock.

Back.

To Lanrock.

54

Why?

Because . . . because . . .

'Old friend, was it?' The taxi driver was in her fifties, chatty and friendly.

'New friend.'

'Well done. He seems very nice. Keen, too. My daughter does that Tinder dating thing, but no luck so far. All she's met is a bunch of idiots.'

'This wasn't a Tinder date. We just happened to get chatting in a café.'

'Even better. Bet you're looking forward to seeing him again!'

'I won't see him again. We didn't swap numbers.'

'Blimey, love, are you mad? Wouldn't catch me turning down a chap like that. Something wrong with him, was there?'

'No . . . no, nothing wrong with him. He was great.'

Silence fell. The taxi continued along the coast road, passing Carbis Bay on the left.

'OK, you're right,' Ruby said finally. 'I've made a mistake.'

The woman grinned, meeting her gaze in the rear mirror. 'Reckon you have.'

'Can we turn round and go back?'

'Well done, love. Sounds like a plan to me.'

Ruby tipped her well, to make up for the brevity of the trip.

'Here, love, take my card. If you can't find him, give me a call. Hell,' added the woman with a wink, 'call me anyway. Always good to know how these things turn out.'

It was only a few hundred yards from the taxi rank to the cottage on Carncrows Street, with its blue window boxes overflowing with geraniums. Thankfully, there were lights on downstairs. Ruby held her breath and rang the bell, then heard the door being unlocked. OK, what could conceivably go wrong now? Maybe if she were to come face to face with an unamused non-lesbian wife . . .

But it was Richard's face she saw when the door opened, and he didn't appear to have anyone else lurking behind him.

'Hello! This is a surprise . . . Did you forget something?'

'No.' She shook her head. He was smiling, which made her smile too.

'Problem with the taxi?'

'No. Although the taxi driver did say she thought you looked really nice.'

'I knew I liked her.'

'She also thought it was a shame we weren't going to be seeing each other again.'

'I thought that too.' He paused. 'Is that why you're here? To ask for my phone number?'

Time to be brave. Ruby said, 'Actually, I was hoping for more than a phone number.'

He reached for her hand and drew her towards him. 'Well, that sounds like something I could go along with. If you're sure it's what you want?'

'It is. Very much so.'

'I want to kiss you.'

She held his gaze. 'That's a coincidence.'

His mouth met hers, and it felt strange but nice to be kissing someone else for the first time in over a decade. His skin smelled different, his body felt different . . . In a weird but good way, it was like being young again.

Drawing away, he said, 'Are you doing this to get back at your husband?'

'Probably.' May as well be honest. She didn't tell him that she fancied him quite a lot too.

'And is that a good thing?'

He was making sure, giving her the chance to change her mind. Which obviously proved he was a thoroughly decent man and meant of course that she wouldn't. 'I'm not going to regret it, if that's what you mean. I plan to enjoy every minute. And there's no need to ask me again if I'm sure about this, because I definitely am.'

Richard's eyes crinkled at the corners. 'Thank God for that.'

From down here on the beach you could see the party still carrying on at the Rupert Hotel. The trees on either side of the broad terrace were lit up with thousands of twinkling white solar lights. Music was playing, the drink was flowing, and people were now dancing with abandon, celebrating the wedding-that-never-was.

Gazing up at the hotel from this distance, you'd never know anything had gone amiss. It looked like any successful reception packed with friends and family squeezing every last drop of enjoyment from the happy day.

Lottie swivelled back round to face the sea. For some people it had definitely turned out to be a happy day, but her own feelings were confusingly muddled. She'd met up with Max again, and seeing him all these years on had stirred up a lot of old, squashed-down memories and emotions. Throughout the afternoon they'd chatted, socialised, laughed and teased each other, and danced with his friends and her own, and it had been giddy-making to the extent that eventually she'd

57

needed space and time alone to think things through without Max, the ultimate distraction, at her side. Which was why, when he'd disappeared into the hotel to order more drinks, she'd slipped away from the party and made her way down the zigzagging path to the beach. It was always the best place to sit and clear her mind; the rhythmic swish of the waves acted like a slow, reassuring metronome. The sky was bright with stars, reminding her that whatever might happen was insignificant in the great scheme of things. What might seem huge in her own life was actually microscopically small. Even the fact that her friend Freya's marriage to Cameron hadn't taken place today wasn't a major disaster, because all they had to do was set another date for the wedding.

Minutes later, she became aware of someone descending the path behind her. Her stomach began to fizz, because how was it possible that she was able to recognise footsteps? But she could, just as she knew without turning round that he'd come to find her.

'Sex on the beach?'

'No, thanks.'

'Just as well that I got you a gin and tonic instead.' Max appeared at her side with white towels slung over his right arm and a drink in each hand.

'How did you know I was here?'

'Why, were you hiding from me?' He sat beside her on the dry sand. 'I went up to my room to put my phone on charge. Looked out of the window and saw you sloping off down here.'

'Not hiding. Just thinking.'

'About how fantastic it is to see me again? That's probably what it was.'

'I was looking at the stars. Feeling tiny. Did you bring these down for us to sit on?' She pointed to the towels, now lying in a heap where he'd dropped them on the sand.

'Thought we might go for a swim.'

'Are you out of your mind?'

'No. Are you *old*?'

'It's only May. That water's freezing.'

'You never used to be scared of anything.'

'I'm not scared, I just don't want to turn into a block of ice.' But even as she uttered the words, Lottie knew what he was going to say next.

'Come on, it'll be fun.' His teeth gleamed white in the darkness. 'I dare you.'

How many times had he dared her, back when they'd been teenagers? How many times had she dared him? And the thing about dares when you were a teenager was you never turned one down. Which, since the two of them had been as competitive as each other, was the reason they'd got into so many scrapes.

'You know you want to.' He gave her a sideways nudge.

'I *don't* want to.'

'It's only water.'

'You once dared me to eat a chilli and said it wasn't that hot. It was a Carolina Reaper.'

'I remember. I also remember the time you tipped a jar of ants into my school bag.'

Lottie kept a straight face. 'One of my happiest memories.'

'And now here we are.' Another playful nudge. 'Race you into the sea. For old times' sake.'

'Absolutely no way.' Getting to her feet, she shook her head. 'Not a chance.' She began vigorously dusting the sand from her legs, took a few steps away from him, then in one smooth movement grabbed the hem of her dress and lifted it over her head.

'You . . .!' With a cry of disbelief, he leapt up and began to tear off his shirt and trousers, but it was too late, she'd outwitted him. She flung the dress behind her and took off, racing down the beach. Shedding clothes along the way, Max chased after her, but she had the advantage and it was too late to catch up. She gave a triumphant whoop, high-stepped her way through the breaking waves, then launched into a shallow dive and submerged herself under the water.

When it was this cold, it was the only way.

Eurgh, and it *was* cold. But exhilarating too, not least because she'd won; she'd tricked Max and beaten him into the sea. As far as feelings went, that was just about the best.

Spinning round and breaking the surface, she shook her hair like a dog and called out, 'I can't believe you fell for it – what a loser!' But he was nowhere in sight; all she could see were his clothes abandoned on the shoreline. Her head swivelling in outrage, Lottie realised he must be hiding behind a rock, leaving her to enter the icy water on her own, which was just typical. She should have known he'd go for the double-cross—

'*Waaahhh!*' She let out a shriek as two hands closed around her waist. The outwitter outwitted. The next moment she found herself being raised out of the water and held high over Max's head like at the end of *Dirty Dancing*, only on her back instead of her front. And in the film, Patrick Swayze had balanced Jennifer Grey in the air, he hadn't deliberately tipped her over backwards . . .

Whoosh! Holding her breath, Lottie found herself meeting

the water again, head-first. All that was left to do was to make a grab for the nearest ankle she could find and pull Max off-balance so now they were both submerged, and it was so like old times that she wanted to laugh, but that wasn't advisable in the sea.

Finally they both regained their footing and came up for air. She wasn't yet shivering, but it would start soon. All she had on was her lime-green bra and knickers, and Max had discarded everything other than low-slung black boxer trunks. They were facing each other now, mere inches apart, their bodies being gently pushed back and forth by the waves.

Chapter 9

'Lottie.' Max shook his head. 'I still can't believe I came down to Cornwall for a wedding and found you here.'

'I know. It's crazy.' The cold was beginning to bite into her, icy tentacles enfolding her internal organs.

'I knew I'd get you into the water.' There was the gleam of white teeth again. 'You never could resist a dare.'

The swell of the next wave moved them closer still, and Lottie's arm brushed against his as she stepped sideways to steady herself.

'I wonder what our parents would say,' Max murmured, 'if they could see us now.'

'Don't.' As scenarios went, it was unthinkable. Her brain was currently too full to want to go there. Plus, her body was starting to protest about the cold by numbing her extremities.

'Come on, I can hear your teeth chattering.' He reached for her hand. As they headed back to shore, Lottie wondered if he'd been thinking of kissing her before realising he was likely to get his tongue bitten off.

Or was she the one who'd been wondering if he'd been about to kiss her?

Having retrieved their scattered clothes, they each grabbed a bath towel and dried themselves as best they could.

'How far away's your flat?' said Max.

'Ten minutes.'

He shook his head. 'My room it is, then.'

It went without saying that everyone found it hilarious when they reappeared on the terrace in their towels, earning themselves much laughter, a round of applause and a few ribald comments as they made their way barefoot across the dance floor and into the hotel.

Max's room was on the third floor. He switched on the power shower and said, 'The coldest person can go first.'

'Thanks.' She dipped past him, closed the door and stepped under the steaming water. *Bliss.*

Then it was his turn, and while he was in the bathroom, Lottie blasted her bra and knickers with the thankfully powerful hairdryer. By the time he re-emerged, she was dressed once more, her underwear only slightly damp, and attempting to at least half-dry her hair.

'Better?'

'Much.' She straightened up and switched off the dryer. 'Thanks. I'm going to go back down now.'

'You don't have to rush off.'

'I know, but I want to.'

He gave her a speculative half-smile. 'Well, it was nice swimming with you. You know, you haven't changed a bit.'

'I have. We both have. Well, maybe not you so much.' Lottie indicated his phone, still charging on the bed. 'A WhatsApp came through while you were in the shower.'

'Right.' He pulled an *ouch* face. 'And?'

There was no point pretending she hadn't glanced at the

screen. 'Cara wonders how everything's going. She also hopes you're behaving yourself.'

'I think I'm behaving marvellously. Don't you?'

'Is she your girlfriend?'

'No. Cara's someone I see every now and again. When it suits us both.' He smiled. 'Ours is a relationship of convenience.'

'Meaning she likes you more than you like her, but she'll take whatever she can get.'

'Maybe it's the other way round,' Max suggested. 'I could be crazy about her but all she wants is a friends-with-benefits arrangement.'

'It doesn't matter either way. You're a free agent.' Lottie shrugged.

The phone went *ting* again and he gestured for her to pick it up. 'Go ahead. You can read it.'

'She says Denny just posted a load of photos on Instagram and she can't see you in any of them, so where are you, and you'd better not be up to your old tricks.'

'What can I tell you? She's insecure.'

Lottie had enough experience with the opposite sex to recognise a classic case of pass-the-blame. She handed him the phone. 'Bye.'

'If you wait, I'll be dressed in two minutes.'

'I'm leaving now.'

'Hey.' Max reached out to her. 'Why?'

'I'm tired. And I have to be at work tomorrow morning.' She gave a casual shrug, although the turmoil in her chest was anything but casual. She'd never been a one-night-stand sort of person – meeting a stranger and hopping straight into bed with them just wasn't her thing. But Max wasn't a stranger, and seeing him again had knocked her for six, sending her emotions into overdrive.

64

There was unfinished business between them, and they both knew it. She'd be lying to herself if she refused to admit to being incredibly tempted. They'd spent the last six hours verbally sparring, the chemistry between them undeniable. Each instance of physical contact had felt like electricity zapping her nerve endings.

And of course nothing could ever come of it, they both knew that, but maybe one night together – just the one, with absolutely no strings attached – would round things off nicely, providing the necessary full stop to an issue that had remained unresolved for the last thirteen years.

Oh, who was she kidding? Of course that was how this evening would have ended. Of course she'd have spent the night here with Max in this hotel room. It would probably have been amazing too; having always taken great pride in excelling at everything he did, she couldn't imagine him being anything less than spectacular in bed.

She looked at him now with a mixture of frustration and regret. The other thing she'd never done in her life was sleep with another woman's boyfriend. And while Max might not classify himself as Cara's boyfriend, in Cara's eyes he clearly was.

As if to confirm it, the phone in his hand began to ring. When he hesitated, Lottie said, 'You can't not answer.'

Max briefly closed his eyes and pressed the button. She couldn't hear what Cara was saying, but it didn't matter.

'I'm fine, I was just talking to an old friend.' He listened, then replied, 'No need to pick me up from the station, I'll get a cab. Cara, I'm about to run out of battery. I'll call you tomorrow. Yes, no, OK. Bye now. Bye.'

He ended the call. 'She really isn't my girlfriend.'

'In that case, you probably shouldn't lead her on.' Lottie moved towards the door.

'I don't want you to go.'

'Yes, well. You can't always get what you want.' She turned the handle and stepped out into the corridor.

Max followed her. 'Do I at least get a goodbye hug?'

With a clunk, the door swung shut behind him. 'Best not,' said Lottie.

'And now I'm locked out of my room.' He indicated his naked upper half, the towel fastened around his hips.

'I'll let the receptionist know. She'll send someone up.' Reaching the staircase, she waved goodbye.

With a brief smile, Max said, 'You're killing me. You know that, don't you?'

It was the kind of thing confident seducers liked to say. Maybe sometimes it even worked. Lottie replied, 'I'm sure you'll survive.'

Downstairs, she acknowledged the woman on reception, then headed outside to retrieve her shoes and say goodbye to the happily unmarried couple.

'I can't believe you went to school with Max.' Cameron enveloped her in a hug. 'That's mad.'

'I can't believe Cameron never told me he had such a good-looking friend.' It was Freya's turn to fling her arms tipsily around Lottie. 'He's gorgeous. Do you think he's gorgeous? Those eyes!'

'I think he thinks he's irresistible. Anyway, I'm off now. Are you OK?'

Freya beamed. 'I'm fine. It's been the best day. Well, not for everyone, obviously. Mum phoned the hospital earlier and Peter's had his op. They wouldn't give any details, obviously, but apparently he's comfortable. Poor Ruby, though, what a horrible thing to happen to her.'

'You don't mind that she messed up your wedding?'

'How could I mind? It's been fantastic and everyone's had a great time.' Freya gave her another enthusiastic squeeze. 'I'll call you tomorrow and we'll have a proper catch-up. I want to know all about *everything* . . .' Glancing over Lottie's shoulder, she did a double-take. 'Including why handsome Max has just come down to reception wearing nothing but a towel.'

Whoops. Lottie ducked out of his eyeline before he could spot her. 'We'll talk tomorrow. Time I was gone.'

Chapter 10

It had been one of those hot, restless nights of endless dozing and waking, and Lottie knew who was to blame; it was one more reason to be annoyed with him. Now, at seven in the morning, here she was, lying in bed and *still* thinking about Max.

She'd definitely done the right thing leaving the party when she had. Her body might have been tempted to stay but her conscience hadn't allowed it, despite the fact that Max's evidently didn't bother him. But he hadn't experienced the trauma she'd endured in her first year at university, when falling for a smooth-talking charmer called Keiron had caused her untold misery. Looking back, of course, she could see now that Keiron had been selfish, full of himself and not charming at all, but at the time she'd been too besotted to notice. For almost three months they'd had the best time together, until one morning a girl had tapped on the door of his room in the halls of residence and started sobbing to be let in. 'Shh,' Keiron had murmured in Lottie's ear as they lay in bed together. 'If she thinks I'm not here, she'll go away.'

Except his visitor didn't go away. She stayed outside the door for hours, until the two of them were forced to emerge from the room and the devastated girl said to Lottie, 'How long have you been seeing him?'

Mortified, Lottie replied, 'Not that long.'

The tear-stained girl addressed Keiron. 'Why didn't you tell me?'

He looked exasperated. 'Because I knew you'd do something like this. It's just typical of you.'

She turned her attention back to Lottie. 'So are you going to finish with him now?'

Keiron reached out at that point and gave Lottie's hand a secret squeeze of encouragement. And Lottie, having heard his whispered explanation about the clingy ex-girlfriend who refused to acknowledge that their brief relationship was well and truly over, had known what she needed to do. As kindly but firmly as possible, she heard herself say, 'Look, he's moved on. I'm sorry, but you need to accept it. He'd rather be with me.'

It had been way out of her comfort zone, but she'd felt brave at the time, like a character in a film, standing her ground and staking her claim on her boyfriend.

After that, the girl had turned and left without uttering another word, and Keiron had been delighted, because she was the bane of his life, a desperate stalker ex from his home town who couldn't take a hint. He told Lottie how brilliantly she'd handled the situation and treated her to a meal at Burger King as a reward.

It wasn't until two days later that he abruptly disappeared, and word reached Lottie via one of his friends that the desperate stalker ex was in fact the twenty-year-old mother of his six-month-old son, and she was currently lying unconscious in intensive care having taken a massive overdose of antidepressants.

The girl had recovered, thankfully. But Keiron had never returned to university, nor had he contacted Lottie again. The abject horror, the shame and the feeling that she was at least partly to blame for what had happened had not left Lottie to this day. Thanks to her out-of-character and horribly misguided decision to believe and stand by her man, she could have been held at least partly responsible for the tragic death of a young mother.

Oh God, how she hated even remembering that hideous episode in her life. It had changed her irrevocably, making her wary of potential boyfriends ever since. And if the timings had been infinitesimally different last night, she wouldn't even have known of Cara's existence. She could have woken up this morning in Max's hotel room, in his bed and in his arms . . . Even picturing the scene, her pulse was quickening, because it was what she'd wanted to happen and—

Drrringgg went the doorbell, and now Lottie's heart rate really shot into overdrive, because who else could be outside at this time on a Sunday morning? He'd obviously asked around last night and found out her address, and now he was here to resume the temptation, because when you were Max Farrell, failure wasn't an option. Except what he still didn't understand was that she had no intention of giving in.

Leaping out of bed and hurtling into the bathroom, she brushed her teeth at lightning speed, splashed her face with cold water and pushed her hair into some semblance of tousled sexiness rather than just side-squashed bed-head. Lip gloss? No. Scent? OK, just a quick squish. And a super-speedy change into a clean oversized T-shirt because the one she'd been sleeping in had a blackcurrant jam stain over one boob that made her look like the type of person who'd eat toast sluttily in bed.

Which of course she was.

The bell rang again, long and loud. Skidding downstairs, Lottie took a breath, then pulled open the front door and came face to face with a little old man wearing an orange cagoule and huge lemon-yellow trainers.

He shot her an accusing look. 'You're not Mary.'

And he definitely wasn't Max. She said, 'I know. Do you mean Mary Jackson?'

He nodded. 'What have you done with her?'

'I haven't done anything. Mary lives up the road at number twenty-six.' She pointed him in the right direction. 'The one with the red front door.'

He tutted with irritation. 'Well, it's not my fault. She didn't tell me that.'

So there it was. Not Max Farrell on her doorstep after all. Probably just as well.

Lottie headed back to bed, ignoring the crushing weight of disappointment in the pit of her stomach.

'Well, this wasn't how I expected the last night of my break to turn out.' Richard pushed a loose strand of hair away from Ruby's face. 'But I'm very glad it did.'

'Me too.' In truth, she was still half wondering if it might all have been a dream. Here on the doorstep of the cottage on Carncrows Street, about to leave at nine in the morning, she still felt completely unlike herself.

'Are you sure you won't let me give you my number?'

'Quite sure. Spending yesterday with you was perfect, just what I needed to get me through . . . everything. But I think

71

it has to be a one-off. From now on I need to sort myself out.'
All she knew was his first name. All he knew was hers. It was
better to keep it that way. Reaching up to plant a final brief
kiss on his mouth, Ruby said, 'I hope you manage to sort things
out with your ex-wife. Don't let her force you into doing
anything you don't want to do.'

'I won't. And good luck to you too.' The smile he gave her
could have broken her heart, if it weren't broken already.

She blew him a kiss, waggled her fingers goodbye, and made
her way back up the narrow street to the taxi rank. It was time
to leave St Ives, time to return to the real world.

Also, probably time to visit her husband in hospital.

Which would be fun.

Peter was lying in his hospital bed with his eyes closed and
various parts of him bandaged. Observing him from just beyond
the entrance to his room, Ruby thought how fitting it would
be if, beneath the white cotton sheet, *that* part of him was
wrapped in a bandage too.

Sensing her presence, his eyes opened and he looked at her with
a mixture of relief and trepidation. Raising a hand and wincing
with pain, he cleared his throat. 'You came. Look, I'm sorry.'

'Don't be. And I'm only here because clearly we have stuff
to sort out.' She entered the room and pulled out a chair to sit
on, keeping it several feet from his bed. 'Has she been in to visit
you?'

'No.' He hesitated, then said, 'I wonder if you could do me
a favour?'

Presumably Margaret hadn't wanted to take the risk of their
affair being found out if she turned up to see him. Ruby said,
'Wow. You have some nerve.'

'I need a phone. Arrangements have to be made. I need to speak to—'

'The Bishop? I suppose you do, to let him know you're resigning.'

'Are you going to do that to me? Is this what has to happen?'

Ruby had no intention of informing the Bishop herself – word would get back to him soon enough – but she marvelled at Peter's attempt to skew the conversation, to make her feel like the one in the wrong. 'You've done it to yourself. You made it happen. I haven't told anyone who you've been sleeping with, by the way. But I can't see it staying a secret.'

He looked stricken. 'Please . . .'

'I just hope she's worth it. How long are you going to be in here?'

'Not long. They operated on my knee last night. They're hoping to discharge me after a few days, but obviously I'll be needing some help.'

'Well, good luck with that. Hopefully the Bishop will let you stay on at the vicarage until you're up and about again. I'll be moving my things out in the next couple of days.'

Her husband's pale face creased with pain. 'Can we talk about this?'

'Not much point.' Ruby crossed her legs. 'Our marriage is over. If I'm honest, it hasn't been the best, has it? Not what you'd call the most fun. But I stuck with you because I thought it was the right thing to do. And now look at us. What a waste of all those years.'

He shook his head. 'I'm sorry.'

'You keep saying that. But only because you got caught. Do you really love her?'

'I don't know. Maybe. I think so.'

'Well, let's hope she loves you, because you're going to need someone to put your socks on for you for the next few weeks.'

'I need a new phone.' He was almost begging, as desperate as any teenager.

'I expect you do. Never mind, Margaret can buy you one. I'm going to be too busy moving out.'

'Where will you go? Home to your parents?'

'What? I'm forty years old, thanks. And why should I go anywhere? I'll rent somewhere in Lanrock. I'm not moving away just to suit you. I don't have to do anything to suit you,' Ruby continued. 'From now on, I can do whatever I like. Sleep with whoever I want to sleep with. Nothing to stop me. Why are you looking at me like that?'

'Now you're being ridiculous. You're just saying that for effect, trying to upset me.' His tone had switched now, to belittling; it was another of the psychological tricks he employed when she stood up to him.

'Oh no, really? Would it *bother* you?' Ruby clapped a hand to her chest. 'Would my unfaithful husband find it *upsetting* if I slept with someone else? Because guess what? I already did! I met someone yesterday and spent all night with him. In his bed.'

Wasn't this why she'd done it, after all? So that she could announce the fact to Peter and, hopefully, cause him a jolt of pain so that he might get a hint of how it felt. What she hadn't expected was for him to produce one of those flat, humourless smiles of his, which meant he didn't even believe her. He thought she was just saying it to get back at him.

'Of course you did.'

Her hackles rose, because how dare he doubt her? 'It's true. It *happened*.'

'Right, of course it did.'

74

Oh, this was beyond infuriating. 'You think I'm lying? I'm not. I met him in a café in St Ives and we spent the afternoon and evening together. Then I was going to come home but I thought, why should I? So I didn't. I stayed at his house.'

'Yes, yes.' Here it was, the slow, patronising nod he reserved for special occasions, like when elderly pensioners started showing him endless photos of their grandchildren. Incandescent with rage, Ruby raised her voice to stop him in his tracks. 'And we spent the night together, having lots and *lots* of sex, and it was *fantastic*—'

Too late, she registered the discreet tap-tap-tap and realised the door had already swung open. 'Sorry, my love. Didn't mean to interrupt.' The middle-aged woman with the tea trolley was doing a terrible impersonation of someone who hadn't just overheard some deliciously scandalous item of gossip. 'Wondered if you'd like a nice cup of tea, Vicar?'

'That would be most welcome,' said Peter. 'Milk, no sugar. And please don't pay any attention to what you may have heard just now. My wife didn't mean it . . . she was joking.'

Ruby shook her head at him, and an awkward silence fell as the woman poured the tea, in her excitement slopping half of it into the saucer.

When she'd left them to it but was probably still lurking within earshot in the corridor, Ruby said, 'I wasn't joking. I meant every word. And it *was* fantastic.'

'In that case, I look forward to meeting him. Now, perhaps we could try to be sensible about this?'

'I think I'm being perfectly sensible.'

'I can't do anything without a phone. I need one. *Please,*' Peter added.

'I'm surprised you don't have a burner one hidden away somewhere. Isn't that what adulterers usually do?'

He gave her a long, disappointed stare. 'Now you're just being vindictive. You have to understand, I never wanted to hurt you.'

'What a coincidence.' Ruby rose from her chair. 'Same here. I thought that was a given, in a marriage?'

'I'm sorry.'

'Are you? I think it's the school you should be feeling sorry for.' Unable to resist it, she added, 'Not that I'd say anything myself, but it definitely isn't the easiest time of year to find a replacement head.'

Chapter 11

Freya's deepest and most shameful secret was that yesterday she'd been due to marry Dr Cameron Bancroft, officially the nicest man on the planet, and when it hadn't happened, she'd been overwhelmed with relief.

Which had to be a secret, because who did she think she was? Someone special, some spoiled princess who demanded the world on a plate? She didn't deserve someone as lovely as Cameron; she knew that for a fact. She'd lucked out three years ago when they'd met in a bar and for some reason he'd decided she was the one for him. Since then, she'd grown accustomed to people telling her how lucky she was to have nabbed such a catch. Cameron was a GP who had time for everyone. He had an open, friendly face, a warm smile and the ability to make people feel as if they were really being listened to, even when they'd stop him in the street to give him a long and detailed update on the state of their varicose veins.

He was just all-round lovely, raising money for various charities in his spare time and generally encouraging others to be a force for good through leading by example. He was a keen cyclist who genuinely preferred food that was healthy, and when the time came, he would make the most brilliant father. There wasn't any way to find fault with him. No, really, none at all.

Freya had felt incredibly guilty when her feelings for him had begun to waver after their first year together. Because you couldn't control your emotions, could you? That was the thing, they controlled you. And much as she liked him – because how could anyone *not* like Cameron? – she'd found herself developing a nagging concern that life should be spent with someone who made your heart race.

But it had been during this period of indecision that something far more important had happened. Her mum, who had raised her alone following the death of her father in a boating accident twenty years ago, had developed acute renal failure. Freya and Tess had always been close, and Freya was panic-stricken at the prospect of losing the mother she adored. At this stage, having Cameron there to explain what was happening and reassure her that Tess was receiving the best possible treatment was something for which she was incredibly grateful.

Sometimes, though, the best possible treatment simply wasn't enough. As Tess's condition worsened, Freya began to really panic. When she learned that her mother's kidneys were no longer functioning and she would require dialysis from now on, she was distraught. She instantly volunteered herself as a kidney donor, but tests showed her to be incompatible.

Four weeks later, Cameron appeared at Tess's hospital bedside while Freya was sitting with her, and announced simply, 'I'm a match.'

They hadn't even known he'd contacted the living donor team and put himself forward for testing. It had been carried out secretly, to avoid giving them false hope. Tess burst into tears of joy and hugged him, and Freya said in a daze, 'Are you sure? Are you really sure?'

Cameron's smile was warm. 'Of course I'm sure. I love you. If you can't give your mum one of your own kidneys, at least I can donate one of mine.' At that moment, Freya thought he'd spotted something on the floor and was reaching to pick it up, but instead he sank down on one knee and produced a small velvet jeweller's box from his trouser pocket. And right there on the ward, in front of assorted patients, visitors and staff, he said, 'Freya, will you make me the happiest man in the world and marry me? Will you be my wife?'

Well, after that, how could she not say yes?

He hadn't deliberately planned it this way for publicity purposes, but of course other people had whipped out their phones and taken videos and photos, resulting in a story that dominated page seven of the local paper. Not long afterwards, the transplant had gone ahead and been a complete success. Both donor and recipient made excellent recoveries, and Tess was overjoyed that her daughter would be marrying a man who'd not only been perfect in the first place, but whose altruistic gesture had saved her own life. The three of them were now bound together for ever, and she couldn't be happier about it.

Freya, meanwhile, found herself left with no choice other than to bury her own doubts and instead accept that she owed it to Cameron to be the loving wife he so wholeheartedly deserved.

Because how could she do otherwise? Imagine being known for ever more as the fiancée with the heart of ice who said, 'Yeah, thanks for risking your life in order to donate one of your precious kidneys to my mum, but now you've done it I don't need to marry you any more, so bye!'

The door to Lanrock Holiday Homes was propped open to bring in a breeze and Lottie was behind the desk typing at warp speed on her laptop when she heard someone pause at the entrance to the office.

'Hi,' said Freya. 'Busy?'

'Of course not! Come on in. It seems really weird that you're here the day after you were meant to be getting married.'

'I know.' Freya pulled a face. 'Leaving the cottage this morning felt like doing the walk of shame in reverse – people kept looking at me as if I should be in bed having loads of wild honeymoon sex.'

Lottie raised an eyebrow. 'And? So why *aren't* you still in bed having wild non-honeymoon sex?'

'Cameron's gone to visit one of his patients. She's not ill, just upset because her little brother's died. I mean, he was ninety and she's ninety-three, but you know what Cameron's like. She was crying when she called him this morning, so he couldn't say no.'

'We all know what Cameron's like. Just as well you didn't have a honeymoon booked – he'd probably have missed the plane.'

'He hates to leave his patients. The plan is to squeeze in a quick trip to Paris later in the year.' Freya was endlessly understanding. Pausing for breath, she began to say, 'Did you hear—' just as Lottie beat her to it with the same question.

'I think quite a few people have heard.' Lottie held up her phone, its screen covered with WhatsApp messages. 'Margaret Crane! God, can you imagine?'

80

They exchanged a look, both imagining it. The Reverend Peter Vale and the buttoned-up, somewhat intimidating headmistress of Lanrock Primary School. Who could ever have dreamed up such a pairing?

Lottie's phone pinged yet again. 'Actually, I bet the whole town knows by now.'

Having spent yesterday afternoon and evening heroically refusing to tell anyone who the vicar had been secretly involved with, Iris Norton had finally enjoyed one glass too many of Lanrock cider and succumbed to temptation at around midnight. She'd whispered Margaret's name to her friend Sally, who worked as a waitress at the hotel, who'd promptly spread the news to the rest of the staff, then, in turn, to her many brothers and sisters. Within an hour, phones had been lighting up non-stop and the irresistible item of gossip was on everyone's lips, the big secret a secret no more.

'It just goes to show, you never know what's going on, do you? And speaking of what's going on.' Freya tilted her head enquiringly at Lottie. 'Max is a bit gorgeous, isn't he?'

Lottie tapped a pen against the edge of her desk; here it came, her own personal inquisition. 'And he knows it. He was always full of himself.'

'You went for a swim together, in the sea . . .'

'That wasn't planned,' she protested. 'It was a dare. Trust me, if you don't accept a dare from Max Farrell, you never hear the end of it.'

Freya wagged a playful finger. 'What I need to know is what happened in his hotel room *after* the swim.'

'I had a shower. He had a shower. Not at the same time. And nothing happened. At all.'

'I bet he wanted it to. Were you not even tempted?'

'I did the sensible thing and walked away.' Lottie ignored the memory of the adrenalin jolt of hope earlier this morning when the doorbell had woken her up.

'Probably a good move. Cameron did say Max had a wicked reputation at uni. Apparently girls were always falling for him.' Freya's own phone went *ting*, announcing the arrival of yet another WhatsApp message. 'It's from Amber. She's just seen Margaret Crane loading a suitcase into her car and driving off. She says Margaret tooted her horn at a family about to cross the road *and* jumped a red light.'

'What a mess. I wonder if her husband knows yet? Maybe he's kicked her out of the house— Ooh.' Lottie pointed through the window. 'Look who it is . . .'

They both watched as Ruby Vale made her way up the hill on foot, wearing dark sunglasses and an emerald summer dress. Her dark brown hair was fastened in a loose bun with a green and white flowered scarf and she was wearing white espadrilles.

'She looks like an Italian film star,' Freya sighed. Peter Vale's wife was curvy, tanned and endlessly glamorous, and it seemed crazy that he would risk everything in the way he had. 'If I were married to her, I wouldn't be having a fling with the local headmistress behind her back, I can tell you that.'

'She's coming in,' yelped Lottie as Ruby crossed the street, heading directly towards them. 'Hello!'

Ruby came into the office and sank onto one of the chairs in front of Lottie's desk. Removing her dark glasses, she gazed up at Freya. 'Hi. Well, at least I can kill two birds with one stone. Freya, I'm *so* sorry about yesterday. I feel terrible about it. The last thing I wanted was to cause so much trouble.'

'You don't have to apologise, it wasn't your fault.' Freya shook

82

her head. 'It doesn't matter about the wedding either. We can get married another time, and the reception at the hotel was great anyway. We're more worried about you,' she went on. 'Such a horrible thing to happen. Are you all right?'

Ruby pulled a face. 'I'll survive. I got a text from Iris apologising for being a blabbermouth. Does everyone know who it is now?'

Lottie nodded. 'Afraid so.'

'Oh well, I suppose you can't expect something that good to stay a secret.'

'How's your husband? Have you heard?'

'Saw him an hour ago. He'll be discharged soon enough. That's why I came to see you.' Ruby gestured at the property details displayed on shelves around the office. 'Looks like I need to find somewhere else to live. Preferably before Peter gets out of hospital.'

'It's so unfair, though,' Freya protested. 'You shouldn't have to leave, not when you haven't done anything wrong.'

Lottie moved across to the machine in the corner. 'Coffee?'

'Coffee would be great, thanks. And yes, it's unfair, but it isn't the end of the world.'

'So you want to stay in the area?'

'I do. Lanrock has everything. I love it here.' Ruby's eyes flashed. 'And why should I move?'

'Exactly,' Freya exclaimed.

'I mean, I suppose people will be laughing at me behind my back.'

'They won't. They're laughing at him, not you. As far as everyone else is concerned, it makes no sense at all. I mean, look at you, he was so lucky to have you.'

For a moment, Ruby's eyes swam with tears. Then she gathered herself. 'Thanks.' After a pause, she went on, 'Well, fuck him. His loss.'

After a moment of stunned silence – *the vicar's wife swore!* – Lottie put the coffees on the desk and said with a grin, 'Fuck him indeed. And it's definitely his loss. Now, let's find you somewhere to live.' She pulled her laptop back towards her. 'Tell me what kind of place you have in mind, and how long you're going to need it for.'

'Oh God, a few months, I suppose. By the end of the summer I'll hopefully have been able to buy somewhere.' Ruby took a sip of coffee, then sat back. 'And I don't have a clue what I want, so long as it isn't a draughty old vicarage. Just show me what you've got.'

Two days later, Ruby moved into her temporary new home. There hadn't actually been many properties to choose from, what with most of the holiday homes being rented for a week or a fortnight at a time and the majority of them largely booked up. But luck was on her side, and two days ago a family who'd planned to spend the summer season in Lanrock had changed their minds at the last minute and were flying to California instead.

'Right, so it's one of these two,' Lottie had told her during their Sunday-morning meeting in the office. 'The first one's a good price, but it's at the far end of Leopard Lane . . .' She'd paused and grimaced, because that meant it was just around the corner from the vicarage.

Ruby had given an exaggerated shudder. 'Maybe not.'

'OK. The other one costs more, but it's way nicer anyway.' Pulling up the details of the apartment that had just become available, Lottie had shown her the laptop screen. 'Right on the seafront with fantastic views.'

The vicarage had been surrounded by mature trees, with no views at all. 'Sounds perfect.'

'The only problem is, you'd be stuck with a bit of a nightmare neighbour.'

There always had to be a drawback, didn't there? Ruby's spirits fell. 'Who is it?'

'Me,' Lottie deadpanned. 'I know, sorry. Do you think you could bear it?'

Oh, the *relief*. Ruby broke into a wide smile. 'Well, I am pretty desperate. I suppose I could manage that.'

Chapter 12

And now here she was, three weeks later, happily settled into the second smallest of the four properties that had been renovated several years ago by Lottie's father, Terence Palmer. Constructed around a sheltered courtyard, the modern apartments had been built on the site of the old indoor market at the junction of Beach Street and Cliff Road, just up the road from Bert's Bar and with only a strip of grass separating them from the beach itself.

From Ruby's living room window, the view was an uninterrupted one of pale gold sand, sparkling sea and small boats bobbing on the water. From the bedroom at the back, you looked out onto the communal courtyard that was shared by the guests staying in the apartments. The fourth one, with the least expansive sea view, was occupied by Lottie, who ran the family's lettings agency while her parents, Terry and Kay, spent their days socialising and sailing, playing golf and generally making the most of their early retirement.

Ruby swirled sapphire paint from her paintbrush in the jar of water in front of her and wondered if she really was happily settled. The apartment was great; despite being on the small side, it was light and airy, and she'd pushed the glass-topped dining table right up to the window so she could simultaneously work at it and admire the ever-changing view.

But happy? No, evidently not, not when she was still finding it hard to sleep at night, and woke every morning with a start and a sense of doom-laden panic in her chest.

Because her old life had been taken away from her like a rug being unceremoniously ripped from beneath her feet. Maybe her marriage hadn't been a giddy apex of joy, but at least she'd been used to it. And yes, she knew she would become accustomed to this unexpected new life in due course, but it was showing no signs of happening yet.

Meanwhile, punishing deadlines waited for no one, and her next book was due on her editor's desk in four weeks. Somewhat problematically, her brain was refusing to cooperate and had gone on strike.

Worst of all, an hour from now, her editor was arriving in Lanrock to take her out to lunch and discuss plans for future books, which meant she would be wanting to see how much progress had been made on this one.

This nowhere-near-finished one, which Ruby had given the impression of being *almost* finished.

The thing was, publishers' schedules were worked out many months in advance, and missing a deadline caused all manner of kerfuffle. Aware of this, she had always prided herself on handing in her manuscripts – both text and accompanying artwork – before their deadlines.

She might be casting off her vicar's-wife persona, but she was damned if she'd give up her career as a writer and illustrator of children's books. She had been a consistently bestselling author for eight years now, and she wasn't going to allow Peter's affair to put a stop to that.

Outside the expanse of window, a flock of excitable gulls swirled and swooped around a fishing boat as it came chugging back to the harbour. A toddler on the beach was trying to eat a long strand of seaweed, and a chocolate Labrador with an orange frisbee in his mouth was having a tug-of-war with his owner. People-watching and animal-watching was how Ruby conjured up her ideas, and she was trying to brainstorm by doodling whatever she could see with watercolours and inks. But today her brain was stubbornly refusing to storm. Wally Bee and Zelda weren't playing ball. And knowing that her editor would be here very soon was just making her anxiety worse.

The initial idea for the books had arrived one Sunday nine years ago when Peter had, without warning, put her in charge of a six-year-old girl while he spoke with the girl's mother. In a panic, Ruby had said, 'But what do I do with her? I'm no good with children!' Whereupon he'd briskly replied, 'Well, maybe it's time to learn.'

Which was a fair enough point. Plus, there'd been no one else available while he took the distraught young mother into the living room to discuss the problems she'd been having with her husband and in-laws.

Leaving Ruby in the kitchen, at something of a loss and required to entertain a withdrawn six-year-old for God knows how long. Worse still, a six-year-old who shook her head and said no when Ruby suggested she might like to watch TV.

Out of desperation, Ruby had sat her down at the kitchen table with a sketchpad and a packet of coloured felt-tip pens. The girl, her bottom lip wobbling, whispered, 'Daddy said my drawings were no good. He threw away the pictures I did.'

Ruby already knew the father was a nasty piece of work and a heavy drinker. Her heart pierced, she exclaimed, 'Oh sweetheart, I bet you can draw brilliant pictures. You do one for me now and let's see how great it is. No one's ever drawn anything for me before, so I know I'll love it!'

'I can't.' A single tear ran down the girl's cheek and plopped onto the table.

'Well then, why don't we do one together? How about that for an idea? We'll think of things to draw and turn them into a story.' As Ruby made this slightly desperate last-ditch suggestion, a bumblebee entered through the open kitchen window and flew around their heads, buzzing noisily. She attempted to guide it back out by waving a tea towel, but the bee deftly avoided her. 'Let's draw this naughty boy, shall we? What do you think his name is? Oh, where's he gone?' She gave up the chase as the bee disappeared behind a pot of yellow geraniums on the windowsill. 'Can you see him? If only he had a name, maybe he'd come out!'

And the girl, showing interest for the first time, said, 'We could call him Wally Bee.'

'That,' Ruby told her, 'is brilliant. Because it means everyone who hears his name will think he's a wallaby.' When the girl understandably looked blank, she pulled up a photo on her phone to show her what wallabies looked like. 'So every time people expect to meet a wallaby, they'll be really surprised when they find out he's just a tiny bee instead. Called Wally. But he can still fly off and have adventures with his favourite friend . . . ooh, I think she might be six years old, and we could call her . . . what do you think? You can choose.'

'Donkey?'

'Er . . .'

'Biscuit?'

'Well . . .'

'I know.' The girl was animated now. 'Let's call her Zelda.'

Ruby wrote it down. 'That's a great name. What made you think of it?'

The girl gave her a look as if she should know that. 'It's the name of my snail.'

This, on an unprepossessing rainy afternoon at her kitchen table, was how Ruby's new career had begun. By the time Megan's mother and Peter reappeared an hour later, she had sketched out Wally Bee and Zelda and between them they had come up with a short story that Megan was happy to show off to her mum. And that evening, Ruby had found herself dreaming up ideas for further adventures. Like magic, a tap that she hadn't even known existed had been turned on. Until then, painting in watercolours had been nothing more than an occasional hobby. Within a week, she had written and illustrated her first short story. The second had taken six days. A month later, the head of the firm of solicitors where she worked as a secretary found her scribbling new ideas on the back of a manila envelope beneath her desk.

'What's this?' Whisking the envelope from her hand, he read aloud, 'In the dentist's surgery, Wally buzzes around making a sound like a drill . . . secret stash of sweets in drawer . . . they start to sing and dance . . . knitted booties for Wally . . . Zelda needs to rescue him from the bin, then climbs out of the window that night to find a star that's fallen into a tree and—'

Bright red, Ruby mumbled, 'Sorry.'

'Never mind sorry. What *is* it? Have you been taking LSD?'

'It's nothing.' The man was officious and unbearable, the one person in the firm of solicitors she didn't like.

'It's also nonsense. And if you want to write nonsense, in future I'd be grateful if you'd do it in your own time. Back to work now.' He'd crumpled the envelope into a ball and tossed it into the nearest bin. 'Don't let me catch you again.'

He'd always been a right misery. Taking him at his word, Ruby had continued noting down ideas when they occurred to her, but had made sure he didn't catch her again.

Three months later, having scoured the *Writers' & Artists' Yearbook* for literary agencies that might be interested, she sent off copies of the eight illustrated stories she'd written so far. The first agent rejected them. So did the second. And the third. It was starting to get seriously depressing. Ruby consoled herself by googling now-successful authors who'd been turned down by more publishers and literary agencies than she had.

Then the seventh agent fell in love with Wally Bee and Zelda and asked Ruby to travel up to London to meet him. He agreed to represent her, and suggested ways to widen the appeal of the characters and their adventures. Within four months, offers to publish the series of books had come in from publishers in other countries as well as the US and UK, and a year later, when publication of the books began to happen, sales took off.

The most satisfying day of Ruby's life was the day she handed in her notice to the head of the law firm, the man who'd thrown away the envelope upon which she'd scribbled some of her nonsensical ideas. He told her stiffly, 'I saw that interview you did with the *Sunday Times*. They seem to think you're going to be some kind of superstar of children's fiction.'

Naturally, Ruby knew every word of the interview off by heart, but she gave a modest shrug. 'There are no guarantees.'

'I said to my wife, if it's that easy to churn out books for kids, she should give it a go herself.'

New though she was to the book world, Ruby had already heard words to this effect dozens of times. She shook her head at the boss she'd never liked and replied, 'Oh, it isn't easy at all.'

By way of contrast, the very best bit of becoming published had been taking finished hardback copies of the books round to Megan and her mum, whose marriage was over and whose ex-husband had returned to live in Trowbridge with his equally horrible parents.

Now, eight years on, Megan was a gangly teenager who was probably mortified each time Ruby sent her a copy of the latest book, and she herself was an author beloved by children the world over for her quirky illustrations, inventive plots and wild humour. Interviewers loved to point out the irony that she'd had no children herself, and Ruby had learned to smile, replying patiently that yes, it was a shame that a family of her own had never happened, but never mind, it was a huge privilege to be able to bring joy into the lives of those millions of young people who'd read her books or enjoyed watching the spin-off TV series.

Away from the interviews, the extra income from her career had improved her and Peter's quality of life, providing a nice safety net and allowing them the kind of luxuries they wouldn't otherwise have been able to afford. Now she wondered if it had been a factor in him staying with her longer than he might otherwise have done.

Probably.

It just made her despise him more.

So yes, life had taken an unexpected turn nine years ago, and now it was taking another one. All she needed was to somehow get her writing mojo back, because at the moment it appeared to have buggered off to Timbuktu.

And here, right on cue, came Morwenna, her editor, emerging from a taxi. Down from London for a week's holiday in Fowey, she had made the most of being in the vicinity to arrange a meet-up and see how work was progressing on the next in the series of books.

The answer was, of course, not by much at all, but first they would have lunch together over at McCarthy's restaurant, and Ruby was determined to enjoy Lachlan McCarthy's fantastic food before making her guilty confession.

After all, everything seemed so much better once you had a plate of garlicky langoustines in Pernod sauce inside you.

Chapter 13

'Absolute bastard,' Morwenna exclaimed when Ruby had finished relaying the whole sordid story. 'Look, sorry if I'm not supposed to say that about a vicar, but *really*, what a nerve that man has. I hope you realise you're better off without him.'

Ruby watched as her editor poured herself another glass of wine. 'Oh, I know I am. It just still . . . you know, takes some getting used to.'

'Like having your comfortable slippers taken away and being forced to wear spiky heels all day long. But eventually you'll get used to those heels, and then there'll be no stopping you, I promise.' Pointing with her fork as an idea occurred to her, Morwenna went on, 'In fact, now could be the perfect time to get you out and about, promoting the brand and keeping you occupied. We could book you to appear at a few literary festivals, school events, that kind of thing . . . Wouldn't that take your mind off—'

'I'm not sure,' Ruby blurted out, because travelling wasn't what she was in the mood for right now. 'Sorry, but I don't think I can.'

'It'd be fun! You'd be meeting loads of new people.' Morwenna took another glug of wine; sometimes her enthusiasm could be scary. 'Having a great time . . . just what you need.'

'I really don't want to meet new people at the moment. Not while I'm feeling like this.'

'Fine then, I won't force you. But don't go turning into a hermit.' Morwenna paused, studying her with an editor's eagle eye for detail. 'You've lost weight, haven't you? And you look as if you aren't sleeping properly.'

Ruby pulled a face, only too aware of the dark shadows beneath her eyes. 'I wake up fifty times a night. And fall asleep during the day.'

'It'll get easier. You do need to look after yourself, though. Right, back in two minutes.'

While Morwenna headed off to the loo, Ruby gazed out of the window at the holidaymakers making their way up and down Beach Street. Idly she watched two small children sorting through a bucket of pebbles outside the café opposite while the women with them chatted animatedly and drank coffee. The children – a boy and a girl? – each clutched a rapidly melting ice cream. The next moment, the boy dropped his cone into his lap and let out a wail of dismay, but the older girl retrieved it before it could roll onto the pavement and handed it back to him.

Ruby's eyes pricked with tears at this show of kindness – oh God, not more waterworks – and she had to turn away. For years, the sight of tiny babies in prams and toddlers falling over then uncomplainingly getting back up again had affected her at unforeseen moments. But Peter hadn't been enthusiastic about the idea of parenthood, had never experienced that visceral pull of longing, so it hadn't bothered him at all when no babies had come along. When she'd tried to talk to him about her own feelings, he'd been dismissive, pointing out that the planet was overpopulated as it was and no one needed to reproduce simply to make themselves feel important.

'Look,' he had said in his earnest, trust-me way, 'if it's meant to happen, it'll happen. If it doesn't . . . well, maybe that's God's will.'

Pressing a tissue against each eye in turn, willing herself to get a grip, Ruby watched as the two children began to squabble over a pebble they evidently both felt belonged to them. Enough of this weakness. She drank some iced water and quelled the anxiety in her stomach. Lunch was almost over, Morwenna would be back from the loo any minute now and had already said how much she was looking forward to seeing Ruby's new apartment. Confession time was drawing near.

Twenty minutes later, they left McCarthy's and made their way up Beach Street.

'This place is gorgeous. I already like it more than that gloomy old vicarage.' Morwenna gave an approving nod as they entered through the gates leading into the central courtyard. 'All clean and modern. This is much more you. Shame about the ankle-biters,' she murmured as the two small children from the café came racing out of the apartment opposite with an inflatable pink flamingo and a stripy beach ball, which promptly got dropped and stumbled over. The boy shrieked with annoyance and made a grab for the flamingo, and a noisy battle for owner-ship ensued.

'Rather you than me,' Morwenna went on as the argument rose in volume. 'Are you allowed to tell them to shut up?'

Morwenna might be an excellent editor of children's books,

but she had zero patience with children in real life. Ruby hid a smile. 'It's probably frowned upon. Besides, this is their holiday too.'

'Well, thank God for adults-only hotels, that's all I can say.'

'MUM, MAKE HER GIVE IT BACK TO ME,' roared the small boy. 'IT'S *MY* FLAMINGO.'

'Oh, stop quarrelling, you two.' The mother appeared in the doorway, clutching an armful of clothes. 'Just play nicely, please, then you can have a banana yoghurt.'

'Good grief.' Morwenna shuddered as Ruby unlocked the door to her own apartment and ushered her inside.

'I don't *like* yoghurt . . . *ow!*'

'No one in their right mind likes banana yoghurt,' Morwenna observed as the battle for the flamingo resumed. 'She should offer them a vodka tonic, that might do the trick.' She gave an exaggerated shudder. 'Doesn't it drive you mad? They're so high-pitched. Like polystyrene on glass.'

'They've only just arrived.' Ruby shrugged, unbothered. 'Today's changeover day. Last week it was two retired couples who sat out in the courtyard every evening until gone midnight, chatting and drinking. The week before that we had a group of thirty-somethings. Now they *were* noisy.'

'Oh well, can't have it all. Except maybe another layer of soundproofing. Right, let's see what you've done so far . . .' Morwenna had already made a beeline for the table by the window and was opening the oversized portfolio carry-case in which Ruby always stored her latest works. 'Ah, this looks great!' She admired the first painting, then flipped it over. 'Where's the rest of them?'

Time to come clean. Reluctantly, Ruby said, 'In my head.'

Morwenna gave her a sidelong look. 'And is that true?'

Ruby shrugged. 'No, sorry. I don't have anything more than that. It just isn't happening.'

They sat down at the table and talked through her crippling mental block, which Morwenna told her was completely understandable under the circumstances, though wouldn't it be better for Ruby to plough on and force herself to work *through* the block, because that way she could distract herself from thinking about Peter's betrayal?

Moving on, she reassured her that the ideas and the urge to create the illustrations would return, while Ruby did her best to agree and sound as if she believed it. It would complicate the schedule, Morwenna continued, but if she really wasn't able to write anything, they could push the publication date back by a couple of months, which was both comforting and panic-inducing in its own way. They then attempted some brainstorming, which just served to convince Ruby that the block was permanent and her career was over. The more Morwenna told her to relax and not to let it worry her, the more unrelaxed she became.

'It's the characters' voices . . . I've just lost them. I can't make them funny any more.'

'It'll come back. Keep ploughing on.' Morwenna knocked back her third cup of espresso. 'As soon as you can come up with the text and a few illustrations, we'll get the art department to start work on the cover design. Right.' She checked the message that had just flashed up on her phone and rose to her feet. 'My taxi's here. Ruby, it's been *so* lovely to see you again. Any time you want another brainstorming session, just give me a call and we can— Oh! Are you OK?'

Ruby had been about to give her a goodbye hug when she'd glimpsed a figure outside who looked as if they might be . . . but no, it couldn't be, and the next moment they'd moved out of sight. It must just have been a superficial similarity. She took a calm-down breath and shook her head. 'Sorry, thought I saw someone I knew, but it wasn't them.'

'Well, thank goodness, I thought I'd scratched you with my bangle!'

Slinging her expensive bag over her shoulder, Morwenna readied herself to leave. As they exchanged a hug on the front doorstep, one of the children from the apartment opposite kicked a raw carrot across the courtyard, causing a herring gull to fly up into the air with a noisy flap of its black-tipped wings. As it soared overhead, it gave an indignant squawk and released a poo that came perilously close to landing on Morwenna's head.

'It might be an idea,' Morwenna announced in a clear, carrying voice, 'if you children could be a bit more careful while you're playing in a shared space. Also, maybe not kick food around in a reckless manner.'

Oh God. Mortified, Ruby saw the small boy's lower lip begin to tremble. *Don't cry, please don't cry . . .*

'Trust me,' Morwenna murmured in her ear, 'if I were in charge of kids, they'd know how to behave and the world would be a better place.'

Emerging from their apartment, the children's mother said quizzically, 'Is there a problem here?'

'No problem at all.' Morwenna's smile was bland and fixed. 'I was just explaining that they might want to be more considerate of other people. And less wasteful of food.' She patted Ruby on the arm, blew her an air-kiss and stalked out to her waiting taxi, just as the figure Ruby had glimpsed earlier entered the courtyard.

It was him. It *was* him. How on earth had he known where

to find her? Ruby felt her heart jackhammering in her chest and thought for a moment her knees might give way.

'There you are,' exclaimed the children's mother. 'See that woman who just left? She was *so* rude about the girls.' Swinging round to shoot an accusing look in Ruby's direction, she added, 'I hope this isn't going to ruin our holiday.'

Shocked, mortified and struggling to get her thoughts under control, Ruby caught the stunned look on Richard's face and realised this meeting was as unexpected for him as it was for her. Shaking her head at the woman who had to be his ex-wife, she blurted out, 'It's OK, it won't, she's gone now,' then spun round and disappeared into the safety of her own flat.

Chapter 14

Max Farrell was more a click-and-collect person. When Lois-the-beauty-therapist had suggested they spend Saturday afternoon shopping together, Max explained that it wasn't really his thing, so they'd gone for lunch at a new and much talked-about restaurant in Chelsea instead.

Yet somehow, with lunch now over, he found himself waiting outside a changing room in a boutique on the King's Road while Lois kept up a running commentary from the other side of the curtain to let him know her innermost thoughts on the outfits she was trying on.

Not just any outfits, either. Nor was it any old boutique. She'd taken a shine to several of the dresses, and none so far had cost less than four figures.

This was his third date with Lois, who was beautiful but turning out to be somewhat exhausting. Max had learned on the first date that *Made in Chelsea* – surprise, surprise – was her favourite TV show. On their second date, she'd told him that her life's ambition was to appear on the show. Today, although she didn't know it yet, was their final outing together.

'You see, the turquoise and gold is more *me*,' she chattered on from inside the cubicle, 'but the emerald green sets off my eyes. I'm just so *torn* . . .'

She'd been going on like this for ages now, without appearing to need any kind of reply. Max zoned out, stretched his legs in front of him and attempted to get comfortable on the ridiculous pink-velvet-upholstered chair. Taking out his phone, he found himself scrolling through the photos he'd taken last week when his parents had come up to London to celebrate their wedding anniversary. His mother would soon be sixty and his father was sixty-three, though you wouldn't think so to look at them; they were in good nick for their age. He scrolled further back, past all the ones Lois had insisted upon during their first night out together; it hadn't taken him long to realise she had a favourite pose: champagne flute held aloft in one hand, bottle at a jaunty angle in the other, head tilted and smile pouty, with newly acquired dazzling white veneers on show.

Back a bit further still, and he came to the ones he'd taken in Lanrock during the dramatic wedding-that-didn't-happen. There weren't that many, because he tended to forget to get his phone out, but there were several of himself with Cameron and the ushers, as well as random ones snapped during the course of the reception.

Finally he came to the photo he'd been pretending he hadn't been looking for, the only one featuring Lottie. There she was, out on the hotel's broad terrace, dancing along with Freya to Elton John's 'I'm Still Standing'. The pair of them had their arms stretched above their heads and Freya's left hand was clasped in Lottie's right as they sang 'Yeah, yeah, YEAH' and punched the air. There were other people around them, but Max found it almost impossible to tear his gaze away from Lottie's face, her eyes lit up and her smile radiating pure happiness in that one magical moment captured in time.

'Ta-daaaah.' The heavy midnight-blue velvet curtain was abruptly whisked back and Lois came out, posing as if a scrum of paparazzi was there to capture every flick of her hair, each wiggle of her hips. 'Well, which one d'you like best? I'm thinking Henley Regatta, I'm thinking Wimbledon . . .' She did an extra shimmy. 'I'm thinking this is my new favourite.'

She looked amazing. Gauzy layers of orange and silver clung to her body, and the colour really suited her. She was swivelling her hips now, advancing towards him and pointing at his phone. 'Don't just sit there, Maxi. Take some photos! Do you think if I promise to tag the shop on all my socials, they'll give me a decent discount?'

Max arrived home an hour later. How he hated being the one to end a relationship, however brief it might have been. God knows he'd ended plenty over the years, but it never got any easier, never failed to make him feel awful. If someone could invent some miraculous way of doing it that was painless for both parties, they'd be made for life.

Anyway, this particular ending hadn't been painless, it had been a miserable experience for both of them. Lois had burst into tears in the car, then begged him not to be so mean and explained he couldn't break up with her now because she'd told all her friends he was The One. Finally, when he still didn't change his mind, she tearfully accused him of tricking her into thinking he'd been serious about her and called him a two-faced bastard.

Still, it was done now. And it had undoubtedly been the right thing to do, because even as he'd been driving her home, she'd been taking selfies of her pale, devastated face.

They'd be up on Instagram, he suspected, within the hour.

Back at home, he put his phone on charge and took another look at the photo of Lottie having the time of her life, singing and dancing under the stars.

He'd expected to hear from her, had anticipated that she would leave it for a few days, then get in touch. It wouldn't even require any clever sleuthing; all she needed to do was get his number from Cameron. But it had been over three weeks now and it still hadn't happened, which was both intriguing and annoying, because now he was going to have to be the one to make the first move, which he knew for a fact would mean Lottie thinking she'd won.

Once competitive, always competitive. Like the time they'd been playing tennis in the park and he'd been at match point, poised for victory. Hurtling across the court, desperate to reach the ball he'd just volleyed over the net, Lottie had gone crashing head-first into the net post and all but knocked herself unconscious.

Her reckless determination – and the resulting spectacular lump on her forehead – had impressed him. Her refusal to accept that she could lose the game had made him laugh. And two weeks later, the relationship between them had changed irretrievably.

Had they known it would happen sooner or later? Max was pretty sure the answer was yes. The gradual build-up of a new kind of connection had seemed inevitable, on his side at least. But making that initial move was high-risk, because this wasn't just any girl, this was Lottie. And it had the potential to go catastrophically wrong.

Up until then, at the age of seventeen, failure with the opposite sex hadn't featured in his repertoire; it simply hadn't been an option. If you kissed a girl, she enthusiastically kissed you back; that was what happened. This, however, was a whole different level of jeopardy. What if he made a move on Lottie and she screamed with laughter? What if she shouted, 'Oh my God, are you out of your mind? Why would I want to kiss *you*?'

The imaginary rejections kept coming, an endless wave of them. What if she pushed him away and said, 'Wait till everyone else hears about this, you'll be the laughing stock of the school!' And this, of course, was Max's greatest fear, because she was right. Imagine the public humiliation. Whatever happened, he mustn't make a move, any kind of move. Time to put those thoughts and feelings away, because he simply couldn't take that risk.

Except he was seventeen years old and his hormones were less convinced . . .

Anders Nilsson's eighteenth birthday party was held a week later. His wealthy parents had arranged for a DJ to man the decks, and outside caterers to organise the food. Eighty friends were invited and excitement levels were sky high. When Max and several of his friends arrived, he saw that Lottie was already there with a bunch of her girlfriends from school. She was wearing a new dress, bright yellow and tight-fitting, and platform shoes that made her long legs look longer still. He acknowledged her from a distance, casually, then ignored her for a while, because his friends were far more interested in the novelty of getting to know the girls from Anders' sister's school, and they were currently outside in the garden.

By the time everyone moved back indoors, 'Don't Cha' by the Pussycat Dolls was blasting out of the speakers and the huge living room was jam-packed. Max spotted Lottie dancing with a tall, broad-shouldered guy sporting a buzz cut and noted how it made him feel. *Not great.*

Glancing casually around five minutes later, he saw that the buzz-cut boy now had an arm around Lottie and was murmuring into her ear.

Two minutes after that, he observed Lottie leaning away, shaking her head. Buzz-cut boy's arm tightened possessively around her waist, and now she was attempting to wriggle out of his grasp.

Max crossed the room in seconds. 'Hi,' he said pleasantly. 'Lottie, could you come with me? There's something I need to talk to you about.'

Buzz-cut boy's eyes narrowed. 'Hang on, who d'you think you are?'

This was Anders' party. Max had no intention of deliberately causing trouble. He said, 'It's OK, I'm her brother. Sorry, it's urgent.'

Guiding Lottie outside, he murmured, 'What an idiot.'

'You didn't have to rescue me.' She glared at him. 'I can deal with boys like that.'

'I was calling *him* the idiot, not you. And I'm sure you can deal with him. I was just being helpful. Why are you limping?'

'New shoes. I've got a massive blister on my heel.' They'd reached a wooden bench in front of a pond strewn with lily pads. Lottie leaned against the arm of the bench and pulled off her left shoe. Heaving a sigh of relief, she put her bare foot down on the flagstoned terrace and they both heard the unmistakable crunch of a snail's shell. She gave a yelp of disgust. 'Oh God, *eurgh*, get it off me!'

He grabbed a handful of leaves and wiped the remains of the crushed snail from the sole of her foot, then supported her while she rinsed the last bits off in the pond. Still shuddering with revulsion, she shook the water off before returning to the bench just as a pigeon launched itself out of a beech tree on the other side of the pond and flew overhead.

'No need to thank me,' said Max. 'You're welcome. No, don't sit there— Oh.'

'Oh what? *Now* what?' She lurched lopsidedly to her feet once more.

'Pigeon poo.' He grimaced at the messy stain on the back of her yellow dress, deposited with deadly accuracy less than a second before her bottom had made contact with the wooden seat.

'I don't believe it! Why? Why does this stuff always have to happen to me?' She let out a howl and twisted round in an effort to see. 'Honestly, I was fine in the house, but you had to drag me out here. And now look at the state of me.'

Max couldn't help it; he started to laugh. 'Are you seriously telling me this is all my fault?'

'Of course it's your fault.' Wobbling on one platform heel, Lottie bent down, wrenched off the shoe and threw it to the ground.

'Fine.' Still grinning, he said, 'Next time you get groped by some ugly guy, I'll just stand back and leave him to get on with it, shall I?'

'Please do.'

'Want me to help you with the dress? Or shall I go inside?'

In response, she shot him a fierce look, and out of nowhere Max found himself desperate to kiss her. His stomach disappeared. 'You caused all of this,' she told him. 'You can stay and help.'

'Wait here,' he said. 'I'll be back in one minute.'

In the utility room, he half filled a small bucket with water and carried it outside, along with a roll of kitchen paper. Lottie turned away from him, holding the material of her dress taut and away from her bottom so he could clean off the worst of the bird poo then try to rinse the rest of it from the back of the skirt.

When his hand accidentally brushed against her thigh, he heard her momentary intake of breath.

Once he'd stopped sluicing, she said, 'Can you still see the stain?'

Even in the evening half-light, it was visible. 'Honestly? Yes.'

'Great, so now my dress is soaked *and* stained. My life is complete.'

'You could wear my shirt over it. Would that work?'

'I'll look stupid.'

It was on the tip of Max's tongue to reply, 'What's new?' because this was the kind of thing they always said to each other. But this time he didn't. Instead, he unbuttoned his blue and black striped shirt and peeled it off, leaving himself in just a plain white round-necked tee.

Lottie put it on over the yellow sundress and shook her head. 'This is ridiculous. *And* it's unfair, because you just look better without your shirt, and I look worse.'

'It doesn't go, that's all. You need to take off the dress.'

She sighed, because they both knew he was right, then twirled an index finger at him and ordered, 'Turn around.'

Max did as he was told, picturing what he was hearing as the yellow cotton dress rustled and was unzipped, then replaced with the striped shirt.

'I still look stupid,' Lottie complained.

He turned back, and there she was with the sleeves rolled up, the collar popped and her long tanned legs bare.

He said, 'You don't, you look great,' but his throat had tightened and the final word came out with a break in the middle that was perilously close to a squeak. Fuck, *fuck*, so now she was going to crack up laughing and take the mickey out of him for ever more.

But she didn't laugh, which was weird for a start. He saw her swallow and search his face before whispering almost with disbelief, 'Really?'

Max nodded; at least he could still manage that. 'Really.'

'People won't make fun of me?'

Something was happening; the night air seemed to have come alive, crackling with electricity as it sparked around them. Max cleared his throat to avoid further squeaking. 'The other girls will wish they could look half as good as you. The boys will wish it was their shirt you were wearing.'

Given their history, it was hardly surprising that she hesitated. 'I'm waiting for the jokey punchline.'

'There isn't one.' What was he doing? What was he *saying*? And which of them had moved closer, because they were now only inches apart and he hadn't even realised it was happening.

Then their mouths met and the crackle of electricity expanded, enveloping them both. The moment Max felt her body quiver, he knew she'd experienced it too. And now that they were finally kissing, all those weeks of fear and trepidation evaporated, because he knew his emotions weren't one-sided after all. The relief was overwhelming and he drew her closer still. After all these years, their relationship had moved on to the next level. This was the best party he'd ever been to in his life. And it was all thanks to a pooing pigeon and a squashed snail.

RIP, snail. Your sacrifice was heroic.

'Jesus, that is *so* sick,' announced a voice from the far side of

109

the lawn. 'Mate, if that's your sister, you're going to end up in big trouble.'

Emerging through the French doors, Anders said, 'What are you on about? That's Lottie and Max. They're just friends.'

'Trust me.' Buzz-cut boy started to laugh. 'They're a whole lot more than just friends.'

Chapter 15

Sometimes a random memory was triggered out of the blue. Lottie, in a hurry to get to work on Monday morning, didn't have time for random memories, but these particular ones had clubbed together and ambushed her anyway, just as she was knocking back a tumbler of apple juice and grabbing her keys.

Yesterday she had bought a bunch of wilting peonies in the supermarket because they'd been drastically reduced for a quick sale and she'd felt sorry for them. And now, just as she was about to leave the flat and head off to the office, Rihanna came on the radio singing 'Umbrella'. The combination sent her spiralling back thirteen years to the night of Anders Nilsson's eighteenth birthday party, because the flower beds in his parents' garden had been bursting with peonies, and while she and Max had been busy kissing each other out by the lily-covered fishpond, seventy or eighty other partygoers had been inside the house, dancing and singing along at the top of their lungs to 'Umbrella-ella-ella'.

The pin-sharp memories came flooding back now, stopping Lottie in her tracks. It had been set to become one of the most unforgettable evenings of her life. Max had been standing with his back to the sprawling, ivy-smothered property, but out of the corner of her eye she'd seen the boy with the almost-shaven head emerge onto the terrace. If he'd come out to find her, did that mean he was about to interrupt what definitely felt like a moment? Because that was the last thing she wanted to happen. If this *was* a significant moment, she needed the boy to be able to see it for himself and realise he'd be wasting his time.

So she'd been the one who'd closed the brief distance between Max and herself, in order to show him. And that was when it had happened. She'd kissed Max, he'd kissed her back, and in the thirteen years since that night, no other kiss had ever managed to match up. Each time she'd been about to kiss someone new, she had wondered if this time it might be bettered. But no, it never was.

Then again, she'd been seventeen years old back then, a seething mass of teenage hormones; maybe it wasn't fair to expect anyone else to have an effect of that intensity and depth of emotion.

The party had ended at midnight. The Nilssons lived out in the depths of the Oxfordshire countryside, and by the time everyone trooped out, there was a long queue of cars lined up along the grassy verge beyond the main gates. Making her way down the driveway, Lottie spotted her dad's blue Volvo and hoped he wouldn't be able to tell that she'd spent the last two hours doing energetic kissing, because he liked to tease her at the best of times and her mouth felt as if it might give her away.

'How was it?' he said when she climbed into the passenger seat.

'OK.' She wasn't about to tell him it had been the best party ever, *obviously*.

He laughed at her. 'This is what I love to hear, all the *endless* details. Meet anyone nice?'

'No.' Did she *sound* different? Were her lips exhausted? Did they look as if they'd been life-changingly kissed? Oh God, and now her dad was lowering his window to chat to other people before they drove off, because he just couldn't help himself, could he?

Right on cue, he called out, 'Derek, how're you doing? I'll see you at the cricket club next week!'

Now they were edging along the narrow lane past the rest of the parked vehicles and Lottie could see Max getting into his parents' car. Glad they hadn't walked out together, she felt her skin tingle and her heart quicken at the sight of him, then winced as her dad merrily tooted his horn to attract the attention of Max's mum. 'Hey there, thought it'd be Will on pickup duty tonight!'

Imelda Farrell pulled a face. 'Will's at a work leaving do. I drew the short straw.'

'Bad luck. Still, off home now. Have a great weekend!' With another wave, her dad greeted the next driver he knew – Brad Jameson, father of twins Maisie and Della – before getting tooted at himself by someone in a black 4x4.

Embarrassed, Lottie rolled her eyes. 'Dad, you're holding everyone up.' By now he'd gathered quite a queue of cars behind him.

'Holding them up for all of thirty seconds? They'll survive.' Her dad laughed at her obvious pain. 'Nothing wrong with being sociable.'

Except, as it turned out, there was.

Max had called her the following morning. He came straight to the point. 'Hi. Look, I didn't want you to think I was ignoring you, but my dad's just sprung this on me. Mum got us two tickets to the motor show as a surprise, so I can't say no, but it means I won't be able to see you today. How about tomorrow instead?'

It was both frustrating and a relief. Lottie had lain awake for hours, unable to sleep, thinking about him and replaying every detail of last night. It had been amazing and spectacular, but she'd also begun to panic that he might decide it had all been a terrible mistake.

He hadn't, though; she could tell by his voice. Adrenalin fizzed through her body like Alka-Seltzer. 'Sunday's fine, I'll see you then.'

His voice softened. 'Are you sure? I wish I didn't have to go. Is everything . . . you know, OK?'

More fizzing. She was ecstatic. 'I'm OK. How about you?'

'Hey. Last night was pretty amazing, wasn't it?' He was smiling, she could tell.

'Certainly different.' This was her feeble attempt at sounding cool.

'In a good way, I hope.'

Her mouth tingled, wishing he was here so she could kiss him again. And again. 'Oh yes, in a good way.'

There was a lust-filled pause between them, then Max said, 'I can't wait to see you again. I'll have the house to myself if you want to come over here tomorrow afternoon.'

Well, that felt like an offer she should probably refuse. But whether she *wanted* to say no was a whole other matter. Sensing her hesitation, he went on, 'Or we could meet up somewhere else. Whichever. Let me know on Sunday morning.'

Her heart broke into a gallop. 'No, it's fine, I'll come over to yours.'

They both knew what would happen tomorrow. She couldn't wait.

The rest of Saturday seemed to drag on for ever. Lottie wondered whether it was doing the same for Max or if he was having an amazing time at the motor show. The minutes crawled by at the speed of mud and she tried to distract herself by going along to help her mum with the big supermarket shop, coming home two hours later with a haul including a new kind of cereal to try, a bottle of pineapple-scented shower gel, and a three-pack of tiny lace-trimmed knickers in shades of pink, pinker and pinkest.

That evening, she painted her toenails with peach polish and watched hours of TV without taking any of it in. She kept touching her shins; never having shaved her legs before, it was freaky how smooth they felt. Well, apart from the bits where the razor she'd borrowed from her mum's drawer had caught her skin, causing more blood flow than she'd imagined possible from a few tiny nicks – the shower had looked like a murder scene by the time she'd finished.

The endless day had been followed by another almost entirely sleepless night, and dozens of imagined scenarios. By six in the morning, Lottie wondered how she was going to make it through the next few hours. But somehow the minutes ticked past and by one o'clock she was ready to set out at last, to catch the bus that would take her to Max's house five miles away, because he'd said his dad would be there until one thirty.

She thought she was looking good and, God knows, had checked in the mirror enough times to be reassured that this was true. She was wearing the new pinkest-pink knickers, her best blue bra, and a strappy navy top with her oldest, softest jeans, because looking her best was one thing, but she also didn't want to seem to be trying too hard. She did have a white bra with thicker padding but had decided against it because it would only seem like false advertising when she – or Max – took it off.

Honestly, there was so much to think about when you were about to move to the next stage for the first time. Who knew having sex could be so complicated?

Five minutes before she was due to head out, she was in the bathroom, trying to decide whether to leave her hair to hang loose or tie it back with a scrunchie – so she could take the scrunchie off at the perfect moment and shake her head like that girl in the shampoo ad – when she heard the doorbell ring downstairs.

Her first joyful thought was that it was Max, so impatient to see her that he'd come to her house instead. The second thought was that it was Max, here to tell her she should forget what had happened at the party on Friday night and they should just carry on as before because he'd decided he didn't really fancy her after all.

Flying back to her bedroom to peer out of the window and see who was outside – *please don't let it be that* – she saw the police car parked by their front gate just as she heard her mum pulling open the front door.

After thirty seconds of mumbled voices, the sound of her mother's scream reverberated in her ears, and that was the moment their lives changed. Having seen her fair share of crime and thriller TV shows in her time, Lottie knew it probably meant her dad, currently away on a golfing trip, had been injured in some terrible accident.

Either that or he was dead.

★　★　★

Her father wasn't dead, but he was unconscious and seriously ill in the intensive care unit of a hospital eighty miles from Oxford. In Bristol, apparently, although that made no sense at all. Terry Palmer had, after all, left home at six o'clock on Saturday morning in order to spend the weekend playing golf with his friends at a course on the other side of Birmingham.

'He brought me a cup of tea in bed before he left.' Her mother was trembling, shaking her head in utter bewilderment. 'He gave me a kiss and said the traffic around Birmingham was set to be snarled up with roadworks. Then he sent me a text last night to let me know they'd had a great round of golf.' Almost hyperventilating, she went on in disbelief, 'He told me he loved me. I'm sorry, but this doesn't make any sense. He doesn't even know anyone who lives in Bristol, so why would he be there?'

It took a couple of hours to reach the hospital. All they knew was that Terry had been found in a rented apartment in the north of the city. A cleaner hired to come and restore order following checkout time had discovered him unconscious and unrousable in bed, and had immediately called an ambulance.

In fact, two ambulances had been dispatched.

Because he hadn't been alone.

The medical staff were discreet; they explained that they didn't know who else had been with him or where the other person had been taken. Their job, they told Kay, was to care for her husband and hopefully get him through this health crisis, because that was their number one priority right now. Tests were being carried out to ascertain the cause of his coma.

Seeing her father covered in tubes and wires, attached to countless machines that beeped and hissed, was traumatic. The nursing staff attempted to console Kay, who was weeping and

117

devastated. Lottie, beyond tears, sat by Terry's bed for an hour, listening to her mum's sobs and wishing for the millionth time that in the panic to get down here she hadn't completely forgotten to unplug her phone and bring it with her. For one thing, Max would be wondering why she hadn't arrived at his house. But more than that, she just wanted to speak to him, to tell him what was going on and hear his voice as he reassured her that there must have been some mistake, that there would be a simple explanation for what had happened.

An *innocent* explanation. There had to be one. She just hadn't been able to think of it yet.

The mythical innocent explanation evaporated ten minutes later, when Kay fumbled in her purse, telling Lottie to go down to the hospital café and buy each of them a bottle of Diet Coke.

When Lottie descended the stairs leading to the open-plan ground floor and saw who was sitting at one of the café tables, the handful of coins in her left hand slipped from her grasp and clattered down the staircase, causing dozens of people to turn and look in her direction.

How had Max known she'd be here? She had no idea, but he had. Somehow he'd heard the news and raced down to Bristol to be with her because he'd known how desperately she needed him.

At the foot of the stairs, an elderly woman called out, 'It's all right, I've got them for you,' as she scrabbled on the ground to collect up the scattered coins. 'Are you all right, love? You look as if you've seen a ghost. Don't faint, whatever you do!'

Lottie barely heard her; she was unable to tear her gaze away from Max. Slowly, slowly he looked up at her, and in that split second she knew something was terribly wrong.

He wasn't here to see her. His shock at the sight of her was as great as her own.

And it wasn't just shock she was witnessing either. It was horror.

As if he'd suddenly realised something she hadn't yet managed to figure out.

Light-headed, she hung on to the banister rail until she reached the bottom step and managed to smile at the helpful woman who'd gathered up the coins. Then, as if sleepwalking, she made her way across the concourse to the café.

She could count on the fingers of one hand the number of times Max had been serious; his default setting was fun, mischief and humorous irreverence.

But there was no humour there now. His eyes, dark and for once almost opaque, scanned her face as he said, 'Do you know?'

'Know what?' Fear engulfed her. She wanted to throw herself against him and feel the reassurance of his arms around her, but she knew it wasn't going to happen.

'It's your dad.' Max paused, his mouth twisting into a faint grimace. 'And my mum. They were . . . together.'

And there it was, the moment she'd discovered the shocking, unimaginable truth that the hospital staff had kept from them for the sake of discretion. Terry Palmer's weekend away from home had never involved golf.

Imelda Farrell, Lottie learned, had bought her husband and son tickets to the motor show, then – allegedly – decided to pay a visit to one of her old school friends who lived in Nottingham, because they hadn't seen each other for ages and it would be so nice to have a long-overdue catch-up.

Except that meeting had also been fictitious. Instead, Terry and Imelda had rented a flat in Bristol in order to enjoy some uninterrupted time together. If there hadn't been a major fault with the boiler in their bedroom, leaking carbon monoxide at a rate serious enough to plunge them both into unconsciousness, their deception might never have been uncovered.

The affair had been going on for almost seven months, it eventually transpired. They'd met at the school Christmas disco while waiting to take their respective children home, what with the school being situated out of town and nowhere near a bus route in the late evening. They'd got chatting and had taken an immediate interest in each other. From that first evening, the die had been cast. Imelda was beautiful and flirtatious, and Terry had found her completely irresistible. They'd tried so hard not to plunge into an affair – neither of them had ever done anything like it before – but the power of their mutual attraction had made it inescapable. They'd fallen under each other's spell. In some cases, apparently, it really was impossible to say no.

This was the information obtained by Max's father, William, and Lottie's mum, Kay, once their respective spouses eventually regained consciousness and began to recover from their joint near-death experience. By the time they were transferred to the hospital in Oxford, word had spread and pretty much everyone they knew was aware of what had happened. Mortified, humiliated and completely unable to bear the sly looks and whispers, William Farrell arrived at the Palmers' home the day after Terry was discharged from the hospital.

'My wife is ashamed of the mistake she made.' He towered over Terry, wrapped in a dressing gown and recuperating in his armchair in the living room. 'I want to kill you for what you've done to our family, except I won't, because it just means I'd be the one sent to prison. But you're never going to set eyes on my wife again. I'm moving my family back to Ireland, and if you even attempt to contact her, so help me God, you *will* live to regret it.'

The hatred emanated from him like a poisonous cloud; he'd come here to have the last word, and Lottie, upstairs on the landing, had felt sick all over again, because this was the end for her and Max too. The beginning of the end had occurred on that first day in the hospital in Bristol, and now here was the final nail being hammered into the coffin of their own relationship.

'Got that?' demanded William.

Silence.

'Don't just nod your head.' The words were spat out through gritted teeth. '*Say* it.'

'Got it.'

'He has,' Lottie's mother chimed in fiercely from the doorway. 'And we're glad you're going. If that bitch of a wife of yours ever tries to contact my husband, she'll have me to answer to, I can promise you that. We never want to see your family again. The further away you go, the better.'

And that was the last time Lottie saw any of the Farrells. Neither set of parents ever knew there had been any kind of emotional connection between her and Max, and because her mother was determined to sever all contact, she deleted Max's number from her daughter's phone.

Max knew her address; he could have written to her. Or got in touch via Facebook, of course. But he didn't, and Lottie couldn't blame him. Her heart might be bruised, but it wasn't broken – there hadn't been time for that to happen – and it was clearly for the best anyway, what with Max hardly being the shy and retiring type. As soon as he turned up in Ireland, he'd be bound to have girls swarming all over him.

Lottie kept telling herself this, over and over, until she began to believe it. What was done was done. She loved her parents and didn't want them to split up. She'd lost a friend, but given time, she'd get over it. Before long, someone else was bound to come along and light up her life.

At least, that had been the plan . . .

Chapter 16

Thirteen years later, back in the real world, Lottie realised she'd made her way to work on autopilot, walking without even being aware of her surroundings because her mind had been full of a million memories of Max Farrell, prompted by those scented peonies and then the Rihanna track playing on the radio.

Now, rounding the final bend in the road, she saw Max sitting on the low wall opposite the office and wondered if this was a mirage magicked up by her brain. But no, he was really here; no way would her imagination ever have conjured up that purple and green striped shirt.

But that was what he was wearing, along with worn jeans, dusty grey flip-flops and a pair of Ray-Ban Aviators perched on top of his head, pushing his dark hair back from a tanned forehead.

Grinning at the sight of her, he waited until she was nearer then tapped his watch. 'Morning. You're late.'

It was three minutes past nine. Working hard to keep her own expression impassive, Lottie said, 'I'm the boss. It's allowed.'

She unlocked the door and he followed her inside. 'Are you going to pretend it isn't great to see me again?'

'I'm just busy marvelling at your choice of shirt.'

'It's an excellent shirt.'

'Why are you here?'

He pulled out the chair facing her desk and settled onto it, right ankle resting on his left knee, as it had always done when he was relaxed and at ease. 'You left the wedding reception without saying goodbye.'

Lottie imperceptibly breathed in the scent of his aftershave. 'I think I did.'

'Not properly. And you didn't tell the girl on reception I was locked out of my room.'

'Oh dear, I forgot.'

'That was nearly a month ago. I thought you might have been in touch.'

See? So entitled. He'd expected her to make the first move. 'I don't know why you'd think that.'

'I've missed you.' There was that glimmer of amusement, accompanied by a light shrug. 'I wondered if maybe you'd missed me too.'

Lottie mimicked his shrug. 'I don't remember that happening. And I know you have a habit of forgetting these things, but you do have a super-keen girlfriend. Did you bring her down here with you this time?'

'Is that what was bothering you? I no longer have a girlfriend of any description.' He tapped his chest. 'Officially one hundred per cent single. Thought you'd be pleased.'

She hoped he couldn't hear her heart thudding against her ribs. 'I still don't get why you're here.'

'OK, you know how every now and again you need to eat, so you go somewhere that sells food? Or you might break your charging cable, so you find a place that sells new ones?' He gave her an encouraging nod, then indicated the office around them. 'I'm here because you have rental properties on your books. And I'm interested in moving into one of them.'

'Are you serious?'

'Always.' One corner of his mouth lifted. 'Well, maybe not always. But in this case, yes.'

'Because . . .?'

'Because why not? Have laptop, will travel. I like this town. Why shouldn't I stay here for a while, see how things go?'

'What kind of things?' Lottie's mouth was dry.

'Who knows? I may need to spend a few weeks here to find out.' Max nodded at her own laptop. 'Which is why I'm here now, bright and early on this beautiful Monday morning. And single,' he added as an apparent afterthought. 'Bright, early and extremely single.'

Not to mention clearly intent on causing havoc.

Lottie said, 'We're pretty booked up. We don't have anything available for long. There's a place that's free for the next fourteen days . . .'

'Beggars can't be choosers.'

He wasn't a beggar. She leaned sideways and printed off the details. 'Where did you stay last night?'

Another shrug. 'Just got chatting to a girl in a bar, she let me stay at hers . . .' He started to laugh. 'The look on your face. Kidding. I booked into the Rupert Hotel. Alone.'

She reached for the printed-out pages. 'Well, if you're interested in this cottage for the next fortnight, just say the word.'

'Could I take a look at it first, before I decide?'

Lottie pointed to the details. 'These are photographs of the property. This is how you get to see what it looks like.'

'But it's right here in Lanrock. Maybe you could show it to me.'

'Marcus will be in at ten. He can do that for you, if you insist.'

Max raised his hands. 'OK, you win. I'll take it.'

'You don't have to. There's another lettings agency on Angel Street. They might have something you like more than—'

'Lottie, Lottie. This is terrible business practice.' He shook his head at her. 'What are you so scared of?'

Everything. *Everything.* She marvelled at the way her own hands were collecting the five sheets of paper containing the details of Jericho Cottage and efficiently stapling them together, while her brain was in turmoil.

Passing them to Max, she said, 'Nothing.'

'It isn't nothing, though, is it? And you still haven't told me if you missed me.'

There it was again, the invisible connection surging between them, the kind of connection she'd never experienced with anyone else. Lottie took a deep breath. 'Honestly? No, I haven't missed you. It was a shock to see you again at the wedding, but not a horrible shock. It was good to catch up and hear how you'd turned out. But when I left the hotel, I didn't expect to see you again.' OK, tiny fib there. 'And I haven't spent the last few weeks pining away, wishing you'd magically turn up. Because . . . well, there's no point.'

Max tilted his head. 'Why is there no point?'

It was too early for this kind of inquisition. She hadn't had time to mentally prepare herself. She blurted out, 'Because nothing can ever *happen.*'

'No? You mean because your dad and my mum had a thing once? Back when we were seventeen?' He raised his eyebrows

126

in disbelief. 'Lottie, that was then. This is now. We're two adults who can do whatever we want and no one can stop us—'

'Mr and Mrs Derham!' Lottie plastered a big smile across her face as an elderly couple came into the office. 'How nice to see you again. Just give me two minutes to finish dealing with this client and I'll be right with you.' The Derhams were a finicky couple who liked to visit the office in order to spend hours choosing the perfect rental for their next break, but right now she couldn't be happier to see them. Taking the payment from Max's credit card, locating the keys to Jericho Cottage and giving him the list of information he'd need with regard to the property, she wrapped up the transaction in record time. 'There we are, all done!' she said cheerfully. 'I hope you enjoy your stay.'

'Thanks. And if I have any questions . . .?'

'Feel free to call the office. Or email us. Someone will always be happy to help.'

'Actually, I already have a question.' As he reached the door, Max turned. 'How about dinner tonight?'

He winked at the Derhams, causing Nora Derham to giggle and go, 'Oooh!'

Taking care to look busy and important, Lottie typed something very fast on her laptop – *lllmpgggaaa bim poooooo* – and said, 'No, thanks.'

'OK. How about tomorrow night?'

The Derhams were watching her avidly. She cast a bland smile at Max. 'Still no.'

'It's only dinner.' His dark eyes sparked with amusement. 'I'm not asking you to marry me.'

Mrs Derham nodded at Lottie and stage-whispered, 'Are you sure you don't want to, dear? You might enjoy it.'

Max grinned at her. 'I think that's what she's scared of.'

'It isn't.' Lottie did some more important typing; this time it was *fffuck fuck fuckfuckfuckkkkk*. 'And the answer's still no. Bye!'

The door swung shut behind Max and she relaxed at last.

'Aahhh.' Mrs Derham gave a sigh of disappointment. 'If he invited me out to dinner, I'd be there like a shot.'

'No, you wouldn't.' Her husband bridled. 'I wouldn't let you go.'

'He's always been the jealous type, has my Malcolm.' She patted his arm. 'It's OK, love, I'd rather have you any day.'

Heroically, Lottie managed not to laugh. Oh dear, poor Max.

Chapter 17

Ruby had spent the entire morning drawing random doodles and trawling the internet for brilliant ideas . . . well, good ideas . . . OK, any ideas at all. But no, it was the end of another week and yet again they'd failed to materialise. Wally Bee and Zelda were still on strike, sitting on the page refusing to do or say anything at all, let alone anything remotely helpful. In the end, she screwed up the page from her sketchpad and threw it in the direction of the waste-paper bin across the living room, where it didn't even have the common courtesy to go in.

Enough. It was a beautiful day. At any other time she would have taken herself outside to the sunny courtyard to read and doze in peace. But if she were to venture there now, the family from across the way would inevitably arrive back from wherever they'd been this morning, and the two children would be racing around and playing their boisterous games.

Except it wasn't the children that were the problem, was it? It was their father, who was more often than not outside with them, keeping his daughters entertained. Yes, the one with the very short hair was a girl; Ruby knew that now.

She also knew that she and Richard had got their timings and reactions wrong, resulting in the complete hash of a situation in which they now found themselves. If they'd been more practised in the art of one-night stands, maybe they could have carried it off. Instead, during that initial crucial moment, they'd both hesitated too long, then said nothing at all about having met before. So now they were stuck in an awkward situation entirely of their own construction.

Ruby was dealing with this in the only way possible, which was making sure she avoided contact with all of them for as long as they were staying here in Lanrock. Every so often, though, she found herself peering surreptitiously over the lower edge of her bedroom window at Richard, his children, his ex-wife and her new partner whenever they sat outside in the sheltered warmth of the courtyard.

They seemed to get on well together, that much was apparent. And Richard was clearly a loving father to his girls. Eavesdropping from beneath the slightly open window, Ruby couldn't quite make out normal-volume conversation, but she did enjoy hearing them laugh together. Richard, in particular, had a wonderful laugh . . .

Anyway, enough of that. Thanks to her own ineptness, the courtyard was out of bounds for the next week, so she'd just have to take herself off to the beach instead.

'Hello, Zelda.'
　'Hello, Wally Bee.'
　'What are you up to today?'
　'Nothing.'
　'Oh.'
　'Right. Bye then.'

'Wait, where are you going?'

'Nowhere.'

'Oh.'

'OK. Bye.'

For God's sake, just leave me alone, Ruby silently begged as yet another tedious non-scene played itself out behind her closed eyelids. Here on West Beach, children were playing happily together, holidaymakers were having fun and the sound of waves swooshing onto the sand was accompanied by squeals of joy from those paddling along the shoreline. The scents of ozone and sun lotion hung in the clean air. Someone nearby had unwrapped a package of fish and chips, and Ruby's stomach rumbled in response because she'd missed lunch and—

'*Ow!*' A kaleidoscope of pain exploded across her left eye as something hit it at high speed. Catapulting into a sitting position and clutching her face, she gasped as whatever it was ricocheted off her face and fell onto the sand.

The pain was enough to take her breath away. With her eyes squeezed shut, she became aware of a woman shouting, 'Oh my God, I'm so *sorry!* Are you OK?'

A wave of nausea rose in Ruby's throat and she took a couple of deep breaths. The woman, crouching beside her now, said, 'Can you take your hand away so I can have a look? I'm sorry, it was an accident.'

'It wasn't me,' blurted a scared younger voice. 'I didn't do it.'

Ruby lowered her hand, glad that at least there was no blood. The throbbing pain was in the socket above her eye, and her vision was blurred, but she was still able to recognise the woman at her side and the small child hiding behind her.

'Oh, it's you!' The woman's eyes widened. 'From the flat

131

opposite ours. Look, how bad d'you think it is? Can you see all right? Are you going to be OK? Should we get you to a doctor?'

It was a hard plastic frisbee, Ruby saw now, and it had caught her at just the wrong angle. Cautiously exploring the socket of her left eye, she could feel it swelling already, but the skin didn't feel broken and the blurring was lessening.

'I'll be fine.' She risked looking up; were the rest of the family there too, gazing on in horror?

'Sasha, say sorry to the lady . . . I'm afraid we don't know your name.'

'Ruby.'

'I didn't mean it.' Sasha, the older daughter, looked miserable. 'It flew out of my hand before I was ready.'

'It was an accident.' Ruby smiled at the girl; the pain was reducing too, thank goodness. 'I'm OK. No worries. Actually, it's time I was heading back . . .'

'Are you sure you're all right?' Richard's ex-wife was still looking concerned. 'Maybe we should walk with you.'

'Honestly, there's no need.' Keen to escape, because people were staring at them, Ruby scrambled to her feet, gathering up her towel and beach bag. 'I've had enough sun anyway. I'll . . . see you around!'

By six that evening, and despite her best efforts with a packet of frozen broccoli, the bruise was in full bloom. The skin around Ruby's eye was blue, magenta and swollen, but it was looking far worse than it felt, and her vision was clear. After taking a shower and changing into a T-shirt and leggings, she settled down on the sofa for an evening of Deliveroo and undemanding TV.

Until the doorbell went and there was Richard's ex-wife and her partner on the doorstep, clutching a huge bouquet of mixed summer flowers from the fancy florist's over on Angel Street.

'Hello . . . Oh you poor thing,' exclaimed the partner. 'I couldn't believe it when Mel told me what happened down on the beach. I'm Dara, by the way. This is Mel. And these are for you.'

Mel thrust the flowers into Ruby's arms. 'I know I keep saying sorry, but we just feel so terrible. And look how swollen your poor eye is.'

'Really, it's OK, it doesn't hurt.'

'Can we come in?' Somehow it was already happening; Ruby found herself backing into the living room. 'Oh, this is a lovely apartment, smaller than ours but look at that stunning view! It's our first time in Lanrock. Isn't it great? Are you a regular visitor here?'

'I've lived in the town for years, but only moved into this apartment a few weeks ago.' As Ruby spoke, she saw Dara nudge Mel and discreetly point something out to her across the room.

'Well, we wanted to apologise for what happened. And Sasha's sorry too.' There was a slight edge to Dara's voice as she turned to face Ruby. 'Um . . . did you happen to find something of Sasha's out in the courtyard and bring it inside? Maybe in case it rained?'

Ruby blinked; they were both looking at her oddly now. Had she found something? Of course she hadn't. She shook her head. 'No, I didn't see anything out there.'

Another exchange of glances. Dara hesitated, then said, 'It's just, Sasha's lost one of her books and she's pretty upset about it . . . and I couldn't help noticing you have a copy of the same one over there on the table next to the window.'

'It isn't Sasha's, but you're welcome to take it.' Ruby retrieved the paperback from the table, where she'd been flicking through the pages earlier for inspiration.

Not that she'd found any.

'Well, not if it belongs to you,' said Mel.

Ruby smiled. 'It's fine. It's only one of mine because I wrote it.' Oh God, did that sound show-offy? But better to be thought of as a show-off than a thief who'd steal from a small child.

Their faces changed in an instant.

'You did?' Mel's eyes lit up. 'You mean, you're Ruby Vale? Oh my goodness, this is *amazing*!'

'And of course we didn't think you'd taken Sasha's copy,' Dara chimed in hastily. 'Of *course* you wouldn't do that. But you have no idea how much Sasha loves your books. When she hears about this, she's not going to believe it. She'll be over the moon! And this one's her absolute favourite.' She waved *Wally Bee and Zelda's Amazing Australian Adventure* at Ruby. 'If you'd sign it for her, you'd make her year!'

'No, not now,' Mel exclaimed as Ruby reached for a pen. 'You must have dinner with us, come over and meet everyone properly! You will, won't you? We're eating outside at seven, you can give Sasha the book yourself. Honestly, it'll mean so much to her, you're her favourite author in the world!'

Talk about bamboozled; there was going to be no getting out of it now. Ruby's protests that there was no need to invite her to join them were ignored. Once again, she realised she'd missed her chance to conjure up a rock-solid excuse the moment it was required.

Once they'd left, she cast a couple of covert glances through the bedroom window and saw the table being laid outside, the chairs drawn up and preparations being made. She wondered what the current situation was with Richard and the two women, and whether he might suddenly remember having met her before. Maybe they could get away with explaining their brief encounter in the café without mentioning the unforgettable night of wild sex. Or maybe he *would* mention it, although surely not with the children there . . .

Furthermore, she still only had his side of the story. Just because he'd seemed honest and truthful about his situation didn't mean it was true, did it? For all she knew, he could still be happily married to Mel, while Dara was nothing more than a good friend or a sister.

She'd known him for one day, that was all.

She'd been married to Peter for ten years.

Men. How could you ever know them enough to really trust them?

'Thank you for inviting me,' Ruby said when she joined them for dinner out in the courtyard just after seven. 'This all looks wonderful. Hello!' She sat down on the empty chair next to Sasha and passed her the paperback, duly signed. 'I'm so glad you like my books.'

'I love them. They're the best.' Sasha was torn between shyness and delight.

'This is Flo, Sasha's sister.' Mel introduced the younger girl, then gestured to the left. 'And this is Richard.'

I know it's Richard, I've seen him naked. We had sex a few weeks ago, lots and lots of sex . . .

'Hi,' said Ruby. God, it wasn't easy to look at someone as if you didn't know them when you did.

'Hi,' said Richard.

'Can I be completely honest with you?' This was Dara, wearing a floaty blue top with a pintucked front and flared sleeves. 'After that other woman shouted at Sasha and Flo the other day, we decided we didn't like either of you. It was Richard who said maybe you weren't as bad as we thought. And then today you were so nice about nearly getting blinded by the frisbee that we realised he was right.'

'By the way, Sasha found her copy of the book,' Richard joined in. 'It was under the duvet on her bed.'

'Oh, that's good.' Ruby helped herself to a slice of quiche from one of the many serving dishes in the centre of the table. 'Told you I didn't steal it,' she added mischievously.

'We didn't think you had.' Dara offered her a bowl of rice salad. 'Although I might have wondered if your friend had taken it.'

'She was only here on a flying visit.' Probably best not to mention that Morwenna was actually her child-hating editor.

'Well, we're very glad to hear that,' said Mel. 'Here, have some guacamole to go with the rice salad. And what do you want on that baked potato, Flo? Mushrooms? And tomato sauce? How about some quinoa?'

'Bleurgh.' Flo pulled a face.

The food was delicious, right up until the moment Ruby took a mouthful of quiche and discovered it was made with goat's cheese, which she'd never liked. Bleurgh times fifty; she would never understand how people could enjoy something that smelled and tasted of goat. But it wouldn't be a good look to spit it out, as Flo might do if forced to swallow a mouthful of quinoa, so she did the grown-up thing, chewing and swallowing as quickly as possible, then taking away the taste with a hasty gulp of orange juice.

'Are you sure you don't want some wine?' Mel was lifting the bottle of Whispering Angel from the ice bucket.

Ruby shook her head; tonight she definitely needed to keep her wits about her. 'I'm fine, thanks. Going to stick to fruit juice. But I'd love another of those crevettes.'

The conversation flowed easily and plenty of food was eaten, then the girls were put to bed and more wine was opened and enjoyed, though not by Ruby. They talked about her career and about holidays good and bad, and the cookery course Dara had taken last year in France. As darkness fell, the solar fairy lights came on around the courtyard and Mel brought out a board piled with various cheeses, crackers and grapes. As they all helped themselves, Dara said, 'As a writer, Ruby, would you call yourself a curious person? Interested in other people?'

'I'd say I am. I think most writers are.'

'That's what I thought too. Which is why I'm wondering if you're at all curious about us.'

'Oh. Sorry, I didn't realise. I mean, you've told me your names.' Thinking fast, glad she hadn't had that wine, Ruby reached for another cracker. 'Sorry, sometimes people think I ask too many questions! Are you actually famous?'

Dara shook her head. 'Not famous, no. I meant, who do you think we are in relation to one another?'

Ruby felt herself flush. 'Well, the girls call Mel and Richard Mum and Dad, so I assume they're a couple. And you're either a close friend of the family, or maybe . . . Richard's sister?'

'No,' said Dara.

'Well then, are you and Mel sisters?'

'No, thank goodness. In fact we're a very modern family.' Dara smiled and reached out to squeeze Mel's hand. 'This is my beautiful girlfriend. We live together. I love her with all my heart.'

'Oh right! I didn't realise! That's great!' Too many exclamation marks; was she even sounding believable, or was she overacting dreadfully? And might this turn out to be a good moment for Richard to confess that actually they had met before? She couldn't – wouldn't – take the initiative, but if he decided to do it, at least the pretence could be dropped.

'Richard and I were married for seven years,' Mel explained, 'but we had the most amicable divorce in the world and we'll always be good friends. In fact, we get on so well together he's going to help us start a family of our own.'

'Gosh . . . wow . . . that *is* amicable!' Ruby smiled brightly at Mel and Dara but couldn't quite bring herself to look at Richard. 'That's fantastic!' *OK, enough with the exclamation marks now. Dial it down.*

'It just makes perfect sense.' Dara took over joyfully. 'We adore the girls, obviously, love them to bits, but we also want a baby to celebrate *our* relationship. And Richard's agreed to do the honours and make that happen, because he's an amazing person and he knows just how much it means to us. We're so lucky to have him. This way, the girls and the new baby might have one different parent but they'll still be full siblings.' She smiled at Ruby, then leaned her head on Mel's shoulder and said, 'It's going to be perfect.'

'Wow.' Ruby nodded and this time managed to catch Richard's eye for a split second. It was none of her business, absolutely nothing to do with her, but was he really happy to be going along with the plan? 'Well, that's . . . wonderful.'

138

Mel dropped a kiss on Dara's temple, then leaned over the other way and kissed Richard on the cheek, less than an inch from the corner of his mouth. 'It really is. I still love Richard. We're still family . . . we'll always be family. I'm the luckiest woman in the world.'

Chapter 18

On Friday morning, Ruby heard a knock at her door and braced herself for yet another unwanted encounter with Dara and Mel. But when she answered it, there was Richard.

'They've taken the girls down to the beach,' he announced without preamble. 'Without the frisbee, you'll be glad to hear. Look, I'm so sorry about this. I had no idea you'd be here, obviously. Dara booked the apartment months ago. I couldn't believe it when I saw you.'

'I know, same. Do you want to come in?' She stepped aside and he moved past her.

'I never thought I'd see you again.'

'Me neither.'

'How's your eye?'

'Bruised, but I'm OK. Don't worry,' said Ruby, 'I'm not planning on suing your daughter.'

'Probably for the best. She only gets three pounds pocket money a week.'

'So you've changed your mind about the baby thing.' When

you didn't know how long you might have to talk about things, it made sense to get straight down to business.

He exhaled, then raked a hand through his hair. 'I know. Surprise.'

'You weren't happy about it before. What happened?'

'I suppose they made me think again. For the sake of the girls. I mean, it does make sense for them to have a full sibling. An anonymous donor wouldn't be the same. That's how Mel feels, anyway.'

'And you, are you sure? This is a baby we're talking about. A whole new human being.'

'I know what you're thinking. But you heard them last night. It's what they want, more than anything. And maybe it is for the best. I'd be there to see it grow up . . . I'd be involved. Like Mel said, we're always going to be a family.'

He was torn; it was one of those dilemmas with no definitive solution. Ruby said, 'Hey, I'm not criticising your decision. Just making sure you're OK with it.'

He looked relieved. 'I'm OK with it. I tell you what I can't get over, though. Reading Sasha's favourite books to her and not realising the author was you. I mean, I just assumed the name was a coincidence. It didn't occur to me for one moment that you could be Ruby Vale.'

She smiled. 'When you come across some stupid woman sobbing in a café, you don't expect her to be an author of fun books for little kids.'

'Pretty much that. And now it's my turn to ask how you are. I know it's only been a few weeks, so I wouldn't expect you to be over what your husband did. But are you coping OK?'

He didn't really want to hear the whole story, not after she'd poured her heart out to him last time. God knows, it was depressing enough having to remind herself that she couldn't even manage to write. 'I'm doing fine. Better than expected, really. My soon-to-be-ex-husband is recovering from his injuries. He left hospital, resigned from his job and moved out of the area with the new love of his life, and she's welcome to him. I'm really not missing him.' She twiddled the silver bangle on her left wrist. 'Just getting used to being single again. You know, doing my own thing. Haven't been going out much,' she added hastily, not wanting him to think she'd been trawling Cornwall, picking up a different man every night. 'Hardly at all, in fact.'

'Well, I'm glad you're all right. And no regrets about what happened in . . . you know . . . ?'

Was this what had been bothering him? Ruby shook her head. 'No regrets.'

His phone rang and he said, 'That's Mel. Sorry, better take it.'

She stood there in the living room as he answered the call.

'Hi. Oh God, really? No problem, I'll bring emergency supplies. On my way.' He hung up. 'It's Flo, not the best start to the morning. They need more nappies and another change of clothes for her.'

'Richard to the rescue,' said Ruby.

'Goes with the territory. Plenty of practice dealing with those kinds of accidents.' He gave an easy shrug. 'Well, it's been good to chat. I'd better head down there, leave you in peace to get on with your work.'

As if that was likely to happen . . .

As she showed him out, Ruby caught a faint waft of his aftershave. She felt a sudden unexpected urge to pull him back and give him a hug, maybe even a kiss.

But she didn't. She couldn't. It wouldn't be right. What was done was done. That night had happened and had served its purpose. It was now a thing of the past.

Although . . .

On impulse she said, 'Listen, do you know about the Pirate Parade? They hold it every year in Lanrock and it's happening on Sunday. The girls will love it! If you want to watch it from the viewing platform, I can get tickets.'

'Sorry, we can't make it.' Richard was already shaking his head. 'We're heading home on Saturday evening to miss the traffic, and Dara's sister's having a birthday party in Oxford on Sunday afternoon.'

Ruby forced a casual smile. 'No worries, just a thought.'

'I'd better go.'

'You had.' To cover her disappointment, she said, 'Is it a bird? Is it a plane? No, it's Nappy Man,' then instantly felt foolish because it wasn't even funny.

'We'll see you before we leave,' said Richard, and she nodded. 'Although if you're dressed as a pirate,' he went on, 'we might not recognise you.'

Ruby slept in on Saturday morning, which was unusual for her. By the look of the apartment across the courtyard, the family had gone out, evidently keen to make the most of the final day of their holiday. By the time she left, it was already eleven thirty, and the sea was a vivid Mediterranean blue glinting with silver.

She made her way to the market in the car park to the side of the art gallery on Beach Street, which on Saturdays became a hive of activity, with assorted stalls selling local produce. There was a bread stall, a cake stall, a pie stall, fruit and veg, home-made jams and preserves, freshly squeezed juice drinks and smoothies, crisps and roasted nuts, home-made Cornish fudge and—

143

'Hey,' said a voice behind her, 'how are *you?*'

Ruby jumped, then braced herself. Until recently she'd been the wife of the local vicar and, as such, had become accustomed to being stopped in the street by local people keen to sympathise with her situation. It was kind of them, but she still didn't enjoy it; plus, while some were genuine, others were bright-eyed with *Schadenfreude*, loving the drama and longing to dig out extra, hopefully scurrilous, details.

But today, thank goodness, she wasn't being accosted by someone she barely knew. It was Iris, wearing a bright orange strappy top, frayed khaki shorts and pink sandals.

'You're back,' Ruby exclaimed, because Iris had been away for the last fortnight caring for her disabled father in Truro while her mother took a break with a friend in Weston-super-Mare. She gave her a hug. 'How did it all go? How's your dad?'

Iris grinned. 'Glad not to have to put up with any more of my cooking.'

'What? But you're a fantastic cook!'

'I know, but Dad only likes stuff like mince and potatoes, fish fingers and oven chips. No foreign muck, nothing as exotic as curry or pasta. He's a grumpy bugger too, but we managed to have a laugh. And Mum had a good rest, that's the main thing. More important, how are you getting on, and oh fuck, who did *that* to you?'

Ruby had pushed her dark glasses to the top of her head, unwittingly revealing her no longer swollen but still colourful bruised eye. Hastily she said, 'It's OK, it was an accident, a six-year-old with a frisbee on the beach.'

'Phew, had me worried there. How about the bastard ex, what's happening with him?'

'Out of hospital, buggered off with Margaret, God knows

144

where. Good riddance to the pair of them.' They were getting in other people's way; market-goers were bumping into them while darting from stall to stall. Ruby indicated the half-full canvas bag slung over Iris's bony shoulder. 'We should probably move. What have you been buying?' She loved that Iris was so adventurous in the kitchen.

'Asparagus, a pot of za'atar, plenty of fresh herbs.' Iris opened the bag to show her. 'And gooseberries to make a fool. I'm going to do a smoked duck terrine tonight . . . ooh, and mustn't forget to pick up some torta di dolcelatte . . .'

'There's no queue over there at the moment.' Ruby shielded her eyes from the sun to check out the cheese stall decorated with fluttering strings of red, blue and white bunting. 'Actually, I might get some mozzarella.'

But as they reached the stall, a waft of goat's cheese reached her, filling her nose, her brain, her whole body. Oh good grief, this was so much worse than the other evening in the courtyard, and that was when she'd been forced to chew and swallow a mouthful of the terrible quiche. It had been revolting, but she'd managed it.

'What's up? Wow, you OK?' Iris looked up as Ruby took a step back and stumbled into her. 'You're white as a sheet. Not going to faint, are you?'

'Feeling sick,' Ruby mumbled, overwhelmed by the intensity of the sensation rushing up from the pit of her stomach. It had to be the heat increasing the strength of the smell. But one thing was for sure, she had to escape, and fast.

'Right, let's get you out of here . . . Let me think where's best.' Iris supported her through the crowds, leading her away from the visibly relieved owner of the cheese stall. 'Take deep breaths, nice and slow . . . OK, we're heading for Lachlan's.'

It wasn't quite midday, which meant McCarthy's restaurant had yet to open, but Iris evidently knew Lachlan would be in there prepping food for the lunchtime service. Still holding on to Ruby, she pushed open the door and called out, 'Bit of an emergency, can Ruby use your bathroom?'

Lachlan, framed in the stone archway between the kitchen and the dining area, said, 'Of course, help yourself,' but Ruby and Iris were already on their way. The cubicle door slammed shut behind Ruby and she made it with seconds to spare.

Oh, though, *the relief*. Within half a minute, her stomach was empty and the nausea was a thing of the past.

'Better?' said Iris when she emerged from the cubicle.

'A million times better.'

Iris waited until she'd washed her hands and rinsed out her mouth, then offered her a mint, which Ruby accepted with gratitude. 'Food poisoning, do you think?'

'I'm fine now. It was just the smell of that goat's cheese. Thanks so much for getting me here.' The public loos were three hundred metres away and Ruby knew she wouldn't have made it in time. She chewed the deliciously minty sweet and smoothed her hair back from her face. 'Isn't it weird how you can feel so fantastic right after feeling so ill? I could murder a can of Orangina.'

Iris said, 'Want me to fetch you a nice glass of cold water from the kitchen?'

Water, water . . . the trouble with water was it was just too watery. Ruby grimaced and shook her head. 'No, I really do fancy a can of Orangina. And a hot Cornish pasty.' She paused. 'Why are you looking at me like that?'

'Oh, sweetheart.'

'What? I promise you, I'm not ill!'

Iris still had that unreadable expression on her face. 'I know. Look, I don't want to give you a shock, but is there a chance you could be . . . you know, pregnant?'

Pregnant.

What?

Ruby's brain began to buzz like a wasp trapped in a jam jar. Had she heard correctly? Was that the word Iris had uttered, or had she said poignant? But no . . . there was no mistake.

Iris had seen her reaction and was reaching out to clasp her hands. 'Oh, that absolute bastard,' she said fiercely. 'He's got you up the duff and buggered off with . . . I don't believe this . . .'

Ruby shook her head, too lost for words to even begin to take in the implications, let alone formulate a reply. It had been many months since she and Peter had last had sex. His excuse had been that he was stressed, with work getting on top of him, although she'd since learned to substitute *Margaret* for *work*.

Not that she'd been bothered by the lack of intimacy at the time; after years of wanting a baby, she'd slowly come to the conclusion that it wasn't going to happen, and her feelings towards Peter had waned accordingly. It was almost impossible now to recall that they must have been happy together once upon a time, when they'd first married. She knew they had been, but since then they'd been slowly, almost imperceptibly drifting apart.

Then again, if she *was* pregnant, everyone would automatically assume the baby was his.

Oh help, this was too much to absorb. And much as she liked Iris, Ruby knew she couldn't trust her to keep a secret for longer than a few hours. Some items of gossip were simply too delicious to keep to yourself.

'It might not be that.' She heard her voice waver; she was desperate to get home.

'When I was expecting my first, I had a thing about Twiglets dipped in honey. Had them for breakfast every day, couldn't get enough of 'em,' Iris marvelled. 'Never had any since. Funny what those hormones do to you.'

'I think maybe it's just a bug I've picked up. I heard a woman in the supermarket the other day saying there was something going around. Anyway, thanks for everything, but I'm going to head off now.'

'OK, darling, but you might want to pick up a test on the way home. Any help you need, just give me a shout. And don't let that bastard ex of yours talk you into doing anything you don't want to do.'

Ruby had no intention of telling her bastard ex anything at all. 'I won't.'

'Oh,' Iris called after her as they left the restaurant, 'and don't go to the chemist just along from here. They're buy-one-get-one-free at the one up on Tresilian Road.'

Ruby wasn't daft enough to visit either of them. Back at the apartment, she racked her brains, desperate to remember the date of her last period, but they'd always been crazily irregular and she'd given up trying to keep track of them long ago. She looked out of the bedroom window and saw there was still no sign of anyone in the apartment opposite. Then she opened a second can from the four-pack of Oranginas she'd picked up on the way home and savoured every moment of its delicious fizzy oranginess as it slid down her throat.

Finally, she drove out of town and all the way to Lostwithiel, where there were chemists and people who didn't know her from Adam.

By the time she returned to Lanrock, it was mid afternoon

and the urge to carry out the test was vying with the urge not to carry it out, because a definitive answer would make it real.

The first thing she noticed when she entered the courtyard was the wide-open front door and open windows in the apartment opposite. The second thing was the sound of a vacuum cleaner roaring away inside. She might only have lived here a month, but it was long enough for her to know the score. Once each holidaying family had left, the cleaning team moved in to ensure the property was pristine before the next occupants arrived.

Spotting her from the front window, Lottie came out holding the clipboard she used when checking properties.

'Everything OK?' she said cheerfully. 'You look confused.'

'I'm just surprised. They said they weren't leaving until this evening.'

'Changed their minds. They dropped the keys back with me at lunchtime, said they were off early while the roads were clear. And Marge and Lena were happy to come over this afternoon to clean up, so they don't have to miss the Pirate Parade tomorrow. How were they, as neighbours? Not too noisy, I hope?'

'No, they were fine.'

'Friendly?'

'Very friendly.' If only Lottie knew how much.

Back in her own apartment, Ruby carried out the test.

Iris had been right. It was positive.

This was what she'd wanted for years. Well, while she'd been married.

Maybe it was just as well the family from the apartment opposite had left early, because it was hardly the kind of news she could have blurted out to Richard in front of the rest of them.

But Richard was gone from Lanrock now, possibly for good.

She gazed down at the test, with its definitive blue line. She was going to have to do some serious thinking before telling anyone what had happened, let alone him.

Poor man, he had enough on his plate; this was the last thing he needed to hear right now.

Her hands went to her flat stomach, her fingers splaying as she imagined what was hidden in there. Did it have a heartbeat yet? Did it have a heart?

Her own was beating overtime.

I'm having a baby. Imagine that.

Chapter 19

It was midday, and the town was jam-packed with locals and holidaymakers as the Pirate Parade made its noisy, joyous way up Angel Street, across Lanrock Bridge and down Long Street on the other side of the river. There were drums and trumpets, there was raucous singing, and there was dancing and applause accompanying them on their journey around Lanrock.

Having left Marcus in charge of the office, Lottie had come down to watch the spectacle as the pirates approached Beach Street. Ahead of her, she spotted Max standing outside Bert's Bar, experiencing his first parade. She hadn't seen him since handing over the keys to Jericho Cottage seven days ago, which had been surprising, because she'd expected him to turn up and invite her out again.

Except it hadn't happened.

She paused now, watching as he answered his phone and chatted for a minute or two. From this distance, tanned, smiling and wearing a white shirt and faded jeans, he looked . . . OK, let's face it, pretty great. Which was the problem, of course. Her heart gave a squeeze, reminding her of his comment when she'd rejected his invitation: 'It's only dinner. I'm not asking you to marry me.'

Because that was the problem; he might be interested in her now, but how long was it likely to last? Probably just long enough to make her think he was serious, before he disappeared back to his real life, leaving yet another broken heart crushed beneath his heel.

Turning him down had been an act of self-preservation. But she couldn't deny the fact that she'd enjoyed being asked.

As she watched, he ended his call and turned to look at a small boy next to him, who was crying because he wanted to be lifted up. The boy's mum was shaking her head, explaining that she couldn't hold him as well as the baby in her arms. Max said something to her and disappeared into Bert's Bar, emerging moments later with a chair and placing it against the exterior wall of the pub so it couldn't be knocked over. A brief conversation ensued, then the grateful mother passed him the baby to hold so she could lift her son onto the chair and keep an arm around him so he didn't fall.

Pinggg went Lottie's ovaries at the sight of Max with an infant in his arms, instinctively rocking from one foot to the other while pulling funny faces to make the baby smile.

Then the drums and trumpets grew louder as the parade reached them, the pirates came streaming down the road, and everyone began to clap and cheer them on their way. The little boy's face was a picture as he watched from his vantage point, and as she saw Max and the children's mother continue to chat and laugh, Lottie began to wonder if they knew each other better than she'd first thought.

But once the parade had passed them by, the mother helped her son down from the chair, then took the baby back from

Max and, with a cheerful exchange of goodbyes, disappeared off in the direction of the beach.

The crowds along the pavement began to disperse. Lottie felt the familiar clamour start up in her chest when she realised Max was heading her way. He hadn't spotted her yet, but when he did . . .

Well, maybe this time she wouldn't turn him down if he suggested going for a drink.

Except he still hadn't noticed her, and now he was crossing the road, looking preoccupied, weaving his way between tourists and—

'Max!' Lottie couldn't help herself; her arm shot up to attract his attention before he could pass by and miss her completely. 'Hi!'

'Oh, hi.' He paused and nodded in greeting. 'Not at work?'

'Came out to see the parade. You?'

'Same. It was good fun. Well . . .' Now it was his turn to raise his hand, only this time to signal a casual goodbye.

'Everything OK with the cottage?' she blurted out.

'It's great, thanks.'

Well, this wasn't going according to plan *at all*. 'Remember, any problems, just pop in or give me a call.' She flashed her easiest, breeziest, friendliest smile. Why couldn't he look at her like he'd been looking at that tiny baby earlier?

'I will if I need to. But it's fine. Right, I'll see you around . . .'

And now he was walking away, up the hill, as if she were a vaguely familiar neighbour who'd just made a passing observation about the weather. Staring after him in disbelief, she waited a full minute, then turned in the same direction and began to follow him. Was he on his way to meet up with someone? Had the woman taken her children to be looked after by her parents and had arranged to have lunch with Max? Or had he found himself some new girlfriend during the week he'd been down here?

That wouldn't surprise her.

The good thing about the number of tourists milling around was the way they helped her to avoid being spotted. The less good thing was, ten minutes later, she'd lost him. One moment he'd been there, the next he'd vanished. Lottie hesitated, peering around her, then continued up the road more slowly, stopping to check inside each shop along the way.

It was while she was peering into a shoe shop that someone tapped her on the shoulder.

'Looking for me?' said Max.

Mortified, she pointed randomly at – oh God – a pair of burgundy sandals decorated with yellow and white plastic daisies. 'What? No, of course not! I was looking at those shoes in the window.'

'OK.' He shrugged. 'Sorry, my mistake. I thought you might be following me.'

And he was off, striding up the road, calling over his shoulder, 'By the way, don't buy them. They're dreadful.'

It only took a slight detour to reach Tess and Freya's store on Angel Street. The tiny shop with its delphinium-blue frontage and sherbet-lemon interior was probably the most colourful in Lanrock. It was certainly the girliest, with its summer wear ranging from crystal-embellished kaftans to rainbow-silk kimonos. There were glittery flip-flops and every conceivable style of hat, there were sunglasses and gauzy wraps and hand-painted silk jackets in jewel shades. The style might not be everyone's cup of tea, but enough loyal customers loved it to keep the business profitable, with holidaymakers returning year after year, and those who couldn't visit in person enthusiastically ordering items online.

Lottie tried on various bangles and necklaces and sniffed her way through the tester bottles of a new range of perfumes while Freya sold one of the spectacular hand-painted full-length jackets to a woman from Sheffield whose dentist son was due to marry his TV producer wife in Milan in September. Lottie knew this because Freya and her mum were renowned for getting to know their customers in record time; give them an extra ten minutes and they'd have discovered everything about this woman from her passport number to her DNA ancestry.

'There you are.' Freya had wrapped the jacket in layers of amethyst tissue paper and placed it in one of the shop's signature blue and silver cardboard carriers. 'You're going to look fabulous! And don't forget to send us a photo of you at the wedding so we can add you to our wall of fame.'

When the woman had left the shop, beaming and swinging her carrier by its silver rope handles, Lottie said, 'How did her son meet his wife?'

'They were queuing separately to pay for car parking tickets after doing their Christmas shopping. Just got chatting, then he asked if she wanted to go for a coffee.' Freya patted her own heart. 'By the time they got back to the car park, it was six hours later. Cost them an extra fifteen pounds each. But eighteen months on, they both say it was the best thirty pounds they ever spent.'

'And? What kind of engagement ring did he buy her?'

'I don't know, didn't ask.'

Lottie shook her head. 'You're slipping. Where's your mum?'

'Popped out to pick up some sandwiches. And to see the parade, I expect.'

'Same.' Lottie picked up another bangle and tried it on for something to do. 'Just saw Max watching it too. Cameron's friend, remember? From the wedding?'

Freya laughed. 'Of course I remember. We had him over for supper last night.'

'Oh!' Lottie couldn't hide her surprise. Freya and Cameron quite often invited her to join them for an impromptu supper. Last night she'd stayed in, used up a slightly out-of-date ready meal of stroganoff and rice, and watched a two-hour murder mystery on TV that hadn't even ended up being any good.

'It was great! He's such fun, isn't he? Fantastic company.' Freya caught Lottie's expression and added, 'I did say we should give you a call, see if you were free to come over and join us, but Max told us you definitely wouldn't want to.'

'Right. OK.' *Hello, karma.*

'He did say he'd tried to be friendly but you just weren't interested.'

'Well, I was busy . . .' He had a point, Lottie reluctantly reminded herself. When she'd been the one turning down his offer, it had felt like the right and sensible thing to do. She could hardly blame him for taking the hint and backing off.

'So what exactly happened all those years ago between the two of you? I asked Max and he wouldn't tell me.' Freya pulled a face. 'Which is quite annoying when you're as nosy as I am.'

For the sake of her parents, Lottie had never confided in anyone the reason behind Max's abrupt departure from her life. And for the sake of his own family, it seemed Max had kept quiet about it too.

'It was one of those teenage things,' she said vaguely. 'We were kind of friends, although we bickered all the time and drove each other mad. And one time it nearly turned into something

156

else, but in the end it didn't happen. Then he moved with his parents to Ireland and we lost touch. After that, we came to live down here.' She shrugged. 'That's just the way it was.'

Freya was rearranging filigree earrings on a model of a tree. 'And when you saw him again in the church, did all the old feelings come rushing back? Because I know there had to be feelings,' she added drily.

'Not really. Maybe a bit,' Lottie admitted, because it would be weird to deny it completely.

'He's really attractive.'

He was. You couldn't deny that either.

'And he's funny, that's always appealing. You can see why everyone likes him.'

Lottie said nothing. It was the way he was so effortlessly able to cast his spell over women that was making her determined not to fall under it.

Freya was now dreamily refolding a fringed honey-blonde pashmina. 'He has one of those smiles that make you smile too.'

OK, enough of the Max-worship. 'So do lots of people.' Lottie gave her the side-eye. 'Not thinking of swapping Cameron for a newer model, are you?'

'No.' Cheeks flushing, Freya smoothed the pashmina like a cat.

'Oh, by the way, I saw the piece about him in the paper last night. I'll sponsor him, obviously.' Cameron was an enthusiastic fundraiser for worthy charities; Lottie sometimes thought unworthy thoughts and secretly wished he could take a break for a couple of months, because feeling obliged to donate to endless good causes could sometimes get a bit much. This officially made her a horrible person, she knew that. On the upside, the surge of guilt invariably forced her to donate more to make up for it.

157

'It's been a while since his last marathon, so he'll need to train like mad,' Freya said consolingly. 'He probably won't be able to manage it.'

When Cameron hadn't been able to complete the last marathon thanks to a fall resulting in a sprained ankle after three miles, he'd offered a full refund to each person who'd already paid, but it would have been unthinkable to take the donations back. Lottie sometimes wondered if she was the only one who inwardly winced each time Cameron greeted her with a cheery 'Here comes my favourite person!' because she knew exactly what he was going to say next.

She changed the subject. 'How did Esther's leaving party go the other evening?'

Esther had retired from the practice on Friday night, having worked there as a receptionist for the last forty years. Scary but efficient, she had ruled the medical centre like a queen, invariably wrapped in a hand-knitted cardigan, and Lottie knew Freya had been dreading the party, which had promised to be a dry, stilted affair in the back room of the café next to the surgery.

'Oh, it was brilliant in the end! Cameron brought Max along and he cheered Esther up no end – you should have seen her, giggling like a schoolgirl. Max ended up herding everyone down to Bert's Bar and teaching us all how to rap! Honestly, if I hadn't seen it with my own eyes, I'd never have believed it. Look at this . . .' Taking out her phone, she scrolled through until she reached a video and pressed play.

Astonished, Lottie watched seventy-year-old Esther on stage with Max, brandishing a microphone and bellowing, 'My name's Esther *Grey*, it's my leaving *day*, I've had a gin and *tonic* and now I'm on my way!' She was waving her free hand back and forth over her head, and goodness knows what she'd done with her trusty cardigan, because her dress was sleeveless and her sturdy white bra straps were on show. She appeared to be having the time of her life, with Max beat-boxing at her side and everyone in the bar cheering her on like she was Missy Elliott at Coachella.

'Isn't it amazing?' Freya was laughing. 'She said it was the best party she's ever had. It was such a shame you couldn't make it.'

Here came karma all over again. Lottie could have made it, but she'd blurted out some fictitious excuse about having a Zoom call booked with a potential client, then stayed at home and congratulated herself on having avoided the dullest leaving party of all time.

'Honestly, you'd have loved it,' Freya went on as the shop door opened. 'It was a fantastic night!'

'Freya, how are things with you?' The new customer greeted her with open arms. 'Have you fixed another date for the wedding?'

'Well, not yet . . .'

'Oh, but you must! My husband bumped into Cameron the other day and he said you'd probably just have a quick registry office do.' The woman mimed horror. 'But I said noooo, that's not fair, it needs to be another church service, otherwise it wouldn't *feel* right.'

'We haven't really decided,' Freya said lightly.

'Well, it's important, so you need to get it sorted as soon as possible. Can't go around being not-married-yet for ever, can you? Ooh.' The woman's eyes lit up as she spotted a frilly-edged parasol painted with cream roses and blue hydrangeas. 'I like this.'

'Isn't it great?' Visibly relieved at the change of subject, Freya reached for the parasol. 'They just came in yesterday and we sold three this morning. This is the last one in the shop.'

'In that case,' the woman grabbed it as if it were a lifebelt during a flood, 'I'd better have it.'

Chapter 20

The mirror had a tiny crack in one corner but was otherwise perfect, a huge rectangle in one of those ornate silver-painted wooden frames with curly edges. It was the kind of mirror people with plenty of money hung in their homes. Baroque, was that the name of the style? Or maybe rococo?

Iris, who didn't have plenty of money, had spotted it from a distance, glinting in the evening sunshine. Her spirits had lifted upon nearing the skip. Maybe she could carry the mirror home and hang it above the fireplace in her flat. Or, better still, flog it on eBay.

Now, having reached the skip, she saw that it was three quarters full of discarded items. OK, some of them were rubbish, but others were definitely eBayable. She could see broken-up kitchen cupboards and rolls of old worn carpet, but also two decent kitchen chairs, a box filled with odds and ends of crockery, several old-fashioned lampshades, assorted cushions, some saucepans, bundled-up curtains, various pots of paint and a purple Dyson vacuum cleaner.

Treasure. Especially the rococo-baroque mirror. And if she didn't take it, someone else would. Iris was on her way back from three hours of cleaning the house of a long-retired scientist who lived on the other side of Lanrock Bridge and liked to accuse her of deliberately hiding his cutlery, so this felt like her much-deserved reward. Since cleaning kept her strong and fit, she lifted herself easily up onto the side of the skip, swung her legs over the edge and jumped in.

This wasn't her first skip-dive.

Ooh, there was a microwave over there in the far corner . . . and a kettle. But it was the mirror that had first caught her eye, and this was what she was going to carry home with her before someone else made off with it. Bending down to grasp the frame by the corners, she began to lift it out and—

'Oi, put that down,' shouted a male voice from the front window of a house two doors along.

Iris swung round, still holding the mirror. 'Excuse me?'

'You heard,' said the voice. '*Drop.*'

'What am I? Lassie?' Her own voice rose in disbelief.

'My God.' He was shaking his head at her. 'You have a nerve.'

Seconds later, the front door was yanked open and he emerged from the house, looking as if he meant business. Iris took in the dusty shorts, the Iron Maiden T-shirt, the cropped blonde hair and the look of pure vitriol in his narrow blue eyes.

'What is your problem?' she demanded.

'At the moment, it's you. Helping yourself to something that doesn't belong to you.'

'I'm not stealing it. You can't steal something that's already been thrown into a skip. Did you put all this stuff in here?'

'I did. I'm also the one who paid to hire the skip. And you're not having that mirror.'

This was completely ridiculous. She straightened her spine

and marvelled at just how stupid some people could be. 'Look, if anything, I'm doing you a favour. I'm leaving you more room to put other stuff into your precious skip.'

'I don't care. You're still not taking it.'

'Do your neighbours know they have a psychopath living next door to them?'

The intensity of his gaze was almost unnerving. 'I don't live here.'

Iris glanced at the houses on either side of the one he'd just come out of. 'They must be relieved.'

His eyes narrowed. 'Do you know who I am?'

'No. Thank God.' Since he clearly wasn't about to back down, she put the mirror back where she'd found it, then climbed out of the skip and wiped her perspiring palms on the sides of her jeans.

'Good decision.' The man gave her a sardonic wave. 'Bye.'

He had nicely muscled arms. If he wasn't such a dick, with a shitty attitude, she might even have found him mildly attractive.

But he was, so she didn't. Not one bit.

'Shame they didn't let you into charm school,' she said.

'Shame you couldn't keep your nose out of other people's business,' he replied. 'And yourself out of other people's skips.'

Seven hours later, at two in the morning, Iris climbed into her friend's white van and drove through the silent streets of Lanrock until she reached the skip. Clouds were obscuring the moon and no lights were on in any of the houses nearby. She parked the van in front of the skip and opened the rear doors, ready to make the trip worthwhile. Because while before the mirror might have been enough, now that she knew her nemesis didn't

163

live here, bringing a van seemed like the perfect answer. She imagined his face when he turned up tomorrow morning and saw how much was missing, and hoped he'd know it had been taken by her.

Maybe she'd leave a little thank-you note, just to rub it in.

The mirror was no longer there, but she helped herself to the microwave, a couple of oil paintings in plain frames – well, they *might* turn out to be by someone famous – and the first of the Shaker-style kitchen chairs. It was as she was on her way back for the second chair that a light came on and she heard footsteps on the pavement behind her.

Purposeful footsteps.

Fuck.

'So predictable,' he drawled. 'I knew you'd be back.'

'Now I definitely know you're a psychopath.' Iris shook her head at him. 'Have you been peering out of the window all night? Staying awake just so you can catch me out? Because that *is* pathetic.'

'I'm still awake because I've been working.'

She gave a snort of laughter. 'I don't believe you.'

'I don't care whether you do or not. I know who you are, by the way.'

'So do lots of people. I live here.' Recalling a comment he'd made earlier, she added, 'And you told me you didn't.'

'I don't. I'm just staying until the house is sorted. Keeping an eye on the place. And its contents,' he added.

'Even the ones you've already thrown out.'

'I don't care who helps themselves to anything from this skip.' He paused. 'Just so long as it isn't you.'

'So you've come out here to take all this back?' She gestured to the van with its rear doors open.

'No, you can keep the microwave. It's broken. So's the kettle.' A faint smile. 'You're welcome to them, and to the artwork. Those paintings were done by a bunch of kids, in case you were planning to take them along to Sotheby's.'

Bugger. She'd hoped they might be valuable abstracts, like the ones that got investigated on *Fake or Fortune?*

'I took them because I like them,' she lied. Curiosity overcame her. 'Why anyone but me?'

'Do you really not know whose house this is?'

They were on Bell Street, one of several narrow roads leading off Wood Lane. When walking home, as a rule Iris used the next one along, because a couple of her friends lived on it; spotting the skip from a distance was what had drawn her down this street earlier today. At a guess, it had to be something to do with an ex of hers who was a good friend of his. Well, she was single, she was allowed to have exes. And some of them had been idiots who'd deserved to be dumped. Maybe he knew Jed, who'd been a prize prat and who'd been particularly outraged when she'd ended their brief relationship. Although Jed lived with his brother over in Westcup and could never afford a house like the ones on this road.

'I really don't know. Until today, I've never seen you before.'

'I'd never seen you either. But I'm betting there aren't too many women in this town with *LOOK UP* tattooed across their chest.'

Iris's skin prickled with annoyance, but this time at herself rather than him. The tattoo was her biggest regret, an act of rebellion she'd booked herself in for a week after turning eighteen because she'd been so sick of men endlessly ogling her over-developed breasts. Having it done had hurt a *lot*, it had cost *all* her birthday money, and at the time it simply hadn't occurred to her that all the words did was draw attention and ribald remarks about her embonpoint.

To add insult to injury, since giving birth to her children, her once-fabulous boobs had sagged, and now required her to wear bras with industrial-strength scaffolding.

Talk about be careful what you wish for. It was like being young and gorgeous and rolling your eyes when men wolf-whistled. Once the passing years had done their worst and taken away your looks, you almost found yourself missing the attention.

'I bet you wish you'd never had that done, don't you?' He was half smiling now. 'Makes you kind of memorable.'

One day, when Iris had several hundred pounds to spare, she planned to get this bloody tattoo removed, or at least inked over. Until then, however, hiding it from view would mean admitting it had been a mistake, so pride forced her to make a point of never covering it up.

'I'm memorable anyway,' she retorted.

'You certainly were when you turned up at the church the other week and interrupted that wedding.'

Ah. 'You were there?'

'I wasn't. But I heard all about it.'

Iris frowned. 'Are you friends with Jed?'

'Who's Jed? Your husband?'

OK, this was getting ridiculous; were they going to end up standing out here all night? Needing to know now, she said, 'What's your name?'

'Drew. Dawson. Probably doesn't mean anything to you.'

'I still don't know who you are.' She shrugged.

'Maybe this'll help. My sister's name is Margaret Crane.'

Well, well. Iris blinked. 'You don't look a bit alike.'

166

'What can I tell you? She's a head teacher who loves Debussy. I'm a builder who's a heavy-metal freak.'

Iris shivered as a cool breeze made itself felt across her shoulders. 'But . . . she's in her fifties.'

'Fifty-one. And I'm thirty-three. Pretty sure I wasn't planned, but there you go. I turned up anyway.'

'So hang on, let me get this straight. Your sister was having an affair with a married man – a married *vicar*, no less – but because I was the one who told his wife what they'd been getting up to behind her back, you think that makes me the bad guy in all this. And that's why you won't let me take anything out of your skip?' Iris's laugh was incredulous. 'Seriously, you couldn't make it up.'

'I already told you. You're welcome to the microwave.'

'You're hilarious.' Stalking across to the van, she lifted out the broken microwave and threw it back into the skip. Despite aiming it to land on a piece of carpet, it still made a loud metallic clunk.

'Whoops,' said Drew seconds later as a light snapped on in the nearest house and a bedroom window was flung open.

'Bloody fly-tippers,' bellowed a man in his sixties. 'Get out of here before I call the police.'

'It's OK, we chased them away,' Drew reassured the irate neighbour. 'They woke us up too. Sorry you were disturbed.'

Us? 'What are you on about?' said Iris when the man had disappeared from view. She shivered again and wished she'd worn a jacket. What a waste of a night this had turned out to be.

'He's a nosy sod. Margaret can't stand him. Look, you're cold,' said Drew. 'If we're going to carry on arguing, want to come in for a coffee?'

167

Iris stared at him in disbelief before starting to laugh at the sheer audacity of the suggestion.

He broke into a grin. 'Hey, where's your sense of adventure? You can keep me company while I work.'

Inside, the ground floor of the four-bedroomed Edwardian villa had been emptied and stripped back following the abrupt departure of the previous inhabitants.

'Margaret and her husband were never into DIY. They've lived here for years without doing anything to the place,' Drew explained. 'The whole house was looking old and tired, but they needed to sell it now they've split up She doesn't want to move back here and her husband's moved to Plymouth. So a couple of estate agents came over to give her a valuation and said if it was done up it'd fetch sixty grand more. I told her I could do the renovation for thirty. And here I am. Sugar?'

With all the units ripped out, the kitchen was echoey and furnished only with a table upon which stood one of those fancy coffee pod machines and a couple of mugs. But when he carried them through to the living room, there was a squashy grey sofa for her to sit on while he climbed the stepladder by the fireplace and resumed painting the coving.

'I thought you knew this was Margaret's house,' he went on. 'I had visions of you boasting to all your friends about grabbing her stuff out of the skip, showing it off like trophies.'

'That'd be a bit sick.' Iris nearly added, 'Almost as sick as having an affair with a married vicar,' but managed to stop herself. She took a swallow of coffee, which was good and strong, just the way she liked her men. No, the way she liked to drink her coffee. Her gaze flickered over his broad shoulders and defined biceps. *Don't even think it.*

'I know what you were going to say.' Drew was observing

her from the top of the ladder. 'Look, I know what Margaret did was wrong. But she's my big sister, and I love her. Don't roll your eyes like that. Haven't you ever made a mistake in your life?'

'I've made hundreds,' said Iris. 'But there's such a thing as sisterhood. I've never slept with another woman's husband.'

'Margaret's marriage wasn't a happy one.'

'That's no excuse.'

'Our parents died when she was twenty-five and I was seven. She brought me up. I owe her everything.'

'What is this, *The X Factor*? Spare me the sob story,' said Iris. 'It's still no excuse.'

'She missed out on a lot because of me. And then she married someone who seemed like he'd be a decent husband, but all he's done is make her life miserable. My sister's a good person.'

'I'm sure she is, when she isn't being an adulterer.'

'If you really knew her, you'd understand.'

Iris drank down the rest of her coffee, so hot it scalded her throat. She was finding it hard not to stare at Drew Dawson's tanned, muscular body and imagine him naked, which meant it was time to go.

'Right.' She rose to her feet. 'Well, excuse me for not wanting to join the Margaret Crane fan club, but I'm sure she wouldn't want me as a member anyway. Thanks for the coffee. I'll be off now.'

'Oh.' He turned, surprised. 'Are you sure? I thought—'

'Quite sure.' He had long eyelashes too. She could imagine what he'd been thinking, and had no intention of falling for it. 'Good luck with the renovation. I'll see myself out. And don't worry, your skip is safe. I won't be diving into it again.'

After closing the front door behind her, she leaned against it

169

for a moment, needing to get her breath back and regain her composure. The whole time she'd been verbally sparring with Margaret Crane's brother – and hating him for *being* Margaret's brother – she'd been aware of her body reacting to him in a quite different way, and with an intensity she hadn't experienced since she was a teenager. Bloody hell, what *was* it about the man that—

The door opened so suddenly she almost fell backwards into the hallway.

'Thought you were leaving?' Drew's tone was amiable.

'I know. I was just . . .'

Fantasising about you, actually.

'Why are you still here? Leaning against my door?'

He'd been watching from the window, waiting to see her make her way down the stone steps. Iris looked at him. 'I stopped to tie my shoelace.'

'I see.' His gaze flickered down to her pale blue flip-flops, then back up again. After a long moment of direct eye contact, he shrugged. 'Well, it's about time I finished work for the night.'

Iris nodded slowly. Could he hear the way her heart was clamouring against her ribs?

'So . . . coming back in?' he said.

Another nod. She followed him inside, and this time he took her hand, his fingers effortlessly interlocking with hers. The physical contact was electrifying.

Together they climbed the staircase. The bedroom he led her into had been freshly redecorated in shades of dove grey and white. The double bed was fitted with white sheets and a silver and pale grey striped duvet.

'It's all clean. I only bought the bedding last week.' He indicated his arms, liberally spattered with white paint. 'I need to get this off me. If I promise to be out of the shower in record time, do you absolutely promise not to run away?'

As if she would. She gave a tiny shrug. 'You'll just have to wait and see.'

He moved forward and kissed her on the mouth, warm and soft and bone-melting. Iris's head swam with the effect it had on her.

He stepped back. 'You're beautiful.'

'I know I am.'

'Don't leave.'

She lightly ran the tip of her index finger down from his throat to his sternum. 'Don't be long, then.'

True to his word, he wasn't.

Forty-five incredible minutes later, magnificently naked and smiling at her across the bed, Drew rested his hand on her hip and murmured, 'Oh dear. I thought you said you didn't sleep with married men.'

Chapter 21

It had been a blustery, sunny afternoon but a sudden squall of summer rain had brought an influx of customers into the Dolphin pub. Freya, smug at having beaten the rest of them to it, had already bagged her favourite table at a booth in the corner of the back bar, cocooned as it was by a high-backed wooden seat upholstered in crimson velvet. Her mum was over at the salon on Wood Lane having her nails redone and would be here in twenty minutes, when they would order their favourite meals for dinner. Right now, though, after a busy day in the shop, Freya was enjoying resting her feet and sipping a glass of ice-cold Veuve du Vernay while idly listening to the chatter of other customers around her. A family from Birmingham to her left had been having a good-natured argument about which garden centre to visit tomorrow, and an older couple were discussing the merits of a rental property over on Long Street that had a bigger balcony but a less spectacular view than the third-floor apartment up on Cliff Road. Then their food order arrived and silence fell, just as someone in the booth directly behind Freya's exclaimed, 'Oh my God, Janey, you should see him – we thought

172

he looked good before, but he's even better in real life. His eyes! His body! He's just so . . . so *shaggable*.'

Freya instantly perked up; never mind boring old garden centres and rental properties, this was the kind of phone chat worth eavesdropping on. Concentrating all her attention on the female voice behind her, she waited for the woman's friend to finish speaking on the other end of the line.

'I know, isn't it crazy? Mum said moving to another part of the country could be the making of me . . . she even said it would do me good and I might end up meeting the love of my life, and I laughed at her. Except now I actually think it could happen. He's just so perfect.' Pause. 'OK, no way, taking a photo of him would be weird, I'm not doing that.' Another longer pause. 'And no, he isn't married. I think there's a girl-friend, but hey, who's to say that'll last? They could break up next week. Anyway, I'm still allowed to flirt with him, aren't I? How else is he going to know I'm interested? It's not stealing another woman's boyfriend if he decides he prefers me! And it's the way of the world these days. Hang around waiting for Mr Perfect Single Guy to make the first move and you could still be waiting when you're too old to do anything with him.'

Freya took another swallow of white wine and waited while Janey said something else that made the woman behind her burst out laughing.

'Oh stop it. I'm going to wow him with my efficiency and dazzle him with my charms. I have to be there at eight on the dot tomorrow morning, all ready for my first day. I'll be drop-dead gorgeous in my new turquoise dress, flashing my irresistible smile . . . What? Ha, well, maybe I'll flash that too. Ooh, looks like the rain's stopped, time I was out of here. No, no wine tonight, want to make sure I look my best for Dr Luuurve!'

Having spent the last few minutes happily eavesdropping away, Freya belatedly discovered *she* was the girlfriend who didn't count. Frozen in her seat, her brain scrambling to rewind and recall every word of the one-sided conversation, she just had time to snatch up the menu and cover half her face with it as the woman jumped up from her own seat and headed past on her way out of the pub while still saying goodbye to her friend on the phone.

Long silky blonde hair, a pink and white striped crop top, and pink jeans. Very pretty, twenty-something, sunglasses perched on her head and with a waft of rather nice flowery scent trailing in her wake.

What was her name? Cameron had mentioned the woman he'd interviewed over Zoom, whom he'd chosen from the many applicants to replace Esther following her retirement. Naomi, was that it? She'd reached the door now, was about to leave. Freya hesitated for a split second; if she called out her name, Naomi would stop and turn. She imagined jumping up and joining her, then introducing herself and telling Naomi that setting her sights on another woman's fiancé wasn't the done thing at all. She imagined the look of horror and guilt on her rival's face upon realising she'd been caught out.

But she didn't jump up; just stayed where she was in her booth. She wasn't really the confrontational type. And seconds after the girl had disappeared with a swish of silky hair, here came Tess, fresh from the nail salon, holding her hands with her fingers carefully splayed because she was always afraid of knocking them and spoiling their perfect shine.

Freya waved to attract her attention and her mum hurried over, sinking happily into the seat facing her. 'I'm starving! I'm going to have the cheese soufflé and chips.'

174

'I just overheard someone talking to her friend on the phone. She was telling her how much she fancied Cameron.'

'What a cheek! Who was it?'

Freya shrugged and said, 'No one I know,' which was technically true. Under the circumstances, it seemed safer not to reveal the identity of Cameron's admirer. Her mum loved him so much, she would be outraged if she found out who it was. She might even decide to say something, which would be wildly embarrassing.

'Well, I suppose you can't stop people liking him. He's such a catch.' Tess gave her daughter a sympathetic smile. 'But you're the one he's chosen. Because he has excellent taste. Has it upset you?'

Freya shook her head. 'No. It was just weird to hear it.' Somehow it had never occurred to her before that other women might secretly – or not so secretly – lust after her fiancé. 'Anyway, speaking of taste, I'm going to have the king prawn risotto.'

'We should sort out another date for the wedding,' Cameron said later that evening. Having returned from his training run, he was now half watching the news on TV while making his way through a mountain of chicken salad. 'I checked the calendar at work, and Monday the eleventh of July would be good for me if we're going to take the registry office route.'

Freya said, 'Why does that date sound familiar? Oh, hang on, the eleventh of July? I can't do that day. I've already arranged to go up to London for a long weekend to stay with Debs, and I can't let her down, not when she's already made arrangements.' She shook her head apologetically. 'I thought I'd told you.'

'No, but never mind. I'll have another look at the calendar.' He looked up as she went to make herself a cup of tea, switching on the kettle and taking a carton out of the fridge. 'Is that my milk?'

'Sorry, yes.' She preferred semi-skimmed, but had used hers up and forgotten to buy more. 'Is that OK?'

After the briefest of pauses, Cameron said, 'Of course. Help yourself.'

It occurred to Freya that he did always pause slightly before telling her it was fine to do something. She poured a splash into her cup and vowed not to forget to buy the normal kind in future. Then she tasted her tea and pulled a face. She didn't even like oat milk anyway.

'How did it go, meeting the new receptionist today?'

'Fine. She's the polar opposite of Esther. Seems keen and ready to work hard.'

Keen . . .

'Is she pretty?'

Cameron chewed and swallowed a mouthful of lettuce, then gave her a playful look. 'Not bad, I suppose. What's this about? Starting to worry?'

'You know me.' She smiled. 'I'm not the jealous type.'

'Oh, while I think of it.' He put down his plate and reached for one of the A3-sized sheets of paper lying face-down on the table. 'I printed off a few of these today. Could you put one in the shop window? We want to drum up as much publicity as we can.'

It was a poster featuring details of the upcoming marathon and the charity that would benefit from it, as well as a colour photo of Cameron in his white coat, with a stethoscope slung around his neck. It looked like a casually snapped picture, but Freya knew it had been carefully posed to show him at his best. She also wished she could be a nicer person who didn't mind about always having to display these quite large notices in the relatively small window of Kaftan Queen, blocking as they did the carefully arranged displays of summer outfits, fairy lights and sparkling jewellery.

By ten o'clock, she was alone downstairs. Between the long hours of work at the surgery and his exhaustive fitness training schedule, Cameron needed his sleep and had gone up to bed at nine thirty.

Freya sent an email to her old college friend Debs, who had given birth to a baby boy a month before the original wedding date:

Debs, how are you and how is gorgeous Alfie? All good, I hope! Now, it's ages since I last saw you and I'd love to come up for the weekend of 9–10 July. No worries if you can't face a house guest – I can book a room nearby. I'd just really like to have a catch-up and give Alfie loads of cuddles, is that OK? xx

She hadn't planned the excuse in advance. When Cameron had suggested this new date for their wedding, the lie – or was it a fib? – had come tumbling out of her mouth of its own accord.

OK, definitely more of a fib than a lie. A harmless fib, that was all.

Practically a microfib.

All she had to hope now was that Debs wouldn't say no.

An hour later, still not tired, she flicked through the TV channels in search of something half decent to watch. Coming across a film featuring a favourite actress, she settled down with a can of Coke and a packet of Twiglets, ready to be entertained. Was it a comedy? A romance? Time would tell.

Except it turned out to be a complete heartbreaker. The gist of the plot was that her favourite actress was playing the part of a happily married woman who, diagnosed with a terminal illness, devoted the last year of her life to finding her husband a replacement wife. She didn't even tell him what she was doing, just drew up a shortlist and casually introduced the two new women into their social circle so he'd be comfortable in their company once he was on his own. And because it was one of those inevitable happy-ending movies, the beautiful woman who'd seemed like the best bet but was secretly a right bitch revealed her ugly side in due course, leaving the way clear for the devastated husband to slowly come to appreciate the friendship of the second-choice woman, who might be less glamorous but was a hundred times kinder and more compatible.

The last minutes of the film featured their wedding, after two years of the man grieving and getting over the loss of his first wife. Everyone was happy. There was laughter and dancing and flowers placed on the grave of the wonderful woman who'd arranged for the happy couple to meet and eventually fall in love.

It was one in the morning when Freya made her way up to bed. Sometimes you just couldn't beat a sad story, a heart-warming ending and a good cry . . .

She was woken at six by the alarm clock blaring in her ear, prompting Cameron to leap out of bed, throw on his shorts and running vest and bring her a cup of tea in bed before setting out on his morning run. He'd even added a splash of the precious – but still weird-tasting – oat milk.

Ninety minutes later, he was back. 'Morning, sleepyhead. Time to get up now.' He dropped a kiss on her forehead as she surfaced from another doze. 'And don't worry about buying more milk. I picked up a carton of semi-skimmed on my way back.'

'Thanks.' Freya smiled up at him. See? How many men would be that caring and thoughtful?

But once he'd showered and left for work, a niggling memory from last night's made-for-TV movie kept tugging at the back of her mind. It wasn't until she was in the middle of hastily ironing her dress – sleeveless, orange and splashed with bright yellow sunflowers – that the realisation struck her.

Maybe she could do a bit of gentle matchmaking herself, subtly encouraging Naomi and Cameron to get to know each other better so that Cameron might gradually come to realise he'd be happier with Naomi than he was with his current fiancée.

It could work out. If it didn't, she'd have to come up with an alternative option. But if it *did* . . . well, what could be nicer than a smooth transition with no need for anyone to feel bad? It was the perfect way to escape her sticky situation without the burden of experiencing a lifetime of guilt.

Bugger, *her dress.* With a yelp, Freya lifted the iron . . .

But it was OK, the gods were on her side and there was no scorch mark.

It was a good sign. No blame, no shame and everyone would end up happier than they were now.

She was feeling better already.

Chapter 22

It was Friday. Max had been staying in Lanrock for a fortnight. His time was up.

Lottie had tried calling and texting him earlier but there'd been no reply. She was beginning to take it personally. Was he doing it on purpose?

Turning up at Jericho Cottage, she banged the front door's heavy lion's-head knocker. Still no answer. Was he inside? She unzipped her shoulder bag and was preparing to scribble a note to push through the letter box when the woman who lived next door threw open a window and poked her head out.

'Hi! Are you looking for Max? He left twenty minutes ago, said he was heading down to the beach for a swim.'

'Oh, right.' Lottie stopped searching for a pen. To go down to the beach or not? Without her even wanting to think about it, the memory of swimming in the sea with Max that fateful evening flooded into her brain.

'If you see him, tell him I'm making lobster mac and cheese tonight. It's my speciality and I'm hoping he'll come over to share it.' The woman's eyes sparkled. 'He mentioned it was his favourite. I'm Karen, by the way,' she added with a perky smile.

Karen had to be fifteen years older than Max, at least. What was it about him that had this effect on women? Lottie zipped her bag shut and said, 'If I do see him, I'll let him know.'

It was only a few minutes' walk down to West Beach. Reaching the top of the stone steps leading down to the sand, she gripped the metal handrail and paused to scan the sea, which was glittering like diamonds in the sunlight. She shielded her eyes, but there was no sign of Max, and her overactive imagination caused her pulse to quicken, because what if he'd sunk beneath the waves without anyone noticing?

Then her gaze shifted to the beach itself, and after a couple of seconds of scanning she exhaled, because there he was, half hidden from view by the lifeguard's elevated chair, chatting to the lifeguard currently on duty.

Of course he was safe. That he might not be was unthinkable.

As she watched, he said something that made the lifeguard laugh. Then he stepped away from the chair, dropped his towel onto the sand and pulled his T-shirt up and over his head. Kicking off his espadrilles, he jogged down the beach in just a pair of faded green board shorts, his back tanned and his broad shoulders tapering to narrow hips. Then he was racing into the water, powering through the breaking waves and raising his arms before diving into the sea.

It was one of those occasions when you wished you had a pair of really good binoculars with you. Lottie watched as he swam past a couple of paddleboarders and a group of holiday-makers throwing a beachball to each other, then struck out into deeper water, making his way towards the pontoon anchored fifty or sixty metres offshore.

It was her lunch break; no need to hurry back to the office. She made her way down the steps and carried her sandals over to a clear patch of sand not far from Max's belongings. When he reached the pontoon, he lifted himself out of the water and lay down. Less than a minute later, Lottie saw two girls in micro-bikinis swim out to join him.

Had he met them before, or were they introducing themselves for the first time? Who could tell? She watched from behind her sunglasses as the three of them engaged in conversation. The darker-haired of the girls stood up at one point to show Max the tattoo snaking down her side and around her left leg. OK, this wasn't a good sign; how long was he going to be out there? If they were still on the pontoon five minutes from now, she was off.

OK, maybe ten minutes.

Before she had time to leave, Max dived off the pontoon and gave the girls a cheery wave before making his way back to shore. Other people noticed him emerge from the waves, shaking his hair and striding up the beach. OK, *maybe* looking a bit like a god.

He spotted Lottie, and collected his things before coming over and dropping onto the sand beside her. 'Hey. Not at work today?'

'I am at work.' She did her best not to look at the drops of seawater sliding down his chest and bumping over his six-pack. 'I've been trying to contact you. You haven't replied.'

'Sorry. Cracked my phone screen two days ago. Dropped it into the repair place yesterday and forgot to pick it up before they closed.' He smiled. 'It's actually a great feeling, going around without a phone. Like being on holiday.'

'Except I needed to see you.'

'You did?' He clapped a hand over his left pec. 'Business or pleasure?'

'Business.' It wasn't easy to look businesslike when you were sitting on a beach next to someone half naked. 'You're about to be evicted.'

'I know. Have to be out by midday tomorrow. But I'm enjoying myself down here, so do you have somewhere else for me to go? Or will I need to pay a visit to Tents R Us?'

Lottie took an envelope out of her bag. So much for having thought he'd come down to Lanrock to see her. What she wanted to know, but couldn't ask, was who he was enjoying himself with, if not her?

'A couple of options.' Since his hands were wet, she shook out the pinned-together details. 'There's a third-floor flat up on Cliff Road. Or a nice cottage a few miles inland.'

He leaned over to see. 'I like the look of the cottage.'

Another surprise. She'd expected him to go for the flat on Cliff Road, to want to stay local. 'Well, they're both available for the next week. Up to you.'

'Can I think about it, let you know this evening?'

'Does that mean you've had an offer from someone else?'

'Possibly.' He tilted his head from side to side, as if weighing up the options. The next moment, he said, 'Fancy having dinner with me?'

How did he always manage to wrong-foot her? Half of Lottie thought *At laaaast*. The other half wanted to say no so she didn't sound like a pushover.

'Go on, say yes,' he prompted. 'I haven't seen you properly yet.'

And whose fault is that?

'OK then. Just a quick dinner.' As if she had so many more important things to do.

'How about the Spanish restaurant down on the quay? Around seven, would that suit you?'

'Fine. Oh,' she added, 'your neighbour told me you were down here. She said to let you know you're welcome to join her tonight and she's making lobster mac and cheese because it's your favourite.' She raised an eyebrow and waited to hear the story about his over-keen biggest fan.

'Karen said that? It *is* my favourite.' Max's eyes lit up. 'Look, would you mind if we moved our dinner to tomorrow night?'

She shot him a look of disbelief and he burst out laughing. 'That was a joke. Come on, Lottie, we used to do this to each other all the time. You're out of practice.'

He was right. Back in the day, endless teasing had been their modus operandi. Lottie, silently exhaled and willed her shoulders to sink back to their normal level. 'I am out of practice. It's been a while.' Getting to her feet, she dusted dry sand from her hands and skirt. 'I'll see you at seven. Let me know before five which place you'd like to move into.'

There it was again, the light of amusement in his eyes. 'Well, my first choice,' he said, 'would be yours.'

It was nine in the evening, and something was happening that definitely shouldn't be happening.

When Lottie had arrived home from work, she'd showered and changed into her least favourite jeans (they just didn't fit right but had been a birthday present from her mum, who'd forgotten to keep the receipt) and a plain pink cardigan. She hadn't put on any make-up at all, not even mascara, so that Max would know she definitely wasn't trying to impress him.

Upon reaching the Spanish restaurant, she'd found him outside wearing a beautifully cut three-piece suit with a white shirt and a deep purple silk tie.

'Why are you all dressed up?'

'Wanted to look my best for you.' He grinned. 'Also, I guessed you'd be wearing something like that.'

'You couldn't guess that.'

'Hello?' He made a spiralling-back-in-time motion with his index finger. 'Remember when Dan Mercer invited you to KFC just after your sixteenth birthday?'

Lottie nodded. Dan had been captain of the school's football team and regarded as a great catch; so much so that she'd been both excited and terrified that he'd done it for a bet.

'You wore a horrible yellow sweatshirt and a flowery skirt with old trainers. To show Dan you weren't trying to impress him.'

Oh God, it was true. This had been her thing, a kind of private game marking her out from the other girls at school, her way of seeming ultra-cool and unbothered. And without even realising, she was still doing it now.

'I didn't tell you that,' she said. She hadn't told anyone.

'I know you didn't. I just knew that was why you did it. Dan took a photo of the two of you. As soon as I saw it, I could tell what you were up to.'

'And all these years later, you can still remember what I was wearing.'

Max shrugged. 'What can I say? I have an excellent memory, when it matters. Anyway,' he gestured to the restaurant, 'shall we . . .?'

Once inside, it wasn't long before the indefinable *something* had begun to happen. The place was busy and atmospheric, with its red and gold decor, eclectic assortment of photos and paint-ings on the walls, intimate lighting, and stirring flamenco music playing in the background. They drank red wine and ordered little bowls of tapas, each one more delicious than the last. The conversation flowed effortlessly as they exchanged stories about work, travel and the adventures they'd each been on during their years apart.

The buzz of adrenalin had begun in Lottie's feet and worked its way up through her body. Max was the drug and she knew only too well how dangerous it would be to give in to him, but when he was being like this and looking at her in that way . . . well, resisting temptation was easier said than done.

'Tell me what you're thinking,' he said now.

She half smiled. 'I'm thinking people must be wondering why you're dressed like that and I'm dressed like this.'

'Is that true?' He slowly shook his head. 'I'm not so sure. Try again.'

'OK. I'm wondering why you really came down here.'

'You already know that. To see you.'

'But you *haven't* seen me. Not for the last two weeks.'

'I wanted you to miss me.' In his jacket pocket, his phone went *ting* as a text arrived. It wasn't the first time this had happened. Ignoring it, he said, 'And it took a while, but eventually you did.'

How could she deny this? He'd played the game to perfection. She was, she knew, skating on wafer-thin ice, but was somehow no longer afraid that it might crack. No one else had ever made her feel this way. Holding out on Max was a feat she could only keep up for so long.

'Do you always get what you want in the end?'

'Quite often. Not always.' His gaze was having that liquid effect on her.

Tingggg.

'You should answer that. It could be important.'

'No worries. I'll turn it off.'

Lottie shook her head. 'No, check the messages first.' After what had happened to her dad, she had never been able to bring herself to deliberately ignore a text, because what if it might mean the difference between life and death?

'If it makes you happy.' He took the phone out, glanced at the screen and turned it face down on the table. 'There, happy now? Nothing urgent.'

She lifted an eyebrow. 'One of your girlfriends?'

He nudged the phone towards her. 'Quite the opposite. Help yourself.'

The messages were all from the neighbour, Karen. They were over-cheery:

Hi! Lobster mac and cheese best ever – I saved some for you!

Me again! No need to bring anything to drink – I have tons here.

Hey, just to say, why don't I bring food and a couple of bottles over to yours when you get back? xx

'She has way too many hormones,' said Max. 'In future, you might want to warn the people you put into that cottage.'

Lottie speared a chunk of yellow courgette on her fork and rolled it in a puddle of smoked garlic aioli. 'Poor you.'

They left the restaurant just before ten. Outside, the quay was still busy with holidaymakers. The tide was in, there was a sliver of new moon overhead and the cloudless sky was pincushioned with bright stars.

'See that?' At her side, Max pointed, and Lottie looked up just in time to catch a tail of light streaking across the sky.

'A shooting star.' Excited, she searched for another. 'And there's one over there too!'

Except this one was winking and making slow, steady progress from east to west. She glanced at Max. 'It's a plane. I can't believe you aren't making fun of me.'

His mouth twitched. 'I'm being nice. We're having a good time, aren't we?'

Lottie felt her pulse quicken. 'When you see a shooting star you have to make a wish.'

'Already made it.'

'And?'

He raised an index finger to his lips. 'Wishes don't come true if you tell. Now, I'd invite you back to my place for a drink, but it could all get a bit *Wuthering Heights*. We might have to put up with Karen climbing over the wall into my back garden, banging on the windows to be let in.'

He had a point. Lottie nodded in agreement. 'I think you're right. Probably time we went home anyway.' Reaching out to shake his hand, she said, 'Thanks so much for dinner. Night.'

His face. She took his hand and shook it, then turned away. After three steps, she stopped and swivelled back round to face him. 'Or if you want, we could go back to mine.'

Chapter 23

The moment the front door closed behind them, Lottie knew how this evening was going to end. What was more, it was the way she wanted it to end. Enough with the game-playing and the self-preservation; she'd waited too long to discover how it would feel to finally – *finally!* – have sex with Max Farrell.

The air inside the flat seemed to be alive with electricity. He was looking around her living room, taking it all in, paying attention to the decor, her choice of furniture, the artwork on the walls and the night-time view through the window of the waves hitting the rocks. Lottie poured wine into two glasses and passed one to him, but Max didn't even take a sip before placing it on the low table. Slowly he turned to face her, and she held her breath, the sense of anticipation almost overwhelming.

'I want to kiss you,' he murmured. 'I want to kiss you so much.'

How long had she been waiting for this to happen? Too long. Far too long. She smiled. 'Go on then.'

'Only if you want me to.'

'Try me and see.'

He moved closer and held her face in his hands. She tilted her head back, lifting her heels fractionally off the floor, and prayed her lips weren't pushing forward, trumpet style, like a character in a cartoon, so desperate was she to reach his mouth.

And now they were kissing, and it was everything she'd remembered and more. The sensations were out of this world. Lottie's eyes were closed and her head was in a whirl. His warm fingertips were caressing the back of her neck. They were toe to toe, their bodies pressing together with abandon—

'Lottie? Lottie! *Helloooo*, it's meeeeee!'

What? Oh God. Oh no, don't let this be happening, not now.

'Lottie, I know you're there, the lights are on! Let me in!' Bang bang *bang* went the flat of a hand against the front door.

'Whoever they are, they have immaculate timing,' Max murmured.

At least they were at the far end of the room, well away from the window and not visible from outside. Stepping back and thinking fast, Lottie tried to figure out what to do.

'Could you ask her to leave us alone?' prompted Max.

'It won't work.'

'Hey, if she's a friend of yours, wouldn't she understand?'

Helplessly, she shook her head. 'It's not a friend. And she's not going to take no for an answer.'

His smile was rueful. 'OK. In that case, I suppose I'd better go.'

Lottie took a deep breath. 'It's my mum.'

'What? *Oh.*'

The clanking of chain-link shoulder straps told Lottie her mother was rummaging through her favourite Chanel bag. Through the door, Kay shouted, 'This is crazy, I know I have

190

the key in here somewhere . . . Why can't I *find* it? Ah, here it is, *at last.*'

In a panic, Lottie grabbed hold of Max's arm and pushed him in the direction of her bedroom. 'She'll go berserk if she finds you in here. You have to hide. I'll do my best to get rid of her, but . . .'

It wouldn't be easy, she knew from experience. And the metallic scratching at the front door signalled that her mother was now struggling in the darkness to fit the key into the lock.

'This isn't quite how I was expecting this evening to end up,' said Max, gazing around. 'Nice room, though.'

It *was* a nice room, and she'd tidied it up before heading out to meet him tonight, but now wasn't the time to let him stop and admire it. 'Don't move, don't make a sound,' she hissed, and shut the bedroom door half a second before the front door flew open.

Exactly like a French farce, only fifty times more stressful.

'So the reason you have a key to my flat is . . .?' Lottie raised her eyebrows as Kay made her entrance.

'Oh, come on, is it such a crime? I had a copy made last year, in case of emergencies. And just as well I did. It was right at the bottom of my bag. I nearly didn't find it at all.'

That would have been too much to hope for. Lottie took in the mascara smudges beneath her mother's eyes. 'So what's happened?'

'Oh, it's your father, of course. He's just impossible. I've left him.' Tears brimmed and her mum did one of her signature dramatic collapses onto the sofa, gesturing with her left hand that she needed a drink, stat. 'Get me a vodka tonic, darling. A large one.'

Returning from the kitchen with a tumbler clanking with ice, Lottie said, 'So you had an argument. What about?'

She could guess. She could always guess.

Kay took a hefty gulp of the drink, then dashed away her tears. 'He's up to his old tricks again, of course. We went out to dinner and he was eyeing up the waitress. Because he can't help himself, can he? It happens everywhere we go and it's so . . . disrespectful! And the women . . . they're just as bad. They flirt with him and he laps it up while I'm sitting right there in front of them. Well, I've had enough . . .'

'Mum, how old was this waitress?'

'That's the other thing. She was *young*. Hardly older than you!'

'Then I shouldn't think she was flirting with him.' Lottie was firm. 'I expect she was just being friendly. Normal-friendly, because that's her job.'

'Well, you would say that, wouldn't you?' Kay's tone was dismissive, bordering on bitter. 'You weren't there.'

Which was true enough, but Lottie knew her mother's ability to trust her husband had never recovered following the traumatic discovery of his affair with Imelda Farrell. Ever since, she'd imagined he was making a play for virtually any female who crossed his path. It made her miserable, but she couldn't help herself, because that was pathological jealousy for you; in her mind, it was always real. As far as Lottie could make out, the only reason their marriage had survived was because her dad knew the situation was of his own making and he was still consumed with guilt. Prior to the events of thirteen years ago, they'd been happy together. Now, Kay's regular accusations that her husband was being unfaithful were the price he had to pay.

'Remember what Hazel told you.' Hazel was the therapist

her mother had visited for several months last year. 'You need to put the past behind you and appreciate what you have.' It made Lottie cringe to say it, but after a while you ran out of options and every comment sounded like a platitude.

'Hazel the so-called therapist?' Kay snorted. 'A fat lot she knows. Her husband walked out on her six weeks ago. Word is, he couldn't stand living with her a minute longer, what with all the nonsense she spouted. And who could blame him? Just the sound of her whiny voice made me want to tear my hair out.'

Lottie briefly closed her eyes. 'But Mum, she was right about putting the past behind you. You can't carry on like this.'

'I know I can't. That's why I've left him.' Abruptly, her mother let out a wail of despair. 'And it's all that woman's fault.'

'You can't blame Hazel, she was trying to help you.'

'Not Hazel. I'm talking about Imelda bloody Farrell. The woman who ruined my life.'

Here it came, the latest instalment of a tirade Lottie had heard way too often over the years. Up until now, she'd been vaguely wondering if Max could hear what was going on out here in the living room, but of course he could. She cringed, hoping her mother wouldn't say anything too horrendous about Imelda, although the likelihood was that she would. And what would happen if Max were to burst out of the bedroom and confront her?

God, it was too terrible to even contemplate. At least she knew that he understood how agonising and inflammatory that would be.

The leaving-her-husband announcement was par for the course, too. All Lottie could do was listen, nod in agreement

193

and top up her mother's drink until nature, in the form of a full bladder, came to her rescue. Which it duly did twenty minutes later. Having taken a call from her errant husband and informed him that no, of *course* she wasn't coming home tonight, their marriage was *over*, Kay stood up and announced that she was off to the bathroom.

The moment the bathroom door was closed, Lottie leapt into action. Thank God, Max hadn't fallen asleep on the bed. With a finger to her lips, she grabbed him by the arm and dragged him out of the bedroom, past the bathroom and over to the front door.

'Sorry,' she whispered.

He grinned. 'It's fine. I've been reading your diary. Now I know all your secrets.'

She didn't possess a diary, thank goodness. She opened the front door and gave him a push. 'Out.'

But Max wasn't ready to go. Turning, he kissed her, hot and hard and with urgency, before stepping back and murmuring, 'We'll stay at my place tomorrow. Can't wait.'

Then he was gone, disappearing into the night like a ghost, leaving her breathless and bereft.

'What are you doing?' Her mother emerged from the bathroom.

'Heard a noise out in the courtyard. Probably just a fox.' Lottie pushed the front door shut.

'I don't have anything with me. You'll have to lend me a nightdress.'

'Why don't you call Dad back? He can come and pick you up, drive you home.'

'Huh, he's probably back in the restaurant chatting up that waitress. I told you, it's all over.' Her mother returned to the

194

living room, gazing askance at her empty tumbler. 'Be an angel and get me another drink.'

It was eleven thirty by the time her mother could be persuaded to go to sleep in the spare room. Her own plans for the night thwarted, Lottie lay awake for the next hour and predicted how tomorrow morning would go, according to past experience. Kay would wake up, apologetic and in need of a couple of strong espressos. She would blame Lottie's father for upsetting her, then slowly come to the conclusion that maybe he hadn't been flirting with the young waitress after all. Finally, she would call him and announce that he could come and collect her, but only if he wanted to. Then she would borrow Lottie's make-up and do her face so she'd be looking presentable when her husband pulled up outside, ready to take her home.

Lottie yawned. Oh well, at least she still had tomorrow night to look forward to. Unless the night Max moved into his new temporary home turned out to be the night *his* parents unexpectedly turned up.

Chapter 24

For their second-attempt-at-sex night, Lottie put on make-up, her favourite bias-cut lilac dress and a sparkly tiara. When she arrived at Max's new apartment up on Cliff Road – he'd decided to stay local after all – he opened the door and gave her a slow up-and-down once-over.

'And there I was looking forward to seeing the terrible jeans again.'

It was the way he always seemed to be holding back laughter, Lottie deduced, that accentuated those high cheekbones of his and made the butterflies of lust take flight in her chest. That and the glint of mischief in those cognac-coloured eyes. She shrugged and said, 'Sorry to disappoint.'

'Don't be. You look amazing. Come on in.'

'How's this place for you? All good?'

'Extremely good. And all the better for knowing your mother isn't about to turn up and let herself in. Unless she has a key to all the rental properties on your books.'

'We're safe. She and Dad have gone to a garden party at a friend's house in Plymouth.'

'She's not left him, then?'

'Dad came and collected her this morning. She never leaves him.'

Max was taking in every detail of her face, just as she was drinking in every last detail of his. Desperate to close the distance between them and kiss his beautiful mouth, she realised he wanted to do this too, but they were both holding back, prevaricating, enjoying the sense of anticipation, because it was the very best feeling, like being given an exquisitely wrapped gift on your birthday and just knowing it was going to be the best present ever.

She couldn't wait to unwrap the one currently standing in front of her.

Max said in a murmur, 'I know what you're doing, by the way.'

'Same. Fun, isn't it?' She found herself mesmerised by the flashes of gold in his eyes, the sweep of his dark lashes, the smell of his skin.

'We could turn this into a competition, if you like. See who can hold out the longest.'

Lottie held her breath. Was she going to end up getting her heart horribly broken?

Maybe.

Probably.

Oh, but when the next few hours promised to be out-of-this-world incredible, how could she resist?

'Sorry to sound like a sex maniac.' She shook her head. 'But I don't think I want to wait.'

Max broke into a slow smile. Moving forward, he wrapped his arms around her. 'Thank God for that. After thirteen years, I reckon we've waited long enough.'

Then they were kissing again, and it felt exactly like the first time, all-consuming, giddy-making and as dazzling as a battery of New Year's Eve fireworks exploding into the night sky.

Except this wasn't the end of the firework display, it was only the beginning.

Unable to bear the thought of breaking apart for even a second, Lottie moved with him along the narrow hallway and into the bedroom, which was blue and white and tidy, with only a single Samsonite suitcase in the corner to indicate that the apartment was occupied.

Max drew the blinds, then turned back to her. As his mouth trailed a kiss across the sensitive skin at the side of her neck, Lottie unfastened the buttons of his white linen shirt. She could feel his heart thud-thudding beneath her fingers. And now he was edging her towards the pristine king-sized bed that wouldn't be pristine for much longer . . .

Lottie's body had never raced with so much adrenalin. As he lowered her gently onto the mattress, her widening smile matched his. Whatever happened, she knew she would never regret this.

Me and Max Farrell.

It's about to happen.

At last.

'Well,' said Max a while later. 'That was pretty amazing.'

'Not so shabby yourself.' She twisted onto her side to face him, loving the sensation of his hand moving lightly down the centre of her ribcage, unable to wipe the grin from her face because that had undoubtedly been the most spectacular experience of her life. She wriggled her toes against his left leg, then slid her foot along his shin. And he smelled even more delicious now. Breathing in, she inhaled the scent of warm skin mingling with the clean scent of the sheets, fresh from the laundry.

'I've just had a thought.' He pushed a damp strand of hair back from her temple. 'I hope this isn't how you test the beds in all your rental properties.'

Was she ever going to be able to stop smiling and get her face back under control? She raised an eyebrow. 'What can I say? We have to be thorough.'

'Just so you know. It nearly killed me, keeping my distance this past couple of weeks.'

'It was kind of annoying for me too. I didn't know what was going on.'

His eyes were bright. 'But it did the trick. Which means it was worth it.'

'So . . .' She traced her hand along his tanned shoulder. 'What happens next?'

Max started to laugh. 'Steady on. Give me a few minutes.'

'I mean, this is just a fling, yes? To finally finish what we started – nearly started,' Lottie amended, 'years ago.'

'Is that what you think?'

'I don't know. That's why I'm asking.'

Suddenly serious, he said, 'Is it what you want?'

She looked at him. Couldn't speak.

'Because it's not what I want.'

There were two reasons why she didn't want to hear this.

'I mean it.' He found her left hand, gave it a squeeze.

'But you would say that. It's what men like you always say.'

'Men like me?'

'The seductive kind. Good-looking, charming, a different woman every week, never serious, never settles down. Your basic heartbreaker.'

He half smiled. 'I can't believe you just called me basic.'

'You talk the talk. But that's just to make everyone fall for you. You don't actually mean it.'

'I've already told you. This time I do.'

Lottie ploughed on. 'We've heard from Cameron what you used to be like at uni. And you said yourself how quickly you get bored.'

'That's true. But now . . . OK, I know you don't believe me, but this is different. And trust me, I'm as surprised by it as you are. I wasn't expecting this to happen, not at all.'

'Right. I still don't believe you, but that doesn't matter right now. It's all irrelevant.' She shrugged. 'Because we both know this can't go anywhere anyway. So we may as well just enjoy it for what it is, while we can.' Trust her to fall for someone capable of causing a lifetime of heartbreak.

'The trouble is, I need you to believe me. I've never felt like this before.' Max paused, thought for a moment. 'OK, I have.'

'Of course you have.'

'It felt like love. I thought it was love.' He tilted his head to study her face in semi-profile.

'What happened?' Ridiculously, a jolt of . . . envy? jealousy? speared her heart.

'Well, I was seventeen. So I'm sure you can work it out.' He gave her fingers another squeeze. 'It was you, Lottie. The thing is, can you actually fall in love when you're seventeen? Or is that too young to count? I knew how I felt that night at Anders Nilsson's party. But was it real? And how can anyone tell? All I know is, it felt real. Like, completely. Then the next day the world caved in, everything changed, and there was nothing we could do about it.'

He'd felt exactly like she had. The memory of that time was as fresh as it had ever been. 'You never tried to contact me.'

'Nor did you.'

Lottie shook her head fractionally; back then, there'd been no point.

'Maybe I could have done,' he continued. 'Later, when I was away at uni. But you know how it is. The years go by and I had no idea if you'd still feel the same way. It was easier to hold on to a perfect memory than take the risk of getting in touch and you saying no thanks very much.'

As if. 'Has anyone ever said that to you in your life?'

'I suppose not.' His mouth twitched. 'Well, apart from you the other week when you left the hotel after our swim in the sea.'

'You poor thing. It must have been terrible for you.'

'It *was.*' He pulled her close. 'But it was also the moment I knew my feelings for you hadn't changed at all. They were still there, as strong as ever. I've never felt like this about anyone else.' He kissed her once, then twice more, on the lips. 'How could I not come back down here? I never want to feel like this about anyone else again.' Another kiss. 'No one else. Just you.' One more kiss. 'And don't tell me I don't mean it, because I do.'

Lottie closed her eyes, trembling with anticipation as the distance between their bodies disappeared. All she could do was go along with it and make the most of every moment while it lasted. She couldn't say no. She couldn't say anything. Even if Max was serious, which was highly unlikely, there could be no future for them, no happy ending.

He might think they could persuade their parents to put the past behind them, but she knew better than he did how impossible that would be.

It was simply never going to happen.

All she could do was live for the moment and brace herself to cope with the searing pain of loss when their relationship inevitably ended.

There was a group of revellers outside the bedroom window, laughing and joking as they made their way down to Beach Street. At the tinny sound of a dropped can on the tarmac, a loud cheer went up.

'Always nice to be appreciated,' Max murmured in her ear. 'But I hope they aren't staying for the encore.'

'You can't leave. I won't let you,' Max protested the following morning. 'It's Sunday.'

'And some of us have to work.'

'Did we get any sleep at all?'

'Hardly any.' They'd certainly made the most of their time together last night. Lottie had already jumped into the shower but still needed to go home and change. Her muscles might ache, but her brain was in business mode; today in the office she'd be running on pure adrenalin. And after the office . . .?

'Come here.' Max patted the side of the bed invitingly.

'Stop it, I can't. I'll be late.' But she couldn't resist leaning over him for one more kiss. 'What are your plans for the day?'

'Catching up on all the sleep you cruelly forced me to miss out on.' His arms closed around her, his tongue teasing her earlobe, making her squirm with pleasure. 'It's your fault. I wanted to get some rest, but would you let me? No, you would not. You were insatiable.'

'I finish work at four.' Already she was missing him, counting the hours until she could see him again. This was ridiculous; it was the madness of lust taking over her body, turning her into some kind of wanton—

'I can't see you this evening. I wish I could, but it's not possible.' He grimaced. 'It's Mum's sixtieth birthday and Dad's organised a big surprise party for her tonight at a hotel outside Bath. It starts at seven and we all have to be there before they arrive.'

'Oh. Right. Of course you do.' Lottie swallowed her disappointment; she would survive without him. It was only one night.

Reading her mind, Max said ruefully, 'If you were anyone else, I'd have invited you to come along with me. But under the circumstances . . .'

'Well, quite. Not the kind of surprise your dad would have had in mind.' Lottie could only too easily picture the catastrophic scene that would play out if that happened. The memory of William Farrell's incandescent fury as he'd raged at her own father wasn't something she'd ever be able to forget; just the thought of it made her shudder. She looked at Max. 'Is he still . . . angry?'

Max nodded. 'He's a proud man. Like, *really* proud. And it's all still there inside him, the wrath and the grief. He forgave Mum because he loved her so much, but it's not the kind of thing you can ever forget. Every now and again it comes bursting out. Not as often as it does with your parents, from what you've told me. But yes, it's never going to disappear.'

And there it was, the reason she and Max could never have a long-lasting relationship. They gazed at each other, each of them silently acknowledging this.

'Well,' Lottie said at last, 'I suppose I just have to hope I go off you sooner rather than later.'

'Or,' said Max, 'we could just be patient and wait. If they all die at around the ninety-five mark, we could be married before we hit seventy. That'd be something to look forward to, wouldn't it?'

She hugged him tightly, then climbed off the bed and tried to brush the creases out of her lilac dress. 'I have to go. Have a great time.' *But not too great.* See? The first twinges of anxiety were starting already.

'No kiss goodbye?' Max was looking innocent.

If she gave him another kiss, he would pull her back into bed and she might be tempted to stay there. She straightened up and moved away. 'I know what you're doing. I'll see you tomorrow. And I hope your mum has a fantastic party.'

He half smiled. 'I'll tell her you said so.'

'Except you can't. Because if you did, she'd have to keep it a secret from your dad. And that wouldn't be fair on either of them.'

'I know.' Max nodded. After a moment he said, 'Do you hate her for having an affair with your father?'

They hadn't discussed their feelings about it, not properly. Lottie paused, then shook her head. 'No. Obviously I wish it hadn't happened. But if I hated her, I'd have to hate my dad too. And I don't.'

'Same,' said Max. 'And no, I won't be mentioning you to anyone tonight. Don't want to set off World War Three.'

Lottie blew him a kiss from the doorway. 'Best not.'

Chapter 25

The surprise party was being held at Colworth Manor, an imposing Georgian country house hotel a few miles from Bath with a reputation for fabulous hospitality. It was owned by Hector McLean and run by his daughter Daisy, and Max knew the restaurant there was his parents' favourite place to eat. As far as Imelda was aware, William was bringing her here this evening for a quiet dinner à deux. Instead, a gathering of seventy or so of their friends would be waiting to surprise her when she arrived.

Max got a surprise too, once he'd parked in the car park next to the picturesque village church and made his way past the churchyard and up the curving tree-lined driveway at ten minutes to seven.

'Well, well, what are the chances?' Lois, looking radiant, was wearing the dress she'd bought in the boutique on the King's Road in Chelsea the other week. Her eyes sparkled. 'Fancy bumping into you here!'

Except it wasn't an accident. Of course it wasn't. He'd been out on his second date with Lois while his parents were celebrating their wedding anniversary with a weekend in London and a trip to the theatre. When his mother had called to find out where he was, she'd exclaimed, 'Oh, we're not far away. Why don't we hop in a taxi and meet you for a drink?'

Which had meant he hadn't really been able to say no, and Lois had been thrilled to spend the rest of the evening with Imelda and William. Now Max remembered Imelda excusing herself to pay a visit to the bathroom and William taking the opportunity to tell him about the plans he'd made for his wife's upcoming sixtieth birthday.

'Oh, she'll be so *thrilled*.' Lois had clapped her hands to her heart. 'I *love* a surprise party!'

Which had in turn resulted in William saying politely, 'Well, you'd be very welcome to come along too.'

As a plus-one, he'd meant. Not as a guest in her own right. Lois had exclaimed at the time that she would be delighted, but Max hadn't given it another thought, because who in their right mind would do something like this?

Lois, that was who.

He blinked. 'Lois. What are you doing here?'

'Same as you! Oh, wait till you see the beautiful earrings I bought for your mum. She's going to *love* them.'

'You only met her for an hour.'

'I loved her, though. And we got on like a house on fire. I can't wait to see her again.'

'Look, we're not a couple any more.'

'And whose silly idea was that?' She gave him a pleading look and reached out to take his hand. 'Oh Max, I've missed you so much, you have no idea. It's so good to see you.'

Max inwardly cringed; he hated it when this happened.

'Lois, we gave it a good try. It just didn't work out. No one's fault . . . sometimes these things happen.'

'But did you see *Made in Chelsea* last week? OK,' she went on hastily, 'I know you don't watch it, but this girl went out on three dates with this guy, then he finished with her . . . but a few weeks later they bumped into each other quite by chance and he realised he'd made a massive mistake and now they're back together again, as happy as anything!'

'But—'

'Don't say it, please! Let's just have a nice evening together and enjoy the party. You never know what might happen.'

Max knew what *wasn't* going to happen. He said, 'The thing is, I've met someone else since I've been in Cornwall. It's serious.'

'Oh, come on, now you're just making up excuses. Here, have a drink and relax.' Lois beckoned eagerly to a waiter carrying a silver tray of glasses fizzing with champagne. 'I've been talking to my friends about you, and it turns out loads of them know who you are. They all say you've never been the serious, settling-down type.'

Hoist by his own petard. Oh, the irony of not being believed. He was about to protest that this time it was true when a voice called out, 'They're here, the car's just pulled up outside! Get ready, everyone – she's here!'

Everyone clapped and cheered as William led his wife into the ballroom and she realised for the first time what had been planned behind her back. Glasses were raised, toasts were made and happy tears were shed by Imelda.

'Darling!' She gave Max a huge hug. 'I had no idea! If only I'd known, I'd have worn waterproof mascara.'

'You look amazing,' Lois exclaimed, throwing her arms

around her the moment Max stepped back. 'Happy birthday. It's so fantastic to see you again . . . and I bought you something I hope you'll really love!'

'How kind. Thank you so much.' Imelda took the ornately packaged gift from her. 'And it's so nice to see you again too . . . Laura, is it?'

'Lois. Like Lois Lane. And Max is my Superman!'

'Lois, of course it is. For some reason I thought you two were no longer . . . together. But here you are! And I love your dress.'

'Max was with me when I bought it. Isn't it gorgeous?'

'We're not together, though,' Max reminded her, in case she'd forgotten.

'We're just here to celebrate your mum's birthday,' Lois said gaily. 'I can't believe you're sixty, Imelda, you look incredible. Now open your present, I do hope you love them. I had them made specially for you . . .'

'But we're not together,' Max repeated when the earrings had been opened and exclaimed over, and Imelda and William had moved on to greet their other guests.

'I know. But we can still have a nice time, can't we?' Lois clinked her glass against his. 'Relax!'

She was knocking back the champagne. Max said, 'Where are you staying tonight?' Because Colworth was a small village and he knew that the hotel was fully booked.

'I have a friend who lives in Bath. I'll get a taxi over to hers. Now come on.' Lois swished back her hair. 'Why don't you introduce me to the rest of your family?'

'Because . . .' Oh, what was the point of arguing? She was evidently dead set on sticking to him like glue. 'Fine,' he said. 'But this isn't going to end up like *Made in Chelsea*, OK? I already told you, I've met someone.'

'From what I hear, you spend your whole life meeting *someones*.' She made wiggly quote marks with her fingers as she said the final word.

'This time it's different.'

'Oh, come on! How long ago did you meet her, Maxi? It can't be more than a few weeks. Give it another fortnight and you'll be over her, just like you get bored with everyone else.'

'So why are you here, if you know what I'm like?'

Lois said lovingly, 'Because you didn't give me enough of a chance last time. I know I'm perfect for you. And if you were really serious about this other girl, you'd have brought her along here with you tonight.'

Max's attention wandered across the ballroom to where some of the Irish side of his family were milling. Maybe he'd introduce Lois to mad Aunt Maeve, who believed in fairies, and ear-splitting Uncle Eoghan, who'd been telling the same three jokes to everyone he met for the last forty years. That would serve her right for turning up this evening.

God, he missed Lottie. If only she could be here now.

Lois gave him a prod. 'Are you even listening to me?'

Did he have any choice?

'Of course I am. Come on, let me introduce you to my aunt and uncle.'

It had been a great evening. By midnight the ballroom was emptying out. Designated drivers were heading home, pre-booked taxis were leaving from outside the main entrance and those guests who'd chosen to stay at the hotel were having one last drink before making their way upstairs.

'Your friend's going to be wondering where you've got to,' Max told Lois.

'Oh, she's such a flake. She WhatsApped me to say she's away this weekend and can't put me up after all.'

Lois wasn't as good a fibber as she thought she was. Max shook his head. 'What's her name?'

She hesitated for a split second. 'Bella.'

'Selfish of her. Can I see the message she sent you?' He observed her reaction. 'Or has it mysteriously vanished?'

She pouted and gave him an apologetic smile. 'I knew you had a room booked here. I checked with reception when I arrived.'

'And if I'd turned up with someone else who'd be sharing the room with me?'

'Then I'd have left, obviously. I'm not some kind of deranged stalker! But you're here on your own and it's too late now to try and find somewhere to stay.' Lois lifted her chin. 'OK, *fine*. Don't worry about me. Off you go, up to bed.'

'What will you do?'

'Oh, I'll just sleep outside on the grass. Or go over to the churchyard and find a bench to lie on. Let's just hope it doesn't rain.'

Max wondered if this was yet another scene that had been played out on *Made in Chelsea*. Having arrived at the hotel only minutes before seven, he hadn't yet checked in and his case was still in the boot of the car. He indicated the reception desk, visible through the ballroom's open double doors. 'You can have my room.'

'And where will you go?'

'I'll sleep in my car.'

'But I don't want to be in your room on my own.' Lois shook her head vigorously. 'I want to be in it with you.'

'Night, darling!' His parents were leaving, about to head

upstairs to their suite on the top floor. Imelda gave them both a tipsy hug. 'Hasn't it been the most wonderful evening? Will we see you down here for breakfast tomorrow?'

Clearly still confident that she could win Max over, Lois smiled widely. 'Definitely. Can't wait!'

Chapter 26

It wasn't too bad really. The car's front seat tipped back; it wasn't quite horizontal, but it would do. Like being on a long-haul flight, only with silence instead of the roar of a plane's engines, and fewer cabin crew coming over to offer you another drink.

Somewhere in the trees, an owl hooted in the darkness. A skein of pale grey cloud drifted across the surface of the moon overhead. Max closed his eyes, feeling decidedly good about himself. See? Already he was a changed man. Doing the right thing, sleeping in his car while Lois occupied the queen-sized bed in his luxurious hotel room. He hadn't even had that much to drink, so by six in the morning he'd be fine to drive back to Lanrock. Back to Lottie. His heart soared at the prospect of seeing her again. He couldn't wait.

It was a couple of hours later that he became aware he had company.

'Maxi, Maxi,' whispered a voice, a hand coming to rest on his knee. 'This is crazy, you can't spend the night out here. Come up to the room.'

Her low voice sounded as if it was coming to him from a

great distance, but the hand was now snaking up to his chest. Warm fingers rested beneath his untucked shirt. Max breathed in the heavy scent of Lois's perfume.

He half opened his eyes and murmured, 'I'm staying here. Go back to the hotel.'

'I can't believe you're being so mean.' Lois's bottom lip jutted. 'I thought tonight was going to be so much better than this.'

It seemed simplest to just close his eyes again and pretend to be fast asleep once more. After slowing his breathing and waiting for another few minutes to tick by, he heard her climb out of the passenger seat. The door slammed behind her and then she was crunching stroppily across the gravel, making her way back to the manor house.

Max smiled, pleased with himself for having dealt with the situation like a good and faithful boyfriend. Once you knew you'd found the right woman, it seemed being honourable was easy.

And now there was a tap-tap-tapping noise on the car window. Opening his eyes once more, Max made the discovery that it was now daylight. When he saw what was on the other side of the glass, he also thought that maybe he'd died and gone to heaven.

A rather attractive woman with long dark hair was carrying something, wrapped in a white linen napkin, that looked very much like a toasted baguette. In her other hand was a steaming white china mug.

Buzzing down the window, he inhaled the mingled scents of smoked bacon, grilled cheese and fresh coffee. Out here in the early-morning sunshine, it smelled insanely delicious.

'Hi, I'm Daisy.' She indicated the black and gold badge on

her shirt, letting him know that she was also the manager of the hotel. 'And my receptionist tells me you're Max Farrell, William and Imelda's son. So, how did you sleep?'

He instinctively liked her. 'Better than expected, thanks.'

'My receptionist also explained the situation, about you giving up your room. Apparently your girlfriend was telling her all about the two of you.' She corrected herself. 'I gather she's an ex-girlfriend now.'

'If that. We went out on a total of three dates. I had no idea she was going to turn up last night.'

'Well, anyway, to put you in the picture, she's just gone into the dining room and joined your parents for breakfast. I don't know if you wanted to see her again this morning . . .'

'Preferably not,' said Max.

'I guessed. So we thought maybe you could do with a take-away instead.'

His stomach rumbled as he took the heavenly-smelling baguette. 'You're an angel. I can't thank you enough.'

'And if you follow the path over there, round to the swimming pool, there's a shower and loo in the pool house with plenty of toiletries and fresh towels.'

'You're more than an angel.'

Daisy grinned. 'I like that you chose to sleep in your car. No one's ever done that before. Couples who have arguments here usually just yell at each other in their rooms before falling asleep in bed.'

Max swallowed a mouthful of baguette and washed it down with coffee. She was a stranger, but he felt a compulsion to share his news. 'I've met the woman I want to spend the rest of my life with. And it's not,' he pointed at the hotel, 'the one in the breakfast room.'

'You have? Well, congratulations. When did you meet her?'

'Almost six weeks ago. Well, over twenty years ago really. We hated each other when we were kids, then we didn't hate each other . . . then other stuff happened.' He couldn't help himself, desperate to tell Daisy everything but aware that it would be weird to do so. 'We lost touch, but no one else ever matched up for either of us, then we met each other again quite by chance and after that I just couldn't get her out of my head. So a couple of weeks ago I decided to take a long holiday in Lanrock, where she lives. And two nights ago, we finally got together properly. For good.'

Did it sound crazy? *Two nights ago* definitely sounded ridiculous now he'd said it aloud. If Daisy laughed, he could hardly blame her.

But she was studying him, not laughing at all. 'You should see your face. You really mean it.'

The relief was overwhelming. Max exhaled. 'I do. I love her. And I've never said that about anyone before.'

'When you know, you know.' Daisy's phone beeped with a message and she pulled a face. 'Damn, I have to get back, I'd love to have heard more. Hopefully we'll see you again,' she went on cheerfully. 'Maybe next time you'll bring the love of your life along with you.'

Max deliberately didn't think about his parents. 'I'll make sure I do.'

'And I'll tell you how my husband and I eventually got together.' Her eyes danced. 'It was quite the journey. When people hear about it, they always say it's the kind of story you'd read about in a book.'

The roads were clear and the drive back to Cornwall was straightforward. Max found himself singing along to the radio

215

at the top of his voice, which wasn't something he was in the habit of doing, but thinking about Lottie made his heart want to burst out of his chest and he couldn't help himself.

When he reached Lanrock at ten thirty, he experienced an overwhelming urge to buy her flowers, and stopped off at the posh florist's on Angel Street, very nearly earning himself a ticket from a grumpy traffic warden. Arriving at Lottie's office fifteen minutes later, he caught sight of her through the window, and his heart lifted. She was wearing a turquoise sleeveless top and white pencil skirt, and was slotting property details into Perspex holders. Her hair was fastened up in a casual bun with loose strands falling around her face and neck. And as for those legs, so slim and tanned . . . seriously, just the legs alone were enough. He wondered how he was going to get through the next seven hours before she finished work and he could bundle her back into bed.

Looking up and spotting him in the doorway, Lottie said, 'Uh oh.'

'Excuse me?'

She pointed to the flowers. 'Are those for me?'

Why wasn't she pleased to see him? He entered the office. 'Of course they're for you.'

'Why? What have you done?'

'I haven't done anything. Nothing at all! I bought them because I thought you'd love them.'

She started to laugh. 'Really? In that case, thank you. They're stunning. You shouldn't have.'

'I *really* shouldn't have if they're going to make you think I've been up to no good.' Dumping the spectacular bouquet on her desk, Max took her in his arms and kissed her in the way he'd been fantasising about all the way home.

'Wow.' Lottie was breathless when he let her go at last. Twisting round, she saw that Marcus had emerged from the back room and was observing the goings-on with glee. 'You, don't say a word.'

Marcus, who was only twenty, mimed zipping his mouth shut, then grinned. 'Wouldn't dream of it. I had no idea those kind of shenanigans were allowed in the office. But now I know, this is fantastic news.' He indicated the flowers. 'Want me to put those in water for you?'

'That'd be great,' said Max, keen to kiss Lottie again.

'How did it go last night?' said Lottie just as his phone began to ring.

'It was, you know, good.' It was his mother calling, and Lottie had caught his slight grimace.

'You should answer that.'

Did she think he had something to hide? Knowing he didn't, Max put the call on speaker. 'Mum, hi, how are you feeling? Great party.'

'Max, I can't believe you left without saying goodbye!'

The expression on Lottie's face was hard to read; it probably felt strange for her to be hearing his mother's voice again for the first time in so many years. Max said steadily, 'I was avoiding Lois. She knew she wasn't invited, she just turned up anyway.'

'We noticed. She told us all about it over breakfast,' said his mother. 'Nearly started blubbing into her eggs Benedict. She seemed a bit devastated, I must say.'

Max held Lottie's gaze as he spoke. 'I finished with her weeks ago. She's having a hard time accepting it's over. We only went on two and a half dates.'

'Well, she was quite dramatic. We did tell her it was pretty much par for the course with you. But then she said apparently

217

the reason you refused to sleep in the hotel room was because you've met someone new and fallen madly in love, all in less than three weeks. I mean, we pretended to go along with it, but it does seem unlikely.' She laughed. 'I have to confess, though, I'm intrigued. Darling, is it actually true?'

Lottie's eyes widened. Max said steadily, 'Yes, it's true.'

'Sweetheart, really? That's fantastic! We've waited years for something like this to happen, but never thought the day would come! Did you hear that, William? Our boy's found the right girl for him at last. Oh, you should have brought her along to the party! What's her name? Tell us all about her . . . This is the *best* news. You've never said anything like this to us before!'

Lottie was shaking her head at him. She closed her eyes and murmured, 'Don't tell them.'

'It's early days, Mum,' Max said. 'Let's give it a bit longer. She's perfect, and that's all you need to know right now—'

'LOTTIE!' bellowed Marcus from the back room. 'Where's the scissors so I can trim the stems?'

'Where are you?' said his mum. 'Who's that?'

Another warning head-shake from Lottie, who spun round and disappeared into the back room.

'Who's Lottie?' Imelda repeated.

Even the name of her ex-lover's daughter had brought back memories; Max could hear the change in her voice. As far as his parents were aware, he and Lottie had never been anything more than playfully bickering friends. He said, 'No idea, I'm in a flower shop.'

'Ooh, ordering something for me?' She laughed, clearly delighted. 'You know the kind of thing I like, darling – lilac roses are my favourite.'

Once he'd ended the call, Lottie re-emerged from the back room. 'Now you have to send her flowers.'

'It makes her happy. And unlike some people, she doesn't automatically assume I've just done something bad.'

'You gave Lois your room?'

He nodded smugly. 'I slept in the car. All night. You can call and check with the hotel if you want. The manageress brought me coffee and a bacon baguette and I told her all about you.'

'Hey, I believe you. I wasn't asking because I'm jealous.' Amused, Lottie added easily, 'Jealousy's a waste of time. And it never helps.'

'Really?' Oh, but she was so right. It wasn't an attractive trait.

'If you want to be with me, you will. If you don't, you won't. It's your choice.' She shrugged. 'Why would I try to nag you into staying if you're not that bothered?'

Max said, 'That makes me want to stay even more.' God, he loved her so much. Lowering his voice so Marcus couldn't overhear, he moved closer until his mouth brushed the side of her neck. 'You have no idea how much I want you. Just so you know, we're going to spend all evening in bed.'

'Just so *you* know,' Lottie whispered back, 'I've already promised Freya and Cameron we'll meet them at Bert's Bar tonight for karaoke.'

'Damn. When do we need to be there?'

'Eight.' She was smiling now.

'So that gives us two hours before we have to leave my flat.' He trailed a finger lightly along the curve of her collarbone and felt her shiver beneath his touch. 'Two long hours. Well, I'm sure we can find something to do to pass the time.'

219

Chapter 27

Freya saw Lottie walk into the bar and rushed over to greet her.

'Thanks for coming along.' She gave her a hug. 'You look fantastic, your eyes are all sparkly!' They really were; in fact her whole face seemed lit up.

She turned to Max, who'd arrived at the same time as Lottie. 'And you look wonderful too. I'm so glad you two are friends again.'

'We were never enemies,' Max said with a grin. 'At least, not since we were twelve.'

'We hated each other up until then,' Lottie agreed. 'But we're over it now.'

'Honestly, you'd make such a great couple,' Freya told her when Max had gone to the bar to get the drinks in. 'Are you sure you don't fancy him? Not even a tiny bit? He is gorgeous.'

Lottie shook her head. 'We're just friends. Anyway, where's the new receptionist? Is that her, over there?'

Freya was proud of her brilliant idea and excited to put it into action. She wished she could share it with Lottie, but it wouldn't be fair to do that. Along with everyone else in Lanrock,

Lottie adored Cameron, and she'd be shocked to the core to discover her plan. She was the one who'd first introduced the two of them, and had since delighted in taking the credit for the happy-ever-after love story between her friend and the most perfect man in Cornwall.

No, this was one secret Freya was definitely going to have to keep to herself.

'Not her.' She pointed to the left. 'That's Naomi, over there, chatting to Cameron. I popped into the surgery in my lunch hour and met her. She hardly knows anyone down here, so I thought it'd be nice to invite her along tonight, give her a chance to meet people and make some new friends.'

'Wow.' Lottie had spotted her and was now boggling slightly, because Naomi, evidently thrilled to be asked, had pulled out all the stops. She was wearing a virtually transparent cream lace shirt over a fuchsia bra, a pair of extremely short pink shorts and pointy cream ankle boots.

'I know. Pretty, isn't she? And so nice!' Freya spoke with enthusiasm. 'I think she's going to settle in really well.'

Lottie raised an eyebrow. 'She looks as if she already is.'

As they watched, Naomi burst out laughing at something Cameron had said and touched his arm, just like the dating experts always tell you to do when you want to create a connection with someone and make them like you.

'She's just friendly.' Freya couldn't believe how brilliantly her plan was going; she really was a genius. 'And far more fun than Esther, which has to be a bonus. Come on,' she added as Max returned with the drinks. 'Let's go over and I'll introduce you.'

Two hours later, the pub was rammed with a mix of locals and holidaymakers, the karaoke session was in full swing and Lottie was starting to have serious misgivings about the wisdom of Cameron hiring a receptionist who had obviously taken quite a shine to him.

But could she – *should* she – warn Freya about it, when her friend appeared to be oblivious to the situation? Would it help, or might it just cause awkwardness and trouble? And why was she feeling so torn?

She escaped to the loo to consider the facts. The last thing she wanted to do was upset her friend or hurt her feelings. She was the one who'd introduced Freya to Cameron in the first place, assuring her that he was amazing, lovely and the kindest man she'd ever met. But in truth, she hadn't actually known him that well back then; it was like enthusiastically recommending a new restaurant on the strength of one brief visit, then discovering that most of the time the food and service wasn't great at all.

No, that wasn't fair. Cameron was a good doctor and he *was* genuinely kind. It was just that he could be a tiny bit holier-than-thou sometimes, a tad *too* nice. And overly modest while at the same time managing to draw attention to his niceness at every available opportunity.

She washed her hands at the sink and studied her face in the mirror to see if she looked guilty. But no, her innermost thoughts were safe. Because the truth was, just occasionally she found herself wishing she *hadn't* introduced Cameron to Freya. Except of course she could never admit it, because he was popular and a local hero and everyone else in Lanrock loved him.

Especially Freya.

But it was OK, the situation was manageable. It wasn't as if he was horrendous. And plenty of people had friends whose partners you weren't one hundred per cent crazy about, didn't they? You just did your best, ignored the niggly annoyances and got on with them anyway, for the sake of your friend.

The door to the bathroom opened and two middle-aged women came in laughing. 'I tell you what, you can't blame her,' one of them was saying. 'If I was twenty years younger, I'd be up on that stage with him too.'

Lottie slipped out and made her way back to the karaoke, where Cameron and Naomi were now performing 'Islands in the Stream'. Cameron had a good voice and loved to perform – especially at charity events, she reminded herself cattily – and what Naomi might lack in the singing department, she was more than making up for by writhing around him like a Pussycat Doll. And there, right in front of the stage, was Freya, happily cheering them on as if she was their biggest fan.

Max discreetly slid an arm around Lottie's waist and murmured in her ear, 'Can we go home yet? It's been two hours and eleven minutes.'

'She's being so . . . obvious. I mean, poor Cameron,' said Lottie, because Max and Cameron had been friends for years.

'Hey, don't worry. He can handle women like that. All part of the job description.' In their dark corner of the bar, he was caressing her hip, which was heavenly but dangerous.

'Stop it,' Lottie protested weakly. 'There might be someone here who knows my parents.'

'All the more reason to get ourselves out of here before we're noticed.' He was smiling now; she could hear it in his voice as his fingers circled the hollow of her spine. 'You know it makes sense.'

'You're the one that I want,' Cameron was singing, up on the stage.

'You're the one that I want.' Naomi wiggled her bottom as she sang the words back at him. 'Ooh, ooh, ooh!'

Dancing along in front of them, Freya whooped, twirled and waved her arms in the air. The evening had turned out so much better than she'd dared to hope. It was eleven o'clock, last orders had been called at the bar, and this was the final karaoke performance of the night. Best of all, several people – including Lottie – had quietly warned her that she might want to keep an eye on Naomi, who evidently wasn't backward in coming forward and appeared to have taken quite a shine to her new boss. In return, Freya had shaken her head and said, 'Oh no, it's nothing like that, she's just having a bit of fun.'

Honestly, though, who'd have thought the evening would be such a success?

As they left the pub to walk home together twenty minutes later, Freya said, 'I really like Naomi.'

Cameron slipped his arm around her waist. 'Do you? I was worried she might have been a bit full-on.'

'Oh, she was just enjoying herself.'

'She made me sing with her three times.'

'Well, she didn't know anyone else, did she?'

'You don't mind, then?' He sounded relieved.

'Of course I don't mind! It was karaoke and she joined in – that's what you want people to do. Better that than hiding away in a corner, don't you think? She's great company. And pretty, too.'

Cameron laughed and gave her a squeeze. 'Well, I'm glad you like her. And relieved that you aren't bothered by the way she . . . you know, *is*.'

'Hey, she's going to brighten up the surgery. All the patients will love her. Plus, it's so much nicer for you, working with someone who's fun.'

Cameron stopped walking and pulled her to him. 'And that's why you're the one for me.' He kissed her. 'You're the only one that *I* want. I love you.' Another kiss. 'When are we going to get married, Mrs Nearly-Bancroft?'

'I love you too.' Did she? Kind of. How could she not love the man who'd so selflessly given her mum his left kidney? She kissed him back. 'Let's think about fixing the date once you've got your charity marathon out of the way.'

Chapter 28

Returning to her flat on Tuesday afternoon after a two-hour walk along the cliffs and back along the beach, Ruby found two unexpected items on the step outside her front door.

The first was a case of twenty-four mixed fruit drinks, because the craving for Orangina had extended to include raspberry, pineapple and passion-fruit juices, and this one had arrived more speedily than anticipated from a small, family-owned company in Kent.

And speaking of family . . .

The second item on her front doorstep was her soon-to-be-ex-husband.

At the thought of opening one of the bottles of delicious, finely carbonated raspberry juice, Ruby's mouth watered.

She eyed Peter, who was wearing jeans and a new salmon-pink shirt that didn't do him any favours. 'Fancy meeting you here.'

He was looking distinctly hangdog. 'Can I come in? We need to talk.'

She took her phone out of her pocket and held it up. 'I have one of these.'

'It's not the kind of thing you can say over the phone. Please, Ruby.'

'How long have you been waiting out here?' His fair skin was showing signs of sunburn.

'Ninety minutes.'

'Should have texted first.' Purely for her own amusement, Ruby said, 'You know how to text, don't you, Peter? I'm sure you did it often enough when you were arranging your secret assignations with Margaret.'

'Please . . .'

'Fine.' She fitted her door key into the lock. 'Carry that box in for me, would you? It looks heavy.'

Once inside, she offered him a glass of tap water, which he gulped down thirstily while Ruby sliced open the well-packaged box and took out the bottle that was most insistently calling her name. God, it was *so* indescribably delicious, the tiny carbon bubbles dancing on her tongue, better than any champagne.

She didn't ask Peter if he wanted one. He might say yes.

'Right,' she flashed him a couldn't-care-less look, 'what is it you wanted to see me about?' Oh, but wouldn't it be hilarious if he'd come to tell her Margaret was pregnant?

'Ruby, I'm here to tell you how sorry I am. And I wouldn't blame you one bit if you think I deserve everything that's happened to me. I suppose I do.' He bit his lip and shook his head mournfully. 'But you have to understand, I never stopped loving you. Not for a minute.'

'Are you serious?' She almost burst out laughing. Was he *deranged*?

'It's all over. I've ended it with Margaret. It was a moment of madness.'

'A pretty long moment. *How* many months was it before you got caught out?'

Peter shook his head, damp-eyed and apparently on the verge of tears. 'I was wrong. I did a bad thing and I'm so sorry. But . . . how many times have I preached in my sermons about the power of forgiveness?'

Ruby didn't often listen to his sermons, and given that he'd been advised to resign from his position, he wasn't going to be preaching any more of them for the foreseeable future.

She said, 'I have no idea. I'm usually thinking about other stuff.'

He used the back of his hand to wipe his eyes. 'I've told her it's over. I want to make this up to you. If you can forgive me, I promise – absolutely *promise* – you won't regret it. I'll do whatever you want, anything at all.'

This was new; in all their years together, she'd never seen this grovelly, desperate side of him before.

'Well, what I want . . .' she couldn't resist it, 'what I really really want . . .'

This sailed completely over Peter's head; Spice Girls references didn't feature on his radar. Eagerly he said, 'Yes? Just tell me.'

'What I really want is a baby.'

His mouth dropped open. She saw the cogs whirring in his brain as he weighed up the available options. Finally he said, 'Fine. If it's what you want, if that's what it takes, we'll give it another shot. Because I love you. And I know how much I hurt you, but I have faith in God that together we can overcome that and put the past behind us.'

'Do you?'

He gave a slow, meaningful nod. 'I really do. We can be a family again, stronger than ever.'

228

'So . . . you'd come and live here, in this apartment? With me?' *And live off the money I earn from my books, presumably?*

'Well, for now, at least.' He gazed around the flat, gave an approving nod. 'It's a nice enough place. But if you want to move away, we can do that too. Go wherever you like. You always used to say you liked the Cotswolds, remember? What was the name of that village you said you'd love to visit . . . was it Foxwell? We could go and explore there and—'

'Except we can't. That isn't going to happen.' It was Ruby's turn to shake her head and look sorrowful. 'Peter, I don't want you back, not even slightly. Why would I, after what you did to me?'

'But . . . but you said you wanted to have a baby. I'll do everything in my power to make it happen. OK, I know I wasn't that keen before, but this time we can make a real effort, explore all avenues.'

'Wow,' Ruby marvelled. 'Will you say anything to get your own way?'

'I mean it. I love you.' A bead of perspiration rolled down his forehead, which was attractive.

'Me? Or the money I make from the books and the TV shows? Anyway, you won't be moving into this apartment.'

'But where else can I go?'

'Don't know. Don't care. I'm sure your brother in Manchester will let you sleep on his sofa for a few days.'

'And what about you wanting a baby?'

'Peter, I don't just want one. I'm *having* one.' And right at this moment, it was craving another hit of raspberry juice. Since her glass was empty, this time Ruby took a swig from the half-full bottle. God, it was heavenly stuff.

Plus, drinking straight from the bottle would definitely annoy Peter.

But he was frowning, confused. 'What are you talking about?'

'Right here, right now.' She pointed to her stomach, still flat but on the verge of expanding; over the course of the last week, the button on her favourite jeans had become increasingly hard to do up. 'In here, safe and sound.'

'Is this a joke?' He was staring at her in disbelief. 'Are you seriously pregnant? But . . . you can't be.'

'I think you'll find I can.'

'How . . . how . . . *how* pregnant?'

'Seven weeks and four days.' She gave her stomach a reassuring pat. 'I wonder if that rings any bells?'

'But we hadn't—'

'Had sex for a while? Correct. And thank goodness for that. At least this way I know for sure it isn't yours.'

'You slept with someone else?' Peter was spluttering, red-faced. 'Are you telling me you were having sex with some other man? And you had the nerve to act all *superior*?'

'Seven weeks and four days,' Ruby repeated, holding up her hands as if counting on her fingers. 'The day of the wedding that didn't happen. The day my marriage ended. I met someone and slept with him that night. I *told* you about it, remember? In the hospital? But you didn't believe me.' She patted her stomach once more. 'Well, it was true.'

His forehead creased in revulsion. 'That's disgusting. You should be ashamed of yourself. What will people think? What are they going to *say*?'

'Well, if they think *I'm* disgusting, what do you suppose they think of you?'

'Margaret and I were in a relationship.' His tone was icy. 'You had a one-night stand.'

'To be honest, most people have congratulated me on having

230

left you.' Ruby was really starting to enjoy herself now; she felt *light*, like a phoenix spreading its wings, rising from the ashes. She added truthfully, 'And you know what? I've never been happier in my life.'

Chapter 29

It was a hot and sunny Thursday afternoon, the last day of June and publication day for Ruby's new book – the one she'd completed back in January, before her ability to write had shrivelled up and slunk off, possibly for good.

Now, though, that was bothering her less; she had the baby to think about instead. Far more important. Plus the joy of having told Peter exactly what she thought of him and his oh-so-generous offer to return still hadn't worn off.

She hadn't particularly wanted to make the long train journey up to London today, but Morwenna had stood firm. An important interview and signing event at a central London bookshop was due to be filmed and posted on her website, and the publicity generated would boost sales of the book, *Wally Bee and Zelda's Fantastic Firework Adventure*.

Which was fair enough, Ruby had been forced to admit. After all, she was only pregnant, not ill. Weird smells were still capable of making her feel nauseous, but she hadn't actually thrown up again.

Sitting on the train, she tried to use her fellow passengers as inspiration for the next book, but her brain stubbornly continued to be an ideas-free zone and she found herself instead gazing at the app she'd downloaded that showed you what your baby was doing at each stage of development, *in utero*.

It was fascinating, and the images on the screen were incredibly detailed, capturing each tiny movement and letting you know everything about the baby, from the size of its tiny pulsing heart to the development of its fingers and toes.

Who are you?

Are you a girl? I feel as if you're a girl.

Whoever you are, I'll love you anyway.

A man came swaying down the carriage with a takeaway cup of coffee in one hand and Ruby felt simultaneously sick and envious, because the smell had become revolting to her but she still longed to be able to enjoy coffee again.

Climbing out of her taxi from Paddington just before five o'clock, she saw Morwenna waiting for her outside the bookshop.

'Ruby, how wonderful to see you.' Morwenna threw her arms around her and, oh God, she was wearing a new and dramatically different perfume. Gone was the light, delicious summery one Ruby was used to; in its place was a spicy, peppery scent with undertones of lily and patchouli. She tried to breathe through her mouth, but it was no good, her nose still knew it was there.

Having taken the decision not to tell Morwenna about her current condition until the twelve-week mark had been reached, she found herself springing back and blurting out, 'I'm pregnant!' Aaargh, that sounded crazy. Hastily she added, 'Sorry, it's your perfume, it's making me a bit nauseous.'

'Oh my God, you poor thing.' Morwenna sounded appalled. 'What a bastard! Is he still with that woman?'

'Well, no . . . they broke up.'

'Typical! So what happens now? Is he back?'

'Um . . . I mean, he came back a few days ago . . .' Caught off guard, Ruby found herself feeling both sick and flustered; she'd managed to spring this situation upon herself with no warning, and the timing couldn't have been worse. Morwenna's phone was dinging and she was automatically reaching for it to read the latest message, they were being jostled by other pedestrians on the crowded pavement, and two women had just emerged from the bookshop and were making a beeline towards them.

'Hi, hello, we spotted you through the window,' exclaimed the bright-eyed older woman with *Manager* on her name badge. 'It's so lovely to meet you! This is Jody, our assistant manager, and I'm Emily. Come along in and thank you so much for doing this, we're expecting a wonderful turnout . . . You have so many fans who can't wait to see you and buy your new book!'

The staff, enthusiastic and hospitable, spent the next twenty minutes plying Ruby and Morwenna with hors d'oeuvres and drinks and chatting with them about bookselling in general and children's fiction in particular, while outside the room they could hear people arriving and taking their seats in the far bigger interview hall.

Then it was time for Ruby to take her place on the platform and be greeted by the audience packed into the high-ceilinged space. There was a glowing introduction from Emily, much excitement amongst the children present, and applause from their accompanying adults. Ruby scanned the sea of faces in front of her—

Oh goodness. She did a cartoonish double-take, because there in the middle of the sizeable audience was Richard, with Sasha beside him.

She hadn't expected this. Today seemed destined to catch her off guard, and now her heart was thumping wildly, her body unsure – yet again – how to react. Because this was the father of her unborn child and it was so lovely to see him, but he had no idea of her situation and was about to father his ex-wife's baby.

If it hadn't happened already.

Morwenna belatedly took her seat on the front row with a look-at-me flourish of her crimson silk scarf and an unwelcome waft of that heady, spicy perfume. Then the video camera was rolling, and all eyes were upon Ruby. She swallowed down another wave of nausea and gave the interviewer her full attention. Imagine becoming known as the children's author who'd thrown up live on stage . . . There were some kinds of publicity you just didn't need.

The interview proceeded smoothly. It was easy to fib and chat with enthusiasm about how much she loved writing her books and couldn't wait to sit down at her desk each morning with wonderful ideas jostling for attention and so many brilliant adventures planned for Wally and Zelda that she wished she could write a new book every week.

The children in the audience loved this. They loved it even more when Ruby asked them what kind of adventures they wished Wally and Zelda could have next. Hands shot up all around the room and she flashed a bright smile at a small boy in the third row, mentally crossing her fingers that his idea might be one she could use.

Well, she was desperate.

'They go into space in a rocket made of fish fingers.' The boy was thrilled to have been chosen.

'Great! And . . .?'

'They eat the fish fingers and the rocket crashes and everyone dies.'

Honestly, hopeless. But you weren't allowed to say that, so she applauded and exclaimed, 'Wonderful!'

The ideas kept coming. They were all terrible. Ruby pretended they were fantastic and kept inadvertently catching mini blasts of Morwenna's perfume despite doing her best to breathe through her ears.

'Yes?' She pointed at Sasha, who'd been waving her arm in the air for the last ten minutes. For a brief moment she fantasised that Sasha might jump to her feet and announce, 'My dad loves you!' like a kid in the final scene of a *really* slushy afternoon movie. But Sasha, delighted to have been picked at last, said, 'My sister Flo cut her hair and Mummy cried because now she looks silly.'

'That's a fantastic idea,' Ruby told her warmly. Well, it might have been, if one of her own writer friends hadn't just published a book on the same theme.

At last the interview and the Q&A were over. Once the applause had died down, Ruby was led over to the signing desk, with copies of the new book piled high on either side. A long line of children and parents snaked around the room, and her stomach did a little flip when she saw that Sasha and her dad were there at the very back of the queue. Had they deliberately chosen to be last in order to have time for a chat? She hoped so. But before that could happen, she had another fifty or so eager readers to get through, speaking to them and signing copies of the book.

Many of the children had brought along painstakingly drawn artwork of Wally Bee and Zelda and were keen to present it to

Ruby while explaining in great detail what each drawing depicted. At her side, Morwenna's assistant, Carys, patiently gathered the masterpieces into a pile and offered Ruby a glass of wine, which she politely declined. Morwenna, steering well clear of the queue of noisy children, was on her phone making arrangements to meet some A-list celebrity client in New York next week.

Fifty minutes later, the queue had finally dissipated and there were Richard and Sasha standing in front of her.

Be still, my galloping heart . . .

'Hello! Thank you for your brilliant idea.' Finding herself unable to look at Richard, Ruby smiled at Sasha instead.

'That's OK. Can you sign my book? Put: "To Sasha, I like you better than Flo."'

'Ah, but that wouldn't be very kind, would it?'

'I don't care. She put my sandwich down the toilet.'

Right, she couldn't carry on pretending Richard was invisible. Having signed the book, Ruby met his gaze. Here came another tummy-flip. 'Hi! I can't believe you came all the way into London to see me.'

'It was me who wanted to, not Dad.' Sasha was keen to get the praise.

Richard pretended to wince. 'Actually, it was both of us. You're looking very well, by the way.'

'Thank you.' *There's a tiny baby growing inside me right now. Is it going to look exactly like you? Your eyes, your nose, your smile?*

'It's good to see you again,' he said.

'You too.' Oh God, this was *scintillating* repartee. She caught another waft of the nausea-inducing scent as Morwenna approached them.

'We caught the train,' Sasha went on chattily. 'And then the Tube. It was full of people not talking!'

'Tube trains can be like that.' Ruby smiled at her.

'Actually . . .' Richard cleared his throat, 'I was wondering if you might like to join us for something to eat, or maybe just for a drink if—'

'How very kind, but I'm afraid that won't be possible.' Morwenna came swooping up to the desk, waving her phone. 'We have a completely full schedule and no time to spare. Ruby, the photographer's waiting for you up on the second floor, and you have your radio interview straight after that. Then as soon as it's done, we're off to dinner at the Dorchester with the people from the TV production company.'

Sasha tugged at her father's sleeve. 'Dad, that's the lady who was mean to us on holiday.'

'I don't think I am. I've never met you before.' Morwenna gave her a terrifying smile. 'Anyway, are we all done here? Carys, have you got everything?' She turned to Emily, the manager of the store, who was busy stacking chairs. 'Could you take Ruby up to the photographer? Now, you've had your book signed, yes?' She returned her attention to Sasha. 'And given Ruby your lovely painting of a . . . gerbil?'

Sasha's lower lip jutted. 'It's Zelda.'

'Of course it is. Marvellous. Right, off you all go. As soon as the photographer's done with you, Ruby, I'll meet you back down here.' She made unsubtle shooing gestures at Richard and Sasha.

As Ruby was whisked away by Emily, she shot Richard an apologetic look. 'Bye . . .'

Chapter 30

As Ruby disappeared with the manager, Richard found himself and Sasha being ushered out of the interview hall. He paused in the corridor, wondering what to do next. Dammit, this hadn't gone according to plan at all.

'That *was* her.' His daughter's expression was truculent and he shushed her while considering his options. He'd seen the announcement about tonight's event on Ruby's website and had left it visible on his laptop screen, feigning indifference when Sasha had seen it and asked if they could attend. In his imagination it had all been so different. Upon spotting them, Ruby would have been overjoyed. OK, it was only in his imagination, so it was allowed, but she might even have rushed over to greet him and Sasha, in such a way that everyone else in the room would know there was a special connection between them and would exchange knowing smiles and nods with the people around them . . .

Except it hadn't happened. If anything, she had looked startled to see him, her mouth twisting into a faint grimace as if his presence wasn't even that welcome. It was now screamingly

239

apparent that he might have spent the last few weeks thinking about Ruby, but she hadn't been thinking about him.

From inside the room, he heard the clink of a glass, then the bossy woman called Morwenna, who he now knew to be Ruby's editor said, 'Eurgh, that wine was warm.'

'Maybe that's why Ruby didn't touch it.' This came from the younger woman who was her assistant. 'She wouldn't even eat those snacky things they gave us.'

'Are you talking about the Brie and cranberry puffs? They're called hors d'oeuvres, not *snacky things*. Hang on, are pregnant women allowed to eat Brie?'

'No, they mustn't, soft cheese can be dangerous for the baby. Oh my God,' gasped the assistant, 'are you *pregnant*?'

Morwenna gave a bark of laughter. 'Me? Are you mad? Of course not, but Ruby is, so that'll be why she steered clear of them. In fact, better make a note of that for future events. Warn the organisers not to serve anything with soft cheese in it. Or wine. Just soft drinks for Ruby,' she amended. 'Wine for the rest of us.'

'I didn't know she was pregnant. Wow, didn't you say her husband was having an affair?'

'Oh, that was just a stupid fling, it didn't last. The usual mid-life crisis malarkey. But he came crawling back.' Morwenna's tone was dismissive. 'And Ruby's always wanted a baby, so now she's getting one at last. Not my idea of fun, but so long as she's happy.'

'Poor thing.' The younger woman sounded upset. 'She deserves better than a husband who cheats on her.'

'*All* women deserve better than that. The trouble is, most of them don't believe it. Life lesson, sweetheart. Men are pigs and women are better off without them.'

240

Richard exhaled silently. And there you had it, the brutal truth. Reaching for Sasha's hand, he turned away. If this trip to London had been going from bad to worse, it had now reached peak *worst*. His skin was clammy and he felt physically sick. And to think Ruby had been so adamant that her marriage to the philandering vicar was over. But that, presumably, had been before she'd realised she was pregnant. Once her husband had broken up with the frumpy head teacher and begged Ruby to take him back, circumstances had evidently conspired to change her mind about him. As Morwenna had pointed out, millions of women didn't have the confidence in themselves to go it alone. Any partner, they believed, was better than no partner at all. And single parenthood was hard.

But at the same time, another thought was niggling away at him. He'd slept with Ruby. Was there any possibility at all that the baby could be his? Although if there was, might the reason that she hadn't told him this be due to the fact that she didn't want him to be the father? Or to be acknowledged as such?

They reached the end of the corridor, pushed through the swing doors and re-entered the bookshop itself. Ruby was busy, had no time to speak to him and in all probability no inclination either. He could loiter for a while, on the off chance, but was there really any point? And Sasha was becoming increasingly fidgety; now her book had been signed, she was hot, tired and ready to leave.

Right on cue, she tugged at his hand. 'Dad, can we go to the burger place now? I'm hungry.'

He headed over to the sales desk, took a business card out of his wallet and borrowed a pen from the lad manning the till. On the back of the card he wrote: *If you ever want to chat, just give me a call. Or text or email. Any time.*

He hesitated, wondering what to do now and who to give it to. Then the swing doors at the back of the shop were pushed open and out came Morwenna and her assistant. Finally, something was going right. Well, at least not catastrophically wrong.

'Hello again.' He smiled at them both and held the card out to the assistant. 'As you know, I was hoping to take Ruby out to dinner, but she's otherwise occupied. So I wondered if you'd give her this instead.'

The girl said brightly, 'Of course! I'm afraid I'm heading off now, but I can pop it in the post tomorrow.'

'Thank—'

'No problem, I'll pass it on.' Reaching for the card, Morwenna said smoothly, 'Thanks for coming along to the event. I'll make sure Ruby gets this. Have a good journey home.'

There was nothing Morwenna loved more than dinner at the Dorchester, perusing the extensive wine menu and choosing a bottle of her favourite Saint-Émilion Grand Cru. Better still, the TV people had texted to let her know they were running late and wouldn't be there for another fifteen minutes.

Best of all, Ruby had ordered a glass of something fizzy, orange and non-alcoholic, which meant she had the delicious wine all to herself.

'So, cheers!' Once their drinks were in front of them, Morwenna raised her glass; she might not be keen on squalling infants herself, but she prided herself on always knowing the right things to say. 'Here's to you, and to the baby, and to you and Peter getting back together again . . . Here's to family!' She tried to clink her wine glass against Ruby's tumbler but only made contact with air.

Ruby was staring at her. '*What?*'

'You know, family! That's what you'll be.'

'Except Peter and I aren't getting back together.'

Morwenna was accustomed to being charming and agreeing with everything her authors said, even when they were palpably wrong. Plus, didn't pregnancy affect women's brains? Patiently she said, 'But when I asked you about him earlier, you told me he'd come back.'

Another look of disbelief, then Ruby spluttered with laughter. 'And then the women from the bookshop interrupted us. What I was going to say was, Peter came back to Lanrock to tell me he'd made a mistake, and to beg me to forgive him. He wanted me to take him back.' This time she did clink the rim of her tumbler against Morwenna's glass. 'But since I'm not completely mad, I said no.'

Phew.

'Well, *that's* a relief. And good for you,' Morwenna announced with feeling. 'I must say, I was shocked when I thought you'd agreed to it. Once a cheating bastard, always a cheating bastard. And he knows about . . .?' She pointed at Ruby's stomach.

'Oh, he knows. It came as quite a surprise,' Ruby said drily. 'I told him I was looking forward to raising the baby by myself.'

'Of course you are. And you'll be fantastic at it. You can do anything you set your mind to.' Since babies weren't her favourite topic of conversation, Morwenna deftly changed the subject. 'So, everything's going well, and the interview tonight was a huge success. Everyone loved it!'

'They seemed to.' Ruby smiled and nodded. 'It was a surprise to see the last couple of people in the signing queue.'

In her time, Morwenna had encountered enough over-eager

fans of her authors to know how to deal with them. With those that were a bit too keen, you needed to be pleasant but firm.

'The guy with his daughter? I wondered how he knew you.'

'He stayed in Lanrock, just across the courtyard from my flat. With his ex-wife and their two girls. You told the girls off, remember? Anyway,' Ruby went on, 'they invited me to have dinner with them one evening.' She paused. 'They were nice.'

And now here he was, turning up at a book event with his daughter, clearly having taken a shine to Ruby and entertaining fantasies of getting to know her better. Morwenna, swallowing another mouthful of the delicious wine, felt a momentary flicker of guilt at having dropped his business card into the bin in the bookshop while she'd been waiting for Ruby to finish her radio interview. Because at the time it had seemed unnecessary and irrelevant. Now it crossed her mind to wonder if she should admit what she'd done, albeit with the best intentions.

But no, of course not. It hardly mattered who the man was. Husband or no husband, Ruby had more than enough on her plate right now. This man was clearly keen on her, interested in more than a platonic friendship, and that kind of complication was the last thing she needed.

No, Morwenna reassured herself, she'd done the right thing. Apart from anything else, what kind of man went away on holiday with his ex-wife? That was bizarre for a start, plus he was already saddled with two kids of his own. *Eurgh.*

Anyway, the bookshop was closed and the bin would have been emptied by now. If the guy was that determined to contact Ruby again, he could always send a message through her website.

Guilt was overrated.

'Ah!' She waved at the two TV producers, who were following the maître d' towards the table. 'Here they are. Nick's the one on the left, he's mad about tennis, and George is besotted with his house rabbits. Whatever you do, don't ask if he has any photos of them, because once he starts, you'll never get him to stop.'

Chapter 31

When Iris arrived at the house on Bell Street the following Tuesday afternoon, Drew was on the phone. Four weeks along from their initial encounter, the skip was long gone and the interior of the property was looking much improved. In another month it would be finished and the For Sale sign would be going up outside.

'. . . No worries, I can sort that out. If it helps, I can come over now. Put the kettle on and I'll be there in twenty minutes. It's fine, no problem. OK, see you soon.'

He ended the call and gave Iris a kiss of welcome. 'Hello, beautiful.'

She kissed him back. 'Hello, not-so-bad-yourself. Who was that?'

'Susie.'

His wife.

Drew had been teasing her when he'd told her he was married, although technically he still was. Having been together for three years, he and Susie had gradually and painlessly grown apart before separating four years ago. It had been an amicable split and the two of them had remained friends. Drew had introduced Iris last week to Susie and her new boyfriend, and the evening had gone well. When it suited both of them, they would obtain an easy no-fault divorce, but there was absolutely no hurry to do that at the moment. In the meantime, they were happy to help each other out whenever the situation arose. As it evidently had done just now.

'The boys next door accidentally broke down the fence between Susie's back garden and theirs. And their garden isn't secure, which means Susie can't let the dogs out because they'll just disappear and never be seen again.' Drew reached for his car keys on the newly installed white marble kitchen worktop. 'If I pick up a fence panel from the DIY store, I can get it sorted right away. Sorry, it means I'm abandoning you.' He tilted his head to look at her. 'But I'll be back in a couple of hours. Is that OK?'

It was a measure of how much she liked and trusted him that Iris didn't even pause to wonder if it might not be OK. Drew Dawson was straightforward, honest and a genuinely decent person.

Pretty decent in the sack, too.

'Of course it's OK. I can get on with wallpapering the down-stairs loo.'

He grinned. 'And to think when I first saw you in my skip I had no idea you were a champion wallpaperer.'

She was, and she loved doing it. 'I'm a champion at a lot of things.'

'So I've noticed. Right, I'm off. I'll be back as soon as I can.'

She gave his left nipple a playful tweak through his sea-green T-shirt. 'Missing you already.'

Sixty minutes later, she heard his key turn in the lock, followed by the sound of the front door opening. On her knees in a corner of the downstairs loo, carefully trimming the bottom end of a length of green and gold wallpaper with a Stanley knife, she called out, 'I know I said I was missing you, but you didn't have to race back so soon. Or are you just desperate for me to tweak your other nipple?'

Behind her, a chilly voice said, '*Excuse* me?'

The voice didn't belong to Drew.

Worse than that, she knew who it did belong to.

Fuck.

She straightened up and twisted round, still on her knees, to look at Drew's sister.

Margaret Crane gave a gasp of horrified recognition. 'You! What's going on? What the hell are you doing in my house?'

OK, off to a good start. Their paths seldom crossed these days, but back when Iris's children had attended the school, they'd encountered each other often enough to know their character types were poles apart.

Iris, holding a glinting Stanley knife in one hand and a thin strip of green and gold wallpaper in the other, said, 'Well, I'm not performing brain surgery.'

'Where's Drew?'

'He had an emergency to sort out. He'll be back in an hour.'

Margaret was still gathering her thoughts. She stared at the freshly papered walls, then back at Iris. 'This is my house. Are you aware of that?'

'I am.' Slowly, Iris nodded.

'And Drew is my brother.'

'Yes. I mean, I didn't know that at first. But he told me.'

'I still don't understand. Are you a professional painter and decorator?'

'No, I'm just brilliant at it. I've been helping Drew out in my spare time, because . . .' She shrugged. 'We're friends. I like him.'

'You like my brother enough to . . . tweak his nipples?'

The words sounded so incongruous coming out of Margaret Crane's mouth that Iris couldn't help it; she looked at the older woman, then, like a mini explosion, gave a sudden snort of laughter.

For a few seconds, Margaret Crane didn't react at all. Then she began to smile . . . then laugh . . . except, oh God, now the laughter was inexplicably turning to tears, and she was sobbing, taking deep gulps of air and making strange honking noises like a rusty tractor wheel being turned against its better judgement.

Alarmed, Iris abruptly stopped laughing. 'Look, I know you weren't expecting to find me here, but I'm really not that bad, I promise.'

'Just g-give me two minutes. I'll b-be in the kitchen.' Margaret wiped her eyes, reversed and disappeared from view, leaving Iris more confused than ever.

She waited, listening to the sounds of movement and a tap running in the kitchen. The next moment, another key turned in the front door and she heard Drew's footsteps come to an abrupt halt as he reached the kitchen doorway.

'Jesus, Margaret! What's happened?'

Did he think she'd *attacked* his sister?

Scrambling to her feet, Iris launched herself like a rocket out of the downstairs loo. 'It wasn't me, I don't even know why she's crying!'

'It's OK, I've stopped now.' Rubbing her face with a sheet of kitchen towel, Margaret shook her head at her brother. 'And she's right, it's nothing to do with her. Any chance of some of that Merlot?' She pointed to the bottle of red wine standing in a patch of sunlight on the marble worktop.

'In that case, what's up?' Drew expertly uncorked the bottle, poured wine into the only two glasses in the house and tipped some more into a clean coffee mug for himself. He patted one of the stools around the newly installed kitchen island. 'Let's hear it.'

'I can go if you want.' Iris *didn't* want, obviously. But it was the polite thing to say.

Margaret took a huge gulp of Merlot, then swallowed, shuddered a bit and shook her head. 'You may as well stay. In fact, you'll love it. I'm going to be the laughing stock of Lanrock once word gets around.' Another mouthful of wine. 'Thank God I don't live here any more.'

'What's happened?' Drew rested his left hand on his sister's wrist.

'It's all over with Peter. I've finished with him, kicked him out of the cottage.'

Iris nodded. Drew had already told her Margaret was renting a place over in Launceston. She left it to him to ask the obvious next question.

'And?' he said gently. 'Why?'

'When it first started between us, he told me I was the only one, and that he'd never done anything like this before. And, you know, I believed him, because he's a vicar.' Margaret shuddered again. 'Except it wasn't true.'

When she'd finished telling them the whole story, Iris let out a low whistle. 'Wait till Ruby hears about this.'

'Apparently she's pregnant,' said Margaret.

'I know. How do *you* know that? It was supposed to be a big secret.' Iris was put out; she'd been proud of having managed to keep this item of gossip to herself, for once in her life.

'She told Peter. He told me. I didn't know it was meant to be a secret.'

'I suppose she had to tell him sooner or later.' Iris shrugged. 'How did he react?'

'Called her a tramp.'

'*What?* Does he know it's his?'

'Apparently it isn't. They hadn't had sex for months.'

'Fuck,' Iris marvelled. Although . . . that was probably a good thing, wasn't it?

Drew topped up his sister's glass. 'I feel like I'm trapped in an episode of *Sex and the City.*'

Iris diplomatically didn't point out that the women in that show were far more glamorous than his older sister.

'According to Peter, she slept with someone she met on the day of the non-wedding.' Margaret grimaced. 'You know, *that* day.'

As if any of them could forget it.

'I think we need to get some answers.' Iris took out her phone; this was too thrilling for words.

Time to send Ruby a text.

Chapter 32

Another week, another craving. Ruby was queuing up at the confectionery shop on Long Street when the first text arrived from Iris. Five minutes later, she left the shop with a party-sized bag of different kinds of liquorice – Catherine wheels, thin laces, fat twisted ropes, and some salty black chunks to try because Nigella Lawson had once sung their praises – then crossed the bridge to meet up with Iris and, of all people, Margaret Crane.

They were already there when she arrived, having commandeered a table outside the Dolphin that overlooked West Beach but was far enough away from the other tables that they wouldn't be overheard.

The last time she had interacted with Margaret Crane, she'd been in a state of shock and Margaret had been wearing a neat headmistressy pale blue blouse and cardigan over a below-the-knee grey skirt. Today, no longer a headmistress, she wore a flowery vest top, jeans that looked suspiciously as if they'd been ironed, and pink trainers.

Once Iris had given her a hug, Margaret rose to her feet

and held out a hand for Ruby to shake. 'Congratulations on the baby.'

'Thanks.' Of course Peter would have relayed the news to her. All Ruby knew from Iris's texts was that Margaret had something to tell her, and not to worry, she was going to like it.

'And it definitely isn't Peter's?'

'Absolutely not.'

'In that case, even more congratulations.' Margaret's smile was wry. 'Did he tell you he'd finished with me? Because he didn't. I told him to leave.'

Ruby nodded; this was par for the course where Peter was concerned. 'Why?'

'I waited until he was asleep the other night, then used his fingerprint to get into his phone. Went through his messages. Did you ever do that?'

'No.'

'He sent a lot of messages. Received a lot too. Were you never curious?'

Had she been idiotic not to be? It genuinely hadn't crossed her mind to be suspicious. 'He told me he was discussing personal issues with his parishioners and had to be careful to protect their privacy.'

'That's what he told me too.' Margaret lifted an eyebrow. 'And to begin with, I believed him. Until I got an inkling that something wasn't quite right and looked at them for myself. No wonder he flew into such a panic the other week when he thought he was about to lose his phone.'

One of the barmaids brought out their tray of drinks at that moment. She'd clearly recognised both the recently separated wife of the local vicar and his alleged lover, the recently deposed

253

headmistress of Lanrock Primary School, so purely for gossip-fuelling purposes, Ruby clinked her tumbler of apple juice against Margaret's glass of red wine and said, 'Well, cheers!'

Once the three of them were alone once more, Margaret said, 'He'd kept them all, too. Hundreds of messages, going back years. Do you want me to carry on?'

'Definitely. Don't stop now.'

'OK, I took photos of some of them. Six years ago he had an affair with someone called Paula, who was divorced and lived in Killigarth. After her it was Denise in Talland. Next came Stephanie, who he met when she was on holiday down here, but she lived up in Nottingham so that one didn't last long. And there are more,' she went on. 'Seven altogether. The most recent is an accountant called Julie whose husband doesn't understand her. She's living with him in Bodmin but keeps telling Peter how she wishes they could both just run away and be together for ever.'

'I had no idea,' said Ruby, stunned. 'He was always busy, driving off on visits to help members of the congregation and anyone in the community needing pastoral care.'

'And all this time,' Iris put it bluntly, 'he was shagging his way around Cornwall.'

The more Ruby thought about it, the more sense it made. 'He was a vicar. It was the perfect cover. Wearing his clerical collar, going above and beyond to tend to the needs of his grateful flock. Well, the female members at least.' She looked at Margaret. 'Unless you know different.'

'Just women.' Margaret smiled briefly. 'And yes, it was the perfect cover. Which is how he's managed to get away with it for so long. I don't imagine he'll ever stop. It's like a hobby for him.'

Ruby nodded. 'In that case, good luck to the women of Manchester if that's where he ends up. And thanks for telling me, too. Looks like we've both had a lucky escape.'

'OK, now back to you.' Iris was clearly bursting to change the subject. 'I didn't ask before because I assumed it was Peter, but who *is* the father? Is it someone we know?' Struck by a thought, she blurted out, 'Is it that fit guy, Max, who came down for the wedding and went swimming in the sea with Lottie? Oh, except you weren't there.' She flapped a hand, belatedly remembering. 'Anyway, he's back down here now. I don't know if there's anything going on between them, but they were doing karaoke over at Bert's the other night. So, is it him?'

Ruby, living just across the courtyard from the entrance to Lottie's flat, knew that Lottie and Max were doing a lot more than just karaoke together. But she'd also worked out for herself that there had to be a reason why, to the casual observer, they were no more than good friends. Since she liked Lottie and respected her privacy, she hadn't even raised the subject with her. It just went to show, though, how other people were capable of leaping to conclusions.

'Max is an old friend of Lottie's, that's all I know. I've seen him around a few times, and yes, he's attractive, but I've definitely never done anything like that with him. Trust me, he's a million per cent not the father of my baby.'

Iris was visibly on the verge of exploding with curiosity. 'And? Are you going to tell us who *is*?'

Ruby hesitated; once the shock of seeing Richard in London had subsided, her foolish heart had leapt with the hope that he might feel more for her than he'd been letting on. She'd even fantasised that he might make contact again, but it hadn't happened. When she had come back down to the ground floor of the bookshop that evening, she'd been hoping against hope that he'd still be there or have left some kind of message for her. But no, nothing, zilch. He'd obviously only attended the event for Sasha's sake.

There was a contact form on her website; if he wanted to see her again, it would be easy enough to arrange. But he hadn't done that either, and why would he? She'd been a brief encounter, evidently pleasant enough but certainly not life-changing, and he had his own tricky family issues to cope with. For all she knew, his ex-wife could already be pregnant by him.

Even more reason not to rock the boat and bring unwanted complications into his life.

Iris and Margaret were still waiting for an answer. Ruby raked her hair away from her face. 'It was an unplanned one-night stand with a man who isn't . . . free. I shouldn't think I'll ever see him again and it's for the best that he doesn't know about any of this.' She gestured in the region of her stomach. 'And that's fine by me. My father walked out on my mother when I was five, but she coped. We both coped. She was a brilliant single mother and I hope I will be too.'

'Damn right. Here's to all us brilliant single mums.' Iris enthusiastically raised her glass to Ruby. 'Men are bastards and we don't need them.'

'*Most* men are bastards,' Margaret corrected her. 'But my brother isn't. He's a good man. I hope you aren't going to hurt him.'

'Are you worried I might? Hey, it's OK, we're having a bit of fun, that's all. Nothing serious,' Iris assured her. 'None of that emotional rubbish and no broken hearts. Just loads of fantastic sex.'

'Oh well, in that case,' said Ruby, because it was nice to know *someone* was getting loads, 'cheers!'

Chapter 33

'What are you doing?'

The voice behind her was so unexpected that Freya almost dropped her binoculars into her plate of chips.

'God, you gave me a fright.' She lowered them and clutched her chest. 'I was just . . . watching people.'

It was the last week of July. The schools had broken up, the summer season was in full swing and the beaches were crowded. There were plenty of people to watch from up here on the spacious terrace of the Rupert Hotel.

'Anyone in particular?' Seizing the binoculars, Lottie swiftly scanned the length of West Beach from left to right.

'No . . .'

'And you're quite sure about that, are you? Because I can see your fiancé training for his marathon, and he isn't doing it on his own.'

Freya felt her skin heat up, because Lottie was giving her one of those sympathetic looks that made her feel racked with guilt.

'Honestly, it's fine,' she protested. 'It was actually my idea. Cameron loves running and so does Naomi, so why shouldn't they train together for the marathon?' It had been the next masterstroke in her campaign, and Naomi had been thrilled when she'd suggested it. Now, almost every evening after work, the two of them would change into their running gear and set out on a five-mile run, urging each other on and keeping progress charts of their times.

'Yes, but are you sure you're OK with it? Maybe you thought it was a good idea but now you're starting to wish you hadn't said anything.' Lottie sat down next to her at the table with the best view of the beach. 'Because keeping an eye on them through binoculars makes me wonder if you're secretly getting a bit worried.'

'I'm not worried.'

'Some people are, though. They've seen what's going on. And they're concerned about you.' She added gently, '*I'm* concerned about you.'

Freya felt terrible. The whole point of the binoculars had been that she wanted to check that the two of them were getting on well, that they were chatting and laughing together as they ran. She wished there could be more chat and laughter and less running.

'Hey, relax. It's me.' Lottie reached for her hand. 'I'm on your side. And if you want me to have a quiet word with Cameron, I will. Maybe he just doesn't realise how things look.'

This was even worse. And Lottie was her friend; they'd known each other for years. Freya's sense of guilt worsened. She hadn't confided in a soul, and it was practically the only secret she'd kept to herself in her life.

Glancing back down at the beach, Lottie went on with a trace of asperity, 'The thing about Cameron is, he's so hell-bent on being the heroic fundraiser, he doesn't stop to think about what other people are seeing.'

259

Wow, this was new; Freya had never heard Lottie so much as hint that Cameron might not be perfect. Her spirits lifting, she risked a smile and a hint of eye-roll, because Cameron's determination to always be seen as the heroic fundraiser *was* annoying.

Lottie smiled too, acknowledging the eye-roll, and Freya knew the time had come to share her secret. The urge to unburden herself was too great. She had to tell someone, and who better than Lottie?

'Chip?' She nudged the plate towards her.

'Of course. Except you know I can never have just one chip. It has to be at least three.'

'Take as many as you like. So anyway, I'm inviting Naomi over to ours for dinner on Friday.'

Lottie frowned. 'And?'

'I'm planning to cook an amazing meal, get the table all set up . . . then at the last minute I'm not going to be able to make it. But I'll insist they go ahead and eat together anyway.'

She watched Lottie's gaze stray back down to the beach, where Cameron and Naomi had reached the far end and were now turning back, running side by side through the shallow surf. Naomi was wearing a shiny lilac bra top and matching Lycra shorts that showed off her toned body, and her blonde hair was tied back in a bouncy ponytail.

'Why? Why would you do that?' Lottie slowly turned back to face her. 'Unless you *want* her to take him off your hands.'

Here it came. Slowly, Freya nodded. 'I do. I really do. And I know it's the coward's way out, but it's Cameron, the nicest man on the planet. And he gave my mum one of his kidneys.'

'Wow,' said Lottie. 'I mean, *wow*.'

'I know. I did love him at first, I promise. But after a while I began to feel kind of trapped, and when he proposed, how

260

could I say no? The thing is, I owe him so much. When someone saves your mother's life, you can't just turn around and break their heart. It'd be too cruel and it would look so bad. Which is why I let it carry on, hoping the love would come back again. But it's never going to happen, I know that now. And the only way I can see to get out of this mess is if someone nicer and prettier and keener than me comes along and makes him realise he can do so much better than me. Then it can be his decision for us to break up, and bingo! All sorted. No guilt, no blame and no shame.'

'Oh my God, this is wild.' Lottie was dumbfounded. 'What made you go off him?'

Freya felt as if she could breathe again; the relief at having finally got it off her chest was overwhelming. 'You promise not to hate me if I tell you?'

Lottie pulled a *yikes* face. 'Is it some weird sex thing?'

'No!' Freya burst out laughing. 'OK, this means I'm officially a horrible person. It's the fundraising.'

'Ah.' Lottie's eyes were bright. She gave her a tiny encouraging nod.

'And endlessly promoting the fundraising, which is obviously a good thing, except it always feels as if he's promoting himself.' The muscles in her legs relaxed as the words spilled out. 'He just seems to really enjoy everyone knowing what an amazing person he is. And sometimes he gets a bit cross if he sees someone else on TV being given an award for something they did for services to charity. It's almost as if he feels he should be the one getting praised. I think what he really wants is an OBE from King Charles. Sorry, is that awful of me? I hate myself for thinking it. I'm a bad person.'

After a long moment, during which a gull flew squawking

261

overhead, Lottie pinched another chip and said, 'Well, if you're a bad person, so am I.'

'Really?'

'Oh yes.'

'It's not just me?'

'Definitely not just you.'

'I've been feeling so guilty.' Freya sat back, light-headed with relief.

'Me too. Although I reckon there's a chance that if you gave everyone in Lanrock a truth drug, they'd all say the same. Cameron's a good guy, but sometimes – well, quite often – it all gets too much.'

'I think he'd like it if he could go around wearing an actual halo.'

'You could buy him one for his birthday.' Lottie mimed wearing a halo at a jaunty angle.

'My mum loves him so much, though. As far as she's concerned, he can do no wrong.'

'She loves you more. If you told her how you feel, she'd understand.'

'I guess. But she'd be devastated. So anyway, there you go, I've told you my shameful secret. Thanks for not being horrified. What?' said Freya as Lottie broke into a grin. 'Tell me what's funny.'

'Not funny. More like ironic. I've just realised something. You can't bring yourself to finish with Cameron because your mum loves him so much. But I can't even tell mine I'm seeing someone I really do like because she'd hit the roof if she knew.' The grin gave way to a wry grimace. 'And trust me, hitting the roof is an understatement. If it ever got serious and she found out who it was, she'd spontaneously combust.'

'Hang on, are you talking about Max?' It was Freya's turn to be stunned.

Lottie nodded. 'There you go. You told me your big secret, so now I'm telling you mine. It's a complete mess. He says he likes me. And I know I like him.'

'You mean you *really* like him.'

Another nod, followed by a sigh. 'But it's like standing in the middle of a motorway watching a lorry come barrelling towards you and knowing it's not going to end well.'

'But . . . *why?*'

'I can't give you the whole reason; it's not my story to tell. But it's kind of a Romeo and Juliet situation. Our families are never going to get on, and that's another massive understatement.'

'Oh Lottie, I had no idea.'

'No one does. But that's the reason we've been keeping things under the radar. Luckily, Mum and Dad hardly ever come over to Lanrock these days, but if they did find out . . . well, it'd be carnage.'

Freya shook her head. 'Poor you. Poor both of you.'

'On the bright side, Max doesn't have the best track record when it comes to staying interested in girlfriends, so with a bit of luck he'll get bored with me and move on to the next one before too long.'

Freya couldn't imagine anyone getting bored with Lottie; she was gorgeous, hard-working, funny and great company – basically the full package. 'God, it's so unfair.'

'First-world problems, as some really annoying people would say.' Lottie pulled a face. 'And I do know that. It's just, you spend years going out with all the wrong men, then finally find what feels like the right one . . . and you *still* aren't allowed to relax and be happy because you know you can't keep him.'

'It's horrible,' Freya sympathised. 'He is lovely. And he does really like you, I can tell.'

'Life never runs smoothly, does it? Speaking of running . . .' Lottie broke off and waved as Cameron and Naomi ascended the steps to the hotel terrace. 'Here they come now. Have to say, it doesn't seem fair that she isn't bright red in the face.'

'We saw you from the beach. Hello!' Naomi beamed at them both. 'Phew, that was a hot one. What a great run.' She tapped her watch. 'And we're getting faster too.'

'You're doing brilliantly,' said Freya.

'I'm not as fit as Cameron. He's a hard taskmaster. Sometimes it's a struggle to keep up.'

'I'm firm but fair.' Cameron was stretching out, ensuring his calf muscles were properly relaxed. Freya knew it was necessary, but even the way he made such a point of publicly doing it had begun to annoy her in recent weeks.

'He is, to be fair.' Naomi laughed. 'We both said fair! That's like this morning in the office, when you said you could murder a coffee and five minutes later I said I could murder a coffee too!'

'Great minds think alike,' Lottie said cheerfully.

'Oh, my mind's never great, especially when I haven't had a coffee!'

'Listen,' said Freya, 'you haven't even been round to ours for dinner yet. Would you be free on Friday? Fancy coming over for the evening?'

Naomi's face lit up. 'Really? I'd love that. Thanks so much!'

'Nothing formal, just a cosy get-together with some good food and wine.'

'That's so nice of you. And Friday's perfect for me.' She gave Cameron a playful nudge. 'Looks like we have a date.'

264

His smile was genial. 'Excellent. Although I'm warning you now, we may end up playing Trivial Pursuit. And I'm not a good loser.'

'Neither am I, and Trivial Pursuit's my favourite game. I *love* it.' Looking past them, Naomi said, 'Here comes Max. Ooh,' she turned to Lottie, 'are you two going to be there on Friday as well?'

Lottie said easily, 'Freya did invite us, but we can't make it.'

Freya gave an inward sigh of relief. Now that Lottie knew the truth, it was going to be so much easier having her onside.

'So it'll just be the three of us,' Cameron chimed in, 'if that isn't too boring for you.'

'You could never be boring.' Her eyes sparkling, Naomi hastily added, 'Neither of you are!'

Chapter 34

On Friday afternoon, Freya shot home during her lunch break and made sure the house was looking its best. She set the dining table with their one and only tablecloth, the best cutlery, polished wine glasses and six candles, because what was more romantic than candlelight? She also arranged fresh crimson and yellow roses in a vase. The scent of boeuf bourguignon in the slow cooker was already delicious, the potatoes dauphinoise would only need reheating later, and the raspberry pavlova was sitting patiently in the fridge.

At five thirty, leaving the shop for the second time that day, she rang the surgery.

'Oh, I'm sorry, he's with a patient at the moment,' said Naomi. 'I'll get him to call you back, shall I? Or can I pass on a message?'

'Maybe that's easier. Look, I'm so sorry but I'm not going to be able to be there tonight — it's my friend Jess, she's having a complete crisis . . . She's desperate and needs me there, and I just can't let her down.' Freya marvelled at how genuine she sounded; sometimes her ability to lie convincingly amazed her. When it was for a good cause, she was brilliant at it.

'Oh no, that's such a shame,' Naomi sounded disappointed, 'but of course you need to be with your friend. It's fine, honestly, I understand. And we can always get together another time.'

'But that's the thing,' Freya went on eagerly. 'Just because I'm not there doesn't mean we have to cancel dinner. The food's all cooked, everything's ready, no need for it all to go to waste. There's no reason why you and Cameron can't still enjoy the meal, is there? Drink lovely wine and have a killer game of Trivial?' She paused, then said hesitantly, 'Unless you don't want to.'

'Oh no, of course I'd like that! If you're absolutely sure?' Were Naomi's eyes sparkling with delight? It definitely sounded as if they were. Her own spirits lifting – was there *anything* better than a plan coming together? – Freya said, 'Of course I'm sure! Have fun, eat all the food, and do me a huge favour – really try to beat Cam at Trivial, because he nearly always beats me.'

Naomi sounded ecstatic. 'I'll give it my best shot, I promise!'

Back at home, Freya packed a little overnight case, then sent Cameron a text:

Jess wants me to spend the night with her, she's had a huge row with Martin and her boss is being a nightmare – you know what she's like when she has one of her meltdowns. Sorry, but I can't not go. I'll be back first thing tomorrow. The boeuf b smells amazing – save me some in a bowl. And don't forget to light the candles – food always tastes better when there are candles on the table! Xx

There, sorted. The other week she'd fibbed to Cameron that her upcoming visit to her old schoolfriend Debs in London had had to be cancelled because Debs's in-laws were coming to stay. This time, all she'd had to do was call and suggest meeting up with another of her friends. Overjoyed, Jess had cried, 'Yay, Friday! Come over and stay at mine and let's have a wild night – Fowey won't know what's hit it!'

It was with a bit of a hangover, then, that Freya let herself in the next day. It had turned out to be a brilliant – and yes, wild – night in Fowey. But now it was eight in the morning, Cameron had set off on his run and the house was empty.

The Trivial Pursuit box was on the coffee table in the living room. The kitchen was tidy, and last night's dinner things had been washed up and put away. The cream pillar candles had burned down a couple of inches, she noted with satisfaction. Excellent. Had Cameron played the romantic music she'd left ready, or had he forgotten? Had he and Naomi gazed at each other across the table, the flickering candlelight reflecting in their eyes as pulses quickened and realisation dawned that the attraction between them was both mutual and irresistible?

Had they abandoned dinner, launched themselves at each other and kissed until their lips were numb?

Had they then headed upstairs and spent the night making mad passionate love, and afterwards, as they lay entwined in each other's arms, had Cameron said, 'I've never felt like this about anyone before. I know it's wrong, but I can't help it. I'll have to tell Freya it's over, then we can be together'?

And had Naomi breathlessly replied, 'Oh, poor Freya, I do feel guilty, but from the moment I first saw you I just knew this was it'?

Freya blinked, wondering if it would be wrong to go upstairs and search for clues: a carelessly discarded condom wrapper under the bed, perhaps, or a tiny smudge of lipstick on one of the freshly laundered pillowcases. But then she heard the sound of Cameron's key in the lock, and here he was in his running gear, bright-eyed and pink-cheeked from his exertions and exuding good health.

'You're back! How is she?'

For a split second Freya thought he meant Naomi. No, obviously not, that made no sense. He was being concerned, asking after major-meltdown Jess.

'Oh, she'll be OK. When things go wrong she just gets herself into a complete panic. Once we'd talked it all through, she calmed down.' Freya touched her temple. 'We sank a fair amount of wine. I could do with a couple of aspirin.'

'All in a good cause.' He gave her a kiss on the forehead. 'I'll get you some. You're a hero. Want a mug of tea?'

Was he being extra nice because he was feeling guilty? But no, she had to admit he was always this nice.

As he boiled the kettle, popped two aspirin out of their blister pack and dropped a slice of bread into the toaster, because he knew she'd want some honey on toast, Freya sat down at the kitchen island. How many men would be this thoughtful? Was she making a monumental mistake? Once they were no longer a couple, would she find herself missing him terribly and regretting her actions for the rest of her life?

But no, she knew that wasn't going to happen. Just as falling madly in love could hit you out of the blue, so could falling out of it. Once the feelings had faded, there was no going back. She smiled and thanked him when he put the tea, toast and tablets in front of her, then said, 'How did it go last night?'

'With Naomi? Fine. The food was fantastic. I remembered to light the candles. And I beat her at Trivial Pursuit. So basically, a top evening.'

'What did you talk about?'

'All sorts. Running. Protein supplements. Ways to publicise the fundraising. Eating healthily.'

'Nice.' *Not really.* 'And you did all the washing-up, even the pans. I'm impressed.' Pans weren't his favourite; he generally left them soaking in the sink.

'We did it together. Naomi insisted.'

'I knew she was nice.' Freya took a slurp of tea and washed down the aspirin. 'I like her even more now. What time did she leave?'

'Oh, around ten. Not late. I walked her home, then came back and crashed out.' He checked his watch. 'Anyway, better jump in the shower, don't want to be late for work.'

Last year, Cameron had asked for a Ring doorbell system for Christmas. Now, while he was upstairs, Freya checked the app on her phone. True to his word, there they were, leaving the house together at six minutes past ten. And here was Cameron returning alone fourteen minutes later. So Naomi hadn't invited him in for a quickie, or even a drink. Or maybe she had but there'd been people nearby, aware of who he was and interested to see what he might be getting up to.

Never mind, they were clearly getting on well and that was the important thing. She closed the app and took another bite of toast. Her brilliant plan was still on track.

Out of the shower, Cameron called down, 'Fancy a curry tonight? We could take those chicken pieces out of the freezer.'

'Great, let's do that.' He was very keen on cooking authentic Indian dishes and had a whole cupboard of herbs and spices.

'I'll give you another lesson in how to cook basmati.' He also liked to tease her because she'd once committed the apparently cardinal sin of lifting the lid from the saucepan and giving the rice a quick stir.

In a good mood, Freya called back, 'No need, we can just use boil-in-the-bag.'

He laughed. 'Over my dead body. By the way, I bumped into the new vicar yesterday. He says if we want to book a date for the wedding later on in the year, we could meet up with him next Saturday to have a chat about it.'

'It's the height of the season,' Freya protested. 'I'll be working flat out in the shop. Maybe some other time, when we're not so busy.'

From the top of the staircase, Cameron nodded. 'OK, but we don't want to leave it too long.'

Well, one of us might.

Chapter 35

Rocked by the gentle swell of the sea, Lottie opened her eyes. Out here, a hundred yards or so from the shore, all she could hear was the lapping of the water against the sides of the tethered pontoon. Above her, the sky was a vivid shade of blue with a single white cloud directly overhead, small and elongated with a hint of an eye, a wonky ear and a puffball tail.

'It's a rabbit,' murmured Max beside her, and she tilted her head.

'How did you know what I was going to say? That's so spooky.'

The corner of his mouth lifted. 'Not really. Not when there's literally nothing else to look at. It's a choice of either blue sky or a cloud that looks like a rabbit.'

'Or a dog. Or a baby llama. Or a sheep.'

'It could be a baby llama. I can see that.' He interlinked his fingers with hers and gave them a squeeze, and Lottie wondered if it would ever stop feeling completely magical. Right here, right now, she couldn't imagine being happier than this. It was a long, slow, perfect moment and she never wanted it to end. Spending time with Max felt like the only thing that mattered.

As the weeks had slid by, the connection between them had grown and deepened. Was it more than just a connection? Was it love with a capital L? It certainly felt like it, but she was too scared to admit as much, even to herself.

'Love you.' He gave her fingers another affectionate squeeze, and yet again it felt as if he were reading her mind. Except, as before, rather than an astonishing coincidence, it was simply the truth, an honest expression of how he felt. Having never said it to a girlfriend before – allegedly – he was now more than making up for it, telling her he loved her several times a day, every day.

'It's turning into a hamster,' said Lottie, because pretending he hadn't uttered the words was the only way she could handle this new situation.

'And she ignores me again.' His tone was good-natured. 'But I won't give up until you say it back to me. One day it'll happen, I just know it. I love you.'

'Can't hear you.'

He gave the side of her leg a playful nudge. 'Good job I like saying it.'

A pair of gulls were soaring overhead, wheeling in a lazy figure-of-eight. Lottie thought back to the one and only boyfriend she *had* said it to. It had been Keiron, of course, the absolute charmer who'd abandoned his ex-girlfriend and baby and neglected to mention their existence. He'd said it to Lottie and she'd said it back, chiefly because it seemed like the polite thing to do, despite the fact that at the time they'd only been seeing each other for a fortnight. It wasn't until many months after he'd disappeared from their lives that one of the other students in their halls of residence had told her that a group of Keiron's male friends had been playing a game, taking bets on how soon they could get a girl to say it to them.

273

By all accounts Keiron had won himself the contents of the pot that night, a grand total of fourteen pounds fifty.

It was the kind of humiliating information that was hard to blank from your mind.

'What's happening?' Beside her, Max lifted his head slightly. Before, there'd been silence, but now they could hear shouts in the distance. Peering across at the beach, he said, 'Can you make out what they're saying?'

Lottie raised her own head and felt a trickle of perspiration slide down from her neck into her cleavage. 'Maybe they're excited because the ice cream van's turned up at last.'

He was shielding his eyes from the sun. 'Looks like they're pointing at us.'

'What? Why would they be doing that?'

The next moment, cupping their hands around their mouths, two men on the beach yelled in unison: '*Shark!*'

Her heart hammering, Lottie sat bolt upright and swivelled round to look behind her. And there it was, a dark fin slicing through the silver water, heading straight for them. She let out a high-pitched squeak of terror as a second fin materialised alongside it. The voices from the beach seemed to grow more insistent, battling to be heard above the ominous sound of the theme tune from *Jaws* currently reverberating through her brain.

'Just because they're saying it doesn't mean it's true.' Max was laughing at her. 'They're dolphins.'

Dolphins. Of course they were. Of *course* they weren't man-eating sharks barrelling towards her, intent on hurling themselves up onto the pontoon and biting off her legs. 'I knew that,' she said.

He carried on laughing, shaking his head at her. 'Of course you did. That film didn't traumatise you at all.'

'Shut up.' But now she was smiling too. It had been a couple of weeks after her sixteenth birthday that they'd watched the film together over at Max's house. Having been so determined to play it cool and take the scary bits in her stride, she'd ended up shrieking so loudly at one point that his mum had come running in from the kitchen convinced there'd been a terrible accident. And Max, of course, had teased her about it for months afterwards; on the bus, in shops, or passing her in the corridor at school, he would suddenly fling out his arms, give a high-pitched scream of terror and cry, '*Nooooo!*'

Now, her breathing back to normal, Lottie pointed and said, 'Oh, look at them, they're adorable.' Because the pair of dolphins had been travelling beneath the water but were now leaping playfully into the air as they circled the pontoon. The next moment, a third one appeared out of nowhere and joined the display.

The lads who'd been yelling 'Shark!' were now whooping with delight along with the dozens of other people on the beach as the dolphins continued their joyous antics, bursting out of the water like beaming synchronised swimmers at the Olympics, then flipping sideways before curving through the air and splashing back down into the sea.

'Is this real?' It was so magical Lottie almost wanted to cry. 'It's like being in a Disney movie.'

'I want to dive in and join them, but I don't want to scare them off. We'll just sit here and watch.' Max put his arms around her waist, drawing her close. In return, Lottie leaned her head on his shoulder and stroked the back of his neck. She loved the interplay of muscles below his collarbone as his skin quivered in response to her touch.

He dropped a kiss onto her temple. 'We'll never forget this, will we? It's going to stay with us for ever.'

For ever. The words filled her with longing and despair, because how long could their relationship really last? She watched the dolphins cavorting around them so energetically that droplets of seawater splashed her sun-warmed limbs and—

'What's that noise?' said Max, just as a faint whirring sound made itself heard. A split second later, looking up, they saw a drone hovering overhead.

'It didn't come from the beach.' Glancing over her shoulder, Lottie saw that a small sailing boat had rounded the rocky promontory and entered the bay behind them.

'They're filming the dolphins. And who can blame them?' Tipping his head back, Max waved up at the drone.

'Don't wave. You're so embarrassing.'

He grinned and kissed her. 'It'd be more embarrassing if we were naked.'

Chapter 36

Lottie was working on her laptop in the office the following lunchtime when the door suddenly burst open and an all-too-familiar voice demanded, 'What in God's name do you think you're playing at?'

Her fingers froze on the keyboard and her stomach clenched; there was no doubt what her mother was talking about. She might have no idea how it had happened, but one way or another it clearly had.

As, sooner or later, they'd always known it would.

It didn't stop her feeling a bit sick, though. This was full-on rage.

Thwack went the newspaper, folded up to make more of an impact as it hit the desk.

'Look at me,' her mother ordered. 'Tell me what's been going on, because I can't *believe* it's happening.'

Luckily Marcus was out with a client, so the office was otherwise empty. Lottie unfolded the newspaper and saw the photograph for herself. There she was in her yellow bikini, on the pontoon with Max, curled up beside him with his left arm around her waist and the other waving at the camera overhead. They were both laughing, their legs entwined, as the dolphins splashed around them. It was an unusual enough occurrence to have bottlenose dolphins this close to the shoreline that the photo had made the front page, and the quality of the video camera attached to the drone meant every detail of the photo was pin-sharp, so there could be no mistaking the identity of the two people out there on the pontoon.

The local paper was always keen to big up local delights in order to boost visitors to the area, and the headline proclaimed: *A Splashtastic Display in Lanrock Bay!*

Lottie scanned the text below the photo, but it was about the dolphins and didn't mention either Max or herself by name. Not that it was necessary in this case; the cat was well and truly out of the bag, which was more than enough damage for one day.

'That's Max Farrell. And don't try to deny it.' Her mother jabbed at the page, her tone icy. 'It's *him*.'

'I know it's him.'

'What are you trying to do to me? How *could* you?'

'We met up by chance at Freya's wedding. I really like him and he likes me. We always did like each other, but I never told you that, because the other stuff happened and then they moved away. But I never forgot him.'

'You were only seventeen!'

'And now that I'm thirty, we like each other even more.' Was this her chance to get through to her mother? With a sudden surge of hope, Lottie said, 'I've never felt this way about anyone else, it's—'

'No!' Kay shouted. 'No, no, NO.'

'But you can't blame him for what happened! It wasn't his

278

fault. Mum, I love him.' She might not be able to say it to Max's face, but she could say it here. 'I do, I really do.'

'Well, stop loving him. Make it stop right now. Because it can't happen. It *mustn't*.'

This was exactly what she'd expected to hear. Feeling sick, she carried on anyway. 'But why do we have to suffer for something that was nothing to do with us? It's not fair!'

'I know it's not fair. Life isn't fair. But if you go ahead with this, what's going to happen? You'll ruin my life as well as your own. Do you seriously think you can be happy?'

'Yes! That's all I want!'

'Well then, you need to find someone else to be happy with, because I'm telling you now, our two families are never going to be together in the same room.' Kay was trembling, shaking her head. 'Imagine the engagement party. If we're invited, Max's family won't be there. And the wedding? Maybe they'll go and we'll stay at home, and how will *that* make you feel?' She was ticking future events off on her fingers now, her voice cracking with emotion. 'Will you have children? Because they'll never see their grandparents together at birthday parties or at any of the other special times in their lives, and if they ask you why not, what will you tell them, hmm?'

'Mum, stop it. Please.'

'Maybe you'd prefer it if they just have *his* parents in their life, then you can all have fun together without having to worry about us.' She snatched a tissue out of her handbag and wiped her brimming eyes. 'In fact I'm sure you've already planned it that way. Well, have a nice life with your new family, *sweetheart*, because cutting ties seems to be the only answer. As long as you're with him, you won't see us again. *Ever*.' She turned on her high heels and stalked out of the office, slamming the door behind her.

Lottie exhaled and sat back in her swivel chair. That was her mother all over, never knowingly under-dramatic.

Then again, she also stuck to her guns like glue, as they'd all learned to their cost over the years.

It was heartbreaking, but it was part of life.

Her phone started ringing. Lottie answered it.

'I just went to the corner shop to pick up a carton of milk,' said Max, 'and the woman on the till showed me the front of the local paper.'

'You're lucky. My mother just turned up and showed it to me.'

'Ah.' He paused. 'And?'

'She isn't over the moon, let's put it that way. So long as I'm seeing you, she never wants to see me again.'

'Shit. I'm sorry.'

'I knew she'd be like this. Oh well.' She managed a smile as two prospective clients walked into the office. 'Just be glad they don't sell our local paper up in Bath. At least your parents aren't going to see it.'

Lottie had been right; they hadn't seen it in the local paper. Instead, the stunning aerial video had caught the attention of one of the popular nationals and been published in their online edition later that evening, racking up hundreds of thousands of views and ensuring that plenty of Imelda Farrell's friends, recognising her beloved only son, had got in touch to let her know about it.

Max took the FaceTime call from his mother the following morning, shortly after she'd seen the footage for herself online.

At least, unlike Lottie's mother, she wasn't completely incandescent with fury. Then again, she was the one who'd had the affair
with Terry Palmer. Plus, he guessed his father hadn't seen the
video yet.

'Darling, you're famous!' she exclaimed.

Here we go.

'It wasn't planned.' On his way to the coffee shop, Max found
an empty bench and sat down.

'That girlfriend of yours isn't going to be thrilled . . . Louise,
is that her name?'

'Lois. And she isn't my girlfriend. I told you that.'

'She seems to think she is.' Imelda paused. 'So, the one with
you in the photo . . . is that who I think it is?'

'Depends who you think it is.'

She raised an eyebrow at him. 'Well, I haven't seen her for
the last thirteen years, but it looks to me like Lottie Palmer.'

'It is Lottie.' Max nodded.

'Amazing. How did this happen?'

'I came down for Cameron's wedding back in May. And Lottie
was a guest too. She lives here in Lanrock.'

'And her parents?'

'They're twenty miles away, in Bodmin. Still together.' He
answered the unspoken question.

'I suppose that's good. Are they happy?'

'Right now? Not particularly.'

'Oh dear, poor you. Still, it's not as if it's going to last, is it?'
His mother laughed as if the idea was ludicrous. 'How is she
anyway? Lottie, not Kay. Sweet girl. I always did like her.'

'She's great. And you'd still like her. I do,' said Max. 'A lot.'

'I'm not surprised, darling. I must say, she's looking gorgeous.
That figure!'

281

Given his past dating history, he couldn't expect her to understand. Keen to explain, he said, 'Mum, listen to me. This is different. She's the one I told you about the morning after your party, remember? I love her. And this time it *is* going to last.'

Two teenage girls giggled and nudged each other as they walked past the bench.

More laughter from Imelda, who no longer seemed convinced he was serious. 'Of course it is. You're so funny, darling! Well, I'm glad you're having a good time down there anyway. And if Kay gives you grief, don't take any notice – just tell her it'll all be over in a month, then you'll be gone for ever, so there's no need for her to get her knickers in a twist about it.'

'Except it isn't going to be over in a month. I've never felt this way about anyone before. What's happening with me and Lottie is completely different.' Max fixed his gaze on his mother's face, willing her to understand just how serious he was. 'She's all I've ever wanted. Now I've found her again, I'm not letting her go.'

But Imelda was clearly humouring him. Her eyes sparkling, she said, 'Well, whatever you do, don't let your dad hear you say that. Can you imagine what would happen if he thought you and Lottie were in danger of ending up together? Total carnage, doesn't bear thinking about! Look,' she went on, 'if someone does show him the photo, I'll just tell him it's a meaningless fling and you're getting bored with her already. And if he asks you, just say the same. But otherwise there's no need to mention it. We don't want to stir up trouble by dragging up the past.'

Max swallowed his frustration; there was no point trying to argue with her when she was like this.

'Fine.' He shrugged. 'It's not true, but you say what you want. Maybe ten years from now you'll believe me.'

'Just have fun with her,' Imelda pleaded. 'Darling, I'm sure she's wonderful and I'm sure you *do* think you love her right now. But let's be serious for a moment and think of the ramifications. How could it ever work? You and Lottie . . .' She gestured helplessly with her free hand. 'It's just not *practical*.'

'Well, this is a disaster,' said Lottie when they discussed it that evening after work. 'I mean, we always knew it would be. But now that it's happening, I just feel . . . sick.'

'Hey, we'll sort it out.' Max held her close and kissed her.

'How?'

'One way or another.'

She sighed. 'That's not an answer, though, is it? It's the kind of thing politicians say when they know there *isn't* an answer.' At that moment her phone went *ting* with yet another text from her mother telling her the relationship had to end because to continue to see Max was simply untenable. All the old insecurities had been stirred up like silt in a muddy pond and the situation was spiralling out of control. Kay had got herself into a complete state and was evidently taking it out on her husband, having convinced herself that his previous ill-fated affair would now start up again.

'Maybe it'd be easier if we did stop seeing each other,' Lottie blurted out now, then held her breath, because what if Max said yes?

'Never.' Another kiss on the mouth. 'And you don't mean that anyway.'

'I know.'

'I love you.'

'I know.'

'And you love your parents. If you didn't, this wouldn't be a problem.' He paused, then drew back and gazed past her into empty space.

'What?' said Lottie.

'Nothing. Just trying to figure something out. Let me give it some thought.' Sitting back, he picked up a pen, then took out his phone and began scrolling with one hand while scrawling notes on a pad with the other at the lightning speed he invariably employed when working on the logistics of a new online game.

Lottie gave him a few minutes, then leaned sideways to take a look at what he'd been writing. Her stomach lurched when she saw what it was. 'That's a bit drastic, isn't it?'

Max shrugged. 'At this stage,' he said evenly, 'I think drastic is what we need. It's pretty much all we've got.'

Chapter 37

'You're doing *what?*'

Beneath her make-up, the colour visibly drained from Kay's face. Her hand flew to her throat and she stared at Lottie, then at her husband. 'No. No, no . . . you can't.'

'Mum.' Lottie remained calm. 'We are. I think we have to.'

'But . . . Oh Terry, *say* something. I mean, New Zealand? It's on the other side of the world!'

'I know it is.' It was six thirty on Wednesday evening, four days since they'd made their momentous decision, and Lottie had driven over to Bodmin to visit her parents straight from work. 'But it's such a great opportunity. And everyone says it's an amazing place to live.'

Kay was stunned, shaking her head. 'They don't let just anyone into the country. You have to jump through hoops, have plenty of money, have a *job* to go to. Margot and John's son applied a few years ago and they wouldn't grant him a work visa. Terry, get me a drink, please. Oh, this is horrendous . . .'

'Max was over there back in April,' Lottie explained. 'He met with the boss of the company in Christchurch, who offered him the position. At the time, he turned them down, but they've just asked him again and it seems like it could be the answer. The visas are going to be taken care of. The company can make it happen quickly, and they're supplying us with a place to live until we buy somewhere of our own. The government jumps at the chance to have people like Max move there. People like us,' she amended. 'And the standard of living is just fantastic. It's the opportunity of a lifetime. We'd be crazy to turn it down.'

'And what about us?' Her mother's face was pale. 'You can't just abandon us. How would we cope, knowing you're thousands and thousands of miles away? Oh, I can't bear it.' Her voice cracked with emotion. 'This is a nightmare. When would we ever *see* you?'

'Mum, don't get upset.' Lottie's tone was soothing. 'It'll be fine. Think how many people emigrate every year. You'll get used to it. It's not like the olden days, when all you could do was write letters that took weeks to arrive. We can see each other as often as we want online.'

'But it's not the *same*.' Kay pressed her hands to her chest. 'I don't want to look at you on a tiny screen . . . How can I hug you through a pane of glass?'

'I'll come back to see you every couple of years, I promise.'

'Every two *years*? Oh my God . . .!'

'You can fly out and stay with us.' Lottie felt a bit guilty saying this; her mother had a lifelong terror of flying that not even hypnotism plus a wildly expensive course on overcoming her fear had been able to cure.

Kay let out a shaky wail of despair. 'You know I can't do that. I just *couldn't*.'

Lottie glanced at her father, who wasn't saying a word. She

286

rested her hand on her mother's arm and said gently, 'Well, I'm sure you'll get used to video calls. It's better than nothing.'

'I can't bear this, I just can't bear it.' Kay's cheeks were wet with tears. 'This is the worst day of my life.'

'Look, it won't be for another few weeks. We'll find someone else to take over the running of the business. I promise I'll get them up to speed before I go. And Mum, thousands of people move abroad every year. Their parents understand that they're doing it for good reasons, and they cope. It really isn't the end of the world.'

'It is to me, though. And how do *his* parents feel about all of this, hmm?' Kay wiped her eyes. 'Or are they not bothered?'

'Honestly?' Lottie paused. 'They're as upset about it as you are. But right now it feels like the only answer to a problem that isn't going to go away.'

'Thanks to your father,' Kay said bitterly. 'And that boy's mother.'

'But it wasn't thanks to us,' Lottie reminded her. 'We didn't do anything wrong. When Max was seventeen, you liked him. You'd still like him now.'

But this was pushing things too far. Kay shook her head in despair. 'What if you go over there with him and it doesn't work out?'

Lottie shrugged. 'Then it doesn't work out.'

Her mother took another gulp of chilled wine. 'But what if it *does* work out?' She swallowed and pressed her lips together, then blurted, 'What if you end up having a baby with him? We'll never see our grandchild . . . grandchildren . . . Oh, *why* did you have to meet up with him again? It's so unfair.'

'Kay . . .' Terry reached out to take his wife's hand, but she shook her head, pulling it out of reach.

Time to go. Lottie rose to her feet. She spoke evenly. 'Mum, I'm sorry you're upset. But meeting up with Max again was the best thing that's ever happened to me. It really was my lucky day.'

Three days later, on Saturday afternoon, Terry Palmer waited at a table in a shaded corner of a café garden in Cullompton, Devon, twenty minutes early for his meeting.

She arrived exactly on time, wearing a pale green trouser suit over a white shirt, and matching heels and handbag. She made her way over to him and he rose from his seat, kissing her briefly on each cheek as if they were distant acquaintances.

Which, when it came down to it, they were.

As always, her make-up was expertly applied. Her perfume wasn't the one he remembered. He felt nothing, not even a flicker of attraction.

Thank God.

'Imelda, it's good to see you again.'

Her smile was brief. 'You too.' And in that moment, he knew her reaction matched his. She might have made an effort with her appearance, but only because it was what she'd always done; the person she was meeting today was irrelevant.

'You're looking well.'

'Thanks. So are you.'

'Well, I'm older. Less hair. A few more inches around the waist.' Wryly, he said, 'I quite often go *oof* when I sit down.'

Imelda nodded. 'We're both older.'

'Thanks for coming today, anyway. I wondered how it would feel, seeing you again. But . . . it's OK.'

She nodded, visibly relieved. 'Same. It's like . . . nothing. Isn't it strange? All those feelings, where did they go? Because they've just disappeared.'

They gazed at each other for several seconds, taking in the weirdness of the situation. Then a waitress appeared and Terry ordered a pot of tea for himself, plus lemon tea for Imelda. Thirteen years ago, swept up in a whirlwind of lust and adrenalin, they'd embarked on an affair that had consumed their lives. Every waking moment had felt like a waste of time unless they were in each other's company. They'd taken great care to minimise the risks of being caught, and for three months it had all worked out perfectly; they hadn't been found out and no one had suffered as a result. It had been wildly out of character for both of them, but at the time the chemistry and magnetism had simply been too powerful to resist.

Until that fateful weekend in the flat in Bristol, when they'd so nearly lost their lives and the world had changed for both Imelda's family and his own.

There had been zero contact between them since, until Wednesday evening, when Lottie had driven over to Bodmin after work to pay them a visit and drop her bombshell, on the same night that Max had broken the news to Imelda and William. Terry, not the greatest fan of social media, had nevertheless searched out Imelda, found her on Instagram and sent her a private message. Within an hour, she'd replied.

And now here they were in Cullompton, pretty much the halfway point between Bodmin and Bath, meeting to work out if anything could possibly be done to fix this latest disastrous turn of events.

'Who would ever have thought it could happen?' Imelda said now. 'Your girl and my boy, meeting up again like this. He says she's the one he's been waiting for all his life. I didn't believe him at first, but he seems pretty sure.'

'Same with Lottie. She's always been happy running the business in Lanrock, but she's never found the right man. Until now, according to her. And all of a sudden they're ready to leave everything behind to start a new life together in New Zealand. All because of us.'

Terry felt a fresh wave of guilt; since Wednesday, Kay had been inconsolable.

'Well, not *us*. We're here to try and resolve the problem. It's my husband and your wife who are the reason they're doing it. But it's thanks to us that we're all suffering as a result.' A tear rolled down Imelda's tanned cheek and she swiped it away, her voice breaking with emotion. 'Is this karma? I suppose so. It's our fault.'

'It wouldn't be happening if it weren't for us.' Terry nodded in agreement. 'Kay's devastated. She just can't handle the idea of Lottie being so far away.'

'And you think I'm not devastated? No parent *wants* that to happen. My only child is moving to the other side of the planet because of what we did. All those years ago we made a terrible mistake, and now it feels like we're being punished for it all over again.'

This was what had been going through Terry's brain on a more or less constant loop for the last seventy-two hours.

'There must be something we can do.' He gestured helplessly. Across the café garden, a family party was in progress, twenty or so people aged from two to ninety-two, all laughing and having a wonderful time together without a care in the world. Once Lottie emigrated, there would be just Kay and himself left, both of them lonely and desperately unhappy. No jolly family gatherings for them, oh no; just bitterness and endless recriminations.

'Whoops, sorry!' cried one of the young mothers in the party as a small child hurled a plastic aeroplane across the grass. It landed at Terry's feet. As he bent to pick it up, he wondered if he would ever be allowed to play with any grandchildren of his own, or if that was the next punishment awaiting him. He was sixty-six and had dodgy blood pressure; maybe he'd die before he ever had the chance to meet them.

When he'd handed the toy aeroplane back to the boy, he looked at Imelda and felt his eyes prickle with heat and desperation. Did the family over there even realise how lucky they were to be together today?

'What?' said Imelda.

'How about if I turn up at your house when you aren't there? I could try and speak to William.'

'You wouldn't stand a chance. He still goes to the boxing gym and trains four times a week. Remember what he was like when he came to see you all those years ago?' Imelda shuddered at the memory; she might not have witnessed it first-hand, but her furious husband had evidently told her about the confrontation. 'Before you could say anything, you'd be flat on your back and out cold.'

It was Sunday morning, the day of the marathon. Cameron had been up since six, crashing around the house so noisily that Freya guessed he wasn't *that* pleased by her decision to stay in bed rather than be there to cheer him on at the start.

'I'll be there at the finish line,' she'd told him last night. 'That's more important, isn't it? After all, anyone can start the race, but not so many get to finish it.'

'I will.' Cameron checked his reflection in the wardrobe mirror, ensuring his race number didn't obscure the photo of himself printed on the front of his T-shirt. 'I'm going to beat my record today.'

'What if Naomi can't keep up with you?'

'Not my problem.' His times mattered to him.

'Oh, that's not fair! You can't leave her behind, not after all these weeks of training together.'

'All's fair in love and marathon running. She isn't a child. I'm going to break the four-hour barrier today if it kills me.'

'Well, make sure it doesn't,' said Freya, 'because that's not the kind of publicity you're after.'

'True.' He handed her his phone. 'Take a few pics of me, will you?'

'Your wish is my command.' She took three.

He smoothed down his hair and changed his pose. 'Now take a few more.'

The race had begun at nine a.m. After dozing for another hour, then having a long shower and a lazy breakfast while catching up with the latest episode of a reality show Cameron mightily disapproved of, Freya got dressed and ready in time to head down to the finish line at twelve thirty. As she passed the rank of shops on Long Street, she discreetly admired her reflection in the window of the fancy wine and cheese store – hair looking good, pink and yellow kimono top worn over narrow paler yellow trousers – and idly wondered what excuse to use next when Cameron mentioned booking a date for the wedding. *If* he mentioned it again; she'd fantasised earlier that he and Naomi crossing the marathon's finish line together might prompt an outburst of emotion and a huge hug, followed by him realising once and for all that she was the one for him. God, wouldn't it be great if that happened, like a scene in a film, with hundreds of people around them to witness it?

Then her phone rang in her bra and she discreetly whipped

it out, agog to discover the caller was Cameron. Surely he hadn't finished the race already? Aaargh, if he'd beaten his best time by that much, he'd be *so* annoyed she'd missed it.

Bracing herself, she pressed accept and exclaimed, 'Oh my God, have you just broken the world record? This is crazy!'

But instead of Cameron's triumphant voice, she heard the tearful, gulping, panicky tones of someone blurting out between sobs, 'It's not him, it's me . . . N-Naomi. I'm so sorry, the ambulance has just taken Cameron off to the hospital. He collapsed during the race and I thought he was going to d-die. It looks like he's had a heart attack.'

Chapter 38

Terry Palmer had never felt less prepared for an encounter in his life. Then again, nor had he ever felt more determined. As far as Kay was aware, he'd set out from home at the usual time for his Sunday-morning game of golf with a group of regulars from the club.

More than likely, she was going to get a shock when he eventually arrived home. If he even managed it in one piece.

'You have reached your destination,' his satnav informed him, and to Terry's ears the voice sounded snide and knowing, as if to inform him that in executing this plan he could be making a massive mistake.

The satnav was probably right, but he was going to do it anyway.

He parked around the corner from the property on Lansdown Road and took a few moments to collect himself. The houses were tall, Georgian and expensive, with only small front gardens, which meant there was no privacy. This might work in his favour. Then again, it might not, depending on whether it bothered William that his neighbours could witness the meeting.

Damn, he should have stopped at the last service station to empty his bladder.

Right. No more thinking. Just do it.

He stepped out of the car and locked it. His other mistake had been spraying himself with too much aftershave before leaving the house this morning. Why in God's name had he even put any on in the first place?

He rounded the corner and paused outside number sixteen, with its emerald-green front door and twin bay trees standing to attention in stone pots on either side of the recessed entrance.

Deep breath. He pressed the doorbell and heard it ring inside the house. Imelda, as arranged, had gone to visit her friend in Bradford-on-Avon. On Sunday mornings, she'd explained, William liked to go to the gym for an hour, then be home by eleven and spend some time working in the garden.

Terry waited, listening for footsteps. None came.

He tried the bell again.

Still nothing.

Oh, for God's sake, this wasn't part of the plan.

Another long ring, then he heard the sound of a door being unlocked from the inside. But it wasn't the door whose bell he'd been pressing.

'Hello, dear, were you wanting to see William and Imelda?' The woman emerging from the house next door was absolutely tiny, white-haired and beady-eyed. She had to be in her eighties, and was carrying bright yellow gardening gloves, a microfibre cloth and a pair of secateurs.

'Uh . . . yes.'

'Well, I'm afraid Imelda's out for the day, and I saw William leave the house twenty minutes ago. He told me he was just popping to the shop, so hopefully he'll be back soon.'

'Right.' Terry hoped so too.

'You could call him,' the woman suggested helpfully. 'Do you have his number?'

'Er . . . not on me.'

She whipped a phone out of the pocket of her gardening apron. 'Well, why don't I let him know he has a visitor?'

'It's fine,' Terry protested, but too late; the tiny woman had already made the call.

'Will, hello! Are you on your way home? Yes? Oh good, because someone's here to see you.' She paused before turning back to face Terry and saying brightly, 'Who are you, dear?'

Fuck. His mind went blank. Then his gaze landed on her window box, filled with herbs. 'Uh . . . Basil.'

'His name's Basil,' she said into the phone. 'I'll tell him you won't be long.'

There followed an uncomfortable ten minutes of polite conversation about ferns, slugs and pesticides while Terry pretended to read something important on his phone and the woman, who'd now introduced herself as Rose, snipped away at the various plants and shrubs in her small but immaculate front garden. With each minute that passed he could feel the tension racking up inside him like a wrench being tightened by a giant.

Finally she said, 'Ah, here he is now.'

Terry turned and watched as William approached them from a distance, wearing a grey polo shirt and jeans. Rose waved at him and William briefly raised a hand in acknowledgement. A moment later, recognition dawned. His expression grew stony, and he switched the carrier bag of shopping from his right hand to his left.

Which was ominous.

'Yoo-hoo, here we are! Basil and I have been having a lovely chat about gardening. Always nice to meet a fellow enthusiast.' Rose beamed as he reached them.

For a terrifying moment, Terry thought William might be about to take an almighty swing at him in front of his sweet elderly neighbour. He held his breath, nodded at William and said, 'Hello.'

A second passed in silence apart from the crisp snip-snipping of Rose's secateurs as she trimmed back the Virginia creeper around her front window. Then William said slowly, 'Hello . . . Basil.'

'Oh, let me cut you some dill,' Rose exclaimed, turning to her window box. 'Imelda said she was going to be marinating a salmon tonight. Here you are!' She passed a generous handful of the feathery green fronds over the wall to William, then turned to Terry. 'How about you, Basil? Would you like some too?'

How could she be so blithely unaware of the tension between him and her neighbour? Terry nodded. 'Um . . . yes, OK. Thanks.'

Rose returned to the window box, sliced off another bunch of the herb and handed it to him. 'There you go. It's a marriage made in heaven, salmon and dill. We had it at our diamond wedding party two years ago because it was Tom's favourite. Remember that party, Will? Such a perfect day. I lost my husband eighteen months ago,' she explained to Terry. 'Such a wonderful man.' She turned her twinkly gaze back to William. 'Just like you, dear.'

Taking his front door key from his jeans pocket, William said tightly, 'Well, we'd better get inside. Thanks for this.' He indicated the fronds clasped in his right hand.

'Yes, thanks very much,' Terry echoed.

'Oh Basil, no need to thank me. It's my pleasure!'

He followed William into the house, closing the door behind him.

In the spacious blue and white kitchen, they stopped and faced each other.

'So, *Basil*. What are you doing here?'

William's manner was brusque and unfriendly, but less explosive than Terry had expected. He realised that Rose's presence had prevented him from reacting as furiously as he might otherwise have done. They'd been coerced by her into feigning politeness, and now the anger – well, some of it, at least – had seeped away.

Still, he'd come here for a reason. No backing down now. Bracing himself both mentally and physically, he said, 'I want you to hit me.'

'*What?*'

'You heard. Hard as you like. I want you to knock me down, punch me, really hurt me. Whatever you want to do, just do it.'

William blinked. 'Why?'

'Because it's the only way I can think of to show you how sorry I am, so we can get past what happened . . . No, I know we can't get past it, but maybe we can come to some kind of arrangement. Because none of us ever planned to see each other again, and that was what all of us wanted, but now circumstances have changed and it's tearing our lives apart. My wife is inconsolable. And I am too. Because of what happened, our girl is moving to New Zealand with your boy, and we don't know how to cope with the thought of her not being here any more. And I'm sure you must feel the same way.' He ground to a halt, steadying himself against the kitchen table. 'They don't *want* to go. They're only doing it to avoid the situation.'

'Caused by you.' William's jaw was rigid, his fists curled at his sides.

'Yes. And I was still too ill last time, which meant you never had the chance to punish me. So that's why I want you to do it now.'

'You're sure about this? You want me to punch you?' There was a glint in William's eye.

'I'm sure. Go ahead. Do it.' Terry braced himself, tensing every muscle in his body. Since looking at William was too unnerving and he didn't want to duck or instinctively try to avoid the moment of impact, he clenched his teeth and closed his eyes.

Waiting . . .

Praying that when it happened, he wouldn't let out a humiliatingly high-pitched shriek of pain.

Come on, come on, get it over with.

'Aaarrrghhh,' came the high-pitched shriek, but not from him. It was accompanied by the screech of metal chair legs against the quarry-tiled floor. Terrified that his adversary had picked up the chair in order to take an almighty swing at him, Terry lurched back, his eyes snapping open in time to see William jumping up onto the pulled-out chair. The next second he saw a mouse scuttling at speed across the floor before disappearing behind the Welsh dresser.

'*Fuck!*' William yelled. 'Get it out of here! I hate rats!' The colour had drained from his face and he was visibly quaking.

'It's not a rat. It's only a mouse.'

'I hate mice too. Fuck, I can't handle this.' He jumped from the chair up onto the table and made panicky shooing gestures. 'I mean it, oh Jesus, *do* something.'

Terry grabbed a broom from the adjoining utility room, stuck it along the back of the dresser and waggled it until the tiny creature shot back out. Then it all got like a video on fast-forward, with the mouse zigzagging like a ninja around the kitchen and Terry chasing after it, while a terrified William yelled at him to get a bloody move on. Terry then yanked open the door that led out into the back garden, but the mouse – surely as traumatised as William – continued its zigzagging and flatly refused to go anywhere near it.

Finally he managed to corner the terrified creature between the bin and one of the cupboards, throw a tea towel over it and scoop it up in his hands.

'Out! Take it out . . . far away,' gibbered William, still visibly squirming with revulsion.

Terry carried the squeaking mouse down to the very furthest end of the garden, then released it through a hole in the fence into next door's vegetable patch.

'Gone,' he announced when he returned to the kitchen.

'Did you kill it?'

'No!'

William shuddered. 'I can't stand mice. It's a phobia.'

'You don't say.' Terry watched as he climbed gingerly back down to floor level. 'Right, where were we?'

William looked at him. 'You still want me to hit you?'

'That's why I came here.'

'Well, it's not going to happen. It never was.' William shook his head resignedly. 'I was about to tell you that when . . . well, when we were interrupted.'

'But you're a boxer.'

'Exactly. I don't fight with people who aren't even trying to fight back. I'm not a monster.' He gestured in the direction of the garden. 'Anyway, thank you for getting that thing out of here.'

'Shall I let you into a secret?' said Terry. 'I don't like mice either.'

'But you dealt with it.'

'One of us had to.'

'Well, thanks again. I really do hate them. They freak me out.'

With a brief smile, Terry said, 'I'd never have guessed.'

Thirty minutes later, he climbed back into his car, ready to begin the long drive home. As he passed the house, William, standing in the doorway, raised a hand in farewell. Terry did likewise.

One down, one to go.

And incredibly, he was driving away without a single broken bone in his body.

Thanks, mouse.

Chapter 39

'They won't tell me anything. They wouldn't even let me sit with him.' Naomi, her face drawn and tear-stained, leapt off her orange plastic chair the moment she saw Freya entering the waiting room through the sliding doors. 'One of the race marshals gave me a lift here and I told the nurses I was Cameron's very close friend. But they still wouldn't let me in with him. I can't bear it, he's all on his own in that cubicle, and what if he's *dying* in there? What's the *matter* with these people?' She cast a pleading look at a middle-aged nurse, who said patiently, 'He isn't on his own, love. He's being monitored by the team. As soon as they know what's happening, his next of kin will be allowed in to see him.'

Freya said, 'I'm his fiancée.'

The nurse glanced at Naomi, one eyebrow raised. 'Oh, I'm sorry, you said you were the next of kin?'

Naomi flushed. 'I only said that because nobody would tell me anything.'

'Is he going to be all right?' Freya's mouth was dry, her heart thumping. What if he wasn't? Oh God, she may have thought bad things about him and wished for their relationship to end, but this wasn't the way she'd wanted it to happen.

'Hello,' said a tired-looking doctor in blue scrubs, approaching them. 'Are you here for Cameron Bancroft?'

Naomi's hand flew to her mouth. 'Oh no, *oh no!* Don't tell me he's dead . . .'

'He's not dead.' The doctor shook his head. 'He's doing just fine. All the tests are clear and we're not keeping him in. It appears to be a case of over-exertion combined with dehydration and a touch of heat exhaustion, leading to a panic attack. There's nothing at all wrong with his heart. He's a healthy chap who wasn't used to feeling unwell and that's what caused him to panic.'

'Oh, thank God!' Naomi promptly burst into noisy tears.

'Hey, it's all right,' said the doctor. 'You must be the fiancée.'

'*I'm* the fiancée,' said Freya.

'Sorry, of course. If you'd like to go through, I'll show you where he is.'

'Can I come too?' Naomi pleaded, and the doctor looked questioningly at Freya, who shrugged.

'I don't mind.'

He led them through a doorway and along a corridor, then ushered them towards a curtained-off cubicle at the far end. Whisking back the curtain like a magician, he announced, 'Here you are, you gave these two quite a fright, but I've reassured them that you're fine.'

'Thank God, thank God.' Naomi was wiping her eyes.

Feeling like the understudy in a play who hadn't learned her lines, Freya echoed awkwardly, 'Um, yes, thank God.'

'I thought this was it,' said Cameron. 'I was so sure I was on my way out, about to lose my own life while raising money to save the lives of others.' When the doctor had departed to attend to his next patient, he added, 'Could one of you take a photo of me? Make sure to get the drip in.' He pulled the drip stand closer to the bed and lay back against the pillows with a weary but heroic look on his face.

'I'll do it,' said Freya.

When Naomi had handed over his phone and Freya had dutifully taken several photos of her fiancé in his hospital bed, Cameron said to Naomi, 'You may as well take some too. Make sure they're good enough quality for the papers.'

At that moment a door at the end of the corridor opened and closed, and a woman wearing denim shorts and a T-shirt passed the cubicle. Glancing across at them, her attention possibly drawn by the flash on Naomi's raised phone, she did a belated double-take and skidded to a halt, then took a few steps back and exclaimed, '*Cameron?* I don't believe this! Is it actually you?'

Cameron, who'd been giving it his best poorly-but-incredibly-brave look, jerked his head up from the pillows and stared at her in astonishment. 'Tan? What are you doing here?'

'I work here! Right here in A&E.' She started to laugh. 'I left my phone behind when I came off shift this morning. Just popped back to pick it up.' She patted her pink raffia shoulder bag. 'But what's going on with you?'

'I'm OK.' The brave face was back as he pointed to the race number attached to his T-shirt. 'I collapsed during the Lanrock marathon and the paramedics thought I was having a cardiac event. But I've been given the all-clear. Bit of heat stroke, that's all it was. Trying too hard to beat my personal best.' He couldn't tear his eyes away from her. 'I'm working as a GP over in Lanrock.'

'And I'm here in Plymouth. I've just bought a tiny flat on

304

Rochester Road. I'm so sorry.' She broke off, turning to address Freya and Naomi. 'Barging in like this and not even introducing myself! I'm Tanya Barton. Cam and I trained together at St Thomas' in London. We were . . . great friends.'

'It's OK, you can say it.' Cameron was beaming. 'It was years ago. And we were more than that. Tan and I went out together for over a year. We only broke up after graduation because she took a job in South Africa. We had a huge fight about it and stopped speaking . . . haven't had any contact since then.'

'And lived to regret it, too,' Tanya continued cheerfully. 'All my fault. What an idiot I was.'

'How was Cape Town?'

'Amazing, but I couldn't enjoy it. Hated every minute because I knew I'd messed up big time. Moved back to the UK a year later, all ready to throw myself at your feet, but Maddy Pearce told me you were seeing her friend Gemma and I should leave the two of you alone.'

'Gemma Mason? The kleptomaniac? She was a nightmare,' said Cameron. 'I dumped her after a fortnight.'

Tanya clapped a hand dramatically to her chest. 'If only I'd known.'

'If only *I'd* known,' Cameron said with feeling.

'And now we meet again, but you still aren't free. You must be Cam's girlfriend,' said Tanya, addressing Naomi.

Really? Although at a guess it had to do with Cameron and Naomi wearing matching running clothes with adjacent numbers pinned to their chests. Freya said patiently, 'I'm the girlfriend.'

'Well, it's good to meet you. And *so* great to see you again,' Tanya told Cameron.

'You too, Tan.'

Tan and Cam, Freya realised.

'I'd better leave you to it. You take care of yourself. We don't want to see you in here again.' Tanya hoisted her raffia bag back onto her shoulder and waggled her fingers at him. 'Bye, Cam.'

'Bye,' said Cameron. 'Maybe we'll bump into each other again sometime.'

Naomi, Freya couldn't help noticing, was looking distinctly unamused. Whereas Cameron suddenly seemed so much more cheerful.

'Right.' With Tanya gone, he reached for his phone. 'Let me give you the number of the news desk at the local TV station. If you let them know I'm here, they might be able to come over and interview me before I have to go home.'

'Why?' Freya already knew why.

'It's all about publicity for a good cause. It might raise more money for the charity.'

'Ooh.' Naomi ran her fingers through her hair and perked up. 'Can I be in it too?'

'I'm the one who could have died,' Cameron told her. 'It's probably better if they concentrate on me.'

Chapter 40

This would be the hardest thing she'd ever had to do, but Iris knew she had to do it. The time had come. The longer she left it, the more agonising the situation would become.

The song she really wished would stop haunting her was playing on an endless loop in her head as she made her way over to the house. 'If you love somebody, set them free,' Sting crooned for what felt like the millionth time, and under her breath she muttered, 'Oh, do shut up.'

She reached the end of Wood Lane and rounded the corner onto Bell Street, and there he was, bare-chested and deeply tanned in just paint-spattered jeans and Timberland boots, tidying up the sloping front garden of Margaret's home so that it looked as well tended as the house itself. Feeling tears prick at the back of her eyes, Iris paused for a moment until she had them under control, because getting weepy wouldn't do at all. She had to be calm and unemotional if he was going to believe her.

Breathe. Blink. She was about to do something that was unimaginably hard, but at the same time only right and fair. She'd fallen for Drew Dawson, never meaning it to become serious, and they'd shared a summer of love. But now it had to end. As she'd come to know Drew and his friends, she'd learned just how much of a family-man-in-waiting he was, a thirty-three-year-old in his prime who was absolutely brilliant with children and had never imagined not having any of his own. And kids in turn gravitated towards him, because . . . well, who wouldn't want to? He was fun, endlessly patient with them, always up for impromptu games on the beach, and never found it frustrating when plates were broken or drinks got spilled. There was an instant rapport between him and children of all ages; even small babies gazed at him in wide-eyed fascination. It was no secret amongst his friends that Drew was more than ready to settle down.

Iris knew she'd left it too long. She might not have outright lied to him, but it was undeniably lying by omission. When he'd assumed in their first week together that the faint silvery scar had been the result of a Caesarean section, she hadn't corrected him, because years ago a boyfriend had grimaced in distaste upon hearing she'd had a hysterectomy. As they'd lain in bed together, he'd said, 'God, I thought that only happened to old people. My gran had one of those when she was seventy-six.'

She'd dumped him, of course, because he was both idiotic and ignorant. But the fear of being thought of as old and past-it had evidently lingered in her mind long enough for her not to want it to happen again.

Especially with Drew.

Straightening up now, then turning and spotting her, he broke into a broad grin and waved. Iris waved back and closed the distance between them, breathing in the clean, salty smell of his sun-warmed skin as he greeted her with a lingering kiss.

'Get a room,' grumbled an old man walking past with his snappy-looking Jack Russell on a lead.

Drew murmured in her ear, 'I prefer it al fresco.'

'Let's go inside.' The kiss had almost undone her; this wasn't getting off to the best start. Hardening her resolve, she drew away. 'We need to talk.'

'Sounds ominous.' He gave her backside a playful pat, which didn't help at all.

In the kitchen, she poured herself a glass of ice-cold water from the fridge, then perched on one of the high stools at the marble-topped island.

'What's this about, then? Something to do with Margaret's birthday?'

'No.' She shook her head. 'It's about us. This house is finished now. It's all done. And we've worked well together. Had some fun. But it's time to be realistic. You and me, we were never meant to be a long-term match.'

The questioning smile faded from Drew's face. 'Weren't we?'

'Oh, come on, it was only ever a fling, admit it. And it's been a great fling. God knows, you're fabulous in bed. But flings don't last. I'm forty years old. You're thirty-three. I've had my kids. You haven't had yours yet. It's time you met someone younger than me and settled down. I'm not the settling-down type. We need to call it a day.' Iris paused; inside, her heart might be breaking, but outwardly she was making a good job of sounding as if she meant it.

Drew was shaking his head. 'I don't believe you.'

'Well, you should. Every relationship I've ever had, I've been the one to end it.' She gave an offhand shrug. 'And now it's time to end this one. Like I said, it was great while it lasted. But now's the right time to move on.'

'Why?'

'Because it's always better to do it before it gets boring.'

A muscle was twitching in his jaw. 'I'm not bored with you. Not even close.'

She looked at him, her mouth dry. 'But it's starting to happen for me. Sorry, I didn't want it to, but it is. I have a low boredom threshold. I've told you that before. It's why I redecorate my flat every year.' Oh God, this was agonising. 'We want different things. You want kids. I can't give them to you.'

'You're forty, not eighty. I know women who—'

'I had a hysterectomy,' Iris blurted out. 'Seven years ago. My periods were out of control. And there were fibroids. I knew I didn't want any more children, so they took it out, the whole lot.' *Don't cry, don't cry.* 'Best thing I ever did.'

'Right.'

'I suppose you think I should have told you. But I didn't because it never seemed relevant. We were enjoying ourselves, having a great time, but we were never going to last, so why would I need to mention it?'

'You never thought we were going to last?' A frown line appeared. 'I did.'

'Which just goes to show, you don't know me as well as you thought you did.' Her throat was tightening. 'Look, I don't enjoy doing this.'

'Don't do it, then.'

'But I have to. Because I *do* know what I'm like, and this is the way it always goes.' She tapped her fingers impatiently on the worktop. 'We had fun, but now it's over, time to call it a day.' There, done. She reached for her glass of water to signal that the conversation was at an end.

'Iris—'

'Please.' She raised her other hand to stop him. 'Don't try to argue, because I'm not going to change my mind. And whatever you do, don't beg. That's just cringe.'

It was the most hurtful thing she could think of to say, and she saw it hit home. Drew stiffened as if she'd slapped him.

'Fine. Don't worry, I'm not going to beg. I'm not the begging type.' He took a couple of steps back. 'Anyway, thanks for letting me know. I guess you won't be coming with me to Stevie's party this weekend.'

'Not really any point. But say happy birthday to him from me.'

'Are you seeing someone else? Is that it?'

Iris paused and took another sip of water. 'I'm not seeing anyone else. But it'll happen sooner or later. To me, and to you too. We'll both meet other people, start new relationships. Mine won't last,' she said drily. 'Hopefully yours will.'

He shook his head, didn't reply.

'Well, I'd better be off.' She checked the time on her phone. 'Places to go, houses to clean.' She hopped off the high stool and gave him a brief, deliberately awkward kiss on the cheek. 'Thanks for everything. It's been great.'

'Don't go jumping in any strange skips,' said Drew, and the fact that he was attempting a joke almost broke her heart all over again.

'If I do,' she managed a brief smile in return, 'next time I'll make sure not to get caught.'

But leaving the house, she was unable to hold back the tears. Was he at the window, watching her walk away? She didn't look round to see. Drew might be feeling bad now, but the one thing she knew was he couldn't feel worse than she did.

No wonder she'd never done this before. Being unselfish and doing the altruistic thing was just shit.

'. . . Now we welcome onto the show one of this country's most beloved children's authors, and a personal favourite in our household, the wonderful Ruby Vale!'

Richard almost crashed into the van in front of him; having only just pulled out of the car park two minutes earlier, he'd had no prior warning from the radio presenter that he was about to hear Ruby's voice again. Luckily, the rush-hour traffic in Henley-on-Thames was heavy and only inching its way along the congested high street.

'Hello, Danny, it's so lovely to be here, chatting to you!'

Was she actually there, in the studio? Or were they communicating over Zoom, two smiling faces hundreds of miles apart? He knew this happened because she'd told him it was often the case. Oh, but it was so good to hear her. It wasn't something he would say aloud, but Ruby's was his favourite voice in the world, as low and beautifully modulated as that of an actress advertising chocolate on TV.

'And you're looking spectacular today, I must say. Positively blooming, if I'm allowed to mention that to our listeners!'

'Not a problem!' Ruby laughed. 'Yes, I'm expecting a baby. Eating for two, which is fun. Especially when there are custard doughnuts in the vicinity!'

So the chances were that she was there in person, rather than at home in Cornwall. Edging the car forward as the traffic lights ahead changed to green, Richard wondered if her cheating husband was currently sitting in the apartment they shared in Lanrock, listening while his wife was interviewed about her life and career. If he was, he hoped the man who'd treated her so

312

shabbily appreciated how bloody lucky he was to have been taken back and given a second chance.

'Mmm, custard doughnuts,' exclaimed the presenter. 'Don't blame you one bit! Well, many congratulations to you and your husband from all of us here at—'

'Oh, we're no longer together,' Ruby interrupted. 'We broke up. But it's fine, everything's fine. I live in a fantastic little seaside town, it's a real community, and I have amazing friends around me. I can't tell you how much I'm looking forward to becoming a mum!'

'Well, that's marvellous to hear. And just think, it won't be long before you're reading stories about Wally Bee and Zelda to your own—'

BEEEEEP went the horn of the car behind him, and Richard realised he was holding up the queue. The traffic lights switched back to red and a man yelled 'Dickhead!' before furiously beeping his horn again.

No longer together.

We broke up.

On the radio, Ruby sounded as if she was smiling. 'I know, won't that be magical? I can't wait.'

Chapter 41

Visiting William at his home in Bath might have turned out better than expected, but that had been the easy part.

Now came the far more difficult one. And much as he could have spent weeks or months waiting for exactly the right moment, Terry knew he didn't have time on his side. On Friday evening, when Kay emerged from a long, scented bath in the peacock-blue silk dressing gown she'd bought herself last week, he waited until she'd settled herself comfortably on the sofa with a bowl of cashews and a gin and lime, then announced, 'We need to stop them leaving.'

'Lottie?'

'And Max. That's his name. It wouldn't kill you to use it.'

A muscle began to quiver in Kay's temple. 'There's nothing we can do. Her mind's made up.'

'There is something. And we need to do it.'

Her chest rose and fell as she took a lungful of air. 'I can't.'

'You can. It's the only way.'

'That woman ruined my life. If you see her, how do I know it wouldn't start up over again?'

'It wouldn't. I can promise you that.'

'You can't, though.'

'I can. I've already seen her.' He uttered the bombshell words as calmly as he could manage and braced himself for the explosion.

Kay looked at him. '*You what?*'

'We met up. And there are no feelings there, for either of us. They've gone,' he went on. 'It was only ever a stupid, thoughtless fling. We both wish it had never happened, but it did. And we both know it's never going to happen again.'

If her tumbler had been a wine glass, it would have cracked under pressure by now. He could see her knuckles gleaming as she gripped it. 'Except you lied to me before, so how can you expect me to believe you?'

This was the back-and-forth argument they'd been having, on and off, for the past thirteen years.

'You could ask Imelda.'

'*Tuh.*' Her snort of outrage would have done a dragon proud.

'Or William.' Terry paused. 'I've seen him again as well.'

'Are you *serious*?' Her voice rose.

He shrugged. 'Never more so.'

'When?'

'Last Sunday.'

'You played golf last Sunday.'

'Except I didn't. I drove to Bath.'

'You mean you told me more lies.'

'For a good reason. We're all on the same side. None of us want our children to move to the other side of the world because of us.'

'Weren't you worried he'd hit you?'

'No. I was expecting it to happen. But it didn't.' There was

315

no need to mention the mouse; the rest of the story was far more important. 'We parted on amicable terms. He's a good bloke.'

Kay stared at him for several seconds. Finally she said, 'Well, well. You have been busy. I wonder what else you've been getting up to behind my back?'

'Imelda would like to meet you.' He watched as she rolled the fine blue silk of her dressing gown between finger and thumb. 'She's happy to drive down here tomorrow. You could have lunch together and talk things through.'

'You really think I'd do that?' She shook her head at him in wonderment. 'My God, you must be out of your mind.'

The Tregarron Hotel, on the outskirts of Liskeard, was medium-sized and elegant, with manicured grounds, a discerning clientele and an ambitious chef hell-bent on gaining stars. Having checked it out online, Imelda guessed it had been carefully chosen by Terry because it was the kind of place where even Kay might think twice before causing a ruckus.

Well, that was the hope. It was to be just the two of them meeting for lunch. Terry would be dropping his wife here, then leaving them to it. The suggestion that the four of them could meet up had been firmly vetoed by Kay. Imelda wasn't looking forward to the encounter, but it was something that needed to happen if their end goal had a fighting chance of success.

Having been dropped at the entrance by William, she made her way up the gravelled drive. Was Kay already here, ahead of her? Or would she choose to arrive late in order to make an entrance and gain the upper hand?

But no, there she was, sitting alone in the restaurant at a table for two, wearing a crisp white shirt-dress with a tan silk scarf

316

around her neck and her hair fastened back in a neat French pleat.

Not a machine gun in sight.

The smartly dressed maître d' led Imelda over to the table, and Kay gave a stiff nod of acknowledgement. Imelda sat and straightened the front of her own high-necked pale grey linen frock; she had deliberately dressed down in order not to look like the shameless, low-cut floozy Kay clearly thought she was.

Well, *had* been. Once.

'Thanks for agreeing to do this.' She spoke as soon as the maître d' had handed them their menus and departed.

Kay compressed her lips. 'I'm only here because I love my daughter.'

'I know. And I'm here because I love my son.' Imelda saw how tightly Kay's hands were clasped together, and went on, 'I want you to know how sorry I am. About everything. What we did to you was terrible, and I've never stopped feeling ashamed.'

The tendons in Kay's neck were taut as she glanced around the busy primrose-yellow restaurant, almost but not completely filled with lunchtime diners. Turning her attention back to Imelda, thankfully still keeping her voice low, she said, 'Good.'

The wine waiter materialised at that point and Kay said, 'A bottle of the Cloudy Bay, please,' without asking Imelda if this suited her. *Fine.*

'We don't have to be friends . . .' Imelda began.

'Just as well.'

'. . . but we both want Lottie and Max to stay here in the UK. And to do that, we need to learn to at least be civil towards each other.'

'I'm sure you'd enjoy being civil with my husband.' Kay gave a chilly half-smile. 'More than civil. How do I know you didn't have sex with him when you met up last week?'

'You don't know. But I didn't.'

'Except you would say that, wouldn't you?'

'We talked about how we felt. And I'm sure Terry's already told you that there's zero attraction there. I don't fancy him any more. At all. And he doesn't fancy me.'

'Why not?'

'He's losing his hair. Growing a paunch. I mean, I am too.' Imelda gestured at her stomach. 'It's mutual.'

And now the sommelier arrived with their bottle of wine, followed by a pretty waitress ready to take their food order. A group at another table burst into a round of 'Happy Birthday' as a cake awash with lit candles was carried out of the kitchen. Other diners joined in with the singing and the applause, but Kay barely seemed to be aware of what was going on; she was clutching her glass of Cloudy Bay and glancing across, yet again, at the other side of the room.

Was a grenade about to be lobbed through the window?

'I love my husband,' Imelda tried again, when the singing and applause had died down. 'You might not believe me, but it's true. I'm grateful every day that we're still together.'

Kay looked distractedly at her, then took another gulp of wine.

'And Terry's glad he's still married to you,' Imelda ploughed on.

'After the hard time I've given him over the years? I doubt it. He tolerates me because he still feels guilty. He thinks I don't know that.' Kay shook her head slightly. 'But I do.'

'He still loves you, though. And you obviously love him.'

'Do I?' She lifted the bottle out of the ice bucket and topped up her half-empty glass.

'Of course you do.'

Kay spoke slowly. 'OK, what if I told you I didn't? What if I said you were welcome to him?' She paused, her gaze steady. 'Would you want him?'

Was this some kind of trick? A test? Taken aback, Imelda said, 'No, of course not!'

'Sure about that?'

'Absolutely sure.'

'Right.' Kay's attention wandered off around the room again. Then, focusing back on Imelda, she said, 'Well, shame.'

'What?'

'Because I really wouldn't care if you did.'

It was presumably an attempt to prove something that didn't exist. Patiently Imelda replied, 'I think you would.' Maybe if she sat here long enough and kept on making her point, Kay would start to believe her. Then again, Terry had been trying his best to do that for the last thirteen years.

Kay took a deep breath. 'I'm leaving him.'

Yet another ploy? 'Why?'

'Because it's time. Our marriage is over. It needs to happen. I should have done it years ago.'

Imelda realised that Kay was looking over to her left again, nodding as she uttered the words. Turning her own head, she saw a man sitting alone at a table, reading a newspaper.

'Why didn't you?'

'Why d'you think? I had no confidence. I was too scared. I didn't trust myself to make the right decision. I didn't trust anyone after what happened with you and Terry. Not my friends. Not my husband.'

Imelda swallowed. It was her own fault. Her actions had been the cause of all of this. 'I'm sorry.'

'And we had a teenage daughter to raise,' Kay went on. 'I was a mess, but I wanted to do what was best for her. So I stayed with Terry because I thought better the devil you know. Except after a while I realised I was wrong. It wasn't better. It was still awful.' She glanced sideways once more and Imelda followed suit. The man had put down his newspaper and was now on his phone, tapping away.

The next moment, Kay's phone chimed in her tan leather bag. She bent to retrieve it.

'Who is that man?' said Imelda. 'What's going on?' Please don't let him be a hired assassin.

Kay took out her phone, then held it up so Imelda could see the screen.

The message, from someone with just the initial A, said simply: *Tell her.*

'His name's Alexander.' Kay took a breath, then squared her shoulders. 'And I love him.'

Chapter 42

This was utterly surreal. Imelda turned and watched as the man, tall and angular, rose from his seat and made his way over to them. Evidently having lip-read Kay's words, he said simply, 'And I love her.'

It took no time at all for their waiter to accommodate Alexander at their table. Their food arrived but remained almost entirely untouched. Meanwhile, the tension in Kay's body visibly melted away, leaving her looking ten years younger.

'How long ago did this start?' Imelda still couldn't believe it.

'Our affair? Six years.' Kay's eyes were shining.

'Six years and four months.' Alexander interlaced his fingers with hers on the white tablecloth. In his late fifties at a guess, he was wearing a beautifully cut charcoal-grey suit. His eyes were grey too, the heavy-lidded kind that turned down at the outer corners, and he had high cheekbones, a slightly cleft chin and a warm smile.

'We met in a newsagent's in Polperro,' Kay went on. 'I

wanted to buy a packet of fruit pastilles, then got to the front of the queue and realised I'd left my purse in the car. So I put them back on the shelf and left the shop. Two minutes later, as I was making my way back to the car park, the man who'd been standing behind me in the queue caught up and handed me the sweets. He'd bought them for me,' she added. 'Not shoplifted them.'

'She insisted I went with her to the car park so she could pay me back,' said Alexander. 'But I wouldn't let her.'

'So I offered him a fruit pastille instead. A black one,' Kay chimed in. 'They're the best.'

He nodded. 'It was a warm day. I was thirsty.'

'Or you pretended to be.'

'And you said you could do with a drink too. That's how we ended up in that tiny wine bar on Fore Street. Even though I was a complete stranger.'

'But you'd bought me fruit pastilles. And I'd had a row with Terry the night before. *Another* row,' Kay amended. 'I think I wanted to go home afterwards and tell him I'd been for a drink with an attractive man. See how he liked it.'

'And did you tell him?' Imelda couldn't believe the change in Kay. All the stiffness and stroppiness had melted away. Even her voice sounded different, lighter and more carefree.

'No. Because by the time we'd been chatting for a while, I knew I wanted to see Alexander again. So it became our secret instead. And I didn't even feel guilty; it seemed completely fair, because it was what Terry had done to me.'

'All these years,' Imelda marvelled.

'I know. I used to wonder how long you and Terry would have carried on secretly seeing each other if the hospital thing hadn't happened.'

'Not six years.' Maybe not even one year. They'd never know, though, would they? 'But all that time you carried on giving Terry grief, not trusting him an inch, endlessly accusing him of looking at other women.'

'I was still jealous. And I still didn't trust him.' Kay shrugged. 'I didn't trust Alexander either. Every single day I worried that he was going to get fed up and leave me, because he was a man and that was what men did. I still expected him to break my heart.'

'She did,' Alexander confirmed. 'I must have told her a million times I'd never do that to her. But she couldn't bring herself to believe me.'

'I've never told anyone else about him,' said Kay. 'Not a living soul. You're the first.'

'Well . . . wow.' Imelda sat back; who could have imagined that today's meeting would take such a turn?

'But you won't be the last.' Kay gazed into Alexander's eyes. 'If you're still sure you really want me?'

His fingers squeezed hers and he said simply, 'I've been sure for six years and four months.'

'OK then.' She nodded. 'We'll do it. I'll tell Terry tonight.'

'He's going to get a shock,' said Imelda.

'He'll be relieved. Glad it's all over at last. I think Lottie will, too.'

Her curiosity piqued, Imelda said, 'Do you accuse Alexander of flirting with other women?'

'No. Because he never has.'

'And . . . would you say you've exaggerated your jealousy, used it as a kind of cover, so it would never occur to anyone that you might be getting up to mischief behind your husband's back?'

A glimmer of a smile crossed Kay's face. 'Maybe.'

'From what I've heard,' said Alexander, 'definitely.'

'Terry's never suspected a thing.' She shrugged. 'It's the perfect cover.'

'It really is.' Imelda shook her head; you had to hand it to her. 'Simple but brilliant.'

Kay raised her glass. 'Well worked out, Sherlock.'

The food on their plates had to be cold now, but it still looked delicious. Her appetite returning, Imelda picked up her own glass and said, 'Cheers.'

Max and Lottie left the beach at seven that evening. Having headed down for a swim after work, they'd sat on the sand afterwards, enjoying the sunshine while drying off and eating ice cream. Now, making their way back to Lottie's apartment, Max pointed and said, 'Isn't that Cameron?'

A bottle-green Honda was pulling out of the car park behind the medical centre. For a moment the sun's glare obscured the windscreen, then the car began to turn left and they were able to see the figure wearing dark glasses and skulking down in the passenger seat.

Lottie's heart sank a bit. Was it bad, if you truly loved someone, to be keeping a secret from him? But it really wasn't her secret to share.

'I don't think it's Cameron.'

'It is. That's definitely him. Hey, Cameron!' Max waved to attract his attention. 'Where's he going? What's he up to? Look at that, he's ignoring me. Who's he with? Because that's definitely not Freya.'

Lottie knew who he was with, because Freya had been keeping her updated. Ever since the day of the marathon,

Cameron and Tanya had been in more or less constant contact. Freya was thrilled but taking care to appear not to have noticed. The thing about Cameron was, he was terrible at keeping his own feelings under wraps. All this time they'd been watching him like a hawk for tiny giveaway hints that something might have been developing between him and Naomi. But now that Tanya had reappeared in his life, the hints were about as subtle as a stampede of elephants.

'Maybe it's one of the practice nurses giving him a lift home or something.'

'Trust me, he's trying to hide. That means he's up to no good.' Max was outraged; he glared after the car as it disappeared off up the road. 'My God, what's he playing at?'

'It could be a harmless flirtation.'

'Well, he shouldn't be doing that either. What a dick. What's Freya ever done to deserve this? You should warn her. And I'm definitely going to have a word with Cameron.'

'Look, let's not jump to conclusions. It might be nothing at all. Don't say anything just yet.' The blonde in the driving seat had been Tanya; this was all good news, but she didn't want Max having a go at Cameron and frightening him into ending the fledgling relationship.

'But it's *wrong*.'

Lottie grinned and pulled him towards her. 'Couldn't do something like that yourself, of course.'

'Not any more.' He kissed her. 'Not now I've found you.'

When the doorbell rang an hour later, Lottie guessed it would be the holidaymakers from across the courtyard with a replacement for the bottle of Barolo they'd borrowed late last night after the off-licence had shut.

She wasn't expecting to open the door and come face to face with her mother.

'Mum!' *Oh God, not again.*

'Hi, darling. No need to look so stunned.'

'Have you had another fight with Dad?'

'Not at all. The opposite, in fact. He's just parking the car and dropped me here first because of my shoes.' Kay proudly showed off the four-inch stilettos. 'So beautiful, but they're killing my feet. Are you going to invite me in?'

This time there was no chance to hide him. Lottie said bluntly, 'Max is here.'

'I know. That's why we came.' Peering over Lottie's shoulder, her mother said, 'Hello, Max.'

Lottie turned to look at him. Max shrugged and said, 'Hi, Mrs Palmer.'

'You can call me Kay. Ah, here's Terry now. We're here because we have something we need to discuss with you.'

More emotional blackmail? Lottie stepped aside to let her parents into the flat. Terry and Max greeted each other politely. Wasting no time, Kay came straight to the point. 'Now, what do we need to do to change your minds about emigrating to New Zealand?' There was a light in her eyes that Lottie hadn't seen before.

'All we want is for you two and Max's mum and dad to be able to be in the same room together.'

Kay gazed steadily at her for a long moment. Then, turning on her heel, she crossed the room and pulled the front door open once more. Sticking her thumb and index finger into the corners of her mouth, she executed a multi-decibel, ear-splittingly high-pitched whistle.

Out on the street, a dog barked.

'What are you *doing*?' It was a trick Lottie hadn't heard her use for years.

Kay beckoned her over, then pointed. Seconds later, walking into the courtyard came two people Lottie recognised instantly but couldn't quite believe she was seeing.

Standing behind her, Max said, 'What the hell? Am I on drugs?'

'You'd better not be.' Kay's tone was crisp but she was almost – *almost* – smiling.

Lottie's mouth had fallen open. She looked at her mother. 'How is this happening? Did you arrange it?'

'I did,' said Terry, from the living room.

'You started it off,' Kay corrected him. 'But it wouldn't be happening now if it wasn't for me.'

Oh God. Lottie's heart began to race. 'Are you about to meet them for the first time since . . .?' Because one wrong word and this could turn out to be apocalyptic.

'Darling, don't look so horrified,' said Kay. 'We've spent the afternoon together.'

Lottie gaped at her. 'But . . . but how? I mean, *how?*'

'Brace yourself,' Terry called out from behind them. 'You haven't heard the rest of it yet.'

Twenty minutes later, with the six of them all together in the living room, Lottie and Max had been brought up to date with everything that had been happening behind their backs: the initial meeting of Terry and Imelda, then the risky encounter between Terry and William.

'Rose, our neighbour, was keeping a discreet eye on the

pair of them for me,' Imelda explained proudly. 'She's ninety-two, worked as a spy for MI5 during the Cold War. She's a crack shot, you know.'

'I'm glad I didn't,' Terry said with feeling.

'Anyway, William drove me down here this morning. Terry brought Kay to the hotel so we could meet. And we talked.'

'Sorted everything out.' Kay nodded in agreement.

From his position on the sofa, Terry said drily, 'Everything.'

'We thought if you didn't see it with your own eyes,' Imelda continued, 'you might not believe it.'

'I'm seeing it.' Max shook his head. 'And I still don't believe it.'

'We know we can't stop you, but we don't want you to go. And now we've done what you wanted,' Kay swallowed, 'all we ask is that you do the same for us.'

Lottie hesitated. She turned to Max. He looked at her. For the first time, the room fell silent.

'*Please*,' Kay begged. There were unshed tears in her eyes. It had clearly been a traumatising experience, making her peace with Imelda, but she'd forced herself to go through with it in an attempt to prevent Lottie from moving to the other side of the world.

Feeling guilty, but not *too* guilty, Lottie reached for Max's hand. 'Shall we stay here?'

'Seems only fair,' said Max with a reassuring squeeze of her fingers.

'Oh, thank God!' Kay gave a noisy sob of relief and threw her arms around Lottie, while Imelda launched herself at Max and hugged him as if she would never let him go.

Lottie murmured, 'Thanks, Mum. I know it can't have been easy.'

'Oh, sweetheart. I should have done it years ago.'

Which was a bit of a weird thing to say, but Lottie didn't dwell on it, because now her mother had moved on to Max, cupping his face between her hands and saying, 'Look at you, and haven't you done well for yourself? Your mum's so proud, she's been telling us all about you.'

After hugs all round, wine was opened and toasts made. Lottie, catching Max's eye, thought that one day they might confess to their parents that the plan to move to New Zealand had only ever been a ploy. But not today. Not yet. Let them enjoy their victory, the miraculous success of their own decision to put the past behind them once and for all.

Everyone made mistakes, didn't they? The real trick was making up for them and seeking forgiveness.

'Mum.' Finding Kay again, she said, 'You look so happy.'

'Oh, sweetheart, I *am*. Happier than you could ever know.'

'I think this is going to do you and Dad the world of good.'

'I do too.' Beaming, Kay caught her husband's eye. 'Terry? Time to tell her the rest of the . . . *you know*.'

Come to think of it, her father was also looking rejuvenated, as if a great weight had been lifted from his shoulders. Intrigued, Lottie said, 'What's the rest of the . . . *you know*? Ooh, are you planning to renew your vows?'

'Well,' said Terry, 'not exactly.'

'We're going to get a divorce,' said Kay. 'But don't worry, it's fine, it's what we both want!'

Terry said jovially, 'It's the best thing that could happen. And it'll definitely make us happy.'

Lottie stared at them. They were both laughing now at the stunned expression on her face.

'This is too much to take in.' She'd known of course that

their marriage had been staggering along, had often thought over the years that a divorce would be ideal, but had never imagined it becoming a reality, given the dynamic between them.

'OK. Let me say it. One of us is in love with someone else.' Terry was visibly relieved to be getting it off his chest.

'Dad!' *Oh God, no, not again.*

'And this time it's not him,' her mother said with barely contained glee. 'It's me.'

Chapter 43

Freya was kneeling in the window seat, rearranging the display of kaftans and jewellery, when someone tapped on the glass. In mid tussle with a mannequin – it wasn't easy to get a bikini top onto a plastic person with rigid arms – she looked up and saw Naomi pointing to the door.

Emerging from the back room where she'd been unpacking boxes of just-delivered stock, Freya's mum said, 'Who's that? Oh, it's Naomi from the surgery. I'll let her in, shall I?' She unlocked the door. 'Hello, love! We're closed, but seeing as it's you we'll make an exception. Got your eye on something in particular? Ooh, we've just had some new silk tops in, the blue and yellow one would look lovely on you.'

'Actually, I'm not here to buy anything. I wanted a word with Freya.' Naomi paused, then said, 'If that's OK?'

'Oh sorry, of course! You feel free, plenty to keep me busy . . .' Tess waved her hands apologetically and disappeared, and they heard the distant sound of cardboard boxes being torn up to fit into the recycling bin.

'Sorry,' said Naomi, 'but there's something I need to tell you.'

Freya could guess what it was, but she put on her innocent face and gave an encouraging nod. 'Oh? Fire away.'

'It's about Cameron. Where do you think he is tonight?'

'Well, that's easy, he's visiting one of his rugby friends to help him promote a fundraiser for—'

'Except he isn't,' Naomi blurted out. 'He's seeing *her*. That Tanya woman from Plymouth, she keeps phoning him and making arrangements for them to meet up. Sorry, but you deserve to know what's been going on behind your back.'

Poor Naomi, she wasn't happy; despite her best efforts, her crush on Cameron had never been reciprocated and now another woman had burst into his life. Plus, because Cameron wasn't a practised philanderer, he wasn't great at covering his tracks. What with Lanrock being the close-knit small town it was, Freya was up to date with pretty much everything he'd been getting up to.

It was the *best* news. She couldn't have asked for more. At home, Cameron had even apologetically moved into the spare room, claiming that his irregular working hours were making him restless and disturbing her sleep.

'Well, thanks for letting me know,' said Freya, 'but I'm sure it's completely innocent. Tanya's just an old friend.'

'An old *girlfriend*,' Naomi retorted. 'If you ask me, she's throwing herself at him. And I've listened in a couple of times when she's called the surgery. Let me tell you, she definitely isn't innocent.'

The door to the back room flew open and Tess appeared, red-faced with dismay. 'Oh my God, I can't believe what I'm hearing! How can he *do* this to you?'

'I *know*,' said Naomi.

'Not *you*. How could he do it to my beautiful daughter? Oh sweetheart, this is so unfair, you must be devastated.'

332

'You shouldn't have been eavesdropping,' said Naomi. 'We were having a private conversation.'

'Didn't stop you listening in to Cameron's private phone calls, though, did it?' Tess responded with asperity.

'Well, anyway, I was just trying to be helpful, updating you with what's been going on.' Naomi headed for the door, then turned back to Freya. 'Because your fiancé has been playing around, and I thought you might like to know.'

It was past midnight when Freya heard Cameron's key in the lock. She turned down the volume on the TV, sat back on the sofa and said, 'Hi, you're late.'

'I'm sorry.' If he was surprised to see her still awake, he didn't show it.

'No worries. It's allowed.'

'No, I mean I'm sorry. About everything.' He stood in front of her, rubbing the back of his head so his hair stuck up. 'Frey, I've never wanted to hurt you, but I'm the one who needs to apologise, because I know I'm going to. And I know Naomi came to see you after work, because she texted to tell me.'

'She likes you.' Freya nodded. 'She's jealous.'

His eyebrows shot up. 'Is she? Does she? Are you *sure*?'

She smiled at his reaction. 'For an observant man, you have an amazing ability to miss some things. She's fancied the pants off you since day one.'

'God, I had no idea.'

'I know you didn't.'

'I thought she was just . . . friendly. And keen on running.'

'She was mainly keen on being friendly and running with you.'

'Wow. Literally didn't realise.'

'Might make it awkward at work.'

He shook his head. 'She sent me another text, said she's going to start looking for another job. I did wonder why, but I guess that explains it.' He stopped and thought for a moment, ruffling his hair with both hands now. 'As for the rest of it . . . God, Frey, I'm just so sorry. The things she told you about Tan . . . it's all true. And I feel terrible about it.'

He looked so sad and plagued with guilt, Freya's heart went out to him. 'I know you do. It's OK.'

'You can't say that. It isn't OK. You've done nothing wrong, nothing to deserve it, and I've never wanted to be the kind of person who'd do something like this to someone they care about. But these things hit you like a bolt from the blue, and that's what happened to me when I saw Tanya again. It was like, *wham*.' He pressed a clenched fist against his chest.

'I know,' said Freya. 'I was there. I saw it happen.'

'And it wasn't just me. It was the same for her. She rang the practice the next day, left her number and asked me to call her back because she needed to speak to me urgently about a patient. Except *I* was the patient. And the urgency was that she had to see me.' Cameron couldn't help himself; his eyes were shining at the memory. 'I knew it was wrong because I knew what was going to happen, but I just couldn't help myself. We've been talking, and texting, every moment we can. We've met up almost every day since then. And I'm so sorry, but Tan's the one I want to be with. I *need* to be with her. And she needs to be with me.'

'It's OK,' said Freya, because his whole body was radiating tension and anguish.

'You keep saying it, but you must be devastated. I can't believe you're taking this so well. You aren't even *crying*.'

Could she cry on tap? No, it was no good, it wasn't going

to happen. 'I did earlier,' she fibbed. 'Loads. Got it out of my system.'

Cameron looked relieved. 'Well, that's good. I mean, you're bound to be upset, but it's probably for the best if we call it a mutual decision. What with me having a public profile, we don't want my charity work to be adversely affected, do we?'

'Definitely not.' She hid a smile; heaven forbid that his saintly reputation should suffer.

'And I'd be grateful if you'd mention that to your mum, too. I gather she was upset when she heard what Naomi had to say.'

'She was.'

'If she could be discreet, that'd be good.' He cleared his throat. 'After all, you could say she owes me a favour.'

I gave her one of my kidneys, he meant. *So don't go bad-mouthing me to the whole of Lanrock.*

Which, really, was fair enough.

'I'll remind her. She was upset earlier, but I'll calm her down. I'm sure she'll understand.' Having spent the evening thinking she would confess to Cameron that her own feelings towards him had changed months ago, Freya was now revising that decision. What would be the point? He would only be offended rather than relieved.

'Well, thanks. Are you sure you're going to be all right?'

I'm going to be ecstatic.

She didn't say this, just thought it, and smiled at him in a mildly heartbroken way. 'I'll be fine. Just as well we didn't get married, eh?'

'That's what Tan said tonight.' He winced, clearly realising it wasn't the most diplomatic thing to say. 'Look, where will you go? You don't have to move out straight away, of course. It's just, you know . . .'

'I'll move out tomorrow. Mum'll be glad to have me back for a few weeks. Then I'll find a place to rent once the summer season's over.'

'You're a great girl, a real catch. You'll find someone else in no time.'

'I don't want anyone else.' No, that sounded wrong. 'I don't want anyone *at all*. Plus,' she went on, 'I know I'm great. I *am* a catch. I'm just going to enjoy being single for a while until I decide I want to be caught.'

He looked at her with a mixture of admiration, affection and relief.

'Whoever you end up with, they'll be the lucky one. And I hope we'll always be friends.'

'I don't see why not. As long as we're both living in Lanrock, we're going to be bumping into each other.'

'You're amazing. Come here.' He held out his arms and Freya rose from the sofa so they could share an it's-over hug. There was no need for him to know that, for her, their relationship had been over for months.

The hug tightened and he murmured into her ear, 'If you like, we could spend one last night together. You know,' he offered, 'to give you some closure.'

Freya almost laughed out loud. The absolute nerve of the man she'd once loved. But that was Cameron all over, reframing the situation to his own advantage, so he came out as the unselfish hero doing her a favour.

'Thanks, but no thanks. I have all the closure I need.'

'Sure?' She knew from the way his mouth quirked down at one corner that he was disappointed, had been keen on the idea, after a fairly prolonged drought, of one last hurrah.

'Quite sure.'

'Well then, that's fine.' He thought for a moment, then said, 'I tell you what we could do, though. Have a chat with the editor of the local paper, offer to do a piece about how to go through a successful break-up. I could contact the radio station too. And you never know, it might be picked up nationally. Look what happened when Max and Lottie were seen on that video with the dolphins, and they weren't even trying to get publicity. People would want to hear how we've managed an amicable split, wouldn't they? They'd love to know how we'd done it, and it'd be great publicity for my next fundraiser. After all, I gave your mum my kidney . . . everyone's going to be so fascinated to hear about that, aren't they?'

'Well, I think you've mentioned it once or twice before,' Freya said innocently. 'So anyone who lives in Cornwall probably already knows about that.'

Chapter 44

Now that word was out, Ruby was discovering that being pregnant was a bit like being a celebrity. Everywhere she went, people stopped to congratulate her, admire her now-visible bump, tell her their thoughts on whether it was going to be a boy or a girl, and chat about how it felt to be pregnant.

And it didn't stop there; they would then go on to regale her with graphic tales of their own experiences, ranging from a craving for honey and broccoli soup, to overwhelming morning sickness, followed by hideous giving-birth details and the horrors of babies who never slept, babies who threw up fifty times a day and babies who screamed non-stop. These stories, told with enthusiasm, always ended up with the women saying, 'Wouldn't be without them, though,' in order to make up for the nightmare scenarios they'd spent the last ten minutes describing with such relish.

The upside of being pregnant, however, was the fact that all the hormones swooshing around her body meant she no longer cared a jot about the ongoing writer's block. Coming up with ideas and producing a new book seemed so much less important than growing an actual human inside her. It was the last week of August, it was hot, she was free to do whatever she liked, and currently what she liked to do most of all was sit beneath a sunshade on her favourite section of East Beach with a cool box holding raspberry ice lollies and bottles of fruit juice at her side. Sunglasses on, a favourite novel on her lap, plenty of suncream to hand and the freedom to take a nap whenever she wanted . . . who could ask for more?

It was one such blissful doze that was interrupted by a nearby group of teenage girls squealing in mock horror when a golden retriever came racing up the beach and shook itself vigorously, showering them with seawater. The dog, giving them a naughty look, then went hurtling back down to the shoreline before plunging joyously back into the breaking waves.

Smiling to herself, Ruby sat up a bit as the retriever emerged once more, gave another whole-body shake, then grabbed the corner of a turquoise beach towel and attempted to tug it along despite there being a small child on it. Laughing, the child called out, 'Wally, *nooo!*'

Wagging his tail, Wally carried on dragging the towel and gave a triumphant bark when the child tipped over.

It was the name that kept Ruby watching. Over the years, many young readers who loved her books had chosen to call their pets Wally. There'd even been a grass snake once, who'd been brought along to one of her signing sessions in Birmingham and had slithered out of its owner's grasp, prompting mass panic amongst the parents in the queue and shrieks of delight amongst the kids.

The next moment, on the beach, a female voice rose above the rest, shouting, 'No, Wally, let *go,*' and Ruby's skin tingled in recognition. Sitting bolt upright on her sunlounger and letting her book slide onto the sand, she shielded her eyes from the bright sun and peered at the woman who was attempting to bring Wally under control.

Without much success, it had to be said.

But yes, it was her, it was Richard's ex, Mel, wearing a black and white striped bikini and a white baseball cap. And the small child on the turquoise towel, Ruby belatedly realised, was Flo. Scanning the area around them, now giving it her full attention, she saw Sasha a couple of metres away, engrossed in building a sandcastle. But that was all. No Dara. Nor any sign of Richard either.

Her heart, having soared with hope, sank with disappointment. Then again, just because they weren't all together on the beach didn't necessarily mean they weren't here at all. But was this her hormones being ridiculous, teasing her into getting her hopes up that she might be about to see Richard again? After all, nothing else had changed. She'd made her decision weeks ago and needed to stick to that. Richard's situation was complicated enough without her adding to it.

She couldn't help covertly watching them for a while, however, until the heat and pregnancy exhaustion swept back over her and she drifted off once more.

She dreamt that a giant water snake was swimming alongside her in the sea, speaking in a high-pitched voice and telling her that life would be so much easier if only everyone could walk around wearing their name, age and personal circumstances on a badge. 'Then we'd all know everything we needed to know about the people we meet,' it explained, 'and there wouldn't be any secrets.'

Ruby, treading water as the snake writhed around her, replied, 'That's a terrible idea. What if you don't want other people knowing all about you?'

'Fine, suit yourself, it was just an idea.' The snake didn't have shoulders but appeared to be shrugging. Then, clearly offended by her lack of enthusiasm, it swam off.

'Ruby?'

That wasn't in the dream. Someone was addressing her. Ruby opened her eyes with a start and saw Mel standing over her, casting a shadow across the sunlounger.

'Oh, hi! Wow, you're back!'

'We are. Couldn't resist it.' Mel grinned. 'What was the terrible idea?'

'Sorry, was I talking in my sleep? I can't even remember.' The dream had already slithered away, out of reach. Ruby hauled herself into a sitting position and became aware of Mel's gaze falling on her tanned, rounded stomach.

'Well, anyway, congratulations on the baby! Richard heard you being interviewed on the radio. Such lovely news.'

'Thank you.' Ruby instinctively rested a hand on her bump. 'I can't wait.'

'We called at your apartment earlier, to see if you were at home. But you weren't,' Mel said with a shrug. 'We only arrived a couple of hours ago, though, so you were probably already down here on the beach.'

'Where are you staying?'

'It was a last-minute idea, coming back to Lanrock, so there wasn't much to choose from. Lottie managed to find us a cottage right at the top of Wood Lane. The thought of staying anywhere else in Cornwall just didn't appeal. This is our new favourite place to be.'

'And . . . where's everyone else?' Gosh, it was hard not to look in the direction of the girls, the dog and the turquoise beach towel. The perils of having to pretend you hadn't already spotted someone.

'Oh, we're down there.' Mel pointed, and Ruby feigned surprise at seeing Sasha and Flo for the first time. 'We bumped into a family we became friendly with last time. They're keeping an eye on the girls while I came over to say hello.'

Ruby nodded brightly. She couldn't ask about Richard. 'And is Dara down here with you?'

Gulls were swooping noisily overhead. Mel glanced up at them, then said, 'No, Dara's not with us. Actually, we broke up.'

'*What?*' This time the surprise was genuine. 'But you two seemed so happy together. God, I'm sorry.'

'No need. It was my decision. May I?' Mel indicated the sunlounger and Ruby nodded, shifting her legs to one side to give her room to sit down.

'What happened?'

'Oh, it was the baby thing. It was Dara's idea from the start. She wanted us to have a child that was ours, but she wasn't interested in being the one to give birth. And she kept trying to make Richard agree to it, but he wasn't that happy about the idea either. The more she pressured him to change his mind, the more I started to wonder if it was really the right thing to do.' Mel pulled a face. 'Dara's a wonderful person in so many ways, but she can be a bit . . . overbearing sometimes. She likes to be in control. I realised I was in danger of going along with what she wanted for all the wrong reasons, and it could turn out to be a massive mistake. So we talked about it, a *lot*. And then we broke up.'

'Wow. And how did the girls take it?'

Mel smiled, her eyes sparkling. 'They were fine. More than fine. They'd kind of noticed that Dara could be bossy. I mean, they didn't secretly hate her or anything, but they still have me, and they still have their dad. And that's enough for them.'

Thud-thud-thud went Ruby's heart. And not in a good way. 'So . . . are you and Richard back together, then?'

Mel burst out laughing. 'Nooo! I'm still a lesbian, so that's never going to happen. But we'll always be co-parents and we're never going to stop being friends. I'm sure Sasha and Flo would have been happy to have another brother or sister, but it was never really what I wanted. And it would have been weird for Richard too, being the sperm donor.' She flicked back her hair, then said playfully, 'So we got ourselves something else instead, something that Dara definitely didn't want.'

'Oh?' God, this acting malarkey was hard work. Ruby didn't know what to do with her eyebrows.

'The newest member of the family is . . .' Mel did a pretend drum-roll, 'a golden retriever!'

'Seriously? That's amazing!'

'He was a rescue, ended up in the dogs' home after his owner died. And his name was Colin but the girls weren't so keen on that, so we changed it to Wally. We all love him to bits. He's over there with them now, if you'd like to come and meet him?'

'I *adore* dogs.' Ruby jumped to her feet. 'Try and stop me.'

Mel's daughters were flatteringly pleased to see her, or maybe happy to be able to show off the newest member of their family. Wally, friendly and delighted to meet anyone at all, woofed and rested his front paws on Ruby's knees before attempting to scramble onto her lap.

'Not much room, I'm afraid.' She ruffled the dog's silky ears and admired his soulful amber eyes. 'You are gorgeous. And what a great name.'

'It's because of the Wally in your book,' Sasha said proudly.

'That's such a lovely compliment,' Ruby told her. 'I'm honoured.'

'Why are you fat?' said Flo.

'Ruby's not fat. She's having a baby,' Mel exclaimed. 'We told you, remember? Daddy heard about it on the radio. So exciting!'

'How do babies get out?' Flo was frowning.

Mel laughed and exchanged a look with Ruby. 'With difficulty.'

Wally licked Ruby's hand and she stroked his head. 'So are you all glad you got him?'

The girls nodded vigorously. 'Dara doesn't live with us any more. So we have Wally now instead,' Sasha explained. 'He's really cuddly. We take him to the park every day.'

'Does Daddy like him too?'

Sasha laughed. 'Oh yes. Even when Wally ate his shoe.'

Mel had wandered over to chat with the friends who'd been keeping an eye on the children. Ruby lowered her voice. 'And is Daddy down here with you?'

'No.' This time Sasha shook her head. 'He's at home. With Christina. She's got a dog too, a black one called Mabel. She's nice.'

'Right.' Not what Ruby wanted to hear. 'So is it Christina who's nice? Or Mabel?' This was how low she'd sunk; reduced to interrogating small children.

'They're both nice!'

'And who's Christina? Is she Daddy's . . . special friend?'

More nodding. 'She lives next door. And she gives us chocolate in secret, when Daddy says we've had enough.'

Bribery. That was a cheap trick. Ruby pictured the next-door neighbour in her mind, blonde and bouncy like a weather girl on morning TV, with an everlasting smile, a chirpy manner, and buttons on her dress that had a habit of accidentally popping open.

'You know when the baby's born?' Flo was tugging at Ruby's arm for attention, clearly intent on getting a proper answer. 'Is it like being sick? Does it come out of your mouth?'

'Oh God, I lost track of time!' Mel rushed over to them. 'We have to get back to the cottage – I ordered a food delivery and if it's left out in the sun the cold stuff will go off. Ruby, it's lovely to see you. We must meet up again, I'll be in touch. Sasha, can you pick up the towel? Flo, what have you done with your shoes? And where's Wally's lead? Honestly, two girls and one dog,' she exclaimed, 'you'd think it'd be easy, wouldn't you? You have all this fun to look forward to!'

Chapter 45

Ruby had been hoping to see Mel and the girls again, and they undoubtedly would have bumped into each other on the beach if only the weather hadn't taken a dramatic turn for the worse the next day and the day after that. Grey clouds rolled in, and every time the more intrepid holidaymakers dared to venture down onto the sand, the wind would whip back up and a face-stinging downpour would sweep in from the sea, reminding them who was boss.

Having spent the last forty-eight hours in her apartment imagining what Richard and his pneumatic neighbour Christina might be getting up to in Henley-on-Thames, Ruby had been forced to go online and buy stupid things she didn't need in order to try and cheer herself up. So far today she'd had three items delivered: a length of stained-glass bunting in shades of red and gold to hang in her front window, a deep purple mascara, and a new set of sable watercolour brushes to encourage her to start painting again rather than just endlessly doodling half-ideas in pencil that never came to anything.

Tak-a-tak-a-tak came a fresh flurry of rain, clattering against the living room window like shrapnel as the next downpour announced its arrival. Outside, the pale grey sea blended so completely with the sky that the horizon wasn't even visible. Only one person was out there, wrapped up in a sou'wester and wellies and carrying a fishing rod over one shoulder. Ruby wondered when her next drinks delivery would arrive, because it was now four in the afternoon and the promised delivery slot was two forty-five to four fifteen. Her mouth watered at the prospect of uncapping a bottle of the fizzy blackcurrant that was her new favourite.

Then a message popped up on her laptop and her heart did a tiny skip, because despite everything, each time it happened she still hoped it might be Richard.

But of course it wasn't. It was an automated missive from the delivery company announcing that the revised estimated time of delivery for her order was now between seven o'clock and eight thirty.

Tears of frustration swam in Ruby's eyes. And yes, she'd read up enough on the subject to know that they were only hormonal tears due to pregnancy. She also knew it wasn't actually a serious problem. But dammit, right now it *felt* serious. Her body was craving fruit juice, she'd finished the last bottle this morning, and it was raining and miserable outside. The *bastard* driver had probably delayed the delivery on purpose out of sheer spite. How was she supposed to wait until eight thirty, and why was it all so *unfair*?

Well, fuck it and fuck *everyone*, she wasn't going to let the bastard driver win, nor was she going to cry. Tipping her head back and gazing up at the ceiling until the tears slid back into her eye sockets, she snatched up her raincoat and stuffed her feet into orange clogs. Rain or no rain, she would go out and

347

buy her own bottles of fruit juice from the deli over on Angel Street, even if they hardly ever stocked the kind she liked.

Who knows, maybe the walk across town would cheer her up.

Ha, said her hormones. *Don't bet on it.*

And they were right. Forty minutes later, Ruby returned home in the middle of the most ferocious summer storm yet. The hood of her stupid coat kept blowing down. What was more, the material was thin and laughably porous, and rain had seeped through to her cotton dress, causing it to cling clammily to her body. Nor did the problems end there, oh no. The orange clogs she'd bought last week were now rubbing painfully against her toes and the tops of her feet, and her hair was both tangled and windswept. Plus, the deli hadn't had any of the drinks she liked in stock, which meant she'd been forced to buy four bottles of lemon and ginger, which was her least favourite and hardly even counted as a fruit.

To cap it all, when she limped around the bend in the road, what did she see through the driving rain as it blasted almost horizontally into her face? Yes, there he was, parked up outside the entrance to her flat, the young driver who delivered her regular order of drinks, lifting the crate out of the back of his van.

She stopped dead. For a split second it occurred to her that if this was a rom-com on Netflix, and if she didn't happen to be pregnant, losing her temper with the driver could be the start of a meet-cute. Then again, that would only be deemed feasible if he was more her age and less scrawny, instead of twenty years younger with limbs like pipe cleaners.

The unfairness of it all meant she was going to yell at him anyway.

Spotting her, he said, 'Oh hey, great timing, I just—'

'No,' Ruby's voice rose, 'it *isn't* great timing, because you sent me a message saying you'd be here this evening, and if I'd known you were turning up now I wouldn't have needed to go out in this weather to buy my own drinks and I wouldn't have got soaked to the *skin.*'

He looked startled as she closed the distance between them. 'S-sorry, I thought I'd be doing you a favour, bringing them early.'

'But you didn't *tell* me!'

'Because I didn't have any phone signal—'

'And now I've bought the lemon ones and I don't even *like* the lemon ones!' She knew she was being unfair to the boy, but there was no way he could understand how she was feeling. Devastated didn't even begin to describe it. A fresh gust of wind blew her hair right across her face, which felt like the last straw, and he couldn't understand how horrible that felt either, because his own head was shaved.

Meanwhile, he was gazing at her in dismay. 'Look, I'm sorry . . .'

God, the poor boy, she'd frightened the living daylights out of him. What must he think of her? Her eyes burning with shame, she wailed, 'Don't make me cry. I'm sorry *toooo.*'

He looked even more terrified. 'Are you OK?'

She wiped the backs of her hands across her face and howled, '*Nooooo.*'

'Hey, what's happening?' A voice came from behind her. 'What's going on?'

'I don't know.' The boy, clearly panicking, clutched the rain-spattered crate of drinks. 'I didn't do anything, I promise. I was just trying to help.'

'Tell me what he said to upset you.' A hand landed on Ruby's shoulder, and for a split second she wondered if she was about to be placed under arrest. How much peace did you have to breach before that could happen?

Then she turned round, came face to face with Richard and let out a hiccupy bellow of mortification.

'Just tell me,' said Richard.

'He didn't say anything, d–didn't do anything wrong. It's me . . . I couldn't wait any more for my drinks and then I bought the wrong ones b–because they didn't have the ones I l–liked. It's all my fault, not his!'

'I swear I don't know why she's like this,' said the boy. 'She's usually normal.'

'I just really wanted the b–blackcurrant ones.' Ruby caught her breath between sobs.

'And I don't know why her face is like that either,' the boy went on fearfully. 'I haven't touched her.'

'H–he *hasn't* touched me . . . he was just trying to be k–kind.' Appalled that Richard might think otherwise, she blurted out, 'He's a lovely lad. I always give him five s–stars.'

'OK, I think I know what's going on here. It's a pregnancy thing,' said Richard.

Horrified, the boy took a step back and yelped, 'No, no, that's definitely nothing to do with me!'

'I mean it's her hormones. Nothing for you to worry about.' Richard reached for the crate. 'Why don't I take that? I'll stay with her until she calms down, make sure she's OK.'

The look on the boy's face signalled that he was thinking, *Rather you than me.*

Inside the apartment, Richard carried the clanking crate of bottles through to the kitchen, then expertly flipped the lid off one of the blackcurrant ones and handed it to her. Thirsty from her walk home, Ruby glugged down over half of the blissful, summery, sweet-and-sharp juice.

It was like ingesting the most magical drug in the world.

Finally, thirst slaked and tears subsided, she clutched the bottle to her chest and gazed at Richard, who was leaning against the fridge, watching her with an enigmatic expression on his face.

'Sorry about that.' He probably thought she was deranged, and who could blame him?

The faintest of smiles lifted the corners of his mouth. 'No need to apologise.'

'I'm not really a horrible person.'

'I know that.'

'I don't usually shout at people. I don't know what came over me.'

'Like I told the boy out there, you're pregnant. It goes with the territory.'

Now that she was calming down, Ruby accepted he was right. She took another swig of juice. 'But how did you know?'

Now he really was smiling. 'Been there, done that, got the kids to prove it. When Mel was pregnant with Sasha, anything could cause her to have a meltdown. She used to burst into tears if she couldn't reach down to unzip her ankle boots. Or if there were too many cornflakes in the bowl. One time, the paper boy delivered a magazine with a creased front page, and Mel walked two miles to the newsagent's to take it back to them, sobbing all the way.'

'Really?' It was *so* comforting to hear.

He nodded. 'And you should have seen the state she got herself into when she accidentally stepped on a snail.'

'This is making me feel so much better.' She'd wept last week when a panicking wasp had struggled to find its way out through the kitchen window, despite her best efforts to help. Even now, just thinking about it was making her well up again. God, hormones were weird.

Richard tore off a sheet of kitchen towel and passed it to her. 'You can cry as much as you want. I really don't mind.'

'I suppose you're used to it. Remember the café in St Ives?' She managed a wry smile. 'The first time you came to my rescue.'

'How could I forget?' He nodded at her bump. 'Congratulations, by the way.'

Ruby wondered how he would react if she blurted out the truth. But no, she couldn't. Flustered, she said, 'Thanks. And how are the girls? Are they both OK?'

'They're fine. You saw them a couple of days ago,' he reminded her. As if she could have forgotten.

'I know. I just wondered why you were suddenly here. Sasha said you weren't with them, that you were staying at home in Henley with . . . well, someone else.'

'I was at home,' he agreed. 'I had a meeting I couldn't get out of. But I drove down this morning and now I'm here for the rest of the week.'

Ruby's brain was brimming with possibilities, all of them hopelessly far-fetched, but she couldn't stop thinking them. 'Right. Well, that's nice. For the girls, I mean.'

'Out of interest,' said Richard, 'who's the someone else Sasha told you I was staying at home with?'

'Um . . . your neighbour? Is her name Christina?' Here it came, the crushing moment he revealed the story of how a stunning young woman had moved in next door, dazzling him with her beauty and vivacious personality and bringing love and meaning back into his life.

352

He was nodding. 'OK, yes. She's an amazing person.'

'Sasha told me you had lots of fun together, that Christina's a special friend.'

'We do. And she is.' After a moment, Richard said, 'She's eighty-seven and has dementia. Her husband looks after her, but neither of them is up to gardening any more, so I help out when I can. Christina tells me off when my pruning skills aren't up to scratch. And she used to be an opera singer, so I get to hear her belting out *La Traviata* and *Rigoletto* . . . Do you want another fruit juice?' He changed the subject, noticing that her eyes were filling up once more.

'No, thanks. She sounds wonderful.' Another thought struck her. 'Were you just passing by when you saw me shouting at the delivery boy?'

He shook his head. 'I was coming to see you. For two reasons.'

'Oh?'

'Mel sent me over to find out if you'd like to join us for dinner this evening.'

Yes yes yes yes yes.

'Sounds great. I'd love that.'

'Good.'

'And . . . the other reason?'

'Just so you know . . .' Another hesitation, then he raked his fingers through his hair and said apologetically, 'I told her about us.'

She blinked. 'You told her *what* about us?'

'You and me. Spending that night together.'

It felt as if tiny frogs were leaping around inside her ribcage. She took an unsteady breath. 'Why?'

'I didn't mean to. I just said we'd met before, gave her the Disney version.' He pushed his hands deep into his jacket pockets. 'Then I told her I hadn't been able to stop thinking about you.'

'Oh.'

'I said I'd had feelings about you. Like, serious feelings. But that you and your husband were having a baby and you'd got back together.'

Serious feelings? Serious feelings . . .

'We didn't get back together.'

'I overheard your editor telling her assistant you had.'

Ruby shook her head. 'In London? Morwenna got that wrong. Me and Peter . . . no, it was never going to happen. God, no way.'

'OK, I know that now, but I didn't back then. And when I left my business card for you, I lived in hope that you'd get in touch. But you didn't.'

'I didn't get your business card,' she told him, and saw his eyebrows lift in response. Had that been thanks to Morwenna too? Presumably she'd thought she was doing her a favour, protecting her from the attentions of a fan with possible stalker tendencies.

Richard said, 'Anyway, I mentioned last week that we could maybe squeeze in another break down here, and Mel was all for it. Then at lunchtime today I told her how I really felt about you.'

Ruby's mouth was dry. 'And?'

'I said I thought I loved you. Look, if you don't want to hear any more of this, feel free to tell me to stop. If I'm on the wrong track, just say so.'

Her body was fizzing all over, like sherbet tipped into lemonade. 'Keep going.'

'And Mel said you should never tell someone you love them

until after you've slept with them, in case the sex turns out to be terrible, a complete turn-off, and you never want it to happen again.'

'She has a point.' By now Ruby was on the verge of hyper-ventilating.

'So I told her we'd already done that, and it hadn't been terrible.' His gaze softened. 'Quite the opposite, in fact.'

Which was flattering to hear. 'And what did Mel say?'

'She screamed. Almost burst my eardrums. Then she said, "Holy fuck," which was fun, because I've never heard her say that before. Are you crying again?'

'Well,' said Ruby, 'it's always nice to get a compliment.'

'OK, so in a long-winded way, that's why I came here to see you this afternoon.' Levering himself away from the fridge, he removed his hands from his pockets and reached for hers. 'I might be the only person feeling this way, but I have to take a chance and say it anyway. I like you. A lot. In fact I'm pretty sure I do love you. Ever since that night, I haven't been able to stop thinking about you. And I know the last few months have been pretty difficult as far as you're concerned, but I just want to say, the fact that you're pregnant makes no difference to me.' He paused to take a breath. 'I want to spend more time with you. A lot more time. And if things work out the way I hope they will, it won't matter one bit to me that this baby isn't biologically mine. I'll love it just as much as if it was.' He touched her face, then gazed deeply into her eyes. 'And I promise you, I'm a good dad. Well, apart from when I'm trying to persuade them to put away their toys. Then according to my daughters I'm really mean and unfair.'

A single tear slid down Ruby's cheek and he rubbed it away with his thumb. Then she reached up and kissed him, her heart

355

overflowing with joy as he returned the kiss, his arms folding around her, his flat stomach meeting her distinctly rounded one. The last time they'd done this, it had happened because she'd been set on revenge, getting her own back on her unfaithful husband.

This time, it was because there was no one else on the planet she'd rather be with.

Finally they drew apart. As she gazed up at him, Ruby's expression turned to one of confusion, because one cheek and one side of his jaw now looked as if he'd gone ten rounds with Tyson Fury. 'Oh my God, what's happened to your face?'

He'd better not be allergic to her.

'It's nothing.' He broke into a grin. 'I should probably have told you before, but I didn't want to interrupt the flow.'

In the bathroom, staring at her reflection in the mirror, Ruby belatedly discovered what she looked like, her entire face a streaked and smudgy mess of aubergine from the deep purple mascara she'd tried on following its arrival this morning, which had claimed to be completely waterproof but was clearly nothing of the sort.

As she scrubbed away with cleanser and a flannel, Richard came and stood behind her, his arms clasped around her waist.

Ruby said, 'I can't believe you said all those lovely things to me while I was looking like this.' No wonder the delivery boy had been so horrified by the sight of her.

'I didn't want you to be embarrassed. I just needed to let you know how I felt about you.' He gave her hips a squeeze. 'It'd take more than a bit of purple make-up to put me off.'

Once she'd finished, she spun round and used a clean flannel to clear up his own aubergine smudges. Richard kissed her again. 'Mel's all in favour of this, by the way. She likes you a lot and really hopes it works out for us.'

Ruby tilted her head back to look at him. 'You know you said you'd love my baby as if it were your own?'

He nodded. 'I do remember. And I mean it. I will.'

'You're amazing.' Incredibly, this time her eyes didn't brim with tears. What had she done to deserve him?

His tone was playful. 'Not so bad yourself.'

'You know something else? The night I met you, I hadn't slept with Peter for months. *Many* months.'

As he took in what she was telling him, she breathed in the delicious outdoors smell of his skin.

Realisation slowly dawned. 'You mean . . .?'

'This baby's nothing to do with him.' She reached for his hand and placed it on her stomach. 'I promise, it's all yours.'

Chapter 46

New Year's Eve

'It's not too late to change your mind, you know. If you're having second thoughts, we can always sneak you out the back way.'

Max grinned at Paolo, his best man and oldest friend, down from London for the wedding. Over the years they'd done more than their fair share of carousing, havoc-making and heart-breaking. Paolo, the darkly handsome son of an Italian footballing legend and a world-renowned Brazilian actress, had yet to meet his own perfect match. 'I'm not going to change my mind,' Max said genially. 'This is it.'

Paolo's jet-black eyes flashed with mischief. 'Shall I keep the helicopter on standby, just in case?'

'I'm going to marry Lottie,' said Max. 'And nothing's going to stop me.'

They were in the top floor suite of the Rupert Hotel, over-looking West Beach. Back in May, he'd booked into this same hotel at the very last minute, unaware then that he was hours away from Lottie bursting back into his life. Later that evening, after the eventful wedding-that-never-was, they'd swum together in the sea and it had felt to him that this was the start of something properly momentous and life-changing.

And he'd been right, although it hadn't been plain sailing, starting from the moment Lottie had walked out of the hotel, putting the kibosh on his assumption that they'd be spending the night together in his room.

Which had served him right, of course, and taught him from that moment to never, ever take her for granted.

'God, you're a lucky bastard.' Paolo surveyed him with envy. 'You found her again. Imagine if you hadn't.'

'I know.' Max nodded; over the years, he'd bored his friend senseless talking about the one who'd got away. If he'd stayed on in New Zealand for a few extra days of sightseeing, it wouldn't have happened. It didn't bear thinking about.

'If you hadn't asked me to be your best man,' said Paolo, 'I'd be in Edinburgh now with Dex and the boys. What if my future wife's up there, getting ready to go out, and I'm supposed to be meeting her for the first time tonight? But I'm here instead, so I never will. Dammit, it's your fault, you've ruined my life.'

'Hello? It's New Year's Eve,' Max reminded him. 'If you were up in Edinburgh with Dex and the boys, you'd be drinking for twelve hours straight and waking up tomorrow with no memory of whoever you might have met. But if you really want to go, feel free. Your helicopter awaits.'

Paolo laughed. 'Mate, I wouldn't miss this for the world. You, properly in love and getting married. Hello . . .' His voice tailed off as he looked past Max, his attention caught by someone outside, hurrying across the hotel's frost-covered terrace.

'Who is it?' Turning his head, Max tried to see who was down there, but the terrace was empty.

'A beautiful woman.' Paolo slapped him on the back and reached for the bottle of Perrier-Jouët in the ice bucket. 'She's gone now . . .'

'Oh my goodness, look at you.' Kay clutched her hands to her chest and gasped as she came into the second-floor suite and saw Lottie for the first time, dressed and ready to leave the hotel.

'Will I do?' Lottie did a quick spin, the hem of the bias-cut velvet dress swirling around her. She was wearing her hair wavy and loose, and stray tendrils flew around her face and neck as she twirled.

'You look stunning. Wait till everyone sees you.'

Lottie hugged her mother, who had been a changed woman since August. Gone were the arguments, the accusations and the outbursts. Ironically, since leaving him, she and Terry were now getting along better than they had in years. Meanwhile, Alexander suited her in every way, while Terry was just glad to be living a guilt-free existence at last. Although, having embraced singledom with enthusiasm and learned to cook rather well, his popularity among the female members of the golf club meant he might not be alone for too long.

'And the necklace is perfect too,' Kay said as she straightened it, the slender platinum chain studded with tiny diamonds glittering beneath the lights of the hotel suite's central chandelier. It had been handed down to Kay by her own mother, and she had now passed it on to Lottie. 'You're a beautiful girl. And Max is a lucky boy.'

'He is.' Lottie gave her a loving kiss on the cheek. 'I'm lucky too.'

'And so are we, to have you both living here instead of on the other side of the world.'

They still hadn't told either set of parents the truth.

Lottie breathed in the scent of L'Air du Temps, the perfume her mother had taken to wearing. 'It's no hardship to stay in Cornwall. Where's Alexander?'

'Downstairs, chatting to Terry about cars . . . or golf . . . or maybe astronomy.'

They exchanged a smile; the deepening friendship between the two men had taken them all by surprise, as had the relationship between Kay and Imelda, who had even gone shopping together in Bath for their wedding outfits – although Kay had later confided with a touch of *Schadenfreude* that her own dress was far more chic and elegant than the one Imelda had ended up choosing. 'Of course I wouldn't say anything, but hers does make her look a bit . . . dumpy.'

Lottie's phone pinged with a text from Freya:

We're heading up to the church in five minutes. Don't keep us waiting too long – we want a wedding that's drama-free!

No couple choosing to marry on New Year's Eve expects the weather to be great, but Max and Lottie had lucked out today. Making her way on foot up the hill to the church, Iris paused at the entrance to the drive, lined with trees, their branches still glittering with hoar frost. Everywhere was white and gleaming in the wintry sunlight, the sky was ice blue, and the only bright colours came from the flowers left on the graves of loved ones in the churchyard.

OK, it might be beautiful, but it was too cold to be hanging around outside. Heading up the drive, crunching over the dried and frozen leaves, she reached the church and pushed open the ancient wooden door, only closed in order to keep the heat from escaping.

And yes, it was warm inside, thank goodness. But that wasn't the reason she was hesitating now. She'd managed to steer clear of Drew for months, but she knew he'd been working on the renovation of the big old house at the far end of Cliff Road, overlooking the sea, that Max and Lottie had bought. She also knew he'd been invited to the wedding, and the thought of seeing him again had been playing on her mind all week. Because her feelings for him really should have gone away by now, but they hadn't – they hadn't even *begun* to fade – and what if she wasn't able to hide them? What if he was here with someone else, someone younger and prettier, who looked at her with pity or disdain? What if she burst into tears and made an absolute fool of herself? The inhabitants of Lanrock all thought she was a tough old bird, plain-speaking and afraid of no one, but what they didn't know was that the last few months had been absolutely brutal, the most agonising of her life.

And yes, there he was, over on the left-hand side of the church. Oh God, and looking wonderful in a dark grey suit and cream shirt. Now she knew she had to sit on the other side, as far away from him as possible. Without looking over at him at all, not even once.

Come on, you can do this. For crying out loud, get a grip.

An usher handed her an order of service and she ducked into the furthest seat in an empty pew at the back of the church on the right. She adjusted the silver scarf tied around the top of her high-necked navy dress, kept her head down and pretended to study the silver-embossed cover of the order of service.

Out of the corner of her eye, she detected movement. Seconds later, Drew sat down next to her.

362

Her heart began to gallop. He was wearing the same aftershave, the same watch, the same signet ring on his right hand.

'Hello,' he murmured. 'Trying to avoid me?'

Just hearing him speak was bringing the memories flooding back. She shook her head. 'No.'

'I think you were. Never mind, I'm here now.' He kept his voice low so they couldn't be overheard. 'I've missed you. So much. You have no idea.'

Iris closed her eyes. She wasn't strong enough for this. 'Don't.'

'I have to say it. I still love you.'

'You should have found someone else by now.'

'Well, I haven't. I don't want anyone else, only you.'

'I'm not interested.'

'I don't believe you.'

She shrugged. 'Really not my problem.'

He reached for her left hand, placed his fingertips over the inside of her wrist. 'Your pulse never used to be this fast.'

'Maybe I should leave.' Iris was so undone by the physical contact that she couldn't even pull her arm away. This wasn't working out at all.

'I've missed you. Every day.'

'Please stop.'

'I can't,' Drew murmured. 'I know you ended it because you think I want children, but you were wrong to do that. I'd rather have you and your children, and none of my own. Your kids are fantastic, and I got on brilliantly with them, didn't I? I'd make a great stepdad, and you know it.'

This was something Iris couldn't deny. She'd only introduced him to her children as a casual friend, but the bond between them had been wonderful to witness and they'd been asking about him ever since.

'You have no idea how much I've missed seeing them,' he went on. 'And being without you is the worst kind of punishment. I just want us to spend the rest of our lives together, be a proper family. Just think, one day we could have grandchildren . . .

The church was starting to fill up now. In the central aisle, Ruby and Richard had stopped to chat to Lachlan McCarthy and his wife, Amber. Ruby, now eight months pregnant and completely over her debilitating episode of writer's block since getting together with Richard, was wearing a crimson dress made of layered silk that made her look like a rose in full bloom. She was laughing, clearly in great spirits as she greeted the McCarthys with hugs and kisses. She was also the only person who knew how utterly miserable and heartbroken Iris had been since finishing with Drew.

Iris shook her head slightly; so much for having poured her heart out to someone who'd promised not to breathe a word about it. Pregnant women; you couldn't trust them an inch. Way too many hormones.

'Ruby told you,' she said with a sigh.

He nodded. 'Last week. She thought I deserved to know.'

'Hmm.'

Turning, Ruby had spotted them and was looking delighted.

'I happen to agree,' said Drew. 'I've spent all this time thinking you'd just grown tired of me.'

'It still wouldn't be fair on you. You want children, a family of your own.'

'I know plenty of children. Pretty much everyone I know has them.' He shrugged. 'And yes, I like them. But I can live without having my own, so long as I have you, and yours.'

She shook her head in desperation. 'You say that now.'

'And I'll always say it. I love you.'

'Oh God.'

'You can say it back to me, if you like.'

'I can't. Not here. Not now.' Her resolve was crumbling. She was only human.

Moving closer, until his mouth was inches from her ear, Drew murmured, 'But maybe later?'

Her wrist was still in his grasp. She slid it free, then curled her fingers between his until they were fully intertwined. It felt . . . incredible. Her mouth curved into a slow, unstoppable smile. Tilting her head so she could meet his gaze, she whispered back, 'Maybe.'

He gave her hand a secret squeeze. 'That'll do me.'

Chapter 47

Occupying the front pew gave Kay the best view of the altar, with the flickering flames from the beeswax candles reflecting off their silver sconces, creamy-white winter roses arranged in glass bowls, and a lovingly embroidered white altar cloth falling in matching folds at each corner.

Next to her, Alexander leaned in and said, 'So, when are *we* going to get married?'

Just the sound of his voice made her happy. Everything about him did. 'Not yet. It's too soon.'

'It's been nearly seven years. Isn't that long enough?'

'Most people don't know that,' Kay reminded him. 'We need to leave a gap between my divorce and getting married again. It's more classy.'

'Well, you've been divorced for almost a month now. We could get married in late spring.'

'We might even manage to find Terry someone nice by then.' Kay gave him a nudge. 'You haven't told me yet how his date went last night.'

'Not great. According to Terry, she talked about golf all night.'

'He met her at the golf club,' Kay exclaimed. 'He loves golf!'

Alexander shrugged. 'Apparently we should have heard her, though. Non-stop. Drove him mad.'

'Just like he used to drive me mad. Now he knows how it feels. Oh well, never mind. We'll keep trying.'

'He did say there's no need, he's fine as he is.' Alexander covered her hand. 'He also said he's enjoying the rest.'

That Terry could make such teasing comments and she no longer took offence was a testament to her own increased confidence. Kay touched her leg against Alexander's; he had brought calm and stability into her life. Since making the decision to trust him fully, after years of not daring to, she'd been so much happier. As had Terry, who would shortly be arriving with Lottie to walk her up the aisle.

'Here come Imelda and William,' Alexander said now, swivelling round to greet them. 'I like her outfit.'

Imelda had bought the swirly blue and green dress and jacket from a little boutique in Bath. And yes, it did make her look a bit dumpy, what with the pattern being so bold, but it still suited her. She was looking good.

'I like it too.' Kay patted the slithery amber silk of her own immaculately cut outfit. 'But I like mine more.'

Freya was having the best time. Because it had been too cold for people to want to mill around outside the church, many of the guests had gathered beforehand at the Rupert Hotel. In the main bar, she'd seen Cameron deep in conversation with two of his favourite people, the editor of the local paper and the big boss from the TV station.

Something about the expressions on the faces of the two men prompted Freya to wander over and lurk in a casual fashion behind them.

'. . . It'd be such a fantastic story for the viewers,' Cameron was saying with enthusiasm. 'If it wasn't for me inviting my best friend since university down to my own wedding back in May, this one wouldn't be happening today!'

'Is it really a fantastic story, though?' The TV station boss sounded decidedly unimpressed.

'We can *make* it fantastic,' Cameron insisted. 'Look, I'm planning to walk the Great Wall of China at Easter. For charity, of course. How about if I get Max to do it with me? We could film a series of episodes following our training progress, then the viewers will see just how much work goes into getting our bodies ready and really appreciate what we do to—'

'If Max is your best friend,' interrupted the editor of the paper, 'why aren't you his best man today?'

'Well . . . er, I mean . . . we're still good friends . . .' Caught off-guard, Cameron floundered for a moment. 'I mean, of course we are. He wouldn't have bought that big house here in Lanrock if it wasn't for me.'

'So you keep saying.' The boss of the TV station was looking bored. 'But I was chatting to him the other day and he told me he's taking Lottie to Greece over Easter. So no, we wouldn't be interested, I'm afraid. I think our viewers have been a bit over-exposed to you and your good works. They deserve a rest. Anyway, nice talking to you.' He and the editor gave Cameron fleeting polite smiles, then moved off.

Turning, evidently outraged, Cameron spotted Freya. 'Did you hear that? What's the matter with these people? Don't they even *care* that everything I do is for the benefit of others? I'll find someone else to work with now.' He shook his head in despair. 'How are things with you, anyway? Found yourself another chap yet?'

Freya rolled her eyes; he asked her this question every time he saw her, and it was *so* annoying. 'I keep telling you, I don't want another chap. That kind of hassle's the last thing I need. But I'm glad things are still going well for you and Tanya.'

'Thanks. I thought I might ask her to marry me during a sponsored parachute jump.'

'Nice,' said Freya. 'So long as you don't drop the ring on the way down.'

The church was almost full now, buzzing with chatter and laughter as people greeted each other. Pausing on arrival, Freya saw Max in the front pew, seemingly looking out for her and beckoning her over.

As she reached him, the man at his side nodded and said, 'That's her. That's the one.'

She hadn't seen him before, but he was pretty obviously the best man.

They both rose to their feet to greet her. Max said, 'Freya, this is Paolo. Paolo, Freya.'

'It's you.' Paolo's dark eyes were sparkling, his smile wide and white in his unseasonally tanned face.

Freya said, 'I know it's me. Hi.'

He gave her a brief kiss on each cheek. 'I saw you earlier, from an upstairs window at the hotel. You were running across the terrace.'

Max said, 'So you're the beautiful woman he spotted. He's been driving me nuts ever since, telling me he had to find out who you were.'

369

'I was panicking, wondering if I'd ever see you again. It was like Cinderella, only with no lost shoes to help me out. And now you're here.' Paolo spread his hands. 'It's a miracle.'

'Well, not quite. I was dressed for a wedding, so you knew I'd be here.'

'Ah, and that's the magic of weddings. You never know, today could be the day you meet the man of your dreams.'

'Except I'm really not looking for him.' Freya surveyed Paolo with an easy smile. 'And I've definitely heard all about you. The ultimate party boy, famous for flirting and breaking hearts all over London.'

Max was laughing. 'I may have mentioned your reputation. Sorry about that.'

'I'm actually very shy,' Paolo told her, a dimple appearing in his cheek. 'People make these wild assumptions. My hobbies are visiting old churches,' he indicated the one they were currently standing in, 'and flower arranging.'

'You know all about flowers? What are those ones over there?' She nodded towards the bowls of ranunculus and hydrangeas on the altar.

He turned to look. 'They are . . . white ones. With green leaves.'

'Wow,' said Freya. 'Move over, Monty Don. You really are an expert.'

'Making fun of me. I like that.' Paolo patted the space next to him in the front pew. 'Come and sit here next to me.'

'It's OK, my mum's saving me a seat over there.' She pointed to the other side of the church, where Tess was chatting in a pew with Ruby and Richard.

'Playing hard to get,' said Paolo. 'This makes me like you even more.'

'Not playing. I *am* hard to get.'

He laughed. 'Go on then, off you go. I'll catch up with you later.'

'Oh, I'm sure you'll have found someone else to dazzle by then,' said Freya.

'I won't. And I know you think I'm playing a game with you.' He regarded her with a knowing smile. 'But I'm really not.'

Same church. Different vicar.

Different bride, different groom.

And this time no dramas or upsets, no secret affairs abruptly revealed, no car accidents, and definitely no late-night skinny-dipping in the sea.

Well, other people could give it a go if they were mad enough, but Max had no plans to join them.

With a flourish, the organist struck up the first notes of the music that indicated Lottie's imminent arrival. Max rose to his feet along with Paolo, and caught sight of his mother's broad smile as she gave him an encouraging nod.

Who would ever have thought this day would come? Imelda and William were holding hands, turning along with the rest of the congregation as the opening chords of 'The Prince of Denmark's March' reverberated through the ancient church and Lottie appeared in the doorway on her father's arm.

Terry was looking ridiculously proud. And Lottie was beyond stunning in a simple dress of ivory velvet, with her mother's necklace twinkling in the candlelight and a circlet of tiny white flowers in her baby-blonde hair. Standing alongside Imelda, Kay was already dabbing at her eyes with a lace-trimmed handker-chief, and Imelda was giving her arm a reassuring squeeze.

371

Max had never felt so overcome with emotion in his life. This was it, this was all he'd ever wanted, before he'd even known he wanted it. Two warring families reunited. The girl he'd loved and lost as a teenager miraculously found again. Lottie had grown into a woman who was beautiful both inside and out, and she'd made him feel complete.

'She's too good for you,' Paolo murmured with a grin, and he was probably right, but Max was determined to do his best to be worthy of her, whatever the future might hold.

Life was an endless adventure, and he couldn't wait for them to spend it together.

A lump grew in his throat as she reached him. Oh God, he never cried; don't say he was about to do it now.

'Fancy meeting you here,' Lottie whispered, breaking the tension and making him laugh instead.

'Take good care of her,' Terry said gruffly as he let go of his daughter's arm.

Max nodded. 'I will.'

'What am I? Fine china?' Lottie raised her eyebrows at the two of them. 'How about we both take good care of each other?'

Paolo winked at the vicar and turned to address the rows of assembled guests behind him. 'Here we go, then. It's actually happening. Ladies and gentlemen, we're about to witness the wedding of the year.'